PAY
THE
PIPER

ALSO BY DANIEL KRAUS

NOVELS
Whalefall

The Ghost That Ate Us

Bent Heavens

Blood Sugar

The Death and Life of Zebulon Finch: Volume Two: Empire Decayed

The Death and Life of Zebulon Finch: Volume One: At the Edge of Empire

Scowler

Rotters

The Monster Variations

The Teddies Saga
They Threw Us Away

They Stole Our Hearts

They Set the Fire

WITH GEORGE A. ROMERO
The Living Dead

WITH SHÄRON MOALEM
Wrath

WITH GUILLERMO DEL TORO
Trollhunters

The Shape of Water

WITH LISI HARRISON
Graveyard Girls
1-2-3-4, I Declare a Thumb War

Scream for the Camera

Season's Eatings

GRAPHIC NOVELS
The Cemeterians

Trojan

Year Zero: Volume 0

The Autumnal

ALSO BY GEORGE A. ROMERO

WITH DANIEL KRAUS
The Living Dead

EDITED BY JONATHAN MAYBERRY AND ROMERO
Nights of the Living Dead: An Anthology

WITH SUSANNA SPARROW
Dawn of the Dead

Martin

FOR CHILDREN:
The Little World of Humongo Bongo

PAY THE PIPER

GEORGE A. ROMERO
DANIEL KRAUS

UNION
SQUARE
& CO.

NEW YORK

UNION SQUARE & CO.

NEW YORK

ISBN 978-1-4549-5089-9
ISBN 978-1-4549-5090-5 (e-book)

For information about custom editions, special sales, and premium purchases, please contact specialsales@unionsquareandco.com.

Printed in Canada

2 4 6 8 10 9 7 5 3 1

unionsquareandco.com

Cover design by Patrick Sullivan and Igor Satanovsky
Cover art: illustration by Evangeline Gallagher © 2024 Union Square & Co., LLC; MaxyM/Sutterstock.com (paper)
Interior design by Rich Hazelton
Interior illustration (eye): bogadeva1983/Shutterstock.com: 1, 169

For Suzanne Descrocher-Romero

COAUTHOR NOTE

For this novel's portrayal of Cajun speech, I have taken my cue from
Mike Tidwell's *Bayou Farewell: The Rich Life and Tragic Death of
Louisiana's Cajun Coast*, in which he writes:

> Clearly, to write all of the Cajun dialogue in this
> book . . . would exhaust the reader and prove, in
> the end, disrespectful to Cajuns. The true color and
> dignity of their speech would inevitably be lost in
> translation. Therefore I've chosen a more limited
> portrayal, faithfully omitting the *th* sound and
> including some of the altered grammar without
> laying things on too thick. This approach serves
> to consistently remind the reader that Cajuns do, in
> fact, sound different from most Americans with-
> out loading the pages down with an impenetrable
> soup of dialogue.

—Daniel Kraus

HOG GUZZLE

~ OR ~

KEEPING TRACK OF NASTY-SUGAR

BOB FIREMAN'S WAGON WHEEL CARNIVAL had rolled its calliope pennants to the outskirts of Alligator Point's green inferno every January 8 since—well, no still-living Pointer could recall it *not* coming. The carny's clockwork arrival honored an event even kids as small as Pontiac knew. Each year since starting school, she'd heard the same tale from her teacher, Miss Ward.

Under the cold, slithering daybreak fog of January 8, 1815— Miss Ward favored a flowery windup—fifteen thousand musket-wielding British soldiers stormed the only defense shielding New Orleans: an eight-hundred-yard mud barricade. We Yanks had one-third the manpower, a hastily sewn blanket of army regulars, free Blacks, frontier riflemen, Choctaw Indians, and swashbucklers under the Jolly Roger of the Pirates Lafitte. Yet the ragtag throng fell into mystical lockstep under Major General Andrew Jackson, who, in these parts, ran second in celebrity only to Jesus. Two hours later, the Brits paddled home, tails twixt legs. Their dead got pitched down a hole in the Chalmette Plantation battlefield, the only gaffe Jackson made. This was bayou country. The steamy soil said hell no to John Bulls, even dead ones, and pushed those rotting redcoats back into the sweltering sun.

According to Miss Ward, the Battle of New Orleans had been a national holiday, called simply "the Eighth," for fifty fuck-damn years! (Miss Ward didn't say *fuck-damn*, but Pontiac did, quiet, so only Billy May heard.) Somewhere, somehow, January 8 lost its prestige, but that didn't surprise Pontiac. Things had a way of getting lost down here in the swamp. Louisianans, though, kept the date; folk down here loved their celebrations. Every backwater holler Pontiac tread, she heard the spongy land breathe life back into the vaunted dead.

Jackson: the susurration of sugarcane.

Lafitte: the algae hiss as gators skimmed.

No one held faster to January 8 than Bob Fireman, a fellow who didn't exist but whose name gamboled across every food stand, sandwich board, and you-must-be-this-tall placard in the carnival. Bob Fireman's Wagon Wheel Carnival wouldn't arrive in Alligator Point proper until June 23—a different Louisiana holiday called St. John's Day. The January 8 carny was a forty-minute walk north in the dry-land town of Dawes, which had itself a Piggly Wiggly, a Greyhound station, and lots of other modern conveniences.

That's where Pontiac was headed, her nine-year-old, four-foot, fifty-five-pound body as agitated as a shaken soda can.

Daddy wouldn't approve of her speed. "Run too fast at night, cher, and you be sayin bonsoir to the bottom of de quick," he often warned in his baritone Cajun. That was the sober version. Half a bottle of Everclear into a blitz, his advice got less folksy: *"Quicksand, fool!"*

Tonight she had no intention of slowing. Besides, quicksand couldn't snag her so long as she kept to the road. More likely she'd fall into one of the holes Daddy dug himself: Barataria Bay was pitted with his telltale pits, those fruitless attempts at finding the pirate booty Jean Lafitte supposedly hid almost two hundred years ago.

That's why she'd swung by Doc's Mercantile beforehand. She'd been saving for the Whiz-Bang fishing rod in the window but had no choice but to blow all she had on a $4.99 flashlight. How else to avoid all ten million of Daddy's embarrassing holes? Up ahead she could see plenty of other Pointers on their way to Dawes. Like will-o'-the-wisps, their flashlights bobbed.

The fingers of Pontiac's opposite hand sunk into the humid cover of a book Mr. Peff the librarian joshed was more'n half her size: *The Complete Cthulhu Mythos Tales* by H. P. Lovecraft.

Like most of the older books in the one-room library, some-body a long while back had carved an octopus symbol into it, this time inside the back cover. Old octopus symbols were all over Alligator Point. On mossed swamp rocks, old tree trunks, the sides of ancient shanties. Pontiac didn't know why. When she asked Daddy, she didn't get but an irritated shrug.

Daddy didn't like not knowing stuff.

Pontiac didn't either. That's why she read all the fuck-damn time, to the exasperation of Billy May and the sullenness of Daddy, who glared at her books like they were better men, none of whom needed hooch before facing the day. Mr. Lovecraft, her current choice, designed sentences as serpentine as anything in the swamp. They had rippling scales, dripping fangs.

It lumbered slobberingly into sight, he wrote.

Armed with a book like this, nothing at Bob Fireman's could spook Pontiac.

This 618-page tome was the only protection she had since her best friend, Billy May, had claimed he was too tired to come to the carny, when the truth was he was too chicken. Pontiac was rip-snorting mad. She and Billy May always went to Bob Fireman's, on January 8 and June 23 both. Billy always said he could hear the carny's trucks rumbling all the way from New Orleans.

A fib, naturally. But fibs aren't quite lies. Fibs are truths stretched taffy-thin to make life more interesting. Bob Fireman's Wagon Wheel Carnival was a cathedral built to the glory of fibbing. You couldn't turn your head without bonking into the best fibs you ever saw.

THE WORLD'S SCARIEST RIDE—she doubted that!

$5 TO SEE INDIA'S BIGGEST RAT—try again, suckers!

YOU CAN'T ESCAPE THE MUTANT MAZE—you wanna bet?

That was the trickiest, stickiest part of fibs. Spit them often enough and they piled thick and crusted hard like wasp nests. Daddy said New Orleans was built on "fibs, lies, and fabrications," the three pillars keeping the city from going glug-glug-glug into the quag. Down here your lungs breathed fibs right along with Bradford pear, Confederate jasmine, Creole mirepoix, and fresh beignets—and the bad stuff too, the flood mold, hot-trash crawfish shells, tourist-buggy horse shit, and Bourbon Street's hobo funk of liquor, piss, and puke. What didn't end up in a New Orleanian's blood ended up filling every pothole in the Quarter—a bubbly black tarn of viscid vice.

Some Pointers called it "nasty-sugar." It'd get you flying high, yes'm, but it'd gobble your insides too, sure as four dogs have four assholes.

Pontiac splashed through a moat of water spangles and ducked under a spruce-pine bend, and suddenly there was Bob Fireman's Wagon Wheel. Carousel lights flashed like wet teeth and greasy treats exhaled like hot breath.

Right inside, waiting for her—and her alone—was the Chamber of Dragons. Pontiac's pores oozed cane sugar. It hurt. She ran her fingertips over the octopus carving in her book and thought about turning tail like Billy May, heading back home.

If things *did* lumber at Bob Fireman's, if things did *slobber*, it was inside the Chamber.

- 2 -

A SLIVER TILL MIDNIGHT, Billy heard his name.

"Billy May? Billy May, you in dere?"

He'd been waiting for this call since school let out. On vine-swallowed Alligator Point, where it was hard to tell if your feet were planted in the dry or the damp, where air was water and the skeeters had learned to swim, it was dark enough while the sun was *up*. When the sun set, round four-thirty this time of year, all things under the Point's green umbrellas went black.

It had gotten dark during Billy and Pontiac's walk home. Two-and-a-quarter miles, a narrow dirt track forged by folk who walked, every day, in and out of the Point. There wasn't no roads. The track dodged opaque pools of stinking sulfur that rose and fell with the Gulf of Mexico tides. There was no telling what was inside—what he and Pontiac had dubbed "hog guzzle," after the dark slime of mud, grass, chicken shit, and dead vermin in Seth Durber's hog sty.

Billy had wanted to confess to Pontiac what was spooking him. It was the *thing* kids whispered about, the *thing* that drank laughter like Kool-Aid, that chewed good feelings like bubblegum. He'd had a hunch, sure as hunger, or sickness, or needing to pee, that it was coming for him.

The Piper, some folk called it.

But the whole walk home, the Piper didn't grab Billy's ankle from inside the coco-yam or drop down from the Spanish moss. Maybe Pontiac's loud, foul mouth kept it at bay. Getting home safe made Billy feel squat-percent better. That was another thing every kid knew: the Piper made *you* come to *it*.

"Billy May," the voice called. "Don't you hear me?"

The window sash was up. The skeeter screen was down. The voice needled through it at a child's pitch. Billy couldn't tell if he was awake or bad-dreaming. Also, there was the smell of lilacs. Mama didn't plant no lilacs.

"I ain't here!" Billy shouted.

Well, shit-balls, that was dumb. Billy cursed himself while the kid-voice chuckled.

Billy backpedaled. "I mean . . . I'm not allowed to come out. Not allowed to do nothin. It's bedtime. Mama and Daddy's right in here with me."

"Dat so?"

"Yup."

"Ask one of dem to come to de window, so dey can tell you I ain't nuddin to be afraid of."

"Who says I'm afraid?"

"Now, Billy May. Anybody wit' half an ear can tell you afraid. Your little girlfriend could tell. Dat's why she up and ditched you."

The thing outside his window knew Pontiac? That scared Billy deep. Unpacking that fear from his chest was like pulling wet leaves from a rubbish bag.

"You go on talking," Billy said. "I'm not waking up my folks."

The voice sounded pained. "I'd hate if it got around dat Billy May sleeps in de same room as his folks."

Lord, there were so many different kinds of fear.

"I don't," Billy insisted.

"So your ma and pa, dey not really *right dere*, are dey?"

The voice's Cajun was peculiar. Most kids Billy's age didn't carry the accent thanks to TV, which flickered to life in these far-flung parts twenty years back.

The skeeter screen shivered. Maybe a breeze. Or maybe the voice was that close.

"Sound to me like you t'ink I'm somet'in bad. Let me ask you dis. How do *I* know who *you* are? I can't see who I'm talkin to eidder!"

Billy lay silent. It was a good point.

"Well, come over here, then," Billy said. "Look in the window."

"Ah, my eyesight's for shit. Can't see one foot in front of my face."

"Then how come you're out at night?" Billy challenged. "Even harder to see in the dark."

"My old man. Whupped me again. Booted me out. Now, look, I got me a pack of Pall Malls. Stole it out my old man's Levi's on de way out. Figured to offer you some."

"Chuck?" Billy brightened. "Chucky Steve Beatty? That you?"

Now this was different! Billy had smoked Pall Malls three times with Chucky Steve Beatty. It was a good feeling. It was a *tough* feeling. He wouldn't mind feeling tough again. Folk might call cigarettes and Big Gulps nasty-sugar, but they sure tasted fine.

Billy swung his legs from the bed. His shin sweat crystallized to ice.

"I'm coming to the window. That's all."

"Ain't askin for nuddin more."

Pall Malls and a friend, right when Billy needed one. He crossed the floor. Leaned his nose into the skeeter screen. Lilacs like crazy. He panted his hands on the sill, the wood so decayed it barely held the shape of an octopus, carved there long before Billy was even born.

~ 3 ~

PONTIAC WAS HER LAST NAME. If you called her by her first, she'd warn you that, if you did it a second time, she'd sock you, swear on her mama's grave. Which she literally did. Each time Daddy survived a real bad bender, he dragged Pontiac to St. Vincent de Paul Cemetery #3 in the city, where he apologized to Janine Pontiac at a tomb so white it made Pontiac's eyes sting. Daddy always gave Pontiac five minutes alone at the tomb, and damn right she used those minutes to swear. *Why the shit did you give me such a punk-ass name, Mama?*

Thankfully, most folk on the Point had lost their birth certificates to flood, fire, decay, or disinterest. Oysterman Gregg Bentley went by "Stale Cookies." Mrs. Burroughs out by Lake Laurier went by "Salazar." A teenager at the Texaco answered only to "A Walk on the Wild Side." The Pointers who saw her standing in front of the Chamber of Dragons just said "Hey-hey, Pontiac," to which she nodded, cool as a Coke.

No one pestered her about Daddy's whereabouts either. First, they knew he somewhere drunk off his keister. Second, all bayou kids tended to wander. That's why *keeping track*, most of all of one another, was a way of life on the Point. Least it used to be. Miss Ward said folk on the Point were in danger of forgetting the lesson of the Battle of New Orleans. We might be as ragtag as Jackson's army, but in the end, we're all kin, so we all got to *keep track*.

That's why Pontiac carried a third item along with her flashlight and H. P. Lovecraft. Mama had given it to her before she went ahead and croaked from a belly full of cancer. "Keep track of your daddy," she'd gasped. "Keep track of *everything*. You got to promise."

Pontiac had no name for her black-and-white composition notebook besides her "log." In her log, she logged stuff, like Mama said. Maps of the places she went (she used a hashtag symbol for quicksand) and notes on the things she noticed, like the suspicious blue flowers erupting from the bear-grass by the Deevers' place, or how Salazar's dog had been limping for two months now and nobody seemed to give a fuck-damn.

She also kept track of the dead. Not a whole lotta folk were left on Alligator Point. Still somebody managed to kick it every few months. Cancer, mostly. Lots of folk blamed it on the offshore rigs. Some toxic runoff, oil in the water, who knew? There was so much cancer on the Point, Pontiac figured if she snorkeled under the bogs with her flashlight, she'd find mounds of it, rubbery black blobs, quivering as it connived ways to crawl up folk's drainpipes.

Made sense the carnival kept rolling down to the damp. *Carnival*, Miss Ward once said, came from *carne vale*, or "farewell to the flesh."

In other words, cancer.

Pontiac slid her log out from the back of her jeans. It was warped from sweat and shaped like her lower back. A pencil gored from her gnawing dangled from a string taped to the cover. Taking notes made her feel nearly five feet tall and one hundred pounds powerful.

That's the boost she needed to take on the Chamber of Dragons.

Three years now Pontiac and Billy May had stood slack-jawed in front of it, cinnamon king cakes forgotten as they listened for the sandpapering of the snakes inside. She'd show Billy May. She'd go in alone and take detailed notes in her log to prove she'd done it.

She walked up to the ticket-seller while scribbling down observations.

Bob Fireman's carnies wore masks. Not the chicken-feather, sequin-glued, polyester bullshits of Decatur Street tourists either. These masks looked excavated from cobwebby old trunks. Real hair, red velvet hoods, curved balsa-wood beaks, crumbling cloth. The man hunched on the stool outside the Chamber of Dragons wore a lumpy red papier-mâché mask with black horns, hollow eyes, and a little round mouth.

"Five bucks," the demon said from the white-circled hole.

"Shh," Pontiac replied. "I'm writing."

"What's so important you got to write it?"

"Details."

The Chamber's steps were as old as time, and carved into the bottom one was another old octopus symbol.

The demon laughed. Papier-mâché flaked. His croquembouche jowls jiggled.

"*Details* you're after? There be details a-plenty inside this truck, pumpkin."

Pontiac scowled. "I'm nobody's pumpkin."

The demon's red head tilted. His black eyes stared.

"Tell me your name so I might properly say it."

Daddy had warned it, Miss Ward had warned it: don't go advertising your name to strangers. Yet Pontiac's name tickled her tongue like nasty-sugar. She longed to hear it aloud. Hell, she wouldn't be happy till the whole *world* heard it.

"Do I know your papa?" the demon probed.

Pontiac doubted it. Most nights Daddy didn't have the dexterity to get farther than the Pelican, the closest saloon. If this demon met Daddy drinking, he'd know right off Daddy was dying. Not from the kind of cancer that did in Mama, but the kind he nurtured like a pet.

"Or maybe it's your mama I know," the demon said.

Pontiac wondered if the demon had been tipped off by her skin color, precisely halfway between Daddy's white and Mama's Black. Bringing up her folks was wicked manners either way. *Gerard* and *Janine* were quicksand words, capable of drowning the courage Pontiac needed to go inside this truck.

"Pontiac's the name," she said in a burst. "And yours?"

"Don't you know the point of this face-hider? Rich, poor, angel, devil—you wear a mask, you might be any one of them. I could tell you my name. But you'd be a fool to trust it."

Skunk! She'd been swindled! Heat climbed her cheeks tight as trumpet creeper. She let it. Anger trumped fear any day.

"You going to let me in or not?"

The demon ripped off a ticket. "Guess I don't know your folks after all. Pontiac, is it? That's a fine automobile, anyway. I'll give you a buck off."

~ 4 ~

IT WASN'T CHUCKY STEVE BEATTY. But it was a boy, and Billy May liked the looks of him. Mud-smudged cheek and chin. Hair cow-licked stiff. Bare feet clumped with mud large as cougar paws.

"Hey dere, William."

The boy's voice slid clarinet-smooth through the racket of frogs, grackles, herons.

"Hey," Billy replied.

The boy smiled, white teeth gleaming in the jungle dim.

"You're not wearing glasses," Billy observed.

"Huh?"

"You said you can't see good. Why don't you got glasses?"

"Hell. Guy like me? I'd break 'em, two minutes flat."

Billy fidgeted. "I don't believe I know you."

"You ain't lookin careful den. I'm at school every day. Well, most days."

"And you want to . . . share smokes? With me? At midnight?"

"Abraham's shit. Midnight is de best time for sharin smokes! Ain't nobody around to go scoldin on you. Not dat I can't take a scoldin. I took a scoldin so bad once I was bleedin out my butt."

Billy knew the panic of being outdone. He felt it all the time with Pontiac.

"I've been scolded," he insisted. "A bunch."

"Dat's what us bayou boys is alive for, ain't it?"

"I haven't heard any *other* reason." Billy smiled. "Remind me your name?"

The boy popped a cigarette from the pack, lit it with a Bic's flick, and took a drag.

"Pierre. T'ough I don't much care for dat name."

"Pontiac doesn't like her real name either."

"We Cajun types love our masks. *Names* are masks too."

Billy May was impressed. "You going to tell me what you go by?"

"Suppose I can't be shown up by dis Pontiac girl. Mostly I go by de Piper."

Riding Bob Fireman's Wombat Scrambler with Pontiac last St. John's Eve, Billy's stomach had done a great big lurch right before it sprayed his po'boy lunch. His gut lurched like that now. Then a nice tingly feeling overtook it, like he was already smoking the cigs. Hearing the Piper introduce himself proper made meeting him not as bad as Billy had imagined. The dirty face, messy hair, muddy feet—this kid Pierre looked a lot like him.

Plus, how dangerous was a boy who couldn't hardly see?

Pierre shook the pack of smokes. Billy never wanted one so bad. He toyed with the skeeter screen's wayward wires.

"What do they call you the Piper for? You smoke a pipe longside them Pall Malls?"

Pierre grinned. "*Pipes* are for fancy-pants, which I definitely ain't. Now rhubarb *pie* . . . I do enjoy a nice slice of rhubarb *pie* now and again." He exhaled a long gray yarn of smoke. "Dat's a clue, Billy May."

"Rhubarb," Billy repeated.

"No, *pie*, you dumb-dilly."

"Oh. Pie." Billy frowned, then lit up. "Miss Ward read us a story about the *Pied* Piper once. Led a bunch of mice off a cliff."

"Dat's de one I mean. But let me ask you dis. If dat ol' Piper was leadin dem, how come he didn't walk off de cliff too?"

"I . . . can't figure it."

"Because it's a lie de size of Texas. Just like all dem stories about me."

The thing in the swamp. Calling folk's names. Dragging them under the quick. Gobbling their bones. It felt like it'd be downright rude to repeat such rude tales in front of Pierre.

"I ain't heard no stories," Billy lied.

"Den how come you won't come out here?"

"I . . . just don't want to."

"First you weren't allowed to, not you just don't want to. Abraham's shit!"

Pierre hurled his cigarette to the ground. Red sparks fanned like switchgrass. He turned and stomped off, and the lilac bouquet went with him. Panic hitched up Billy's throat like vomit. If he was ever going to keep up with Pontiac, he had to start being braver.

Billy pulled up the skeeter screen, made himself small, rolled over the ancient octopus, and leapt into the weeds below. He got up and sprinted. The swamp was black, blue, and pink, and it curled around Pierre like a mama cat.

"Wait!"

When Pierre turned, he was grinning big, like he'd never doubted Billy was coming.

~ 5 ~

THE CHAMBER OF DRAGONS HAD nine exhibits, four down each side and one at the end, each illuminated by black lights screwed to the tin hoods of terrariums. Hoods that looked like they could be popped right off by any critter that got gumptious enough. It stank as bad as Daddy coming home from the Pelican: sweat, smoke, and sweet things, but cold and salty too. She didn't want to smell it; she quit breathing and, right away, got dizzy.

Up front, the Komodo dragon, forked tongue flashing. Next, the Gila monster, as fancifully beaded as a Mardi Gras suit. After that, it got familiar. Baby gators: she'd seen them in the wild, fresh from their eggs, cute if not for their yellow-eyed madness. A thirteen-inch snapping turtle: Daddy once made soup from an eight-incher he caught using sparrow-bait.

Finally, snakes.

Pontiac's fingertips found the log's current page by the textures of her handwriting. If it wasn't so dark, she could keep track, and that would help. Instead, all she could do was wait for another carnival-goer to enter and keep her company. It didn't happen, and kept not happening. She couldn't even hear the carnival anymore. She pictured a black hill of cancer flopping out of the marsh and absorbing the whole outfit.

Pontiac wanted to skedaddle.

André Saphir's voice, calm as ever, slid through her skull.

Any little t'ing can be magic, catin.

Hellfire. If there was anyone Pontiac liked to impress, it was Saphir.

Pontiac stepped up to the first snake. Blacklight irradiated the peeling stickers: PYTHON. The snake was burly, tiger-spotted, twenty feet long, and burnin' thunderwood. As it moved, its scales created the illusion of going backward, like hubcaps on a speeding car. Pontiac didn't like it. It was a trick. Same kind the demon ticket-taker tried to pull.

RATTLER next, betraying all laws of physics, diamond-patterned body levitating while its larva-white tail shivered. After that, MAMBA, green as duckweed, lithe as an overlong finger, motionless but for its darting black tongue. After that, CORAL, loose as roadkill guts, its yellow, black, and red stripes bragging how it didn't even need to hide. Finally, at the end of the truck, the snake Pontiac knew in her heart had been waiting.

Her fear, another scaled thing, broke from its jar and slithered up her throat.

Inside the final tank, sawdust and wood chips.

And something beneath.

It lumbered slobberingly into sight.

Cottonmouths were the bayou's evilest critters and that was saying a lot. Their worst feature was their lying. Lying, not fibbing. They looked like harmless black snakes except for itty-bitty white marks between their eyes and jaws. Black snakes came at you slow, nothing but curious. Cottonmouths acted just the same. But a quarter of a second was all it took for one to lash out and plunge its fangs.

Here's what happened next, according to Daddy. Pain like you never knew. Spurting blood. The bite swelling up like bread. Falling down clumsy. Throwing up. Gasping. Going numb. Turning yellow. A cottonmouth bite could end you in five minutes. If Pontiac ever got bit, her fate would hang on a coin toss. *Eidder you got de stuff to survive it or you don't,* Daddy said, after which somebody would be obligated to dig a little-girl-sized grave.

The cottonmouth slid from the sawdust, flat head rising, golden eyes locked. Even absent of poison, Pontiac's blood itched. She thought of Billy May, coward, and André Saphir, hero, and leaned closer. She was brave. The bravest. Her sweaty forehead squeaked against terrarium glass.

~ 6 ~

MOST OF ALLIGATOR POINT WAS "damp"—at sea level or lower. Billy May skirted it, moving through the cool reeds of Chickapee Hollow, halfway to Guimbarde Beach, the site of the old baseball diamond. That's where Pierre wanted to go. The boy was a born troublemaker, as bold as Pontiac. Even better than Pontiac, he seemed satisfied with himself. Billy didn't think he'd ever met *anyone* who felt like that. Life fell on Pointers like a sled of bricks.

But Pierre needed Billy's perfect eyes. Billy was proud to lead the way.

Unfortunately, Chickapee Hollow cut straight through the hog guzzle.

The dirt track was thin as a bicycle tire and, like anywhere else in the damp, subject to the surprise traps of Gerard Pontiac's treasure-digging holes. Moist fronds reached out like churchgoers trying to shake hands. Billy pushed them aside only for them to rebound and spank his backside. Some fronds he ripped out only to sense, from the corners of his eyes, replacement fronds springing up.

If Pierre noticed his foibles, he didn't say, and Billy was grateful. Twice Billy noticed old-ass octopus markings, one scraped into a cow-sized rock and one carved way too high on a water oak, but he didn't want interrupt Pierre's chatter. The boy, redolent with lilac now, handed a lit cigarette over Billy's shoulder. Billy took a drag as fast as he could. It helped with his growing worry. What if Mama woke up and found Billy gone? Worse, what if Daddy did?

They'd be mad—though not mad enough to wade through the hog guzzle, not at night.

Smoke curled inside Billy's lungs, hot as a desert sidewinder. Pall Mall paper sizzled. That's what he needed to do: burn away the fear, keep talking.

"If the Pied Piper story's a lie," Billy asked, "how come you use the name?"

"Assuming I don't smoke a pipe, you mean."

Billy laughed. Smoke ribboned past pearly mistletoe into the green-black universe.

"I figure we established that much," Billy said, relishing the big word in the middle.

"You're de one who got schooled my story. You tell me."

Billy pictured Pontiac, scrambly fast except when weighed down with books. Billy thought reading was the pits. Even when the TV fritzed, messing with the rabbit ears was funner than staring at a page of letters. Listening to Miss Ward read, though, that was all right.

"Like I said," Billy began, "first there was the mice."

"Abraham's shit! I'm sick of dem mice!"

"Why you yelling? You told me to tell the story!"

"Get to de part after dat. De part wit' de children."

"All right, so the Piper got rid of them mice for the townfolk but when he came to collect his fee, the townfolk said, 'You didn't do shit. Just went off playing your flute.' Piper says, 'Hey, them mice are gone, ain't they?' The townfolk say, 'Yeah, but they ain't gone because some stupid flute. We don't owe you dirt.' Piper says, 'My flute music ain't ordinary music. It's got magic that makes who hears it follow along.' The townfolk go, 'Oh, yeah? If you got that kind of magic, why don't you blow the flute on *us*?' Piper says, 'I could, but I ain't going to. If you don't pay up, I'm going to play my flute at your children. And they're going to follow along. And they're going to die, just like them mice.'"

"Rats," Pierre said. "It was rats."

Billy stopped and turned toward the boy.

The giant cypresses shivered.

Pierre was wobbling. Billy was surprised. Pierre seemed like the kind of boy who could tight-rope ten miles of fence. But Billy watched Pierre drift into prickly ironweed on one side of the trail before floundering into sticky dixie tick on the other. Billy reached out to steady him, but Pierre caught himself.

Must be his eyesight, Billy thought.

Problem was, Billy no longer saw Pierre's eyes. Couldn't see the kid's face at all. All he could see was the red dot of a cigarette as the boy took a pull.

"It was rats the whole time?" Billy asked. "Why didn't you say?"

"I will take the story from here," Pierre replied.

His voice had changed. It was deeper, fussier, how Miss Ward tried to teach them to talk.

"The children followed the Piper's music," Pierre continued. "Every single child, right through the sooty, stinking old town, past its bounteous farmland and through valleys cupped inside imperial mountains. Only then, in sight of Earth's full splendor, did the children walk themselves over a cliff. And all because folk did not pay the Piper."

Night creature noises filled the silence. Until a delicate pattering joined it: rain, which didn't make sense. It'd been blue skies all day, dry all night. Billy looked up and saw individual drops catch moonlight like tossed pennies.

Unless he was wrong, the rain only fell on top of the boys.

"I have been done wrong," Pierre said. "Very wrong."

Billy's heart leapt to the pace of the hiccupping toads.

"Not by me, Pierre," he insisted.

"What did I tell you about that name?"

The lilac scent, so soft and sweet, thickened with rich, gamy rot.

"Piper, I mean." How stupid Billy had been to open his window to *the Piper*, to chase after *the Piper*. That must be how those mice—no, those *rats*, those *children*—met their fates. The Piper got them to lead *themselves* off the cliff.

The rain fell harder. Pierre, the Piper, whatever this thing was, looked up to the hard drops of rain and drank. Billy saw wet teeth, a worming tongue, the gloss of slurping lips.

"No, Billy. You didn't do anything wrong. But your people *did*."

- 7 -

THE COTTONMOUTH STRUCK.

It did not get its name on accident. The white interior of its mouth had transfixed a millennium of victims. Pontiac, too, in the quarter-second before it bit.

The snake's fangs clacked against the terrarium, squirting venom down the glass. Pontiac hurled herself backward and tripped. Toward the floor. The dark floor. The extremely dark floor. While she'd been caught in the cottonmouth's white, the other beasts had escaped. Only now, too late, did she imagine hearing the crackle of splintering glass, the cymbal of tin lids tipped to the floor.

She was halfway fallen when she saw a thing a blacker than the black floor, coiled and waiting.

Odd thoughts in the last seconds before untold fangs bloated her with poison. Church bullshit: snakes in the Garden of Eden.

Bayou bullshit: snakes spoken of like they were rainbows in the sky. New Orleans bullshit: the Great Serpent, Li Grand Zombi, skaters of land and water, travelers between realms. The scariest ride, the biggest rat, the mutant maze—she believed all fibs now, for everything had come out of hiding, no more *lumbering*, no more *slobbering*.

The coiled thing turned out to be a drain. She saw that when carny lights filled the truck through the open door. *Fuck-damn*, she thought, as adult hands hoisted her by the armpits and she scrabbled for her log, flashlight, and book. *Things never turn out to be what you expect.*

In this case, it was the demon dragging her ass, cackling, adding humiliation to the fright. But it wasn't his bright-red mask burned into her vision. It was the cottonmouth at the instant of attack, so white, so white.

~ 8 ~

THE BOY-THING, ONCE PIERRE, now the Piper, stepped from the rainy shadows. Its pink flesh cracked to pieces. For a moment, its face looked like a dried-out salt flat. Then the shattered bits of boy-skin were sucked into the jelly of the thing's real face—a dark, eyeless mass.

Hog guzzle, Billy thought as urine scalded his leg.

He was sad about dying. Real sad, real quick. He didn't think about Mama or Daddy. He thought about Pontiac. Folk always said he and she were two sides of a silver dollar, one light, one dark. By dying he was letting Pontiac down. A silver dollar missing one of it sides wasn't worth fifty cents. It was worth nothing.

The Piper raised a hand. A boy's hand, until its fingernails started growing. Not into the pinlike stabbers you get from a testy cat. These were more like seal tusks, thick and yellow, so big they split the fingers like bursting hot dogs. After that, the whole hand tumbled into gristly meat.

Only the thumb stayed normal, and for a reason.

The tusk-fingers sunk holes into Billy's chest. Billy watched it happen like it was part of the scary movie shown late nights on Channel 3. The thing's human thumb secured a grip on Billy's throbbing heart before tearing it free, leathery and spurting, and bringing it to the Piper's mouth.

It *did* have a mouth. It was the last thing Billy May saw. The black jelly of its face split open. It was surprising enough to override the wires of pain jammed through Billy's body. He marveled as the thing ate up his beating heart.

Its mouth, so white, so white.

~ 9 ~

Now and again, Pete Roosevelt was seen apart from Spuds Ulene, but rare were the times Spuds Ulene was seen apart from Pete Roosevelt. Pointers said they were "longside" each other, a word indicating more than togetherness: they were unified in purpose. When the longsiding began, there'd been jibes about queer goings-on. It didn't last. People respected Pete as a professional, and were impressed by how Spuds, under the older man's tutelage, had redirected his ill-omened life.

The duo was longside each other in the most common of ways on January 11, except when the backwater track grew too narrow, or pitted with Gerard Pontiac's infamous pirate-gold holes, and Spuds dropped behind. How Spuds kept up at all was, to Pete, an enduring mystery. Spuds was what Cajuns called a *peeshwank*: five-foot-zero with the stride to match. Five-foot-two in racing boots, Spuds insisted. Spuds had, in fact, had a short career as a horse jockey. Didn't like to talk about it much. All he got for three years jockeying was a poorly inserted prosthetic left knee. Pete could identify his limp a mile off, a weird wiggle-skip dance step that kept nearly all weight off his left leg.

Only Spuds's stream of chatter assured Pete the deputy was keeping up. Pete often interjected a John Wayne quote from *Big Jake*: "'You're short on ears and long on mouth.'" Today, Pete didn't blame the kid's nerves. This weren't a stolen toaster oven—yesterday's big drama. This was serious business.

"Goll, Pete, you think we're walking into something bad, don't you?" Spuds was twenty-seven and evidenced but a smidge of the local accent. Pete was fifty-two and loved the yo-yo-ing Cajun, but having spent his first fifteen years in Texas, it weren't his to borrow.

"I don't know," Pete replied. "You *never* know."

"But it sure *looks* bad, don't it?"

"Boys run off. Me and you collared our share."

"Not *nine*-year-old boys we haven't. Nine-year-old boys that ain't shown up in three days. Even I know that's bad, Pete. What do you figure happened?"

Pete sighed. He had a big chest, and the exhale shook a clump of pondspice.

"Got ill at his ma or pa—both worth gettin ill at, by my recollection. After that, J'connais pas. Hidin out with a buddy, I expect."

"But his buddy was that girl Pontiac, iddn't that so?"

"Yeah."

"And you said you went by the Pontiac place this morning and Pontiac said she ain't seen him, iddn't that so?"

"It is."

"And Pontiac's not the type to go fibbing to the law, is she? Goll, every time I see that girl, she's scribbling smart stuff in her little book. She's the honestest girl you're bound to meet in the damp, iddn't that so?"

"That is so."

Chinaberry leaves shushed against Spuds's exasperated shrug.

"That only leaves a couple bad endings, Pete, don't it?"

Sighing this deep in the swamp hurt. Each inhale raised dots of moisture on every bronchiole of the lungs. Hell, maybe Billy May *did* hightail it through the damp, right past Doc's Mercantile and over the border into dry-land Dawes. Pete's understanding was three Pointers had already signed the papers the Oil Man was hawking.

The Oil Man: the only name folk knew him by. Some kind of rep from the offshore oil rigs or coastal refineries. New Year's Day, the Oil Man had started poking around the Point's shanties, offering contracts for land that folk had owned since the eighteenth century. Pointers were proud, flagrantly in many cases, of the exciting pirate history behind their shanties. But rumor was the Oil Man's offer was good. Which didn't bode well for Alligator Point. Too many more takers and joints that mattered would start shutting down. The store. The school.

Maybe Billy May's pa had signed. Maybe that's what upset Billy.

Pete decided to see how well his deputy had gamed it out.

"I'm listenin, Spuds. Tell me those couple of bad endins you're speculatin."

"Gator," Spuds said instantly. "Or bear. Or coyote."

"Puppy-dogs," Pete pshawed. "Unless you egg 'em on first."

"How about a snake? Snakes aren't puppy-dogs, are they, Pete?"

Points to Spuds, though Pete didn't think a snake was the culprit. From what he recalled, Billy May weren't the sort to stray off a trail, not without Pontiac doing the bushwhacking. If Billy had taken a couple snake fangs, his body would have been on a trail, swollen to adult size.

"Not buyin it," Pete adjudged. "What's your other bad endin?"

Spuds, still a kid himself, kicked the ground.

"You know what," he murmured.

Pete did, and he knew why Spuds didn't want to speak it aloud. The deputy had a paralyzing phobia of quicksand. Some childhood incident, Pete figured, having to do with the monstrous Pa Ulene. Pete wondered if quicksand was the real reason Spuds kept longside him. If Spuds blundered into the quick, he'd have old Pete to pull him out.

"Doggone it," Pete said. "We ought to be there already."

"We lost, Pete?" Spuds fretted. His natural cheap-newsprint color went paler.

Always a possibility in the damp, but right then Pete spied a chunk of termite-gnawed wood smothered in burry coastal sandbur. Pete knew tearing up such burrs was a no-no. It ripped them open and scattered more dastardly seed. Pete reached for his Colt .45 to nudge away the plant before remembering he'd had to surrender the sidearm back in '93 when Bullock Parish went bust, the sheriff department with it.

Gently, he moved aside the sandbur with a pinkie.

Carved deep into the softened wood, barely visible now, was an octopus. Plus four words, three of them misspelled.

MAY'S
PRIVUT! KEEP OWT!

"'We all get off on the wrong trail once in a while,'" Pete said. A quote from *The Big Trail*, 1930, John Wayne's first big starring role, a hell of a picture that only tanked because theaters refused to alter their screens for the new 70mm format. The Duke was the one who paid the price, relegated to a decade of Poverty Row flicks until he hit it big with *Stagecoach*.

John Wayne esoterica kept Pete cool when times got tense.

Spuds tapped the old sign. "Anytime I been to the Mays' before, right about this spot here is where I got a shotgun pointed at my—"

"*Hands to de sky, intruders!*"

Pete ducked his big Stetson under a gnarled branch. William May Sr. stood on the gray shambles of his half-sunken porch sixty feet off, a rusty shotgun lodged to his overalled shoulder. Pete waved his hands and smiled as big as he could. One thing he knew about William May Sr. was he was blinder than a decapitated bat.

"Tirez-moi pas, William," Pete said. "We ain't intruders."

"Gat-damn sneakin bandits," William growled. "First you take my propane. Den you take my air mattress."

"We ain't done no such thing, William. This is Pete Roosevelt you're confabbin with. I helped pull your pirogue off that mudbank two years back. I got with me Spuds Ulene. You know Spuds better'n you know me. Short fella? Funny way of walkin? He helped prop up the west side of your shanty not six months back."

The shotgun didn't lower.

"If dat's you, Spuds, holler out de name I call my wife."

Pete glanced at Spuds.

"Goll, Pete," Spuds whispered. "I don't remember."

This was worrisome. But Pete took pains to never look worried. He formed a set of wrinkles high on his brow, just like the Duke. John Wayne's signature expression came off like grim amusement, though in truth, Pete was speculating on how good a shot William May Sr. might be even with headless-bat vision.

"Think harder, Spuds," Pete whispered. "You think sandburs are sticky, wait'll you see our brains all over the damp."

~ 10 ~

PETE ROOSEVELT AND SPUDS ULENE met four years prior. August 1, 1994, at Juicy Lucy's, a grease-sheened twelve-seater burger joint that poured watered-down beer like a spring cloudburst, despite a liquor license that expired the same day that Squeaky Fromme tried to kill President Ford, as Lucy herself like to say. The old broad didn't sweat it. No ATF hard-ass was gonna tramp this far south into the delta. The joint was damned to keep living, just like Lucy was damned to keep slow-murdering Pointers with the nastiest nasty-sugar around: booze.

Pete ate there a lot. He ate there a lot because he parked there a lot. He might have given his rickety Crown Vicky a nautical name—the Melbourne Queen—but that didn't mean it could float. Road vehicles got no farther into the Point than the headland. Even four-wheelers were too wide for the trails. Some folk rode horses or mules. A few had airboats. Many had dinghies or canoes. Mostly folk walked, getting to know the terrain through the grip of their bare toes.

The Melbourne Queen was a tank soldered together in late-seventies Motown. A hundred creaks, groans, and pings. Dozens of dents furred with rust. What was left of its chrome accents pitted from gulf-water salt. Not once in all the years Pete had driven the thing had he gotten bodywork or painting done. He liked the idea of keeping the original crests emblazoned on the doors along with the foot-tall lettering: SHERRIF.

Pete had been allowed to keep the car after Bullock Parish went belly-up. Who else would drive the rattletrap?

He'd sheriffed the hell out of the Point for fifteen years. No one was going to forget that. Including Pete. He still thought of himself as holding the office of sheriff. So did the de facto leaders of the Point known as the Saloon Committee, an inebriated syndicate of elders who got liquored up every Tuesday at the Pelican. Most the Point's forty-seven families stayed liquored up most nights. Well, forty-four since the Oil Man had started handing out contracts.

With the Saloon Committee's blessing, Pointers kept Pete going. They chipped in for his groceries and gasoline. If Pete missed a cookout, somebody ferreted him a tinfoil-covered tray of the choicest bits. He could get a free cup of joe anywhere, and a free beer at any of his regular haunts—Juicy Lucy's, Plum Peppers, or the Pelican, where he threw down with the best of them: Pink Zoot, Gully Jimson, Rawley Deevers, and Gerard Pontiac—the patron saint of all local drunkards.

So: Juicy Lucy's, August 1, 1994. Pete climbed out of the Melbourne Queen, no badge, no .45, pulling on a windbreaker. Eleven years of sheriff weight had made it the only usable remnant of his old uniform—that and the Stetson. He lumbered inside with an inrush of humid air that fluttered several of the tiny, low-grade cotton Jolly Roger flags sold all over the bayou. Pirate's Pride, the product was called.

Pete shot a hello finger at Lucy behind the bar and took a seat in the darkest booth. Didn't feel much like socializing. He was having indigestion, and about to fight fire with fire with a grenade of greasy meat.

That's when he spotted Spuds Ulene. He'd seen the kid before, doing what he was doing now: snorting food like he hadn't eaten in days. The word *kid* weren't real charitable, but Spuds was as small as a kid, with kid mannerisms to boot, scratching at pimples that needed left alone, chewing with mouth agape, slurping electric-yellow soda through a straw. He kept an arm curled around his grub as if a rival gorilla might try to nab it.

Four gorillas had, on cue, loped their way into Juicy Lucy's, agitating the same little Jolly Rogers. Pete didn't recognize them, which meant they were jobbers, edging into the swamp to transport equipment, repair a cistern, run a telephone line, something. They didn't act like they knew one another well, yet had unified as members of a brotherhood. The Brotherhood of Good-Ol' Normal, forever chartered to rain shit down on anyone they deemed Abnormal.

Pete threw beer after burger and watched the brotherhood's razzing of Spuds. Pete knew the brotherhood would grow bored pretty quick. Unless Spuds Ulene stood up, planted his feet, and talked back to his tormentors. That shit might work in movies, but in real life, it got your ass kicked.

Because nothing ever went right on the Point, that's exactly what Spuds did.

Spuds faced them. "The hell y'all over me for? I look funny or something?"

"Yeah," said a man in an oil-stained Astros cap. "You look *real* funny."

"I cleaned up before I came! Checked myself in the mirror! I look fine!"

The brotherhood's radar wasn't busted. This Spuds Ulene kid was slow.

Over the next four years, Pete would learn all about Spuds's capacities—mental, emotional, physical, and, most of all, constitutional. The years Spuds spent as a jockey remained fuzzy as a baby possum, but Pete dug up Spuds's birth certificate from Holy Charity at St. Beatrice Hospital, filled out by a Sister Parissima.

Along with a birth name so heartbreakingly fancified Pete made himself forget it, the words *mentally deficient* had been added in the notes area.

Spuds's ma had died from placental abruption. Spuds lived but had been damaged by a lack of umbilical air. His illiterate pa beat the daft boy for sixteen years before dragging him to the Army recruiting office in Dawes. During Spuds's few weeks in the Army, his C.O. could find no use for him besides kitchen patrol, where Spuds earned his nickname. Far as Pete could tell, that was all Spuds came away with when he was discharged with a familiar curse on his record: *mentally deficient.*

Pete deduced the broad strokes at Juicy Lucy's, where the calculus of fairness was changing fast.

"You thought you looked fine?" Astro continued. "Guess you didn't see it then."

"See what?" Spuds demanded.

"That shit all over you. That yellow shit."

"You calling me yellow?"

"Naw. I'm just saying you got yellow shit all over you. This *here* yellow shit."

Astro picked up a plastic bottle and squeezed with both hands, shooting a stream of French's Mustard. As promised, the yellow shit got all over Spuds, splatting him face to foot.

"Here we go," Pete muttered. He napkined his fingers clean.

While the brotherhood cracked up, Spuds wiped his face and got his bearings. What Pete, Lucy, and the brotherhood didn't know was that sixteen years of taking whuppings from Pa Ulene had taught Spuds a few things. Placid by nature, Spuds could be forced into a blinding red zone, and that's when what he'd learned came flaring out.

Spuds planted his one good leg and fired across the bar like a pinball. The mustard-squirter found himself faceup on the floor, the target of a flurry of unskilled but powerful punches. Pete was caught off guard too; all he'd accomplished was standing up. Here was the magic trick of it: the Astros cap was now on *Spuds's* head.

The brotherhood attacked with the grace of stampeding cattle. A hundred-and-twenty-nine dollars worth of Juicy Lucy property went blammo in seconds. The costliest item was the chair shattered over Spuds's head. The kid didn't seem to feel it. He kept raging till somebody's lucky kick sent him skidding across the floor, coming to rest longside Pete. Pete was the only Pointer who didn't go barefoot on the regular. Didn't think it proper for a sheriff. He wore boots—big, black, leather, shit-kicking cowboy boots.

"Nuts! Nuts! Nuts!" Lucy shouted from behind the bar.

Pete helped Spuds up, getting yellow shit on him too. He gave the four panting gorillas the Duke's patented smirk.

"'Fill your hands, you son of a bitches,'" he growled.

Two were helping up bloodied, dehatted Astro. The third gave Pete a frown.

"The hell's *that* mean?"

Mother Mary, Pete loved this part! He put his boot heels close together, stuck out his hips, lifted arms loosely bent at the elbows, and let his torso sway a bit. Just like the Duke.

"Them's the immortal words of Rooster Cogburn. Ain't none of you uneducated cusses seen *True Grit*?"

One of the others jumped in. "Stay out of this, old man."

"Four big fellas against one little fella." Pete pushed back his Stetson. "Them scales seem tipped."

"That sumbitch stole my hat!" Astro shouted, spraying blood.

Pete eyed the cap Spuds was wearing. "That right, boy? You make off with this feller's chapeau?"

Spuds scowled at his feet, took off the cap, and held it out to Pete. "I shouldn't have started no fight, sir. You can give it back to him."

Pete copied the Duke's famous half-grin.

"Way I see it, that hat is yours, son. Seems to me it was right manly of you to go grabbin it."

"Now wait a darn minute!" Astro barked. "Who the hell you think you are, mister?"

Pete looped his thumbs into his belt. "If you look real hard, friends, out that door yonder, you might see a beat-up old Crown Vicky with a meaningful word on it. Now, I'm not inclined to use the power of that word right now, not when I still got half a burger here left to eat. What I'm *inclined* to do is to put my two-hundred-and-seventy pounds on this little feller's side of the scales. That's what ol' Rooster Cogburn was tryin to say. If that plan sounds good to y'all, then all right—fill your hands with what you got and let's get goin."

The Brotherhood of Good-Ol' Normal backed off, exited, and made donuts in the parking lot. Pete and Spuds helped Lucy clean up, after which she closed for the day. That left Spuds's stomach still growling, so Pete took the kid to Plum Peppers, where he watched Spuds wolf two fried fish sandwiches.

Pete prided himself on his eye for clues. While Spuds gobbled, Pete gave him the ol' twice-over. The kid had a wiry natural health befitting a former jockey, yet showed every sign of surviving out of Alligator Point trashcans. He had the shaley pink skin of unremitting skeeter bites. He had strips of sunburn from sleeping outdoors with scimitars of sun roasting through leaves. He was clearly homeless, and before midnight, Pete had it worked out for the kid to stay temporarily (and soon permanently) in a room attached to the Fontaines' horse stables.

By the time Spuds was licking his utensils, Pete felt solid on the other clue too. The kid's calves were coated in dried dust. Verdict: Spuds had swept and mopped for Lucy in exchange for dinner. Pete thought that was sad until he realized that he survived by the same model.

Truth was, it was Pete Roosevelt who started thinking of Spuds as a deputy, long before Spuds tripped over the same idea.

~ 11 ~

Spuds removed his Astros cap, yellow from four years of swampland sweat, and waved it high. Looked to Pete like he was giving William May Sr. something to aim at.

"I don't remember what you call your wife, but I'm Spuds Ulene, honest! Ask me something only Spuds Ulene would know!"

The shotgun didn't budge.

"C'est bon," William May Sr. said. "When you was here hoistin my house, you told me de name of de little pup you had when you was small. What was dat pup's name?"

Pete gave spuds another Duke-wrinkle.

"Pete," Spuds hissed. "I forgot that too."

"Oh, for the *love*," Pete growled.

The sheriff burst from the brush and stomped across the lawn. The shotgun cocked, nearly as loud a gunfire, but Pete kept coming.

"William May, will you set that bean-spitter aside so I can do me a proper investigation on your missin boy?"

Pete might only have fired his old .45 nine times, but he'd faced an open barrel more times than he knew. Pointers were poor. Poor led to desperation. Desperation led to nasty-sugar. Nasty-sugar led to more fistfights, split-ups, divorces, affairs, and revenge per capita than New York City. Pointers were liberal with threats, though few had the stomach to carry them out.

William May Sr. was the same. He crashed into a rocking chair, which set off the Pirate Pride flags stabbed into either arm. With the nearest dentist an hour's drive north, plenty of Pointers lacked choppers, and William's configuration was a total absence of upper teeth, which allowed his lower lip to curl way up to his nose. He gripped his rifle with two calloused hands and gunned the chair, *skrink, skrink, skrink.*

"Who went and told you about all dat?" he groused.

Pete took off his Stetson and wiped his brow.

"Curious way to start off, William. I was sort of expectin 'Help me find my son,' somethin long those lines."

The bottom lip crept higher. "Some t'ings dere ain't no purpose in huntin."

Pete took the four stairs in two steps and decided to entrust his weight to a metal chair tiger-striped with orange rust. What shade the patchy porch offered felt good, but that was the feint of bayou heat. The sun weren't your foe. Your foe was the wet heat, rising from the offal of soggy soil and the jumping jugulars of a billion breathing things. Spuds wiggle-skipped after, choosing to perch on the porch's rotten wooden rail. Pete anticipated slapstick: cracks in the rail widened with every *skrink, skrink, skrink.*

"I ain't disagreein," Pete said. "That air mattress you're missin? That's not a thing you pawn. Probably stolen by a fellow goin through a rough patch."

"Like I used to be," Spuds added. "Got a regular bed now, though."

"Now, the propane tank, dollars to donuts that's drugs," Pete continued. "You look at the label, you'll see the words *anhydrous ammonia.* Popular drug ingredient right there. You want to save yourself some grief, put locks on your doors, William. The world's different now, even down here in the damp."

"Locks." *Skrink, skrink, skrink.* "How'm I supposed to put locks on doors dat don't even close?"

"I figure that's a problem for you and the missus," Pete said. "Don't you think it's time we got to Billy May?"

Skrink, skrink, skrink. "Who said Billy was gone? I never said it."

Pete quashed a skeeter midair between finger and thumb. It squirted more blood than a skeeter oughta squirt.

"Your missus said it."

The rocking chair stopped sharply. The Jolly Rogers drooped flat.

"Louise said dat?"

William had one eye popped wise. Pete didn't like the look of it. He reached into his shirt pocket and took out the same spiral-bound book report he'd been toting since 1983. Unlike the Pontiac girl's log, he didn't actually write in it. He only pretended. It had a way of getting people serious.

"Not so directly, Mr. May. I heard it from Gully Jimson up at the Pelican last night. Round five in the a.m., your missus came in and told Gully about your missing boy."

"Gully Jimson's a shit-drawers, scrotum-draggin, cabbage-breat' liar dat kisses his poop-eatin dog on de mout'," William said.

William clenched his shotgun. Maybe arthritic spasm, Pete thought. Maybe not. Pete would feel better if that rocking chair got rocking again. He shaped a Duke grin, spread his big hands, and made some Duke wrinkles.

"That's all true about Gully. What he does with that dog, it borders on the unnatural. But it weren't just Gully we confabbed with. We had ourselves a whole parliament of witnesses."

"Drunkards, you mean! You probably soûl, too, Pete!"

That stung Pete a bit. Three, four nights a week, it's true, he got sauced right good.

"You add any ten or twelve drunky accounts together, they're as good as two or three stone-cold sober ones," he grunted.

William's lips plunged into a frown of unbelievable depth. "You ask me, and I believe you askin, dem Pelican drunks are effrayé. T'ings aren't right in dis here swamp. Always been bad but dese days it's gettin badder. Dey tastin fear at de bottom of dey bottles. You tastin it too, iddn't you, Pete?"

Pete blinked to clear the sweat on his eyelids and, in doing so, noticed William's left hand creeping closer to his rifle's trigger. William only had to swing that barrel fifteen inches to take a four-foot shot at Spuds. Spuds, meanwhile, weren't paying any mind. He was busy being spooked; the deputy believed in *everything*, swamp monsters included.

"Lookie here." Pete conjured the Duke's lazy caution. "You and me either's gonna talk about Billy May Jr. right here and now, or I'm gonna go inside and ask Louise about it."

Skrink, skrink, skrink, the sound of resumed confidence. "She won't say nuddin. Not against her own famille she won't."

"That warms the old ticker to hear. So close and cozy a marriage after so long."

Skrink, skrink, skrink. "Dat's right."

"Hey, Spuds. Our parliament of witnesses, they didn't say nothin about Louise havin no fat lip and no blood crusted up her nose, did they?"

"Goll, Pete, your memory *is* going bad," Spuds said earnestly. "That's exactly what they *did* say."

Skrink—and then the chair stopped. Pete didn't believe in God, magic, or miracles, but when it came to glorifying the abilities of the human body, he was an evangelizing zealot. He noticed the twitch of his own arm hairs, the cold roll of sweat down his back. Same kind of signals that allowed the Duke to outshoot any quick-draw scalawags.

That's how, as William May Sr. leapt to his feet, leveling the shotgun toward Spuds, Pete Roosevelt was able to clamp down on William's right wrist, bashing it from the shotgun. With no counterweight, the gun's barrel dripped, and Spuds Ulene, bless him, side-kicked that barrel—with his bad leg, even—showing the same fighting instinct he'd shown at Juicy Lucy's four years back. The weapon pinwheeled across the porch planks.

And then, bless Spuds Ulene twice, the deputy pulled William into an embrace. The goal, Pete knew, was to prevent any more violence. The effect, however, was just the kind of hug you give a father who just lost his son.

Pete never had to leave his chair. The fight drained out of William's body.

"I wuddn't gon' hur nuhbuddy." His voice was muffled in Spud's jacket.

"I figure that's true," Pete sighed. "I'd put my chips on that rusty cannon of yours blowin up in your hands."

William extricated himself and leaned on the stairs rail.

"Don't go in and see Louise."

"You know we have every right," Pete said, though it wasn't true, not since '93. Louise May had to be the one to show her face, whatever condition it was in, and Pete doubted she would. Patterns ran through Alligator Point deeper than any swampland trails.

"It was t'ree nights ago." William's voice trembled. "De night of de carny."

Pete shut his report book, the signal the real interview was starting.

"The holiday. The Eighth."

"I don't know de day, but it was late, and I heard Billy gabbin out in de yard." William sucked his upper lip in over toothless gums. "But dat ain't no crime! Boys are always up late. I was de same, and I bet you, Pete Roosevelt, was worse."

"You bet right."

"Billy was—Billy *is*—honteux. Timid. Reflects poorly on a pa. But dat was de first time I hear him talkin to invisible friends!"

"That what he was doin? Talkin to himself?"

"Sounded so. I told myself, William, you have a word wit' dat boy come chorin time."

"That was the last you saw him."

William nodded. "Louise come fetch me de next day and say Billy's gone."

"Anyplace y'all can imagine he mighta went?"

William shook his head. "Anyplace sensible to look got looked."

"Until you stopped lookin."

"Yes, sir."

"At which point, you weren't fixin to tell nobody."

"Le Bon Dieu! You know we all leavin de Point sooner den later. Dat Oil Man left papers here wit' a mighty tall number on dem. I be takin dat Oil Man's offer and I reckon you be—"

"Until Louise *insisted* you tell somebody. At which point you gave her a little tenderizin. At which point she snuck off to the Pelican anyway. At which point word got back to me." Pete shrugged. "I'm just ruminatin for information."

It was his favorite line from *3 Godfathers*, starring the Duke as a bank robber fleeing across a desert with a newborn baby. It weren't Pete's favorite John Wayne picture—heck, it weren't even his favorite John Wayne picture directed by John Ford—but of all his memorized Duke quotes, none came in handier in the line of duty.

William whirled around. Pete was ready, big paws open for cuffing. A sheriff's duties included rounding up the periodic mad dog, and even after you collared the cur, it generally gave you one last lunge. Didn't come to that, though.

"You *not* just rumifyin, Pete! You sittin your unofficial ass on my porch askin if I went out like Abraham on Moriah and slayed mon fils! And all because de boy woke me up? Or embarrassed me wit' his girly ways? Dat's shit, Pete! You know me better'n dat! You want to know why I zipped shut bout Billy? It de same reason dose Pelican drunkies be drinkin demself mort. Dat t'ing out dere, it finished hidin, Pete. It creepin out of de damp, Spuds. You start talkin bout it like you two talkin bout it, it disposed to start talkin back. And you know what happen after it starts talkin. Folk start *followin.*"

~ 12 ~

"Cher? C'mere? S'il vous plaît?"

Gerard Pontiac wanted to give his daughter a hug but his right arm didn't show up. Where'd the sucker get off to? Pinned under his body, felt like. He blinked and his eyelashes stroked his cheek, soft as the sleeve of Janine's nightgown when she used to turn pages in bed. The sensation told him his face was flat on the floor. And *that* told him he'd passed out and the sticky on his lips was Old Crow, the worst rotgut Doc Devereaux sold.

His brain throbbed. Nausea boiled his belly.

"Pontiac, cher? C'mere?"

Her hand, small as a daisy, was on the screen door, about to depart. She drifted back across the shanty in that little-girl way, barely grazing floorboards. She held something, and for a instant Gerard believed it was the machete he used to chop back the invading jungle. At age nine, already more mature than her daddy, Pontiac had taken it upon herself to chop him down too. Nothing personal. Invasive species gotta be stopped, that's all.

What it was was a fishing pole. A bamboo-styled piece of plastic chintz with the world's simplest line reel. Pontiac liked it because it was telescopic, meaning she could take it apart and stow it in her satchel. Kids loved building and unbuilding stuff. Gerard always played along—*Coo-wee! Now dat dere's some clever gadget!*—when in truth, it was a skosh better than a dead branch. If Gerard didn't piss away his pennies on Old Crow, he could buy her that rod she wanted down at Doc's. Then she'd feel pride and build self-esteem, all that junk little girls needed.

With his free hand, Gerard took Pontiac by the wrist. Her skin was bathwater, her pulse a birdie's heart.

"Going fishin, cher?" Sounded like he had straw in his mouth. Tasted like it too.

Pontiac nodded. "I heard Guimbarde's got blue cat."

Gerard's smile was a novelty-shop costume. "Blue cat grow bigger'n you."

"A lot less smart, though."

"A feller down de bayou once caught a blue cat two-hundred-fifty pounds big."

"That's only a story, Daddy."

"Just because it's a story," Gerard said, "don't mean it's not actual."

Why'd he need to drink himself flat before he could talk so wise? His whole begotten life was a tale better off as fiction. Once upon a time, down in the Atchafalayan dark, a poor, penniless white man named Gerard Pontiac lived in a god's-honest pirate shanty. That shanty had a magic to it. You could tell because Gerard had it all. A fix-it livelihood that made him feel good about his sweat. A woman who made every day, night, winter, summer, porch, kitchen, and bedroom interesting. A little girl so smart he lived in fear over what a wrecking ball they'd loosed upon the planet. But pirate magic was *pirate* magic—troublesome magic. Death came, followed by drink, disorder, descent. The storybook of Gerard's life was wilting fast into the quick.

He pulled his girl close. A sapling spine, shoulder bones like china cups.

"You're slimy," she said. "I'll fetch you water."

"No. Écoute-moi."

Folk on the Point, the Saloon Committee most of all, paid Gerard for odd jobs, but you couldn't rely on it. Two or three times a month, Gerard plunged his bare hands into the muculent clay of outer-reach bayous, digging for chests of gold stashed by the Pirates Lafitte. Two centuries of desperate dreamers had squandered their lives chasing down such hearsay. Gerard knew all the legends. The priceless cache along the Sabine, somewhere near a grove of gum trees. The brick storehouse crumbling on a forgotten island off Lake Borgne. Some rock-lined gulch near Timbalier Bay.

Gerard had yet to wrap his fingers around a single doubloon. At least dirt and clay felt good in his hands. Better than those cold, sharp papers dropped off by the Oil Man. He'd slept through the Oil Man's knocking and only spotted him receding into the distance, suit and tie all geometric against the swamp's loopy tangles. But the manila folder the Oil Man had left was irrefutable. When Gerard nudged it with a bare toe, it popped open like a trap. Dollar signs wove like snakes through legalistic bêtise.

He should have burned the folder in the stove. Instead, he stowed it in a cabinet, where it, and the possibilities it represented, grew like lichen.

Gerard hadn't spoken a word of the papers to Pontiac. She loved their stretch of swamp more than anybody who lived so poor had a right to. To her, the omnipresent mud might as well be her mother's dark brown skin, warm with life in a way the crypt at St. Vincent de Paul Cemetery #3 wasn't.

Gerard sunk his fingers into the clay of his girl's back, digging for a different gold.

"Cher—did Pete come talk to you?"

"He the man in the hat?"

"De big hat, yeah. He come by asking after Billy May?"

"Yeah. He had real decent manners too."

"Écoute-moi. You don't have to talk to *nobody* dat come to dis shanty. To whom dis shanty belong?"

"Us, Daddy."

"And we proud of it, ain't we?"

"Yes, Daddy."

"Maybe dis shanty nuddin but firewood, but it *our* firewood. Next time somebody come by, and he ain't de ghost of Jean Lafitte himself, you come fetch me."

"But Daddy, you were . . ."

The delicacy of this girl, unwilling to speak his curse aloud! When she ought to belt it till the Spanish moss straightened. Maybe then the failures of her no-good daddy would stop smarting.

"What you tell Pete? Ain't Billy May sent no word?"

She shook her head. "Billy May didn't go to the carny. Now he's not anywhere."

The girl wasn't saddled with a Cajun drawl folk in the outside world would mock. Hers was the voice of possibility, of sound of the whole country stretching north. He had to find a way to get her there. The Oil Man's papers might be the first step.

"You hear from Billy, you tell me. Tell me *first.*"

"He's *gone*, Daddy. Gone into the hog guzzle."

Gerard didn't think his girl had ever sounded surer.

"You miss him longside you?"

He saw Pontiac pause, quick as a cricket but languid with loss. She covered it up fast, so fast it broke Gerard's heart. A peeshwank like her ought to be allowed to be sad.

Pontiac frowned. "That boy was a puss."

Gerard's brain made a fist, squirting poison down his spinal cord. *Puss*—that one was his fault. He'd told Pontiac once that Billy May was doomed to wear lawyer stripes in the city. He'd only said it to draw a contrast to Pontiac, who'd he said was "swearing like a ten-dollar hooker." Naturally, Pontiac wanted to know what a hooker was, so Gerard, who'd known some fine hookers, backtracked and said hooking wasn't necessarily *bad*, only to backtrack again to clarify he wasn't saying Pontiac should *be* a hooker. What the hell was he doing talking to a seven-year-old girl about hookers anyway? Ended up drinking that day too.

"He may be a puss, but you don't get to choose dem dat crawl inside you." Gerard squinted through a red film of agony. "Dat why you Guimbarde-bound, non? Dat's near de May place."

Not offering to fetch him water now, was she? When Pontiac got caught, she went as quiet as a career criminal. Sick as he was, Gerard got a laugh at her icepick stare. The laugh set off his gut, lurching like a knot of toads. Suddenly his body was an inferno. His brain ballooned against his skull. His spit sizzled. His instinct was to clamp tight to Pontiac, so he did the opposite and let go.

He heard Pontiac shuffle out of reach. She was as good as out the door. Gerard settled his scalding cheek against his arm and tried to focus. He had shit to say. He didn't know what, but it was building, racing the puke to see which got out first.

"If you got to go, cher, listen to what-all I say. While I still got de power to say it. You watch your step out dere. Specially when a storm's a-brewin. You can never tell a storm brewin from de water. Go by de trees, cher. Dey de only ones dat tell de truth. De turn up t'eir leaves, like beggar hands after a nickel. They hopin and thirstin for rain, and sometime dat rain bring along wit' it her old friend, de wind. And sometime dat wind go mean enough to rip roots right out de ground. Wit' wind like dat, de gulf can rise up quick as a rabbit. And den, well, dere's udder t'ings out dere too."

"I know."

"I don't mean quicksand or gators."

"Kids *know*, Daddy."

"Maybe dat's true. Maybe de young know it twice as good as de old because it comes up from de ground, closer to y'alls eyes and ears. Listen all de same. Dat *somet'ing* out t'ere, it de root of all de awful on de Point. Why nuddin grows. Why pig, cat, dog, dey all croak when dey still babies. Why all a man can do is t'rash around and sink fast. Or grab him a bottle and sink slow. You t'ink your mama died natural? Dat any folk here die natural? I t'ink dat t'ing out dere reached inside her and laid eggs."

Pontiac was at the door looking back. She'd taken apart her rod and slotted it into her satchel. In her back pocket she'd stuffed her log, which Gerard despised. The order of that log mocked the disorder of his life. But he didn't doubt she'd heard him. He'd do anything to still have ears like that.

"It lay eggs in you, too, Daddy?"

Gerard choked. Tears, snot, piss, puke. All of it, coming.

"I don't t'ink so, cher—"

"What about bottles? What if it laid eggs in all the *bottles*?"

Gerard pictured a clot of rubbery eggs sliding down his throat and that was all she wrote. *You don't get to choose dem dat crawl inside you*, he'd said, but maybe it was also true that sometimes they wanted out. Vomit leapt from his belly in a thick mass. It didn't splash, it *thumped*, and Gerard roared for Pontiac to get out, he didn't want her to see this upchuck of liquor and shame. Alcohol was quicksand down here, and he was hip-deep in it, being pulled down and not even fighting.

~ 13 ~

PONTIAC FISHED NOTHING BUT SWAMP GRASS from home plate, but had better luck wading knee-deep by first. Caught a perch with a nub of wax worm. Once that fella was fussing in her bucket, Pontiac dug some grubs from the first base hummock and set her sights on bluegill. Bluegill didn't normally bite till afternoon, so this bunch must be especially dumb.

Five minutes after she'd plunged her bare feet into the pudding of mud, she felt it. Something under the water. Something soft. It tickled her leg a few times, and each time she looked down and saw a pale round thing dropping into the murk. At first she didn't worry. All sorts of trash got sucked into bayou waters. Could be a shallow-dwelling fish, a redfish or sheepshead.

Pontiac, though, got thinking. Why she'd hoofed it to Guim-barde in the first place. Who she'd been hoping to find. What if the next time she felt that soft nudge . . .

. . . she looked down panther-quick . . .

. . . and found, grinning back up at her, Billy May?

The rotten jack-o'-lantern of Billy May's head. Eye sockets hollowed out by hungry fish. Lips nibbled off to make a toothy, silent sob. Pontiac imagined mud bubbling from her best friend's throat, his blub-a-lub of panic.

Why'b you'b leabe me behinb, Pontiab-b-b?

She jerked in fear. Her line popped from the water, the grub parasailing.

"Saphir!" she cried.

The cry echoed, and she was ashamed, because the echo didn't say *Daddy*.

André Saphir was out past the right field marsh, kneeling on Guimbarde Beach, the only place on the Point to have a nice, pretty stretch of sand. He wasn't fishing. Pontiac couldn't tell what he was up to. Once, Pontiac saw Saphir pause in the middle of a sentence, snatch a copperhead out of the water by the tail, and crack it like a whip, just once, hard enough for the snake's fuck-damn head to fly off.

Pontiab-b-b? Why won'b youb look at meeb?

The swamp gas burbling, that's all it was. It made Pontiac feel better to know Saphir was close, keeping track in his own way. He didn't need a log. His noggin was a better record-keeper than a whole Kmart rack of notebooks.

Save meeb, Pontiab-b-b, before the wabber washes my head awabe!

It felt like losing Billy May a second time. Billy May, who'd maybe been a puss, sure, but had been longside her for as far back as she remembered, and she missed him, it came on fierce, like a black widow scampering from nowhere and biting.

"Saphir!"

Saphir lifted his face from the beach and stood. His skin was the exact same shade as Pontiac's, a wheat-field blend of folk both white and Black. That was one reason Pontiac liked to pretend Saphir was her daddy, but not the only reason.

Saphir was made from all the parts Daddy wasn't. He was ten or twenty feet tall, slender as wood shavings, shoulders like a sailboat's boom. Tattoos peeked from under the rolled sleeves of a white cotton shirt buttered with age. The sleeves ballooned like a ship's sails in coastal winds. Leather bands, studded with what looked like gems, clung to his wrists. His denim trousers, scoured by salt, were held up by a three-inch leather belt studded like the wristbands. His left ear was pierced in eight places. Golden trinkets dangled from pins in each of those piercings, one of them, so he said, a coin salvaged from a sunken galleon. Hs head was shaved bald. On it he wore a black, hand-knit cap.

Most the families on the Point claimed a lineage to Lafitte's pirates but only André Saphir looked like a pirate. The rest . . . well, they looked like Daddy. Pot-bellied and sausage-fingered, faces sun-screwed into doleful squints, clad in the regalia of saggy tank tops, stretched-out gym shorts, dog-chewed flip-flops, shrimper aprons, and neon-colored wraparound shades.

Residents prided themselves on their shanties as much as their blood. So said legend, they'd been built by Lafitte's privateers, who'd used these wetlands to offload corsairs and send stolen goods upriver on pirogues, until Andrew Jackson pardoned them in exchange for fighting on January 8, 1815. Alligator Point had started all white like the pirates, and was still mostly so, but over time other blood mixed in too. Black, Hispanic, Native. It was the Louisiana way.

According to the pickled brains of the Saloon Committee, sixty-four shacks had survived two centuries of tidal surges atop their original ten-foot cedar stilts. Pontiac had never seen Saphir's shanty, but it was probably like everybody else's: two or three small rooms, a thousand-gallon cistern for drinking water, a rainwater shower, a bucket-flush toilet, a butane stove, and an electrical current thin as a cockspur bristle. Truth was, it was hard to imagine Saphir snoozing anywhere but inside a boat.

"Couyon," Saphir called. "Dis shoutin gonna spook de fish."

But the fisherman gathered his bag and bucket and waded toward first base on legs as long as an ibis. Pontiac ignored her peripheral vision—the white thing still bobbing—and focused on the relieved lob of her heart. Only when Saphir reached the hummock did Pontiac get embarrassed. Bawling for help was a Billy May move.

She shook her pole to save face.

"Skunk, man. Need that Whiz-Bang! Can't catch a cold with this junk."

"Oui, oui, you can. You just have to out-t'ink Mr. Fish. He not so smart."

"Smart enough to stay away from first base."

"Dere's a barbue fais do-do at second. T'ickest barbue in dis whole swamp."

Second base was a six-foot-wide hummock, a low hill of solid ground like a tiny island. Somewhere beneath it was an actual base. Five years ago, at the edge of Pontiac's memory, there'd been a whole diamond at Guimbarde. She used to watch older kids leap around on legs she could only dream of having. It wasn't totally dry back then. Baselines smacked when kids ran them and ne'er an inning passed without an infielder gloving a frog out of the way.

The marsh had crept in, yard by yard, till the whole field was submerged. It was coincidence that hummocks had formed where the bases had been. Probably.

"I'm not tall enough for second base," Pontiac muttered. "I'd get my log all soggy."

Saphir brought a handful of bright-red mudbugs from his bag. He held out a handful and Pontiac took one. She could eat mudbugs, what dry-land folk called crawfish, in her sleep. She licked the seasoning, sucked the sauce, peeled the tail, and with her teeth dragged the meat onto her tongue. Hellfire! Not in the whole delta was there nothing tastier. It made her feel strong. Less gullible. The white thing in water *definitely* wasn't Billy May's head.

Saphir's blocky jaw chewed sadly. His voice slid like swamp fog.

"None of dis diamond shoulda sunk. Dem oil folk, dey de culprits. Slicing and dicing de playree up wit' t'eir canals. What dey t'ink was gonna happen? De paper says every year de bayou lose land de size of New York City."

"Those oil rigs are pretty, though," Pontiac said.

A year back, while Daddy was nine rounds into boxing himself to a drunken draw, she'd begged Saphir to take her away in his aluminum flatboat with the puny Evinrude motor. First law of the bayou was that any map you drew of it was trash two years later. You had to work the swamp to know it, and no one knew its loch hearts, estuary arteries, and inlet vessels like André Saphir.

Off they sped through Caminada Bay, beyond Grand Isle, all the way past Port Fourchon. *Keep going*, she'd ordered, licking crusts of sea salt from lips already salty with tears. Coming upon the elevated oil rigs and towering derricks at night was like seeing

one of those lost New York Cities rise from the ocean, a mega-
lopolis of glaring lights, white-gas-flame towers, a million jostling
hardhats. It was ungodly yet humbling, like meeting the species
that had come to replace you.

The oil rigs were closer to the Point than New Orleans. Pontiac
knew she could join them one day if she had to. A handful of
Pointers had done it and never been heard from again.

Saphir spotted the oncoming tempêtes through the darkness. The lumpy clouds looked like black gums and foretold
waterspouts—water tornadoes able to toss boats like leaves. Mèt
Agwe, Saphir said. If you believed everything you heard, these gulf
waters were full of divinities, wraiths, monsters, devils, and titans.
In Vodou circles, Mèt Agwe Tawoyo was king of the sea, patron
to fishermen and sailors. If Saphir was evoking Mèt Agwe, things
were dire.

He gunned the Evinrude. That day, they outran the tempêtes,
and who knew what gods or monsters. But Pontiac felt no joy. She
could have gazed at the oil city all night. She could have dog-
paddled out to it, shimmied up the steel, ingratiated herself to
the locals, lived a life.

"If dem upriver hadn't built dem levees," Saphir said, "if dey let
dat ol' Mississip flood like what was natural, dis swamp here, she'd
build herself back. Dat's all de baya is, you know. Sand and mud
from de Mississip just . . ."

"Puked up," Pontiac finished, and regretted the image she saw.

Her daddy, beached by a stomach-acid sea, praying to sink.

Saphir sucked a mudbug. "I was gonna say somet'ing fan-
ciful like *expunge*, but oui, oui—*puked up* is right. Dese waters got
magic, catin. No tellin if it bad magic or good. Or if dere's any difference to de ones who make de magic happen."

He tossed the mudbug shell. Wind snatched it and flung it past Pontiac, so close she smelled the crab boil, and into the water. Saphir followed the shell's path until he was looking right at the white thing bobbing in the bilious marsh. Pontiac tensed. If Saphir saw it, it was real, and all her worst thoughts about Billy were true. She'd lose control and cry like she'd hadn't since Mama's funeral.

"Look at dat," Saphir said. "He crawled back from de grave. To remind us what we done."

Pontiac's body filled with heat, like Bob Fireman's cottonmouth had gotten her. She knew there was moving on till she sucked out the venom. She followed Saphir's gaze and looked down.

Not a head. A baseball.

~ 14 ~

BEST GERARD COULD DO WAS to flop like the two-hundred-fifty-pound blue cat he told Pontiac was real. That only got him a couple feet from his upchucked slime. With Pontiac gone, sunlight seeped through the shanty's screen door and added texture to the puke. It was too chunky to be liquor alone. He must have thrown up his guts, muscle, and bone, reducing him to a slug to be slurped up by the next varmint.

He wasn't going anywhere soon. Fine. Gave him time to think.

He winded back his memory to five that morning. He'd been glued to a stool at the Pelican when Pete Roosevelt swung by to hear Gully Jimson's missing-child report. Gerard had run out of booze coin round midnight, but his pals Rawley Deevers and Pink Zoot had kept the hooch flowing.

Pals—was that what you called folk who twisted the knife in your belly while you twisted the knives in theirs?

Pete talked to Gully, what little that was worth, then shared words with Moses Goingback, the Pelican's owner, then Rawley, Zoot, and Gerard. Gerard copped an attitude. It rubbed him the wrong way when Pete would do the whole lawman dog-and-pony, when one night before, he'd been sloshed right here on the stool longside Gerard.

"You searchin for a scum-sucker dat mighta swiped a child, shérif, you ought to take a look at André Saphir."

Pete's raised eyebrow showed nothing but pity for the accusation. Gerard untangled his bare feet from the stool and hurried off. Tears burned his throat worse than the Pelican's rotgut.

Nothing cut through Gerard's crapulence like his hatred for André Saphir. For starters, the rogue was as renowned a teetotaler as he was a fisher. Everybody else on the Point drank. Or smoked. Or chewed. Or did crack, or tripped balls, or any other nasty-sugar they could find. Elbow-crawling through this cancerous bayou, you didn't have many better choices.

Gerard tried to believe the fifty-some-year-old Cajun was doing something improper with Pontiac. It never held. The only thing Saphir had done wrong was to replace Gerard. Every time Pontiac came home jabbering how Saphir taught her how to pick sticktights off her hair, or demonstrated how to paddle a standing skiff, or this, or that, Gerard's throat went so raw he just *had* to drink. If Old Crow had taken flight, time for cough syrup. If the cough syrup was gone, uncork the vanilla extract. If all cookery cheats were kaput, it was all Gerard could do not to lap up the closest briny pool. Mightn't that pool be spiked with toad toxins?

With all Gerard's crashing about last night, the twenty-minute walk home took forty-five, and the whole way he'd practiced for what he'd tell Pontiac come dawn.

Somet'in got Billy May, it true, but I won't let it get you. Dis here's my last drunk. Wit' God as my witness, I goin as bone-dry as de swamp is blood-wet.

The promise was like the roof of every Alligator Point shanty. Sagging, oui—but there was hope in them sags, wasn't there? Pointers should've cancered themselves out decades back. But folk here kept going, kept going.

He got home. Had to be six-thirty. And Pontiac wasn't there. And he got worried. And he opened cabinets. Looking for grub, he told himself, but he was a shit-ass fibber. He found some Old Crow. And set it in the center of the floor, like a flame to keep warm by. He walked outside. And shouted Pontiac's name. And wondered if he was too late and she was gone like Billy May. And went back inside. And throttled Old Crow by its neck. And drank. And became a crow himself, black feathers, black eyes, black scream. What did it matter? There wasn't no saving Pontiac any—

Pip! Gerard looked at the puddle of vomit. A bubble had popped in it.

Yeast in his stomach acid? C'est bête. Yet other bubbles began to form. They grew, expanded, and caught the light. Gerard pulled himself to his skinned elbows. These weren't the kind of bubbles he'd seen in the corn-and-barley mash of backwater stills. These were the bubbles of a gator about to surface.

A tendril of vomit jetted two feet from the puddle.

The marshland faked like everything was fine. Cicadas cycled through their incantations. Fish gurgled in the water between the shanty's stilts.

Gerard tried to focus his eyes. But the evidence didn't change. The extended arm of nasty-sugar bubbled like pancake batter on a griddle.

Last night . . . had he eaten something . . . alive? God knows he'd done it before, swallowing a flying palmetto bug on accident, gobbling a caterpillar on a dare. He didn't recollect consuming nothing yesterday but Moses Goingback's stale peanuts. It had to be liquor. Some bottles at Doc's Mercantile were too dusty to read the label. The Old Crow must have curdled. Gerard prayed that was it. Because the other option—Pontiac's idea—was unthinkable.

What if it laid eggs in all the bottles?

~ 15 ~

THE GUIMBARDE TIDE RIPPLED WITH DADDY'S VOICE.

Dat somet'ing out t'ere, it de root of all de awful on de Point.

Pontiac took out her log and pencil, found the driest clump of hummock, and started keeping track. What Daddy had said about the thing in the swamp laying eggs. What Saphir had said about levees, which kept folk dry in the city even as they tortured the bayous to death. She took notes on the ball field itself, the depth of the water, where she caught the perch at first, the catfish fais do-do at second.

Track-keeping was the best way to ignore the peeled baseball she'd set inside her bucket. A deep black cleft had given it a puffer-fish mouth. A few clumps of loose threads hung from the cleft, giving it the octopus shape of all the old markings around the Point.

"De sheriff," Saphir said. "He come charre wit' you, huh?"

"How'd you know?"

"Dat's easy. Sheriff Pete got overheard by de sand flies, who landed on de otter, who scrapped wit' de muskrat, who chased off de mallard, who dove after de mackerel, who told me de whole t'ing while danglin off de end of my line."

Saphir smiled like he knew Pontiac was too old for stories but liked them anyway.

"Tee Billy never knew dis playree like you," he said.

"You hardly knew him," Pontiac said.

"Comme ça. But I know you, ain't I?"

She sketched a baseball diamond and improvised symbols for fish.

"What you catching out there?"

"I don't got to catch nuddin for a spell. I took a big boat of ouaouarons into de baya."

Ouaouaron was French for bullfrog, what Saphir called sport fishermen. They came from all over the country for a "bayou adventure," usually hiring a local to glide them through the moory maze. Pontiac could spot them a mile off. Fancy tackle boxes, waterproof windbreakers, energy bars with wrappers that always ended up in the water. Pontiac once spotted Saphir guiding some ouaouarons, steering an eighteen-footer with his toes and acting simple-minded. He didn't point at a splash and say, "Dat's garfish," or point at a swell in the water and say, "Dat's a puppy drum." Big shots, Pontiac figured, only tipped well when they *felt* big.

"What were you doing out there if not fishing?" Pontiac pressed.

Saphir jostled his bucket with a bare foot. The insides clinked like china.

The ache of Pontiac's smile informed her she hadn't smiled since January 8. She pocketed her log and leaned over the bucket. It was filled with the sandy hues, raindrop ripples, and cosmic spirals of seashells—cockles, whelks, olives, coquinas, angel wings, cat's eyes, periwinkles, and wentletraps. To one side was an old handkerchief nestling a single shell with an ice-cream-cone shape and a fold as delicate as a dog's ear.

"Is that a fuck-damn Junonia? Can I hold it?"

Saphir chewed mudbugs and gave her a look: *Sure, if you can do it adult.*

Gently as picking up a newborn kitten, Pontiac scooped up the shell with both hands and held it close. Most shells had the sharp, crystal smell of salt. This one smelled like milk. Usually only shrimpers trawling the deep Gulf turned up Junonias. On land, they were as as rare as the pirate booty Daddy kept digging for.

"You can get two hundred for this at She Sells Sea Shells," she said.

Saphir dismissed the notion with a ringed hand.

"Well, if you ain't going to sell it, let me have it!" Pontiac scowled. "Don't tell me you can *read* these things."

Saphir shrugged.

"The lady at See Shell She Sells says that's a fib," Pontiac said. "Or a fable."

"A fib's different from a fable, catin."

Smelled like horseshit to Pontiac. She gave the Junonia a closer look anyway. Its cream-colored surface was covered in orderly lines of brown squares that made the shell resemble a small, rolled-up scroll. Some folk claimed it was writing, but no kind of writing Miss Ward taught at school.

"Dere's all sorts of writin," Saphir said, reading her mind. "Dis kind's been set by dem who stands over us while we go a-barefootin. Writin dat means to tell us what to do, which-a-way we ought to turn. You find a Junonia and you can be sure you found a message."

"From who?"

"Dat's de question. Is it a good somebody, tryin to help your soul along? Or a bad somebody, tellin lies so you follow dem into de dark? Eidder one is bigger den us folk. And den sometimes . . ."

"What?"

He fussed with a bracelet. Picked at an earring. Slapped a skeeter.

"Time to time, I read tales on dese shells from folk who got lost in de waves."

"Like who?"

Saphir scratched at his hat. It sparkled with salt.

"Fishers. Sailors. Travelers. Folk dat sailed dese waves on t'eir own risk. Dey ain't got much to say but *oops*. But dese udder ones, ones who drowned for no fault of t'eir own, dey de ones who ain't restin peaceful."

"You're talking about slaves," Pontiac said. "I ain't dumb."

"No, you ain't."

"Mama told me slaves brought shells with them over from Africa. From Haiti. Used them like money."

"Dat's true."

"Said they wore shells too. To send secret signs. You wore a cowrie shell, that meant you were planning to revolt."

"Dat a powerful shell."

"Or they'd blow a conch to signal their friends when trouble was coming."

"Trouble was always comin."

"That's the folk you say put words on Junonias?"

A wrathful muscle, rarely seen, twinged Saphir's cheek.

"Hundreds of dem poor folk ended up on de bottom of de sea."

Pontiac frowned at the shell's brown spots.

"Is this how those dead folk keep track? Like me and my log?"

Saphir shrugged. "I t'ink it more likely *we* lost track of *dem*."

Pontiac turned the Junonia over. It was so lotiony soft she could barely feel it.

"How'd you learn to read these?"

"You just got to have de eye."

"Well, what's this shell say?"

"You tell me. You got de eye too. Lotta ladies do."

Pontiac frowned. "That's the kind of shit-butt skill they're always giving girls. Boys get to drive race-cars and fight ninjas and all we get to do is read shells."

Saphir smiled. "Junonia is named after Juno. A goddess and warrior. De protector of all de ladies of Rome. She's gonna lead you into battle one day, long after we men are all busted up from race-car jumps and ninja fights."

Mixing Roman myth with Crescent City hoodoo didn't bother Pontiac one speck. If New Orleans had any magic at all, it was its knack for taking the world's oddments of augury, conjury, devilry, wizardry, astrology, alchemy, necromancy, prophecy, witchery, and trickery, and stirring them into a gumbo that tasted better than any of those ingredients alone. If Juno stood guard with her spear so Pontiac could learn to read shells, then she ought to get learning.

She knotted her forehead and gave the Junonia a harder look. It had felt smooth at first, but really its texture was as tortured as elephant skin. And the brown spots weren't identical at all. Some were shaped like gumdrops. Others, hamburgers. Some spots touched other spots to make figure eights. Not even the brown was brown when you got technical. It was a mix of gold, red, black, and orange.

Being the cleverest kid in the swamp was all Pontiac had. But the shell language made her feel stupid, like Miss Ward was lecturing and she was the only kid in class not getting it. Who cared if the Junonia was a fable? It was a fib *first*, and like the World's Scariest Ride, or Biggest Rat, or Mutant Maze, she was sick of fibs.

She shot to her feet.

"Nobody can read this! All you're doing is lying!"

Saphir held up his hands, a gesture soft as mud. It made Pontiac madder.

"I can't take you lying on top of all the lying Daddy does!"

"Your daddy don't have a lyin heart, catin. All he's got is a demon vine in his belly dat he keeps on waterin. He's gonna pull dat plant by de roots one of dese days."

How would Saphir know? About her daddy? About the kind of smells and sounds that suffused their shanty? Saphir wasn't even looking her in the eye anymore! He was staring down at the Junonia, all worried. Pontiac realized she had the shell in a tight fist. Any tighter, the shell would break. A sultry swamp breeze whispered in Pontiac's ear.

She reared back with the Junonia.

"No!" Saphir cried. "Dem words aren't yours to—"

Pontiac hurled the shell into the bucket, same as if it were a shrimp, or snap bean, or mudbug. The Junonia hit a whelk with a *clink* almost too light to hear. Both shells shattered into pieces the size of teeth.

There was only the patient tide, the whisper of Saphir's breath, and the thrush of blood in Pontiac's ears. She bore it for ten seconds before daring to peek up at her friend. Saphir didn't look much like her friend right now. His lips were drawn back at what she'd done. Pontiac was prepared to accept anger. But that wasn't the look Saphir was giving.

He looked disappointed. Bone-deep disappointed.

Too fuck-damn much to take. Pontiac snatched her bucket and ran. Except her fishline caught, dragging her back, making her look even dumber, an indignity so foul she flung her crappy rod into the depths and ran. From longside Saphir, yes, but also from longside Billy May, longside the gods and ghosts in the waves, longside the dying Gulf and its conquering kingdom of oil.

~ 16 ~

GERARD STARED SO HARD AT the moiling vomit his eyeballs wobbled at the rims of their quivering lids. Bayou folk, the saying went, had swamp in their veins. Maybe it was more than an expression. Maybe the swamp was truly inside them, microscopic bugs dictating what they ought to do, and now he'd gone and barfed his out. The bubbling was its laughter.

Slowly, as if going for a gun, Gerard dug for the item he kept in his front pants pocket.

Not a day passed, even drunken ones, that Gerard didn't think of the single time in his hexed life he'd bucked the odds. It throttled his memories like torpedo grass, tighter with each pass of Pontiac's birthday. To keep his girl out of St. Vincent de Paul #3 longside Janine, he'd need that kind of luck one more time.

When Gerard was in sixth grade, two years before ditching school, he and his friends shot marbles day and night, winning from one another a treasury of immies, clearies, milkies, steelies, corkscrews, benningtons, cat's eyes, onion skins, and giant aggies. The best marbles you could hold up to your eye on a sunny day and see whole universes inside.

Boys didn't comport with girls in 1960. Gerard's crew was all male and half-naked nine months a year, shoulders sun-streaked, bare feet caked in slippers of dried mud. They said you could hear the crack of Gerard's marble shots a mile off. Once a week, he lost on purpose so he didn't clean out his friends. Still, his collection dwarfed theirs. He had fifty-five marbles, his prized possessions, kept in a dress sock he'd stolen from his daddy, DeLoach.

Back then, not even Lafitte's buried gold could out-value picture marbles. Picture marbles were what he and his pals called *hardtoget*—stuff you had to stumble across rather than buy. Picture marbles were regular size, but embedded inside were actual pictures. The three Gerard won from other boys contained the Green Hornet, Sergeant Preston of the Yukon, and Hopalong.

But the first he'd acquired meant the most. He'd never forget watching it tumble from his box of cornflakes, wrapped in cellophane. It contained a picture of Dan-El and Natongo, the teenage heroes from the "Brothers of the Spear" comic printed on the back pages of *Tarzan*. Gerard vowed to never part with it.

Things changed with the arrival of Karl Rusnak in sixth grade. He came bearing a German accent and some *two thousand marbles*, including variations foreign to bayou boys: peppermint swirls, micas, clam broths, latticinios—all of them hardtoget. German Rusnak, as he was quickly renamed, was an ace shooter, a sudden rival for Gerard's crown.

German Rusnak had a racket: a lidless shoebox into which he'd carved holes of different sizes. You took your shots from a dirt line six feet off. The biggest hole paid even money. Shoot in one marble, win one marble from German's stock. Smaller holes paid two, three, or four-to-one. The smallest hole had perfect, crisp edges: it had never been touched. It was the precise dimensions of a standard marble, not a sixteenth-inch wider. It paid hundred-to-one.

The game engulfed every marble-shooter's mind. They shot constantly. Usually they lost. Dynamics began to change. The crew was angry all the time. Lunches got hurled into mud. Mouths got blooded by knuckles. Nicknames sharpened from affectionate to hurtful. Gerard came to despise the game. There wasn't no sport to it. Just that damn box and German's face, smugger with every marble he harvested, chuckling *Ze house alvays vins.* Gerard kept away.

"Zis iz your champ?" German taunted. "He vins by betting nothink."

Gerard was still smarting from the insult when DeLoach returned from collecting crab traps and found his son brooding on the porch—with DeLoach's sock of marbles. Rotten timing: somebody had unloaded DeLoach's traps and he was pissed. With wife Eulalie watching in horror, DeLoach snatched the sock, marched through the downpour, and dumped eleven years of fairly won spoils into the steaming sump.

DeLoach would die of bone cancer nine years later to the day.

That night, Gerard snuck out to get his marbles back. He lowered himself into a lagoon squalling from a hot-rain deluge. He fished beneath the surface with his hands, touching all sorts of slippery things. Moss, sweetgrass, rocks. Finally he felt a single marble cradled in mud.

Before he could make a fist around it, an electric slither passed through his fingers.

A second later, a snake lifted its head from the boggy boil, so close to Gerard he could see steel-rivet eyes and a white-diamonded jaw as smug as German Rusnak's. A cottonmouth. The swamp was the snake's house and *ze house alvays vins.* Glued to the mire, soaked to the skin, and having lost his marbles in both senses, Gerard broke.

"Do it, snake! You hear?"

The snake swelled like it had swallowed up every hard, round piece of Gerard's soul. The legendary fangs emerged from the lipless mouth. The apocryphal white mouth, a hole smaller than any in German Rusnak's box. Gerard inhaled pints of rain and coughed them out, his own sticky venom.

"You t'ink dat scares me, snake? You t'ink you can take somet'in from me dat everybody else ain't already took? Y'all ain't shit, snake! Y'all ain't shit!"

The cottonmouth's flat head tilted like that of a bewildered dog. It retracted six inches. Gerard was the snake now, darting forward to snatch the marble from the mud, then claw back onto the peaty bank. From there he rolled away, panting and gasping, watching the rain reveal which marble it was.

Was there ever any doubt?

The Brothers of the Spear. Gerard saw his own face, reflected by moonlight, miniaturized longside Dan-El and Natongo.

All gamblers, even little ones, can feel when their luck shifts.

"Hundred-to-one," he said the next morning, right to German Rusnak's face. For the first time, German looked taken aback, like last night's cottonmouth. Gerard liked it. He kneeled at the six-yard line, lodged the Brothers of the Spear into the curl of his pointer finger, and fired the picture marble with bullet force. It cut across twenty shadows: boys who'd come to cheer on the defeat of the kid who'd nearly ruined them. One single miracle and they could be friends again.

Gerard won a hundred marbles that day. Realizing he'd never fare better, he retired on the spot, divvying up his winnings so his pals could rebuild their collections. To this day, Gerard could hardly pay for a drink on the Point. One of his old buddies would be at the bar and he'd pull a marble from his pocket, one that Gerard won back that fateful day. Gerard always accepted the drinks. They helped hide his tears.

You'll always be our hero, those marbles said.

Some kind of hero. Butt molded to a stool, slurping swill.

Gerard kept only one marble: the Brothers of the Spear. Now he clutched it. The glop he'd puked wasn't just bubbling now. It fizzed and frothed, a dozen fronds of congealed vomit extending several feet into the air, twitching like antennas. The feelers dripped the former contents of Gerard's belly, with every other *plip* onto the floor sounding like a word.

I *plip* saw *plip* your *plip* little *plip* girl *plip* at *plip* the *plip* beach *plip*

she's *plip* with *plip* that *plip* fisherman *plip* who *plip* ain't *plip* you *plip*

no *plip* sir *plip* he *plip* ain't *plip* you *plip* at *plip* all *plip*

What the vomit-thing said was true: that son-of-a-bitching André Saphir was out there, usurping Gerard's God-given daddy duties. But spilling the fisherman's blood wouldn't do any good. Would it? A few drops of blood wouldn't make the swamp turn red. He had to fight through the sickness, resist this thing's taunt.

He squeezed the Brothers of the Spear till it felt like a bone spur in the center of his palm. He growled at the vomit-thing how he'd growled at the cottonmouth a million failures ago.

"Love you, swamp. Always have. But you slidder any closer to my girl, don't t'ink I won't wrestle you down. Straight down to de bottom of de eart."

I *plip* could *plip* have *plip* killed *plip* you *plip* that *plip* night *plip*

Instead *plip* I *plip* helped *plip* you *plip* win *plip* back *plip* your *plip* marbles *plip*

Win *plip* back *plip* your *plip* pride plip

You *plip* owe *plip* me *plip* Gerard *plip*

He squeezed the marble tighter, tighter, tighter.

"You may have helped me make dat shot. But dat don't mean I can't make it again. Sink your teet' into me and I'll sink my hands into you—dose mangrove roots, dem lotus leaves, dat mud. If I'm a-goin down, I'm pullin de whole damp down with me. If dat don't work, I'll open my mout' and drink y'all down. Because drinkin's what Gerard Pontiac do best."

The vomit's tentacles swayed, and twisted, and in a blink, melted back into the puddle, if they had ever been there to begin with. Gerard panted, and hurt, and moaned, and rolled the Brother of the Spear's cool glass over his hot, sticky face, and tried not to think of André Saphir out there on Guimbarde Beach with Pontiac. Gerard snaked to the undersink cabinet and withdrew a rag, a bucket, and a corroded old bottle of Comet. Before Pontiac got back, he had a whole lot of cleaning to do.

~ 17 ~

IN MISS WARD'S TWENTY-FIVE YEARS at Bullock Elementary, she'd seen nothing elicit more chaos than wild animals on school grounds. If the animal appeared at recess, children bolted in so many directions it took hours to root them out. If it manifested while class was in session, children rushed to the windows, like they'd never seen a gator sunning in a parking lot before.

Today it was a three-hundred-pound black bear on its hind legs investigating the trash bin by the flagpole.

Miss Ward considered it a major professional achievement that she'd so far kept the children's attention from the window. She was teaching fractions, as she did every March 10, the school's Halfway Day, which marked the semester being half over. Bullock's school year and ended earlier than most. Once shrimping season began May 15, half the kids vanished to work on family trawlers.

When God made shrimp, shrimpers liked to say, *he made enough for everybody.*

Nice thought. Except you had to catch them first. That job God left to poor bayou folk.

Thirty minutes after the bear rolled in, the Melbourne Queen rolled up.

Miss Ward's chalk crumbled against the blackboard. Seeing Pete Roosevelt was like swallowing hot coal. Her belly burned. Her nerve endings crackled. That useless, incompetent, so-called sheriff and his hopeless deputy. They'd turn this low-key bear situation into a five-alarm fiasco.

They did, tout de suite. Bullock Parish had no sheriff's office, much less an animal-control unit. That meant no live traps, no leg snares, no tranquilizer darts. Between dictums on fractions, Miss Ward adjusted her thick-lensed glasses to catch glimpses of idiot Pete, who matched the bear pound for pound, circling the beast with a weather-beaten oar. Was he planning to paddle the bear off to safety? Spuds and his butterfly net made even less sense.

Most likely, Pete and Spuds would prevail in chasing the bear into the woods and the students, who by then would have their noses flat to the windows, would erupt in applause. Pete Roosevelt, our hero. Miss Ward didn't think she could stand it. She lowered her glasses an inch so the bumbling fool blurred out of focus.

One child's gaze was already drifting toward the flagpole. It was Renée Pontiac—or just *Pontiac* if you didn't want to set her off cussing—too restlessly intelligent to have her attention held by boring math. Miss Ward needed to abandon the subject, fast.

"La-la-la-la-la-la-la-la-la-la-la-la-*la—la-la*."

For twenty-five years, Miss Ward had used the opening melody of Strauss's *Voices of Spring* to call for the class's attention, just as she used the opening fanfare of Bizet's *Carmen: Les Toreadors* to celebrate a correct answer and Mozart's *Symphony No. 40: Molto allegro* to signal she was growing impatient for a reply. Students loved it, not only for its good humor, but for the fact that Miss Ward had the loveliest voice in the swamp.

The bayou's best-known voices were idiosyncratic, mostly old bluesers with nicotine rasps, like Zydeco Chowder's Pink Zoot. Only Miss Ward sounded classically trained. She wasn't; the capabilities of her voice box had been a mystery since birth. She'd stunned worshippers at her Baptist church until moving to Alligator Point at age nineteen. There she'd drawn inward and shared her voice only with Jack O'Brien and her students.

Jack died four years ago. Now only Miss Ward's students had the pleasure.

Twenty-four sets of eyes in the room looked her way. Twenty kids in desks, the other four on the floor. Ages ranging all over. Most faces as white as paper towels, others as pinecone brown as Miss Ward herself. More kids than you'd expect in a flyspeck town, but Pointer wombs were as fecund as the swamp itself. Legend had it that exotic pollens rendered birth control pills inert and the wet heat dissolved condom plastic.

"Mm-*hmm* . . . mm-*hmm* . . . mm-*hmm* . . . mm-*hmm* . . ."

The opening to Erik Satie's *Gymnopédies* was the signal to put away current materials. Eighteen desktops creaked as children took their fraction work, accordioned from aggravated erasing, and chucked them inside.

"Dum—da-da-da-da—da-da-da-da-da-da-da . . ."

Ravel's *Boléro* was the specific signal for *charcoal pencil*, and though the class was a well-trained lot, happy yips escaped a few. Rustling erupted as fresh pieces of construction paper were withdrawn and slapped to desktops and charcoal pencils were hoisted high into the air.

Pontiac had hers up first, as usual, not to show off (though Miss Ward believed the girl was plenty proud) but because the child was *organized*. Before Pontiac, Miss Ward had never seen the inside of a student's desk that wasn't horrifying. Pontiac's desk contents were stacked by descending size. Small supply boxes were repurposed for pencils, crayons, markers, paper clips. The overall tidiness created room for the weighty library books Pontiac carted everywhere.

Since January, Pontiac had made space for a new item. Miss Ward had seen her share of strange desk contents. Origami folded from *Hustler* centerfolds. A live mouse. A handgun. A bottle cap full of fingernail clippings. Too many of those little Jolly Roger flags. An octopus etching or two, half-a-century old by the looks.

The newcomer to Pontiac's desk was a baseball. Miss Ward respected student privacy but just had to pick up the ball one day after school, push her glasses to her scalp, and scrutinize it with naked eyes. The baseball was so warped and softened it resembled a human organ. Something wedgelike had speared the ball to its core. Clumps of loose stitching gathered at the cleft mouth.

The ball was related to Billy May. Miss Ward knew it. The boy was missing two months now. His desk was directly in front of Pontiac's and Miss Ward had wondered if it was cruel positioning. But she couldn't force another child to sit at the cursed desk and removing it felt egregious. No, Billy May's desk had to remain. Children, especially on the Point, learned to accept spaces left by loss.

Miss Ward, though, did *not* accept it.

By turning up nothing on Billy May, Pete Roosevelt had failed. Again. Same as he'd failed Jack. It still hurt every day, *every single day*, never more than when she saw Pete accepting goodwill from a citizenry that lionized him.

Miss Ward no longer felt like singing. She pushed her glasses up.

"I have a riddle for you, class. An art riddle. I want you all to draw . . ." She drew out the suspense until she had every eye. ". . . a Coke bottle."

The children gasped, thrilled by her use of a dearly held icon.

"There's only one rule. Don't look at a Coke bottle. If you have one at home, don't set it in front of you and copy it. What I want you to do is make a drawing from memory. You've all seen a Coke bottle a thousand times. What exactly did you see? Imagine you are an alien. A little green being from outer space who lands right here on the Point. Imagine you know what bottles are, but not this particular *kind* of bottle. Here's the important part. The bottle has no label. So how do you communicate what it is?"

Pontiac's eyes gleamed. So did those of grade-grubber Alice Chilcote, Miss Ward's least favorite type of student: intelligent only via ambition, absent of creative spark. As usual, Alice's arm was up and waving while Pontiac listened and processed. Miss Ward took some small joy in ignoring Alice.

"I'm going to give you the whole rest of the semester to work on it. The last day of school, I'll gather the drawings and pick the winner. The winner gets a painting drawn of them. By me."

More gasps. None of them had ever met a finer artist. A low bar, Miss Ward knew, but she was happy enough to take it.

"For now, take out your art tools and start sketching ideas. Look at your paper really closely, and *think* about it."

In other words, *Don't look at the grown men outside being chased by a bear.*

She heard the frustrated sighs of children forced to think this late in the day, the scratches of students who couldn't follow directions, and the slapping drop of Alice Chilcote's neglected flipper.

With the kids at work, Miss Ward peeked outside. Pete had nagged the bear all the way to the road while Spuds waved off nonexistent traffic. It was more progress than Miss Ward had expected. She dug her nails into her palms. She didn't like to think of Pete Roosevelt as having any skills. If he did, why hadn't he shown any back in 1984, the year Jack was killed?

~ 18 ~

MISS WARD SPENT HER WEEKENDS outdoors but hidden in her backyard, where no one could make the tragic miscue of trying to chat. She couldn't converse with anyone but children. Last time she tried was 1989, five years after Jack died, a spur-of-the-moment thing, trying to order an ice-cream cone from Gwill Alexander's rolling cart. Old Gwill had seemed honored, even offered her a freebie, but Miss Ward's mind snapped shut at his first question—*What'll it be?*—and that was that, she had to run, weeping in shame, incapable of choosing between a Choc 'n' Nut Cornette and an Orange Super Split Pushup.

Jack's death did this to her.

No, Jack was perfect, in his way. Better to blame Pete Roosevelt.

Her only backyard companion was a sheet of thirty-pound-absorbent taped to an old cutting board. She worked in watercolors. Unlike oils, once a stroke of watercolor was applied, it couldn't be painted over. If you were unhappy with the results, you had two choices: destroy the painting or store it away for reassessment after the passion of the day subsided.

Miss Ward had completed 974 watercolors since she'd begun teaching and had yet to destroy one. But reassessment? Her whole life was one of reassessment. She stacked her paintings in a hall closet. Out of the 974, only 12 hung in her walk-up apartment, located over the one-room library of Mr. Peff, who'd been her landlord until she bought the apartment outright from him in '85.

Old-timers aware of Miss Ward's past wondered why she lived so humbly. Her daddy had gotten rich, or the backwater version of rich, as a shrimper. After he passed, Miss Ward had auctioned off his fleet for $360,000. The rest of Mr. Ward's estate, less funeral expenses and inheritance taxes, netted another $137,000. Miss Ward, by then a twenty-five-year-old spinster, figured that $497,000 would see her through to the end and pay for a respectable tombstone—so long as she "kept track" of that money, as locals said.

Miss Ward had no children and never would; babies forced you to let too many people into your life. Yet she thought of herself as a mother to the over six-thousand kids who had passed through Bullock Elementary. Every payday since her daddy passed, she endorsed her check over to the school's bank account.

Hence the necessity to live frugally. It made her a better painter, forcing tough choices. Despite being atrociously nearsighted, she had an artist's eye, and knew the addition of a thirteenth painting to her walls would create visual turmoil. With each new finished painting, she obligated herself to vote upon a new top twelve.

Only once had her heart prevailed over objective judgment.

The portrait in question hung in the kitchen/dining room, where she spent most her time. It was a head-and-shoulders of Jack O'Brien, painted in August 1980 when he was thirty-six and Miss Ward had just turned thirty. Technically it was clumsy. Compositionally it was dull. Functionally it bore little resemblance to its subject.

What drew the eye was a flagrant flaw. An errant streak of raw umber—Raw Umber W550 to be exact—shot from Jack's left sideburn, across a cheek the shade and smoothness of acorn, to the corner of his mouth. It should have ruined the painting, but instead, Miss Ward viewed it with overwhelming affection. It never failed to bring her back to the moment when the brush had gone awry.

Jack O'Brien had been sitting for his portrait for nearly two hours. The only other time he'd sat longer in one spot, he complained, was when he'd gone to see a reissue of *Ben-Hur* at the Paradise over in New Orleans, and even then there'd been a halftime to stretch his legs.

Halftime was a joke. He'd been cracking wise the whole time in hopes of distracting Miss Ward into a break. Even back then, Miss Ward wasn't known for her sense of humor. But that summer afternoon, she'd laughed a dozen times at the strange man's humor.

"Don't you think it's hot in here?" Jack nagged.

"Don't you unbutton a single button," Miss Ward replied. "I'm perfectly comfortable."

"You're worse than the gators I fish. You're a banshee, I swear."

Miss Ward continued to paint. "What's a banshee?"

"You know what a banshee is. You're just trying to distract me."

"Maybe I'm seeing if *you* really know."

"Well, first off, a banshee is a female."

"No male banshees?"

"Oh, there are. Only we call them demons. Ugly red things with white mouths, mon père used to say."

"So a banshee is a female demon."

"Lord knows they exist. You, for instance. Making me sit and swelter just so's you can make a picture. While there's thirteen-foot gators out there that need trapping and I got one hundred and fifty tags burning a hole in my pocket."

Miss Ward completed a stroke, put the brush in her teeth, walked to the nearest window, and threw it open. "There," she said as she returned to her stool. "Happy?"

A Louisiana breeze ruffled the curtains as it swept in.

It only seemed to make it hotter.

"Lord above," Jack pleaded. "Surely it's time we took some lemonade or something? You got any lemonade? Or something?"

Miss Ward pretended to focus on her painting. "I've got lemons. Assuming the taps are working, I've got water. But I don't have any sugar. I used it all up."

"Sugar? Or *nasty*-sugar? Used it up on the last fellow you painted, I bet."

Miss Ward's brush hand hesitated. "I never . . . had a fellow up here before."

Jack grinned more widely than a portrait model was allowed. Rather gatorlike.

"That a fact?"

Miss Ward's watercolors couldn't keep up with the perspiration on Jack's face, a perspiration she felt rising on her own skin. Her glasses fogged, just a little. She had only let Jack O'Brien up, she told herself, because the library below was having an outdoor book sale. If she screamed, people would hear.

"Not to sit, no," she replied.

"Ah, but you had guys up here for other things, that it?"

Miss Ward stopped painting, spun on her stool, and looked Jack O'Brien square in the eye. Like plenty of bayou folk, his ancestry was as artfully mixed as anything she swirled on her palette. Lot of African in him, a smidge of Yank, and a copper undertone suggesting one or two other kind of folk too.

"Do you take me for a trollop?" she asked.

"A what now, miss?"

Miss Ward blew out air, peeling hair from her hot forehead. This was followed by the strange sensation that her hair might look sexy. What a foreign thought.

"I suppose a trollop, Mr. O'Brien, is a kind of banshee. You should know all about evil things, seeing how you are clearly an evil man. Honestly, I don't recall why I felt the need put you down in paint. Perhaps I wanted to capture your unique depravity."

She anticipated either additional jibes or the pouty recalcitrance of a scolded student. Instead, Jack's brow rolled like poured dough over his eyes. He held his hands behind his back like a man restraining himself. Miss Ward stared at her easel and kept her brush high; it had a pointed end.

"Evil, am I?" Jack's voice had deepened an octave.

She'd been a birdbrain to extend an invite to this man, who stunk of the spoiled chicken he used for bait and the bloody iodine of dead gator flesh, after running into him at Doc's Mercantile and getting overly excited by eye contact.

"I'll thank you to leave now, sir," she said.

"Wouldn't be the first time I left. I was born on this bayou. Ran off to sea when I was thirteen. You know why? To *escape* evil. Not the kind of evil of the folk I grew up with; I learned to make meat of them in time. I'm talking about a different kind. The kind specific to these parts, that rots folk inside-out. I was a kid when I ran. Now I'm back and I'm a man. My gator lines? The treble hooks? The shotgun? They're for a purpose higher than bagging some thousand-pound tree-shaker. It's *Evil* I came back to fight. I'm sick of seeing folk from the Point succumb. I guess I get a little touchy about the word."

Curtains rippled, grasshoppers sang. Miss Ward still wasn't looking at Jack. Her eyes flitted about the thin washes she'd made. None hinted at the man's fiery insides.

"*Succumb*," she managed.

Jack exhaled through his nostrils. A sound of humor.

"Ten-dollar word, huh? Add that to *banshee* and *trollop* and we got about thirty bucks in the kitty. That a good rate for a model, Miss Ward?"

She looked at her palette. Not knowing what to say, she dipped her brush into a dollop of Raw Umber W550 and returned to her painting. In the next instant, her eyes watered from the odor of bad chicken and worse gators. Jack was upon her. He took her arms in his calloused hands. Her skin was darker than his, but the shades looked nice together, a dappling of autumn leaves. The paintbrush jerked, running a streak across the portrait's cheek. The brush left the paper and dropped to the floor as Jack turned Miss Ward on her stool and kissed her.

"Evelyn," he breathed into her mouth, and that was all it took, she came to believe, for her to fall in love. She'd come to Bullock Parish in '69, started teaching in '73, and had never been anything but *Miss Ward* to anyone, herself included. *Evelyn* never had a chance to breathe in this stifling sog and until that second, she'd never cared.

Four years later, Jack was killed pursuing that Evil, a murder Pete Roosevelt declined to pursue. When Jack died, Evelyn died with him. Her singing, which he'd adored, died too, except in the front of her students. Quiet, nervous, lonely Miss Ward, on the other hand, was reborn, glad for the cloak and veil of her former name.

She had her apartment, her paintings, and her students.

That would have to be enough.

And it *was* enough. Till the Oil Man came calling.

She'd only heard the man's smooth voice purring through her locked door, but after he'd slid the papers under the crack and left, she'd cleaned her glasses and pored over them. Uniquely among locals, she didn't need money. But seven kids in her class had told her that their families had signed and were uprooting from bayou mud. That'd leave fewer than forty families on the Point.

Soon enough it would be zero.

Long before that, probably before the fall semester, the school would shut its doors for good and there'd be no more point in living. On that day, she planned to wander off the trail into the swamp's steamy ether, until she sunk, and disappeared, just like Billy May, just like Jack.

~ 19 ~

LIKE MOST FOLK ON THE POINT, Pork Fat thought poorly of herself. She was a tangle-haired, flat-chested, acne-suffering fifteen-year-old subsisting on plastic-wrapped junk food from Doc's Mercantile and living alone in a raccoon-infested shanty. Pork Fat didn't have much. But she had one thing no other swamp rat had, as far as she knew.

She had herself a plan.

It was hard to go deep, musically speaking, when your instruments were a tambourine, cowbell, corrugated-metal rubboard, and cajón. But when Pork Fat started making an honest clatter, she turned any of Zydeco Chowder's off-tune honkers into what Pink Zoot called *jumpin fun*—what zydeco music was all about. Pork Fat trusted her eyes even more than her ears. When she got going, folk's faces relaxed and the burdens they carried melted away.

The band played as far as Biloxi, but their regular gig was at Plum Peppers, a rat-tail joint barely a hundred yards from the high-n-dry.

On Friday and Saturday nights, owners Honey Plum and Sneezy Pepper welcomed a rifle-toting tour guide leading touristes across those "deadly" hundred yards, warning all the way "to keep an eye peeled for gators." Just a little razzle-dazzle before the guide ushered them into Plum Peppers, saying, "Y'all lucky ducks are about to witness enough pluckin and puffin and squeezin to raise Jesus himself."

One night, while Pork Fat was putting her funky axes into her duffel bag, a man dressed like a TV professor (tweed jacket, felt hat, goatee, tobacco pipe) introduced himself as Mr. Donaldson. He asked how old Pork Fat was, which she knew was shifty, but when she said fifteen he didn't get lecherous. He said he was a vice principal—not a professor, but close—at an arts academy in New Orleans's Garden District.

That was mishmash to Pork Fat. Mr. Donaldson explained it was a high school for the artistically talented. Pork Fat, he said, was a *supremely talented percussionist steeped in the improvisational Creole-Acadian folklorist dance-hall tradition.* More mishmash, but long after the man left, leaving her with a pointy-cornered business card, one word kept lingering.

Percussionist.

Rubbing a washboard in a moldy backwater bar longside an amp that blew sparks when rainwater dripped from the tin roof was an all-right way to push through to the next day. Percussionist, though? Heck, that sounded like a *career.*

Anytime Pork Fat thought about contacting Mr. Donaldson, she full-on fainted. Once she pitched into the damp and woke up a few seconds later gagging on duckweed. Another time at home her falling body broke through the floor and landed on the hummock below. If she was going to call Mr. Donaldson, she needed to do it before she killed her damn self.

She'd also need some weed first, which meant scoring from Pink Zoot, which meant tidying up his camp in trade.

She did all that, got good and baked, and barefooted to Doc's Mercantile. If Plum Peppers was a hundred yards from the dry, Doc's couldn't be more than five. You could chuck a coin and have it fall inside Dawes territory. Not that she was chucking any coins. Doc would let you use his phone but he made you pay, same as if it were in a booth.

Pork Fat's shaking fingers failed the first three times calling. By the time Mr. Donaldson answered, her throat was the driest thing in the bayou. Lucky for her, the VP did most the talking. What she had to do was come to the school and audition. If the instructors felt she had merit, she'd be invited up, and if her financial need was severe, they'd foot the bill. Her financial need was severe, all right, but she didn't say a word, just nodded a whole bunch, a stupid thing to do on a telephone. The audition was arranged: Wednesday, April 1, at 1:15 p.m. April Fool's Day, and boy, did she feel like a fool after hanging up.

What could a frottoir scritcher like her possibly play solo that wouldn't sound like a toddler bangin on pots? To make a noise worth hearing, she needed her band.

But she didn't dare speak a word of this to Zydeco Chowder.

She was the baby of the group by a good twenty years. There was BTF, aka Blue Tuna Fish (named for a tuna-fish sandwich that went bad over a three-day Summer Jazz Fest) on piano. Bunny Rabbit on staticky pedal steel guitar. Suck-Up on rusty sax. Bottle-o'-Gin Jerry on not-quite-upright bass. Six A.M. sawing at the remains of a Cajun fiddle. Their band leader, accordion player, and vocalist was none other than Pink Zoot (named for the large-lapeled, shoulder-padded, lace-trimmed, rhinestone-studded pink suit he'd bought secondhand on Bourbon Street for fifty bucks).

Pink Zoot could fly on that squeeze-box, and gigged longer and drank harder than anyone. Even slobbery drunk, he divided all proceeds square with the band.

All he asked was loyalty.

Pork Fat was on her porch practicing for her audition when Pink Zoot glided up on what folk called a Lafitte skiff to pick her up for a gig, Pirate Pride flags whipping hard from the gunwales. She'd been going for hours, coaxing all sorts of strange new noises from her duffel-stuff.

Pink Zoot saw and got quiet. Pork Fat had never seen Pink Zoot quiet. She knew why. She'd never *practiced* before. She'd only *played*. Soon as they hit dry ground at Plum Peppers, Zoot threw a fit, sobbing how Pork Fat was plotting to leave him. Him, who'd practically brought her up! That wasn't wholly true, but he'd done her some good turns. Pork Fat found herself spitting lies, how she'd never leave him, how could he even think it?

BTF suggested Pork Fat treat Pink Zoot real polite for a while, so she doted on him at the Pelican the very night Billy May was reported missing. While Pink Zoot and Rawley Deevers upended bottles, Gerard Pontiac drew Pork Fat into a chat she could tell he wouldn't recall come morning.

But she'd remember it for a good long while.

"I gotta get my girl out of dis here bog," Gerard said. "Quickest way is to off myself. Orphan life gotta be better den dis. But I can't do it. She already lost her mama. An udder way just gotta be found."

Emboldened, inspired, Pork Fat whispered back, "I'm getting out of here too. Gonna sign those papers the Oil Man is peddling. Gonna use the profits to set myself up in the dry. Gonna become . . . a *percussionist.*"

~ 20 ~

PETE ROOSEVELT SIFTED THROUGH HIS tub of VHS tapes from the foldout sofa in his Airstream. John Wayne movies, the whole lot. He needed one tonight, bad. He'd run into Louise May outside the post office outpost at noon, and her frosty glare had colored how Pete received every other Pointer's howdy. Coming up on eight weeks now since Billy May had gone missing, and Pete hadn't shoveled up a single clue. The whole town was starting to doubt him. Just like Miss Ward.

So he'd gone down to the Pelican. Tied one one. Sat next to Gerard Pontiac and tried to buy him a shot, though as usual other drinkers beat him to it, holding up marbles to their falling hero. Pete took the shot himself and got good and drunk, but it didn't do shit for his guilt.

No matter which movie he slotted into his VCR—a dusty RCA with a faux-wood cabinet—his nineteen-inch Hitachi TV would bleach it into an array of purple grays. It only made the films go down smoother. It soothed Pete's pounding head to see all the titles that meant so much to him. *Rio Bravo. The Longest Day. The Quiet Man. El Dorado.*

Pete had seen every film John Wayne appeared in save one: *The Conquerer.*

He vowed never to watch it. In the film, the Duke played not a sheriff, not an outlaw, not a rancher, not a Civil War hero, but twelfth-century Mongol emperor Genghis Khan. It weren't just the idea of the role that put off Pete. It was what he'd read in a dime-store paperback about Hollywood legends.

Shooting *The Conqueror* killed the Duke.

The film featured battle scenes with hundreds of horses galloping across the Utah desert, kicking up clouds of sand that constantly had to be wiped from cast and crew and rinsed from their eyes and mouths.

What no one knew was the sand was radioactive from atomic bomb testing one year earlier. The Utah desert was as poison as Alligator Point. Ninety-one people—nearly half of the 220 people on set—died of cancer within twenty years. That included stars Susan Hayward, Agnes Moorehead, and Pedro Armendáriz (the last of whom shot himself rather than suffer a slow death), director Dick Powell, and the Duke himself.

The Duke was handed his lung cancer diagnosis in 1964. He had a doc yank his left lung and four ribs, and got back to work. It attacked again eleven years later, threading stomach cancer through his body like estuaries through the bayou. The illness was so grueling the Duke tried to follow Pedro Armendáriz's lead, begging friends to smuggle his .38 into the hospital. They refused. The knew the Duke couldn't go out like that, even if the Duke himself had forgotten.

Wayne had a nickname for his cancer.

The Red Witch.

The nickname referenced a picture the Duke made in 1948 with Gail Russell and Gig Young: *Wake of the Red Witch*. Not a famous flick, but the Duke had come to equate the cancer he got on *The Conquerer* with the sunken ship *The Red Witch*, which ultimately kills his character, Captain Ralls. Shortly before the Duke died, he took his assistant's hand and said, "I guess the Red Witch finally got me."

When Pete read this in the Hollywood paperback, he had to sit for a spell.

Wake of the Red Witch had been the first John Wayne film Pete had ever seen, age nine, September 23, 1955, at the Liberty Theater in Lacombe. That was also the last time Pete ever saw his mother,

Rose. She'd sat five rows behind Pete with Gee Putnam, a man young Pete believed was his mother's boyfriend but was actually her pimp. It was a tremendous film, highlighted by the undersea battle between the Duke and a giant octopus called Tarutatu.

The emotional climax, however, was the death of Captain Ralls's beloved Angelique. Ralls carried her to the balcony, where she sighed her final words.

Wherever you go, whatever you do, I'll be beside you.

This isn't the end. It's the beginning.

Pete was glad the theater dark hid his tears. When the words *THE END* surfaced, Pete struggled for meaning. Maybe the people you loved didn't have to love you back in this lifetime. Maybe they'd love you in the next. Pete's missing daddy. Pete's distant mother. He needed to allow them to not love him for now. The house lights came up. Pete wiped his face and turned in his seat, ready to forgive.

His mom was gone. Gee Putnam remained. A giant red frond had been painted across the projector booth wall, blood from Gee's sliced throat. His flashy suit was so soaked it was nearly black. As black as the blood of the octopus Tarutatu. On Gee's chest lay his wallet, less fat now, all the money gone.

Pete stared. No one else exiting the balcony noticed.

He'd never see his mother again. He'd never have a father either.

That last part didn't have to be true, he thought, as he turned back to the screen.

He'd heard of "John Wayne" before.

John Wayne probably made a *lot* of movies.

After the foster system had Pete, he never spoke of the incident again. The Duke had served as the only parent Pete needed for forty-three years. Tonight, Pete decided, not a single VHS in the tub would do. He removed a cigar box from his bedside table drawer. Inside, wrapped in a clean handkerchief, was the one tape Pete prized over all the others: *The Shootist.*

The Duke shot *The Shootist,* his last film, while in the final grips of the Red Witch. It was about an old gunslinger who—wouldn't you know it?—was dying of cancer. It had no right being Pete's favorite John Wayne flick. It had little action, no epic cattle drives, zero Indian skirmishes, not even a frisky frontier lady with sweat beaded along her bosom. All it had was a sad, lonely, overweight geezer who'd fought as hard as a man could fight against the Red Witch.

It got Pete. It got him deep. He'd seen *The Shootist*—skunk, it had to be close to a hundred times now.

Pete pressed play on the VCR. The booze in his blood helped him drift off midway through the flick. That didn't mean he weren't still watching. As tough as the film was to bear while awake, the dream version was much worse.

Pete would come to see it as a warning.

~ 21 ~

MARCH 30, THE DAY BEFORE the audition, Pork Fat's palms were bruised from tambourine, wrist bones sore from cowbell, knuckles shredded from rubboard, back aching from cajón. Pink Zoot prided himself on five-hour sets, but Pork Fat had been going for ten, mixing the clatter of her duffel-stuff in hopes that it might sound like music to sophisticated ears.

What it sounded like was an ungodly mess.

She broke off when night fell round eight. She went inside and banged a rhythm on the cabinets, her cue for the mice to get lost. Could that be her audition piece? Banging on cabinets? She took a column of saltines and a bag of M&Ms, got a can of Natural Light from the icebox, and returned to the porch for the sort of dinner Mr. Donaldson's art students would surely disparage.

She was going light on the crackers and heavy on the Natty Light when a basso profondo echoed through aviary twitters, duck skronks, and the teardrop splishes of leaping frogs.

"Eidder dat's Jesus de carpenter himself fixin up a vacation home, or we got ourselves a genuine board-banger hidin here in de damp."

Pork Fat wiped beer foam with her arm.

"Who's there? I don't see you."

"I'm standin right a-front of you. Maybe de dark's got me hid."

"Anybody comes by trail, there's a *squish*. Anybody comes by boat, there's a *plunk*. I lived here all my life, mister."

A raspy chuckle.

"I do move slower den a banana slug. On account of me bein blind. Look again. Don't you see me standin?"

Pork Fat turned her head ever so slightly and there he was, standing at the foot of the tottery stairs.

The dude was seventy if a day, a wrinkled fedora screwed low on his head, and crooked all over. Friendly brown freckles fanned out from a crooked nose. A crooked grin stretched under a crooked mustache. Crooked shoulders held aloft a crooked old suit: brown corduroy top and bottom, cream vest with gold buttons, sweat-spotted gray shirt, and red striped tie. Too many layers for the night's membranous heat. Even the man's milky eyes were crooked, staring in two distinct directions, neither one at Pork Fat.

"You say you blind?" she asked.

"Fraid so!" the man laughed. "But plenty of music-makers were. Blind Willie Johnson. Blind Lemon Jefferson. Blind Willie McTell. Blind Boy Fuller. Blind Joe Reynolds. Blind Joe Taggart. None of dem too shy bout advertisin de fact neidder."

"You play? What do they call you?"

The man clutched his cane in a swollen-knuckled hand. Unless Pork Fat was seeing poorly, the cane's ornamental handle was reptilian. In the man's other hand was a dinged-up instrument box, a smaller version of Suck-Up's saxophone case. The man grinned.

"Not many call me, not no more. But when dey do, dey call me Blind Bull-Belly." He jabbed his cane into the muck and used his free hand to tip his hat. "What drew me way de tarnation out here was some of de finest bangin and janglin I ever heard. I don't see good, but I *hear* better den most. Girl, you're practicin up! You got yourself a big ol' gig, am I wrong?"

Pork Fat tightened up. If this gent's next stop was the Pelican, he might mention her practice session to the fellow on the next stool, who might be Pink Zoot.

"No," she lied. "I'm just messing around."

The man bowed his wrinkled head.

"Dat's all right. Dat's all right. Dere ain't any good reason to share your big ol' plans wit' ol' Blind Bull-Belly. I just passin t'rough. You go on wit' your bangin and janglin, young miss, and give dis here swamp de what-for. I just shuffle off to de next hummock, yes ma'am."

Blind Bull-Belly planted his cane. The mire sucked at its hoof and the man's crooked spine helixed. A long pin pierced Pork Fat's heart.

"Je m'appelle Pork Fat. Least, that's what they call me."

Blind Bull-Belly stopped. Even in the dim, his blind eyes twinkled.

"Tout va bien. Don't it warm de old ticker to hear dat sweet Cajun French? And from a fille wit' a good and proper musicienne name." His grin widened to display eight equally spaced teeth. "Forgive a vieux garçon for sayin so, but it sounds like you in need of a song in dat heart."

The statement flew as true as the Brazilian bats Pork Fat had seen earlier, snapping moths from the night sky.

"A song in my heart?"

The ground squished as the man fully turned. It was dark now, real dark. Still, Pork Fat got the feeling some of Blind Bull-Belly's crooked parts had straightened.

"Les tambours. Les cuillères. Le 'tit-fer. Dey go awful good longside a down and dirty band. But on t'eir lonesome, dey a chop wit'out de pork. A pepper wit'out de bell. If you intendin to bang and clang tout seul, den you need a song in your heart to play along wit."

Pork Fat took off her vest frottoir. She pushed aside her cajón. Atop it she set her tambourine. Instead of flailing with her noise-makers, she should be playing along to a song running in her mind! What good luck this old man had waddled up.

Blind Bull-Belly nodded his approval. He must have heard her set down her instruments through his wild white ear-hair.

Pork Fat cleared her throat. "Do you . . ."

"Got a song in mind? Now dat you ask, I do. It simple enough to keep track of once you get a-goin. But it got open spaces big as Nebraska so you can stretch and scritch and scratch till your heart content. All I ask is you follow me to dat clearin yonder. Sound just don't carry good inside dese weeds."

Pork Fat leaned forward. "Can you play it for me? What instrument you got in there?"

"Oh, dis ol' t'ing?" Blind Bull-Belly patted his case. "Dis here my pipe."

~ 22 ~

LONG AGO, BACK WHEN PORK FAT was Gillian Marie Le Blanc, a smoggy epoch during which she ate her mama's grilled gator and breaded frog legs, and sipped her daddy's chicory coffee, and each day was as blinding bright as the sun spearing through marshland foliage—even back then, there'd been a darkness. Light attracts dark, Mama used to say, and anybody that got snooty about feeling cheerful was speedboating toward a crash. That's what happened, too, a literal crash, the Le Blanc family fanboat tossed by a waterspout that killed everybody but ten-year-old Gillian, stuck home with the flu. Next morning, she followed a trail of the cruelest clues: foot, thumb, nose, ear, eyeball, kidney, intestines, penis, big toe, throat, breast, heart. She collected what she could in burlap sacks. At the funeral, folk whispered what she already knew: the thing in the swamp had punished the Le Blancs for thriving. Nobody spoke the thing's name. They didn't have to.

"You the Piper," Pork Fat said. "Ain't you?"

Blind Bull-Belly, if that's who he was, took a mighty inhale of sticky air. A gold button popped off his vest. His red tie ribboned out like a long, slobbering tongue. Sweat the color and viscosity of butter oozed from under his fedora. His exhale smelled like the last thing Pork Fat expected: a whole field of lilacs. She'd smelled lilacs in stores before but in Louisiana, they didn't grow natural.

He gazed into the jungle canopy and small things chittered in response.

"Dere magic in music, iddn't it so? How's it folk alone make sounds no better den a rat screechin or a cockroach hissin, but when you put dem sounds togedder—we music folk call 'em *chords*—all a sudden we got an almighty power? You and me, Blind Bull-Belly and Pork Fat, we part of same secret order of sorcières."

Pork Fat ought to be horrified. She knew it. Yet tears heavied her eyelashes. If she failed her audition and got booted from Zydeco Chowder, who would she have left? Nobody, unless she claimed her place in this union of musical sorcières.

She considered the ten rickety steps leading to the ground. Built by pirates, repaired over the decades by their descendants. On the bottom step, a deep carving of an octopus gleamed white from rotten black wood. She'd passed over it uncountable times and never thought on who might have put it there, or why.

"What'll you do? If I follow you?"

Blind Bull-Belly laughed. "My solemn oat', child, I won't do to you a t'ing none of us sorcières haven't done a million times over. Cajun music didn't sprout out of de quag whole, you know. It took Irish. It took Seminole. It took French. It took African. It took Spanish. It took Cuban. All dem folk had to be taken apart, like a child takes apart a bug, den blended and stitched back togedder. Oui, a few folk get hurt in de doin. Hurt a lot, trut' be told. But it wort' it, ain't it? What you t'ink, Gillian?"

Gillian. Tears spilled. She heard the name echoing in the auditorium where she aced her tryout; reverberating in high school halls by friends who saw her as an equal; buzzing from speakers as she was introduced on stages, real stages, where salt water didn't make amps burst into fires you had to stamp out while still playing. A single song could make all that happen, and she'd give anything, it turned out, to have it in her heart.

She crossed over the octopus carving same as she ever did.

The walk to the clearing must have taken time, what with Blind Bull-Belly having no sight and using a cane. Pork Fat didn't recall. All she recalled was that lilac scent growing richer, making her head swim. All at once, they were beside a burble of chocolate-brown water, skeeters humming, egrets squealing, muskrats squeaking like balloons. She stood in the direct shine of the moon, rain coming down pretty good. Yet only onto her and Blind Bull-Belly. And she was sinking.

She looked down. Not quicksand. It was boue pourrie, the gooey rotten mud that bubbled up anyplace bayou land touched water. It was hot against her bare feet, then ankles, then calves.

Pork Fat blinked at the Piper.

"The song?" she pleaded. The boue pourrie slurped at her thighs, her stomach.

The Piper opened his instrument case. His cataracted eyeballs were gone. One dry, fleshy socket contracted like a sphincter— a wink.

When it came to zydeco, *pipe* could mean a lot of things. Clarinet, flute, recorder, panpipes, oboe. But as the boue pourrie tongued Pork Fat's chest, she saw inside the Piper's case a human head. Distended from bloat, pickle green with putridity, dribbling obsidian slime from orifices and wounds, the head was recognizable anyway. It was that boy, little Billy May, missing since January 8, though any born-and-bred Pointer knew what had happened to him.

The Piper lifted the boy's head. Billy's spinal cord was still attached. Wet ligatures of weeds kept the bones together as the Piper brought the lowest vertebrae to his lips. *It's a pipe after all,* Pork Fat thought as the boue pourrie reached her neck. The Piper blew once into the spinal cord, real hard, to clear the valves. A single sour note belched from Billy's brown-gummed maw. The boy's scalp, peeled in the exact pattern of baseball cowhide, flapped once.

The lilac aroma became a sickly stench.

"Cozy down there?" The Piper had shed his Cajun twang. "Good. Now get yourself a big old earful of *this*."

~ 23 ~

THE SHOOTIST BEGINS WITH SIXTY-NINE-YEAR-OLD John Wayne paying a visit to his physician friend, played by another Western legend, sixty-eight-year-old Jimmy Stewart. The Duke's character suffers from awful back pain, so Jimmy Stewart tells him to disrobe and bend over the exam table, a humiliating position. After a career of facing Indians, Japanese fighters, and Nazi soldiers, the Duke looks scared for the first time.

As screened in theaters, and now on plastic cassette, there's a tasteful fade-out before Jimmy inspects the Duke's backside.

But in Pete Roosevelt's dream, the scene proceeds uncut, with the Duke replaced by Pete.

"Ain't nothin'," Pete protests. "Just some boils from too much time in the saddle."

"Now, now, now," Jimmy says in his trademark stammer, "you j-j-just hold yourself still while I give this a good look."

"I ain't afraid, you understand," Pete says, because that's what the Duke would say. "It's just that everybody down here, everybody on the Point . . ."

"I know, I know. Now keep still, keep still."

Pete holds his sweaty head into his cold hands as a series of icy steel instruments probe his insides. Finally, Jimmy relents.

"I-I-I wish I could tell you this ain't no cause for worry. But I can't. We known each other too long, Pete. So I'm going to give it to you straight. What you got . . . it's cancer."

Pete sobs. "The Red Witch."

"I wouldn't lie to you. Not me. Not your good friend Jimmy Stewart."

When the Duke received this news in the real scene, he'd taken a shot of laudanum and walked tall from Jimmy's office. Pete, it turns out, has none of the stuff of his hero. He leaps off the table and starts tearing apart the office, punching, kicking, flinging things, hoping he'll bash straight through plywood and discover it's all just a movie set.

Jimmy, meanwhile, stammers in anger, asking Pete what did he expect? Gallivanting through the poison Utah sands?

Each of the four walls of Jimmy's office has a window. North, east, south, and west, sandy flatlands stretching toward infinity. All four horizons ignite with white light. Typhoons of energy suck away all sounds and drive across the flats the way rip currents drive across sea bottoms. Quickly the blinding flash fades and reveals four mushroom clouds. A second later, the shock waves hit.

Jimmy's office is blown away in a blink.

Pete remains standing beside the melted hulk of the exam table. A thousand window shards are embedded in his body. Because his pants had been down, his pecker hangs out, chopped by glass so it dangles from a strand of skin.

Pete looks up to find Jimmy still standing in his spot. He's untouched, stethoscope around his neck, shaking his head. His lips barely move in that Jimmy Stewart way, but a nuclear scream pours from his throat.

"There, you see? You see at long last? When the Red Witch comes for you, Pete, it's gonna get you, no matter what! You hear? THE RED WITCH IS GONNA GET YOU!"

~ 24 ~

PETE JERKED HARD. HE THOUGHT it was a pane of glass slicing him in half. Then he saw the foot of his sleeping cot, his Navajo blanket kicked aside, his hairy legs shining with sweat. *The Shootist* was still running. The climactic gunfight unfolded quietly, red blood turned gray by aged cathode ray tubes. What jerked Pete was a hand connected to a person he recognized.

"Who said you were dying, boss?" Spuds asked from above.

Pete wiped his face with cold, trembling palms, and took a steadying look at the Airstream. Toppling stacks of VHS tapes. Plates crusted with donated food. Loops of inside-out socks. No sign of any living thing but him, because that was his life, as lonely as the Duke's during his final weeks, when he'd surface from a narcotics haze all alone except for the hospital TV, usually playing some hokey old shoot-'em-up starring a smirking young god named John Wayne.

"Spuds." Pete's voice was scorched raw by atomic blasts. He fumbled a cup off the floor and took a slug of day-old coffee.

"I'm real sorry to wake you," Spuds said. "My daddy told me if you wake up a fella nightmaring that hard, they wake up insane. You insane now, Pete?"

"Probably." He stared at his deputy. "Why'd you do it?"

"Because there's another one."

Pete tossed the cup and with a grunt lifted his carcass from the foldout bed. Gunfire crackled from the Hitachi like the echoes of the Red Witch's cackle in his skull. *Was* he insane? He turned on tepid tap water and splashed his face.

"Another what, Spuds."

"Another Pointer gone missing. You know that zydeco girl? The scritcher?"

~ 25 ~

"I'm dead. I done died in de night and broke in two. One part's out dere wanderin de playree, huntin after a squeeze-box he iddn't never gonna find. Cuz dat udder half a him found it first and is in de damp pushin music out of it longside Pork Fat. Can't you hear it, Pete? Spuds, can't you hear it? Mixed up wit' de cicadas and sand flies? Maybe you got to have dat Cajun ear. Laws, me and Pork Fat are raisin de roof! Gonna be hearin dat duet de rest of my days. Half of me gonna be out dere every night chasin dat music, sweeter den any nasty-sugar I ever tasted. Chasin but never catchin. Not dat it'd do me good. You catch up to Pork Fat now, you catchin up to somet'in else too. Mind yourself dat, Pete. You mind it too, Spuds. Dis ain't no business for de law. Lest you end up like Jack O'Brien."

Pink Zoot sat like a tire-free jalopy on a plywood bench. His pink rhinestone suit lay over his knee like he'd just skinned it from a mythological beast.

His considerable weight, added to Pete Roosevelt's considerable weight, had Pork Fat's porch drooping like one of the Saloon Committee's jowls. Pete figured they'd be plunged into the quick any second now. Fine. Some nice, cold slime might allay his hangover. Spuds kept to the bottom of the stairs per his fear of quicksand.

Pete snorted and spat, and watched the goober vanish into air even thicker and wetter. Would Jack O'Brien ever quit haunting him? Bad enough some Pointers considered the dead gator hunter some kind of martyr. None one seemed to recall how many times Pete had saved Jack O'Brien from himself. They only recalled the one time he didn't.

It was the only murder Pete ever had in Alligator Point. Till now. When he and Spuds had arrived at Pork Fat's place after Pink Zoot's call, they'd found the band leader on this bench and a single set of barefoot prints pressed into the mud, headed into the swamp. Pete and Spuds had followed the footprints to a clearing. They hadn't found Pork Fat.

What they'd found was a pile of human ribs.

Pink Zoot helped himself to one of Pork Fat's beers and explained how he'd come to find the ribs first. He lived farther south than anyone on the Point. That meant a long walk with a big, bejeweled, thirty-pound accordion. He often stowed the squeeze-box at Pork Fat's. When he arrived today to pick it up, Pork Fat was gone. Every instrument in the place was cleared out, too, including the accordion.

"Just look how flat dem ribs be," he said. "Ribs don't get dat flat unless dey got a frottoir pressin down night after night."

"You don't think Pork Fat's off giggin somewheres?" Pete asked.

Pink Zoot waved away the stupid question.

"No one played le chinqui-chinque like my girl. Not t'ree mont's back, I asked how she found dem rhythms she played. Girl says, *Zoot, rhythms never walk alone.*"

"Could be she just plain took off," Pete said. "Maybe she signed the Oil Man's papers."

"Mais non! Somet'in had its eye on Pork Fat. Wanted her picked apart like a mudbug, same as her kin. You know how it watch from de water, Pete. Lookin like a cottonmouth, bout eight inch tall. Deep under, t'ough, it eight *feet*. Squeezin what left of folk down it t'roat. It watchin right now. Listenin too. Music-makers know how to listen. You really can't hear it?"

Pete shook his head. That didn't mean it weren't out there. Everything was, living and dead both. If Pork Fat had been murdered, maybe Billy May had been murdered too. Abraham's shit. Pete sighed.

"Spuds and me are gonna gather them bones. Find us a city forensic who can tell us how fresh they are. You're gonna have to answer questions, Zoot. From folk whose badges got the might of the law behind them."

Pink Zoot nodded. Tears dripped off his face, blotchy red from the nonstop cutty-and-sodas Pete had watched him swill, usually from the next bar stool over. Somehow he'd drilled through two more of Pork Fat's beers.

"Gonna rot your liver," Pete warned.

"Tryin to," Pink Zoot sniffled. "Tryin to blow it like a ten-year-old tire on a cross-country haul. But dis damned body keeps rollin. Yours, too, Pete. De drink, de cancer. One or de udder is fillin our livers up wit' de blackest stuff dere is."

Pete didn't want to think of the booze, the Red Witch, none of that. He screwed his Stetson back on, the sweat cold now. He gazed over Spuds's Astros cap at the swamp, the blackness under all that green. He knew that blackness pretty well, but not like Jack O'Brien had known it. That burned Pete a bit. He weren't a Pointer by blood and that was a stigma he'd never be done fighting.

Spuds quit kicking the shanty's bottom step, which had one of them old octopus carvings on it, and turned toward the swamp as if he'd just heard what Pink Zoot had been reporting. Music. A duet. A rhythm, maybe, that didn't walk alone.

Pete slapped his thigh and stood. The porch groaned in relief.

"We better get gatherin the bones. Zoot, you're not gonna fly the coop, are you?"

Pink Zoot used the frilled edge of his celebration suit to dry his tears.

"I ain't going nowhere. Got a funeral to plan, after all. Guess that'll be Zydeco Chowder's final show. For de best. My fingers don't play liked dey used to. My voice all dried up too. Oughta ask de schoolteacher to join us for our last shindig, eh? Miss Ward she go by? All de children say she got de voice of an angel. Pretty rare t'ing in dis here sewer, where all we got us is devils."

~ 26 ~

IN WHAT PASSED FOR THE GOOD OL' DAYS, the Melbourne Queen had been outfitted with a radio to keep in touch with the main office. Still was, though now there was nothing but ghosts on the other end. Of late Pete had seen New Orleans coppers using mobile phones. Seemed like magic, and the kind of magic Pete wouldn't mind trying. By the time that technology was suitable for the backwater, Alligator Point would be in the hands of the Oil Man, or underwater, or both.

Making the call he had to make right now meant borrowing the phone at Doc's Mercantile. A fourteen-minute drive was all, but that was plenty of time for Spuds to cut to the quick of things like no one else could.

"Goll, Pete. You see that octopus on the stairs?"

Pete delayed his answer by trying to roll his window down more than was possible. The wind was as hot and wet as dog breath.

"I saw."

"I seen those octopuses before. You seen 'em, Pete?"

"Time to time."

"Well, who put 'em there?"

"Any folk old enough to know are dead."

"The Saloon Committee's old. And *they're* not dead."

Pete smirked. "Agree to disagree."

"Did there used to be octopuses here?" Spuds looked worriedly out his window and closed it.

"You listen to the Committee, they'll tell you anything was possible on the Point. They say this place used to be different. Full of life. Full of death too. But *full*. That's one thing the Point sure ain't no more. The Oil Man's pickin us off one by one. Might as well be a sniper."

"You think it coulda been an octopus that got Pork Fat?"

Pete glared. "You heard a thing I said? Those ribs in our trunk, you think an octopus slurped down the rest of Pork Fat like a cochon de lait flesh and spat out the bones?"

Spuds crossed his arms, a scolded kid. Stubborn one too.

"The thing that got Billy May got Pork Fat too. You know it, Pete."

"We had us this talk before, Spuds."

"What talk is that, Pete?"

"The boogeyman talk."

"What about the boogeyman, Pete?"

"It don't matter if you're talkin bout the Piper. Or Bigfoot. Or the Rougarou. The only evil out there is the evil men do. Now, look here. What they can do with bones today will turn your hair red. They might be able to tell us how old the victim was, if they was a man or a woman, how they died, how long ago, and, hell, I don't know. Their favorite candy bar, maybe." He slapped Spuds on the shoulder. "Some old missing person from 1950s, I'll bet you a burger."

The squish of the mud road—muddier every year—was the only reply.

Pete let it be. Few minutes later, Spuds spoke, and real soft for him.

"If the Piper ain't real, what happened to Jack O'Brien?"

Pete shivered. Happened automatic like that. There weren't nothing felt cruddier than shivering while the rest of you was glossed with sweat. He jabbed the AC button that quit working eleven years back.

"Jack O'Brien was a Pointer, Spuds. Born and bred. Spent fifteen years fishing the remotest waters of the Earth. Least that's what he liked to tell people."

"You think he was lying, Pete?"

"Hell if I know. The fellow had a screw loose, I can tell you that. Six or seven screws. Came back to the Point like General MacArthur, dragging a wagon packed full a gator gear. Only it weren't gators he came back to hunt. Claimed he learned things out in the world. Things that taught him what kind of stuff was going down on the Point."

"What kind of stuff is that?"

"You ever seen *Bride of Frankenstein*?"

"You know I don't got no TV, Pete."

"*Gods and monsters*—that's what Jack O'Brien was after." Pete mopped his neck with a wadded kerchief and shook it dry out the window. "He'd tie up his gator boat and go stompin through the *buscoyos*, the cypress knees, the whole swamp, kit out like some kind of guerrilla, shoutin for what he called Evil to show itself. Remington 870 on his back, big old Bowie knife, sugarcane machete in a holster. Gris-gris bags on his belt too, hoodoo nonsense he picked up in his travels. I told him to show me. He wouldn't. No matter how many times I dragged his ass outta the quick. Or scared off a cottonmouth. Or boated my butt through a hurricane to fetch him from a tree. Evil he was after. But I tell you, Spuds, when you make local lawmen risk their tails like that, over and over, not to mention what it did to Miss Ward each time he nearly bit it—who's evil?"

"Is that how he died, Pete? Hurricane?"

Pete sped up as much as he dared. He'd like to outpace these questions.

"Jack O'Brien only called himself a gator hunter. What he was was a professional trespasser. Evil don't keep to property boundaries was his excuse. One day he crawled over the wrong fence." Pete hesitated; he didn't relish this shit. "Got shot by a prostitute. She thought he was a jealous spouse come to kill her. You know what a prostitute does, Spuds?"

"I know, Pete. It has to do with your willy."

"Most the time, yes. Anyways, that lady called me and Doc Devereaux to come, and while Doc tried to save Jack's life, I went into the lady's shanty. And it was . . . Shoot, Spuds, you live in a horse stable and that's nicer than most these shanties!"

"I love it, Pete. I found a poster of a swimsuit lady and put it up."

"That's real good, Spuds. This lady that shot Jack, her place was the worst thing I ever saw. No electricity. No toilet. Eating swamp weeds for food. She had a little girl. Little girl covered with vermin bites. This lady begged me not to jail her up. Pleaded me. The little girl, too, begged and pleaded to stay with her mama." Pete let the mustard sun sting the memory from his eyes. "I been in the foster system. It weren't gonna do no justice to haul that woman off."

"You let them go, Pete?"

The sun failed to scorch his retinas. Pete could still see the little girl peeking around the shanty's corner, legs slathered in mud, scabs like a pox. Pete avoided sharing secrets with Spuds. The deputy was too trusting, he'd tell anything to anybody. But Spuds had earned a secret or two. Spuds had taken the chance Pete had given him and grown into a decent deputy.

"I told them to run," Pete said. "Even showed them the path to take."

He didn't say the secret part. This lady had shared the same profession as his mother. A life saved for a life lost. That was how he looked at it.

Spuds chewed it over, literally from the look of his grinding jaws.

"That's why Miss Ward hates your guts."

Pete nodded. "Can't properly blame her. I let Jack's killer go. Pretty much ruined Miss Ward, far as I can tell. She ain't spoke to a soul over ten twelve years old since. That's on me. I accept it. I accept all of it. How it don't let me sleep good. How it gives me bad dreams all day. I'm just a person, Spuds. Same as that lady I let go. Same as Miss Ward. Same as Billy May, same as Pork Fat. We're all just people doing dark things to each other. We're doing bad enough without any Piper."

The Melbourne Queen peeled around a twisted crucifix of osage orange trees and Doc's Mercantile slid into view. It teetered on the very edge of town, a parking area of white gravel cleanly demarcating the borderline of Alligator Point and Dawes. Lots of Pointers caught their own grub, and those with functioning vehicles mades jaunts to the Dawes Piggly Wiggly. For everybody else, there was Doc's: a broad shack that legend held had once been a Pirates Lafitte auction house. Among its four aisles of oddments were record player needles, nonprescription glasses, off-brand Spam, typewriter ribbons, propane canisters, candy cigarettes, bullets, and nonperishable foods, half of which had perished.

Pete pulled up and killed the Queen. On instinct, he didn't get out. He knew his deputy's silences. Spuds Ulene had more to say.

"When I was up at Fort Pendleton, I peeled a lot of taters," Spuds began. "Sometimes there'd be three thousand taters to peel. I chopped them up when they were good. But sometimes the brown spots went way down inside."

The Melbourne Queen's engine ticked, ticked, ticked.

"What you gettin at, Spuds?"

"What I'm saying, Pete, is it might look like it's just Pointers doing evil to other Pointers. But we ain't evil folk. I know we ain't. Look how you helped that lady and her little girl. Look how broken up Pink Zoot was about Pork Fat. There's something else in this swamp, Pete. A brown spot. One that goes way down past the ones of us living now. There's no way to know what it is till we peel and peel and our peeler comes out the other side."

~ 27 ~

IF YOU WENT TO DOC'S MERCANTILE, there was no ducking Doc. Not only did the seventy-five-year-old white dude own the joint, he was the sole employee, and lived in the back room, which was about as big as the interior of a van. Doc didn't let anyone see it. Still had a few crumbs of pride. Back in the day, he had a doctor's office right across from the library, nicest place in all the Point. Fancy doors that didn't warp from humidity. Clean floors, plus little booties for all the barefooters. Even a few art prints on the wall, pictures of cool, open spaces nobody on the Point would ever see.

For twenty-eight years, he'd been the only G.P. the Point ever had. If you didn't count the folk healers, faith healers, and such. Doc Devereaux, of course, *did* count them. He'd had his mind opened to alternative forms of care—physical, mental, emotional, and spiritual—long before he'd shipped off to med school and traded his Cajun for Latin. By the time he returned, all other healers were gone, their medicines no match for the Point's virulent strains.

Doc was nearly gone too. All he had left was this junk mart. The final stubborn stand of a stubborn old man. The swamp had no lack of ways to end it all. All Doc had to do is take off his shoes and walk in a straight line till something bit, stung, strangled, infected, or drowned him to death. But he didn't deserve that kind of end.

He deserved an elongated agony, the same kind Emily suffered. On that front? So far, so good.

The entry bell had lost its clapper in 1978, but its brass lip clonked well enough against the door to get Doc's attention.

Gopher shit. Pete Roosevelt.

The door swung shut behind Pete and Doc caught his own reflection in the glass. He liked to think he didn't give a poop about his looks anymore. But when a person he hadn't seen in a spell ambled in, Doc couldn't help but see himself through their eyes. Eyeballs big as satsuma fruit behind thick bifocals. Overalls so starchy they could run the store themselves. Two puffs of white hair rising from either side of a bald head. And a frown like the cleft a hoe makes in hard dirt, in place since 1981 and guarded by echelons of wrinkles.

Pete tipped his Stetson and gave the smile all rural folk know, more like a wince, as if instead of saying *hello*, Pete was saying, *Looks like things are going rough.*

Well, Doc might say the same about Pete!

"What are you doing here?" Doc grouched.

The grouch, like the frown, came automatic. He knew being a crabby old fart shielded the bits of him that were still tender. Plenty of those tender bits involved Pete Roosevelt. One of the last acts Doc did before closing his practice was tending to the shotgun wound of Jack O'Brien. Doc got Jack all the way to Lady of the Sea General Hospital, Jack sputtering a single phrase, over and over, through a mouthful of pink foam.

. . . shoot your shot . . .

. . . shoot your shot . . .

. . . shoot your shot . . .

Doc tried to get Jack to explain the phrase as a means to keeping himself conscious. He figured it had to do with gators. Solo hunters like Jack reeled in a gator line with one hand and used their other to deliver a killshot to a golfball-sized area right behind a gator's head plate.

But Doc never found out what Jack was blabbering about. Jack died in the hallway of Lady of the Sea. Doc didn't even have time to wash off Jack's blood before intercepting Miss Ward, breaking the news, and watching four years of sunshine drain from her in a single second. Worst thing Doc ever saw, and he'd seen a lot. No way the woman who shot Jack O'Brien had escaped the Point without Pete's permission. Doc didn't see much justice in that.

Things had been tense between Doc and Pete ever since.

"Gotta use Ma Bell," Pete said.

"Local?" Doc challenged.

"City." Meaning New Orleans.

"Business or pleasure?"

"Shoot," Pete said. "Don't even recall what pleasure even is."

Doc shrugged and felt an arthritic pinch at his shoulder.

"Your quarter," he grunted.

Doc hoisted the heavy black telephone onto the counter. Nothing at the Mercantile was free. Even when folk brought back a pack of corroded batteries, Doc only refunded the price minus the going rate of steel and copper. He picked up Pete's quarter and gave it a counterfeiter's squint. Then he gestured like it was Pete holding up the proceedings.

Pete stuck a thick finger into the rotary dial and spun it.

Shhhhhhhh-tat-tat-tat-tat-tat.

Doc turned back to the door to wait for Pete's longsiding deputy. Spuds Ulene skulked in with a twirling limp and dodged Doc's eyes like a kid fixing to steal. Spuds was straight-up scared of Doc, which was how Doc liked it.

"Hi, y'all," Pete said into the phone. "This here's Pete Roosevelt over Bullock Parish. I'd sure like to have me a palaver with Terry Thurmond."

Spuds eyes widened at the glories of the candy rack.

"Oh." Pete's southern charm fell away. "When did that happen?"

Doc didn't like giving Pete the satisfaction that he was interested in his call. But he knew the sound of somebody getting word of a death. Doc had broken such news to a lot more folk than just Miss Ward. It took the wind out of a soul. Not just the hearer but the teller too.

"I'm real sorry to hear that," Pete said softly. "Terry always did right by us down here in Bullock." He listened. "Yeah, I suppose you better. Uh-huh. Sergeant Pat Wilkes. Yeah, have him give me a ring. Oh—all right then. Have *her* give me a ring. Mighty obliged."

Pete settled the receiver in its cradle with a far less force than he'd drawn it out. Doc made it disappear behind the counter. Too often, one call begat others. Doc tried not to care, but hellfire, what else was there to talk about?

"Friend of yours dead?" he blurted.

"Pork Fat," Spuds piped up. "The scritcher girl from Zydeco Chowder."

"That's not who we're talkin about, Spuds." Pete shrugged at Doc. "Found some ribs in the damp is all. Don't mean nothing yet."

Doc felt another candle blow out inside him. He turned from Pete, spotted his feather duster, and got to flicking it across cigarettes, cigars, and chew.

"That makes two," he grumbled.

"Now, Doc," Pete said. "Don't get going like you do."

"Twice now the Oil Man's left papers for me to sign. Wants me gone. Wants us all gone. Can't quite figure why I'm still resisting. Ain't a single one of us worth the land we're sitting on."

"Not if there's oil under it."

"You know what oil is, Pete? Spuds, you know?"

"Sure I do," Spuds said. "It's the black goo that makes your car go."

"Crude oil," Doc proclaimed, "is made of dead critters who lived millions of years ago."

Spuds, excited now, checked with Pete. "Dinosaurs, Pete?"

"Those critters sank to the bottom of the waters and got buried in rock. Add some heat, a little pressure, and there you go. We don't move our butts onto the dry sooner or later, we'll be oil too. Some of us are already on our way. This pal Terry of yours. This girl Pork Fat. Those offshore derricks are going to get all of us one way or the other."

Spuds gulped audibly. Doc felt his face heat up. He shouldn't have said it. But, hellfire, truth was truth!

Pete sighed. His back rounded like he was Atlas.

"Goddamn it, Doc. I got enough problems without you spookin my deputy. We got a few years till our bodies start bein pumped into gas tanks."

Doc shook his feather duster at Spuds.

"That boy will follow you to the depths of hell if no one tells him the truth of what's happening in Alligator Point!"

"The truth?" Pete looked around, snatched up a plastic St. Christopher selling for a buck and a half. "Is this the truth? Pray to your plastic saints and they'll set you on the golden path?"

Doc showed his palms. "I don't tell folk what or what not to believe."

Pete flung the saint to the ground. It shattered. He plucked a dusty voodoo doll from a rack of similar cloth figures.

"Or is this the truth? These poppets? Add a lock of your enemy's hair, fill it full of pins. Maybe that's what we oughta do to the Oil Man."

Pete flung the doll against the wall.

"Damn it, Pete! That's my merchandise!"

Pete dug both hands into two boxes of candy and threw the whole mess at Doc. Doc lifted an arm against the salvo of M&Ms, Almond Joys, and Butterfingers.

"I seem to recall when Emily was dying, there wasn't *nothin* you wouldn't try!" Pete roared. "Evil-eye candles! Van Van Oil! Mojo hands! Jalop roots!"

Doc's bones went ice cold. His knotted, rheumatic fingers ached.

"Emily's name stays out of your mouth until it can come out respectful," he warned.

"Emily's dead, what? Sixteen, seventeen years? I'm sorry, Doc. Everybody is. But her dyin, bad as it was, ain't no excuse to give up on the Pointers still livin!"

"I had no obligation to keep practicing medicine. Especially when it wasn't doing anybody any good. Not down here it wasn't."

"Why you think that is, Doc? You think the Point is cursed? Spuds does!"

Spuds nodded sagely. "I do."

"Or could it be the refinery toxins?" Pete continued. "Or the oil spills gettin in our water? To hell with the Oil Man, Doc! What he's peddlin ain't any stronger stuff than the plastic crapola you're peddlin! You wanna close up shop, then close. Not me, Doc. The Oil Man's gonna have to hire him a militia to pry me from my Airstream."

Doc reduced his anger to a glower. Oh, he had retorts. And Pete had retorts to those retorts. You lived on the Point long enough, you collected a bucket of hurtful things you could use against your neighbors. None of that changed the fact that Doc *had* quit doctoring when it had gotten too hard. Pete, meanwhile, had done the opposite. Even after he quit drawing a paycheck, he kept sheriffing.

They'd been friends once. Good ones. Hellfire, Doc had given Pete that Stetson. Came into the Mercantile as a sample back in '86, round the same time Doc added the wall of VHS rentals. Pete rented a lot of westerns and Doc figured he'd like a cowboy hat to match. Doc could see splinters of that friendship in Pete's face. He could feel them in his own heart. But once something's been fractured to splinters, not all glue in the world can hold it together.

Doc felt like a scarecrow. Stiff, dry, abandoned.

He drug his eyes over the broken wares and felt for his broom. "I'm putting this on your tab," he said.

- 28 -

One hundred and sixty-three Pointers had died under Doc's care. Many had been middle-aged. There had been seven teenagers. Six women lost in childbirth. Nine infants whose engines Doc was unable to get up and running. A whole mess of old folk. And almost all of them had been taken by the heavy black marbles of cancer.

It was the loss of the oldest that hit Doc the hardest. Couldn't quite say why. Maybe it was the fact they had lived so long, come through so much, and gathered the wisdom of eighty, ninety, or a hundred years. A lost newborn, by comparison, didn't lose any knowledge at all. All it lost was potential—a potential which, in Doc's experience, paid off about as frequently as a certain breed of cicadas resurfaced.

Before Emily died, he'd had a way of fighting the despair. He'd kept track. Like no one else on the Point, he'd kept track.

He'd learned it from his grandfolk. Little notes and sketches they'd scratch down on receipts. Papers they'd tape to walls. Fold inside books. Slip into mailboxes. Hand to neighbors. Other folk their age did the same, as far as Doc could recall. Even while laughing, his grandfolk's eyes had been diamond hard, staring deep into kudzu thick as as clay, up into yellow chinaberry boughs, down at the marsh grass weeping mud-water beneath their toes. Doc didn't know the details of all those communiqués, but he got the gist.

Folk needing help: food, wise words, helping hands.

Gods needing tribute: cake, liquor, purification baths.

When either folk or gods went bad, they could become monsters.

In med school, he'd find himself doodling octopuses on the sides of exams. He didn't see any conflict in it. Doctoring was keeping track of somebody's insides. But humans were only cells in the larger body of the universe. Somebody had to keep track of that too.

Doc returned to the Point in a truck towing a prefab house from the city. He wasn't going to live in a pirate shanty, not anymore. He found things had changed on Alligator Point. Folk were distracted. By TV. By celebrity magazines. By their collapsing homes and their flooding lands. By the dwindling of their people, some decamping to the rigs or refineries, others growing sedentary with what felt like old age but ended up being piles of turgid tumor.

Where Doc's grandfolk kept track religiously, Doc's parents had stopped altogether. Less than a year after Doc came home, Mama and Daddy were dead—cancer, cancer—and their double tomb was the last piece of proof Doc needed. He was the first G.P. who ever lived on Alligator Point, and something down here didn't like it. Something wanted to show him who was boss.

So Doc picked up where his grandfolk left off.

He treated a case of trench foot for a local artisan whose medium was gatorskin and paid her the going rate to make him fifty one-hundred-page alligator-leather journals, hickory brown and gleaming, prettiest things you ever saw and sturdy as a good pair of boots.

Same day the journals were delivered, Doc started filling them with observations. No overriding sense to it, really. Just making a record was the thing, and few people were better suited to know what was going on in a place than the local sawbones. Who went where. How they got there. Why they went. Who did what to whom. Injuries, tragedies, births, and deaths, the last category sprinkled with 163 asterisks marking every case where he, Doc Devereaux, was partly to blame.

Number 163 was the one that broke him.

Doc and Emily had been wed not half a year after he'd set up his bayou practice. He could have changed course and filled the gatorskin journals with the things he loved about her. A smile that felt private. The way she rubbed his neck, almost without thinking. How the sun, what little got through the trees, turned her sweat into little crystals.

In other words, the same shit a billion others felt about the ones they loved. To history, it wasn't worth the paper he would have written it on. To him, though, it worth everything, until it was worth nothing.

Doc couldn't reliably say how many Pointers he'd sent to oncologists in New Orleans. He'd sniffed out every kind of tumor there was. Throat, tongue, lung, stomach, kidney, pancreatic, prostrate, testicular, ovarian, bladder, colon, thyroid—whole covens of what Pete Roosevelt called the Red Witch.

How could he have missed the Red Witch right under his own palm?

What Doc dreamed about in his crusty old age was sex. Sex and regret, what all old fools dream of. He was in bed with Emily. This was how it went. He was on top, missionary. What tipped it off as a dream was the position of his hands. In real life, he had to support his upper body with his hands on the mattress. That was just physics.

In the dream, though, he had both hands planted on Emily's breasts.

He'd always come faster than he wanted in real life. In his dreams, he had the opposite problem. He couldn't come. He pumped away, sweat pouring, joints screaming, forever hoping the next stroke would release him. He thrust again and again, greedily, selfishly, not feeling the woman at all beneath the breasts.

Only feeling the lump in the left breast.

And not caring.

The lump was the size of an egg and hard as a clam.

How had he missed the tumor in Emily? In *Emily*?

Six months that egg lay undetected, time enough to grow, and hatch, and spawn a blacker swamp inside her than what waited beyond the trails. The monster that hatched was merciless. It took Emily's eyesight, her equilibrium; it took her ability to eat, to breathe; it took her mind, turning her from a murmuring lover into a raving hellion. It took her life, and took its time doing it. Really, though, the cancer was only doing what it had been born to do.

Doc was the murderer here.

Emily died in 1981 at age forty-eight. Doc closed up shop the same year, then in late 1982 opened a different shop, Doc's Mercantile, just to keep body and soul stapled adjacent. The prefab house he'd lugged into the swamp he left to rot. He didn't need but a mouse hole to live in anymore. He stowed his clothing beneath his bed, and on the shelves above, hidden by an old sheet, he stacked the forty-nine gatorskin journals he'd filled up and the single one he'd never gotten to, wrapped tight in cadaver plastic.

What good had all that spent ink done? All keeping track did in the end was supply irrefutable proof of your bankruptcies, every bitter variety. He ought to toss the journals. Burn them. Maybe he'd get lucky and the swamp would catch fire. Maybe the oil gurgling beneath would explode. He couldn't imagine a happier ending. Maybe this was the meaning of Jack O'Brien's last words.

Shoot your shot.

First Doc needed to find his balls, missing now for seventeen years. He peered into corners while sweeping up the shattered saint, the ripped poppet, the spilled gris-gris. The only balls he found were made of dust. Pete Roosevelt was right about one thing: Doc wasn't going to find his mojo in tchotchkes. He might as well give up trying, same as he'd given up doctoring, same as he'd given up keeping track.

Would have done it, too, if Gerard Pontiac's little girl hadn't barnstormed in.

~ 29 ~

PONTIAC, OR SO THE TWERP WENT BY, struck a split-legged pose. She had a thick blue book nestled into an arm crook. With her other hand, she shot a finger at the window and made her declaration.

"I need me that Whiz-Bang fishing rod."

Doc got furrowing his brow. Better to gripe than despond.

"In my day, we began with *Hello, sir, how are you today?*"

Pontiac frowned. "You work at this store, don't you?"

Doc went as straight as his broom. "I do."

"Then my money's what says hello. That's what my daddy says."

"I'm not sure I accept money from devils like you."

"That's fine," Pontiac said, "because I don't got any."

"Then what are you on about purchasing that Whiz-Bang?"

"Not just the Whiz-Bang. Also need me a Spindrift reel and a set a bobbers. Lost my whole kit out at Guimbarde."

"What a wonderful story. You learn it from that big book?"

"It's all true. Ask Saphir. The fisherman."

"The fabulist, more like. I wouldn't trust a word from that falsifying prevaricator."

The girl squinted and gave Doc a reevaluating once-over. She removed a warped notebook from the back of her pants, caught the attached pencil, and started scribbling.

"Now what are you doing?"

"*Falsifying prevaricator*," Pontiac read aloud. "That's pretty good."

Doc scoffed. "If you're such good pals with our fisherman fabulist, why don't you use one of his rods?"

Pontiac's scowl looked to Doc more like a mask.

"We ain't friends no more," she muttered.

Doc felt a tick of sympathy, then swallowed it whole.

"Little-girl tears don't work on me. The Whiz-Bang, the Spindrift, the bobbers . . . I figure it'll set you back a hundred and twenty-five."

"Like I said, I don't got it."

"Then let me direct your attention to the *No Loitering* sign."

"I'm not loitering. I'm here on business."

"Why didn't you say so? I would've fetched my briefcase."

"I'm thinking maybe there's chores you'd like to put off on somebody like myself."

"On you? You of skeeter size? Fetching things for me?"

"I been fetching pirogues that drifted down the bayou since I was five. If I can fetch a big old pirogue, I can fetch anything around here needing fetched. The way I figure it, you're making about 3,300 bucks a week. That pretty much the size of it?"

Swamp steam filled Doc's sinuses. "You been peeking at my books?"

"I ain't done no such thing."

"You're just the size of one of my back windows!"

"You're a falsifying prevaricator, is what you are!"

Doc removed his glasses and rubbed his eyes. Long day and getting longer.

"You aiming to tell me you calculated that figure yourself?"

"I been here plenty. I write down what you sell. I write down how many people come in. I write down what they usually buy. Wieners. Chaw. Smokes. Soda pop. Aspirin. You sell a lot of aspirin. Probably the thing you sell most is videotapes, and you don't even sell them, you just rent them. That's smart business. Also, I know exactly how many folk live on the Point."

"Down to forty families now."

"Thirty-nine. The St. Pés signed the Oil Man's papers on Friday."

Doc harrumphed. He hadn't heard that. The St. Pés were steady buyers too.

"Look here, skeeter. You got me swimming in gold. Let me educate you. For me to bring in that $3,300, I have to lay out, last week for example, $2,908. Don't bother ciphering it; I'll tell you. That leaves me $392 a week, before taxes, to pay for my own food, my own propane, my own phone, my own smokes. I'm barely getting by. And you want me to hire a gopher?"

"Yeah, but that's $18,816."

"What is?"

"You gotta times $392 by four cuz there's four weeks in a month. That's $1,568. Then you gotta take that times twelve cuz there's twelve months in a year. That's $18,816. You can spare 125 bucks of that, easy. Especially for all the aspirin money you'll save for giving your sore back a break."

Doc slitted his eyes. "You just figured all that in your head?"

"It's multiplication. Miss Ward can teach you if you want."

Pontiac closed her notebook and slid it back into her pants. Doc recognized it. The same generic composition pad he'd been selling for fifteen years. It bore little resemblance to the oversize, high-dollar, one-of-a-kind gatorskin journals he had in back. Yet he knew it served the same purpose.

The stories Doc had collected back in the day fluttered at the edge of his awareness. Stories about a thing that beckoned people into the swamp at night and ate people's hearts right out of their chests. He'd never seen it himself, never heard its noises. He wondered, though, if it hadn't crept through his window over the years while he slept.

Doc still had his heart. But it'd been plenty chewed on.

He gestured at a dusty castle of boxes behind the ice-cream freezer.

"Those boxes have gone unpacked for six years. Unstack them. See what's inside. You do that without breaking anything, I'll give you a try."

The girl took off. She plunged face-first into the cobwebs, man-handled boxes into stair-step shapes, and climbed them to reach higher ones. Doc was impressed all over again, but didn't advertise it. He shuffled behind the counter as Pontiac started ripping open boxes with rat ferocity. Periodically she shouted the contents.

"Canned beans!"

"Shelf," Doc called back.

"Circus peanuts!"

"Trash."

"Travel Kleenex!"

"Shelf."

Thirty minutes it went on like this.

"Fuck-damn! Doc! Voodoo junk!"

Doc muttered, mostly for show, and walked over with the stiff-legged shuffle that preserved his arthritic knees. The girl was doubly right. It was voodoo stuff and most definitely junk. Doc fuzzily recalled a trip to the city to stock up on the kind good-luck paraphernalia Pointers turned to when they got desperate. Pontiac showed her judgment yet again. She shoved aside painted chicken feet, skeleton-key talismans, raccoon penis bones, and tarot decks to zero in on the only item of intrigue: an old glass bottle.

"What's this, Doc?"

He made a stage show of wiping his specs, leaning, peering, frowning.

"Could be a *zombi*."

Pontiac looked doubtful. "Zombie? Like the old movie with the farmhouse?"

"Zombi astral. A raw spirit. A human soul."

"How'd it get in a bottle?"

"A bokor put it there. A sorcerer."

Pontiac shook it. Matter shifted inside. She gasped and got quiet.

"Is that the soul?"

"Could be cemetery earth. Or skull shavings. Hard to know."

Doc snapped his fingers for the bottle. Pontiac handed it over. It was colder than Doc expected. Heavier too. The bottle was painted black. A metal stopper festooned with tiny shells was screwed tight into what looked like dry tar, and lashed to the shoulder of the bottle by a lacework of twine that held four coin-sized mirrors. Looked awfully authentic for a box full of mass-produced junk.

"How much you going to sell it for?" Pontiac asked.

"I can't sell this."

"Can I have it?"

Doc shrugged and handed it back.

The second the cold glass left his fingertips, he hissed in regret.

"Shit!"

"What?" Pontiac asked.

"Well, dammit. Now you own that zombi."

Pontiac rolled the bottle between her hands. "Cool."

"No. Not 'cool.' You really want to own a human soul?"

Pontiac blinked and held the bottle away from her.

"Fuck-damn! Is that like owning a slave? I don't want it!"

Doc held his hands out to calm her.

"Not *just* like. Some say vodouisants make these bottles to turn their pain into a ritual. Something they can hold, you understand?"

Pontiac gripped the stopper. "Can't I just let it out?"

Doc waved his arms. "Don't you open that bottle in my store!"

Pontiac looked aggrieved. "What am I supposed to do with it, then?"

"I believe you're supposed to care for it. To feed it."

"Feed it? Like with humans?"

"Stop being so dramatic. Unsalted rice, if I recall. Beans."

"Can I have one of those cans of beans I just found?"

"You can buy one."

"Man! You're a hard-ass, Doc!"

"No one said taking care of a zombi was easy."

"I just came to here to get a fishing rod! Now I gotta feed a zombi the rest of my life?"

"Not forever. Just until it goes back to its ancestral homeland."

"When will that be?"

"When it's ready."

Pontiac scowled. "You made me open this box on purpose."

Doc ruffled his plumage. "I did no such thing."

He didn't think he had. Doubt, though, came clawing like the other kind of zombies, the ones in several of the videotapes he rented. During the period of Emily's rapid decline, Doc had sought out healers of every stripe, just as Pete Roosevelt had claimed. None of it had helped Emily, but it had helped Doc some. He'd learned to take a step beyond the hard line drawn by med school professors. The other side was as close as the Dawes border was to the Mercantile, a simple stone's throw, even for an old man. It was a place where all things were possible—good, bad, and the very bad alike.

"If I have to start buying rice and beans," Pontiac griped, "you *have* to hire me."

~ 30 ~

WHAT ELSE COULD HE DO? The pest agreed to barefoot over after school each day to muscle around moldy boxes and defunct equipment, and mop the menageries of crap that had agglomerated in their oily wakes. Doc didn't lay off his crotchety complaining and Pontiac didn't turn down her impudent curiosity, and within days of sealing their odd confederacy, Doc Devereaux knew his hunch about Pontiac had been correct.

Different as they were, he and the girl were kindred.

Oh, he had adjustments to make. Doc didn't have a radio in the shop. He preferred the clicks, snorts, clucks, snuffles, and drones of the damp, how the smacking mud told him when folk, beasts, or otherwise were creeping close. Silence was good for hearing shop-lifters too. Pontiac, though, brought with her a piano factory of new noises. The girl simply did not shut her yap.

There were, of course, endless updates on her zombi bottle, a punishment Doc figured he deserved. According to Pontiac, a zombi astral was less fun than a goldfish. Just sat there, ignoring its daily portions of rice and beans, doing jack shit.

Mostly, though, Pontiac blabbed about other stuff. Nearly took Doc's wheezy old breath away how she blabbed. He'd forgotten the fleetness of the young, how they could catch an idea like a hot gulf wind catches a plastic bag. She talked nonstop about the Whiz-Bang like she was fearful he'd sell it from under her. Seemed crucial to her that he understand she didn't intend to be a "Sunday fisherman." She would use that rod to catch food right alongside André Saphir— but not *longside* him—to prove she was his equal. Then she'd have Doc over for remoulade featuring whatever the hell she caught. Remoulade so good it'd make you slap your grandma. Didn't that sound fine? And didn't Doc feel like cutting the Whiz-Bang package price to an even hundred so he could get to eating that remoulade quicker?

He did not. Doc acted like he was teaching the girl a lesson. The truth was a lot gluier. The sooner Pontiac earned her $125, the sooner she'd stop coming by. Doc checked the clock all day long, impatient for 3:30, when Pontiac would come barging in, log in hand, going full speed about all the crap she'd noticed that day, crap that would bore the tears out of anybody in Alligator Point.

Except Doc.

Only he knew how important that crap really was.

He speculated on how Pontiac might react when she uncovered the stockpile of gatorskin journals and was the first to look upon their contents. He wondered if it might unscrew his dry old body like one might unscrew a zombi bottle, releasing the spirit of the old Doc Devereaux, trapped in the void for too long.

He mopped sweat from his forehead. Stuck his face an inch from the fan. Massaged his lower back, half-hoping for hard egg shapes, the cancer he was owed. How'd it get to this point? Where the approval of a nine-year-old brat had the power to change his opinion that his whole life had been a waste?

Day after day, though, Pontiac didn't find the journals. It didn't make sense. The girl invaded everywhere she shouldn't be. Stuck her hand behind the milk cooler and got her thumb mouse-trapped. Popped the cap off the fence post outside and got a face full of wasps. Crept past the curtain to where he kept the adult videos to gape at the box covers till he scared her off with the broom.

What was so difficult about lifting a goddamn sheet?

Harder than it looked, in truth. He'd tried. Weighed more than the whole delta.

Friday night, six o'clock, closing time, he sat on the stoop, eyes stinging with sweat. High foliage made night come on viper-fast in the swamp and Doc preferred to see Pontiac head home before the sky went full obsidian. But tonight the girl lollygagged beneath a crepe myrtle's purple boughs, half of which dangled over the Dawes side of the border. She was copying into her log something carved into the bark. Doc spat. He used to do the same thing. Damn near every tree on the Point had *something* carved into it.

Pontiac stomped back through the mud. Doc snapped his fingers to see.

The girl gave him a hot look of warning, then cautiously displayed the log's active spread. Doc's eyeballs, no good to begin with, vibrated with the assailment of notes, sketches, maps, grids, and sigils, all put down in pencil lead of maddening slightness. Doc looked down his nose at the last thing on the second page.

An octopus.

Doc knew good and well the crepe myrtle sported an octopus carving. He'd just stopped seeing it over the years. *Octopus*—there was something about octopuses he'd forgotten or misplaced. The answer might be inside those gatorskin journals. But the idea of digging through them to find it? You could shave off nine-tenths of Doc's age and he'd still be older than Pontiac. He had neither the energy nor courage to face his idealistic younger self.

Pontiac shut her log, the free sample expired.

"I ain't coming by tomorrow. Weekends are for fun."

Doc's heart sank into the quag.

"Makes no difference to me," he grunted. "Your zombi's probably lonesome."

Pontiac sat next to him. "You think zombis get lonely?"

Doc bristled. "Don't everybody?"

"Gopher shit. Now I feel crummy. I put that zombi under the sink behind the Clorox and Drano."

"The hell you do that for? What did that zombi ever do to you?"

"My daddy collects bottles for money. If I didn't hide it, he'd take it."

Doc wiped his face of sweat. "You gotta give that thing light. Air. Christ on a cracker."

"It didn't come with an instruction book! Damn!"

"Instead of having *weekend fun*, how about you learn something? You ever been to the library?"

Pontiac held up her big blue book. "Where you think I got this?"

Doc swiped it from her hand and adjusted his glasses.

"Lovecraft. You're really a dumb kid, you know that?"

Pontiac glared as hard as Doc had ever seen her do it.

"I read that whole book. I bet you ain't ever read a book that big."

"Lovecraft was a racist. Did you know you're reading a racist?"

The girl's eyebrows tented with uncertainty.

"I thought it was about monsters and going crazy."

Doc opened the book to the table of contents and paged for the passage he hadn't laid eyes on since college. The swamp hissed and rattled. It didn't like being flayed.

"'The Statuette, idol, fetish, or whatever it was, had been captured some months before in the wood swamps south of New Orleans during a raid on a supposed voodoo meeting; and so singular and hideous were the rights connected with it, that the police could not but realise that they had stumbled on a dark cult totally unknown to them, and infinitely more diabolic than even the blackest of the African voodoo circles.'"

He looked expectantly at Pontiac.

She shrugged. "What?"

"*Hideous? Diabolic?* Does that sound like the zombi you have at home?"

"No," Pontiac admitted. "That bottle's pretty."

"So pretty you keep it by the Clorox and Drano."

"Man!"

Doc's trembling finger found other lines.

"Your favorite author describes these so-called cult members as 'a very low, mixed-blooded, and mentally aberrant type. Most were seamen, and a sprinkling of negroes and mulattoes.'" He paged again. "'Primitive but good-natured descendants of Lafitte's men.'" Doc tapped the page. "Lafitte blood? That's us he's talking about."

Pontiac sunk into herself. "We sure ain't *good-natured.*"

"You start thinking of others as the monsters and you as the hero, why, that excuses taking them over, doesn't it? Chaining them up, wiping them out, whatever you want."

Doc pinched the offending story and ripped it from the book's binding. He tossed fifteen pieces of white paper into the air. They turned black the instant they touched mud. Pontiac hopped around like the mud was burning coals.

"What! Doc! That's Mr. Peff's!"

Doc sniffed. "Now it's Mr. Swamp's."

Pontiac fell to the steps and held her face in her hands.

"Abraham's shit! First I gotta buy a Whiz-Bang. Then I have to feed a zombi. Now I have to pay for a whole new book!"

"Mr. Peff tries to make you pay for those missing pages, you send him to me. He's got a tab here long as an otter tail. I can call his ass on it any day I want."

Pontiac glanced at him doubtfully.

"All right. Still mad, though. I liked that story."

"I don't give a rat's fat patootie what you like. A child's got to learn fact from fiction."

"What's fiction about it? Miss Ward tells us the Battle of New Orleans story every year. Major General Jackson couldn't have won that thing without the Pirates Lafitte."

Doc squared his sloped out shoulders at the girl.

"You can like Mr. Lovecraft's story and still hate his racist ass. Same as you can be grateful to Andrew Jackson for saving New Orleans on the one hand, and on the other hate his stinking guts for tossing Indians off their own lands when he was president. And those Lafittes? Sure, they helped Old Hickory push out the red-coats. But that's not who those pirates really were."

"I *know* who the Pirates Lafitte were!"

"What were they?"

"The Lafittes are heroes!"

Doc stared—and Pontiac's eyes took on a nutria's shine.

"Weren't they?" she asked.

Doc's heart broke a little. The girls' buckling belief sounded like warm Coke poured over ice. Doc sighed and clasped his hands, eight knotted knuckles fighting.

"Folk like to cherry-pick history. Remember only what feels good to remember. An event like the Battle of New Orleans is packed fatter than a stuffed wild duck with all sorts of sound and fury. Easy to get lost inside that. Who doesn't like rooting for David when he meets Goliath? But what if David's got a disease that's going to infect the whole nation? That's a tale's not nearly as fun to tell."

"Miss Ward didn't say nothing about the Lafittes being bad," Pontiac protested.

Doc heard the pride Pontiac had in her teacher. He didn't wish to chip away at it. Fact is, Miss Ward's version of events probably didn't conflict with Doc's. His version only scraped at the charac-ters till they matched the swamp's natural shades. Doc had learned some of the story from his own marms, plus books he read, plus TV he watched, plus two whole movies he saw in theaters, one fancy enough to star Yul Brynner, each iteration inching the Battle of New Orleans further away from the truth.

How could you tell what was truth? Doc had learned how in the doctor's office. Truths *hurt*. They were traded like legal tender by old Pointers lacking the funds to pay for Doc's medical care or, once Doc opened the Mercantile, customers who were dead broke but needed milk for grandbabies. Gratons of hearsay, étouffée of legend, secrets dusted like confectioners' sugar over beignets.

New Orleans—La Nouvelle-Orléans—had a rich, rotten heart from the start. Fertile soil and a fecund climate were native, but not the strong backs needed to alchemize it into gold. Enslaved folk from Africa and Haiti were shipped in for the task. Millions died on slave ships. The ones who died in the bayous were left to sink, and decompose, and rise again as part of the trees and moss and fungi, all while their surviving families back in the city gave the gifts no colonizers deserved: food, music, culture, and spirits that wouldn't quit, even after their bodies did.

They fuck-damn *deserved* that land, as Pontiac might say. Without the Haitian slave revolt draining Napoleon's coffers, there wasn't a Louisiana, because there wasn't a Louisiana Purchase. By the time Louisiana became a state in 1812, New Orleans was singular in the world, seventy muddy, rat-filled, horse-shat blocks of whites, free Blacks and Creoles, and the enslaved, all twenty thousand breathing air tacky with rose petal and bladed with sugar, intermingling, screwing, rebelling, smelting together their languages, ways, loves, and hates, creating something maybe fucked up but, anyhow, entirely new.

Wasn't any kind of civilization the Brits recognized. So they attacked it with hopes of taking the city. Own the city, the ports, and you owned a million miles of trade routes. Did the Pirates Lafitte help Jackson dispel the threat? Damn right they did. Pirates had a way with artillery. But the Lafitte boys were likely to have done anything for the full pardon Jackson gave them. Didn't change the kind of folk the Lafittes were. They hid deep inside Alligator Point not because it was romantic and adventurous. They did it because they were evil.

"If you ever wonder why the Mercantile don't include any of those little Jolly Rogers, that's why," Doc said. "Them Pirates Lafitte weren't selling eyepatches. They were selling people."

"But there's whole *towns* down here called Lafitte," Pontiac protested. "You drive up through Dawes there and you'll see them. Parks called Lafitte too. And hotels, and restaurants, and gas stations!"

"Lies are always prettier than truths."

Pontiac slid from the stoop with a hiss.

"Daddy's proud of his pirate shanty!" Pontiac cried. "And so am I!"

Doc tried to see the girl in the dark, but only heard gravel scuffling under her backpedaling feet. He cussed himself. He'd done worse than ruin Pontiac's weekend fun. He'd told her too much, too fast, forgotten she was still a girl held together with fontanelles of pure belief. Doc called out for her to come back but it was too late. She was gone, past the white glow of the octopus carving and into the black swamp at the blundering speed favored by gators, quicksand, and curses.

~ 31 ~

PONTIAC LOVED THE LAFITTE SHANTIES for the same reasons an outsider would order them burned. Yeah, they were filled with holes. But those holes let in nice breezes and, now and then, interesting wildlife. True, rain fell right through the roofs. But rain was good to drink and was handy for cleaning up filthy accretions. Pontiac knew Doc wasn't an outsider; he'd been born in the Point's moist heart. But he hadn't lived in a shanty for fifty-some years. He'd forgotten what it was like, that's all.

The finest quality of shanties was they often contained pirate junk. Pontiac knew folk who had found corroded cannonballs. Sword hilts. Grindstones. Bronze ship's bells. Glass flacons. Gum Jenkins had found a flintlock pistol he'd sold to a collector in the city and made enough to buy new cauldrons for his moonshine still.

These artifacts went unmolested for so long because of how the Lafitte shanties valued secret spaces. False floors. Double walls. Hollow trusses. Concealed crannies. Pointers didn't find the hiding places so much as they eventually rotted through.

That was Pontiac's problem. Any hiding spaces that had been revealed, Daddy already knew about. That meant accepting a less satisfying place to stash the zombi bottle. Behind the toilet might have worked, but if she were a zombi, she wouldn't take kindly to getting sprayed by pee. The roof seemed like a fine idea until Pontiac climbed up there and witnessed how good squirrels, raccoons, and possums were at stealing things. Nowhere was safer from Daddy than the shanty's underside, but each day the swamp got swampier, and Pontiac couldn't vouch for the bottle's seal. She didn't want the zombi astral drowning.

So the bottle stayed right where it began, under the sink behind bodyguards of Clorox and Drano. Pontiac brought it outside for fresh air whenever she could, which wasn't often. Daddy was home most the daytime, drunk asleep or drunk and stumbling. Pontiac had to wait till night and whispered apologies to the bottle the whole while.

Pontiac got home still stinging from Doc's vitriolic opinion of the Pirates Laffite. Doc was off his geriatric rocker. She should have known it when he ripped the pages out of her Lovecraft. Destroying a story because you didn't like its message was plain arrogance. Least she thought so till she remembered destroying André Saphir's Junonia.

Pontiac took the zombi bottle outside for a good long sit, gazing up at the two or three stars that nosed from between palmetto leaves. No apologizing to the bottle this time. Instead, she talked to it. If it was ancient, it might have knowledge. More than Doc, even.

She asked the zombi what the shit-balls was wrong with Alligator Point these days. How she'd lost both Billy May and André Saphir as friends and was now in danger of losing Doc too. Was it the Oil Man, riling folk up with the potential end of the Point? Or was she, Pontiac, "the common denominator," as Miss Ward liked to say? Maybe she was just too much of a bossy asshole to keep friends.

The zombi bottle didn't reply. It was nice to talk to anyway.

Pontiac went back inside and opened the under-sink cabinet. Though she was alone, she checked for witnesses before giving the bottle a quick kiss. After she crawled into bed, she could still taste the bottle, like cold ink. Still, it was the first time she'd kissed anybody but Mama. Felt weird. But kinda okay.

She went to bed dreaming about kissing. Kissing all sorts of different folk.

Had to be after midnight when she was awakened by a soft voice.

"Pontiac?"

Pontiac's bed was a thin, stained mattress she'd outgrown two birthdays back. Her feet stuck off the end, which she hated ever since a rat bit her toe last fall. She drew her knees up and stared toward the sink. Had the voice escaped the bottle? The flutter of the drapes pivoted Pontiac's attention to the window above. Purple drapes. Mama's doing, damp and cobwebbed now. Daddy kept them closed. Said daylight burned holes in his brain.

Pontiac sniffed. Huh. Weird.

Lilac. Real strong too.

"Ponnnn-tiac . . ."

Pontiac knew the voice. Though she'd never heard it so kittenish.

"Miss Ward?" Pontiac whispered. "That you?"

Nobody ought to be outside her window at this hour, Miss Ward in particular. Pontiac had never seen the teacher outside Bullock Elementary. As far as she knew, nobody had. Kids said Miss Ward had a phobia for talking to adults. Now, though, Pontiac had a different thought.

Maybe Miss Ward simply preferred to travel by night.

"I can't see you, Ponnnn-tiac . . ."

That part made sense. Miss Ward had weak peepers.

A lovely hum hummingbirded through the marsh drone. Mozart's *Eine kleine Nachtmusik*, Miss Ward's musical request for students to *come closer*. A low-burn part of Pontiac's brain told her to refuse, to stay in bed, but she had been trained to obey her teacher's music like a dog does a whistle. Her body moved. Her feet were of equal temperature to the wooden floor and she barely felt it. She seemed to float to Mama's drapes. She brushed them back. They felt like Mama's hair.

Yep. Miss Ward. Standing yonder beside a bubbling tarn.

Sure enough, missing her glasses too.

Miss Ward typically wore mid-calf polyester dresses with demure collars and modest bows, usually gray, on bold occasion blue. To a girl of ragged jeans and Salvation Army tees like Pontiac, it came off real ladylike. Tonight Miss Ward was wearing nothing but a gauzy robe. Looked like white smoke when it fluttered, making it hard to see the teacher's dark brown skin.

"Miss Ward," Pontiac said. "I can see your . . ."

Miss Ward smiled like Miss Ward had never smiled.

"Yes, Pontiac?"

Pontiac's blush made her grateful for the dark. She'd seen countless naked chests in her day, but nearly all of them male. Plus there was the hair. The hair grown-ups had around their privates.

Pontiac saw it right through Miss Ward's gown. Pointing it out, though, felt disrespectful.

"Nothing," Pontiac mumbled. "What you doing out there?"

"I'm checking up on my favorite student."

Pontiac's blush changed, a different warmth, new tingle.

"Yeah? More favorite than Alice Chilcote?"

Miss Ward nodded, slow, a lock of hair falling over her face.

"Mmhm. A lot more favorite."

Pontiac's whole body blushed now.

"What are you wanting to check in on, Miss Ward?"

"I thought if any student had figured out the Coke bottle assignment, it'd be you."

Cold sweat turned Pontiac's blushing body clammy.

"I will. It's just, I got me a job. I haven't had time for thinking about bottles."

Miss Ward tilted her head. Her robe slipped off one shoulder. The lacy material would have fallen to the brown muck but the strap caught on her nipple. Pontiac knew she ought to look away but she didn't. Miss Ward's skin glowed like stained chestnut.

"But you *do* have a bottle in there, don't you, Pontiac?"

Pontiac pressed her lips together. No one was supposed to know about that. Not even Miss Ward, who looked so pretty and whose nipples were showing and whose laugh was like rain plinking on piano keys.

"Now, Pontiac, what did I say about looking at a Coke bottle before drawing your picture?"

Pontiac opened her mouth to protest, then realized her teacher was right. Underneath the thick coat of black paint, the zombi bottle was a Coke bottle! That explained why it felt so familiar in her hand. Those swirling ridges in the glass. That raised squiggle.

"That's the secret!" Pontiac cried. "The word Coke is shaped right into the glass!"

Miss Ward winked. An infinitesimal movement, yet enough to make her robe fall from its nipple peg. It whispered down her belly, stroked her pubic hair, and puddled over her feet like a silky pile of lotion. Miss Ward was full-on naked. In the swamp. At night. Pontiac was too dumbfounded to revel in the Coke bottle revelation.

"You're gonna get all bit up," she managed.

"How nice of you to worry," Miss Ward purred. "Now, Pontiac, you *did* solve the riddle. But you also cheated."

"But I didn't realize it was—"

"I think you better bring that bottle out to me so I can dispose of it. It's only fair to the other students."

Pontiac paused. The whole swamp paused in response. Shaking fronds went still. Blurting toads inhaled all together. The zombi bottle had been a burden since Doc gave it to her. Here was a chance to give it up to adoption, let Miss Ward figure out how to raise it. Felt wrong, though. Big-time wrong. Like walking to the window in the first place felt wrong.

"I think I'll stay in," Pontiac said. "Pure hog guzzle out there."

Miss Ward put her hands on her hips. Kind of thing she did every day at school, but now, with no clothes, Pontiac saw how one hip cocked forward in a nice way, and how the slight twist of Miss Ward's torso brought one breast high while pulling the other to the side.

"Now, Pontiac. It's no different than when I made you spit your gum in my hand. Or when I made Billy May hand over those sex pictures." Miss Ward's lips curled into a smile of startling wickedness. "You got a peek at those pictures, didn't you? I know I did. Going through Billy May's desk after class let out. When I was all alone in the room."

Pontiac shrugged, but of course she'd seen the pictures. Billy May had ripped them from one of his daddy's magazines, real neat so William May Sr. wouldn't notice, far neater than how Doc gutted the Lovecraft. Whole bunch of naked folk in those pictures, women and men both, personal parts all out in the open and touching.

"You know, Pontiac . . ." Miss Ward adjusted her legs enough that Pontiac could see moonlit bayou water through in the space between the teacher's thighs. "You could touch me like in those pictures."

Pontiac heard paint chip off the windowsill. That's how hard she was clawing it. Fact was, she *did* want to climb through the window. She *would* like to touch Miss Ward that way, if only to see what it was like, to see what happened. All it would cost her was one stupid bottle. Only two words stopped her from throwing up the skeeter screen and doing it.

Billy May.

Miss Ward, or whatever this thing was, had blundered by bringing up Billy's name. The pleasant tickle in Pontiac's loins quit the moment her best friend's face surfaced from her memories like the baseball bobbing up at Guimbarde Beach. It was monster boogeymen, not naked teachers, that lumbered slobberingly on the Point.

Pontiac dipped down from the window and reached under her mattress. It wasn't a super comfortable place to hide something, but the zombi astral had taken up the usual spot. She pulled it out: the soggy, sliced baseball she'd come to think of as Billy May Part II.

She'd gotten the idea from the VHS boxes at Doc's. *The Karate Kid Part II. Meatballs Part II. The Hills Have Eyes Part II. Rambo: First Blood Part II.* Past the curtain, *Deep Throat Part II.* If anyone deserved a sequel, it was Billy May, who hadn't lived but nine shitballs years.

"Hold on to your taters, Billy May," Pontiac whispered.

Pontiac gripped Billy May Part II like a pitcher.

"Go away, Miss Ward."

The Miss Ward thing only grinned.

"I know a lotta positions, Pontiac. Positions what'll make both of us feel gooooood."

Pontiac ripped her mind from the interlocked limbs of the sex pictures and forced herself to redefine Miss Ward's term. *Baseball* positions, she thought. First base, shortstop, right field, catcher. Nothing sexy there at all. She drew back her arm, displaying Billy May Part II, while Miss Ward's last sentence echoed in her skull. She sounded choked. Sounded spitty. Sounded *stupid*, the most horrifying part of it. Miss Ward was the least stupid person Pontiac knew.

"I'm warning you, Miss Ward. Daddy says I'm a dead-eye."

And it was Miss Ward's eyes, indeed, that went dead, sparkly browns irising down to flat gray nickels. Her skin pulled away from her mouth, harder and harder, cheeks rippling back like skin sloughing off a roasted turkey. With a limpkin screech, inches of red, drooling gums were revealed.

"*We gon hab us a goooooood time, Pon-tee-ack! Ya cun tutch ma puss while I eat up yors!*"

"Go away, Miss Ward!"

"*Eat it till it all et and DURR AIN'T NUTTIN LEFF!!!!*"

The thing's bottom jaw fell off and music blasted from the stygian throat, not the delicate Miss Ward songs the children of Alligator Point adored, but the diesel shriek of a dump truck dropped atop a church organ, sixty-one atonal notes, the yowl of eighty-five twisting brass pipes as they bent like cattails in a typhoon.

Pontiac's arms cracked forward like a slingshot and released Billy May Part II. She toppled like a relief pitcher unable to handle her own power, crashing into the wall, tangling into Mama's drapes. But she knew her aim was true. She heard the meaty thump followed by a noise like the last big suck of milkshake through a straw. When she pulled herself back up to the sill, there wasn't anybody outside.

Only a lacy white robe sinking into loose brown mud.

~ 32 ~

GERARD GOT HOME AS DAWN'S first feather lightened the swamp's black mass into shades of green. Thick as his noggin was with the Pelican's liquor, he knew his shanty from floor to beam and rafter to roof, from the crowfoot grass reaching through the rickety stairs to the beehive tucked under the eaves. He always could tell when something was amiss. After all, the shanty was the only thing that belonged to him. Besides Pontiac, he supposed.

And Pontiac was dead.

That's what he figured when he saw the child's head plopped in the mud twenty feet north of the shanty. The shade of the skin matched up pretty good with Pontiac's, and the blood was the kind of ruby red that came from deep inside.

Gerard shuddered once. He closed his eyes, commanding tears to hold off till after he confirmed the severed head and had called Pete Roosevelt. He'd known this day was coming. His girl never had much of a shot of escaping Alligator Point. The bog got jealous when folk grew too clever, and they didn't make girls cleverer than Pontiac.

He made his way over, dodging the treasure holes he'd dug and never filled, all while enumerating the likely murderers. Gators, probably. Gators didn't have a real appetite for skulls, and nobody was harder headed than Pontiac. But Gerard hoped André Saphir was the killer. Oh, to have a solid reason to hate the man! Vengeance would be something to live for. He imagined equipping himself up like Jack O'Brien, getting himself a Lafitte skiff, and spending the rest of his days executing the most twisted revenge the Barataria region had ever seen.

Gerard wasn't disappointed to find the head was only a baseball, fabric torn open so it lay flat as a face. He loved his girl and was glad she was okay. He felt the loss of purpose, though, the spark of invigoration he'd felt gone like a swatted skeeter.

He picked up the ball. Big grin-shaped sliced cut into it. Soppy innards like guts about to plop. Gerard looked at the shanty. The skeeter screen over where Pontiac slept was open. Had she chucked the baseball out the window? Abraham's shit, that girl was odd.

Gerard found her asleep inside. Which made this homecoming a repeat of the one before, and before that, a doomed chant. He only ever saw his daughter in these liminal hours, right before he collapsed himself.

He took hold of the sink and forced himself give her a nice long gander. She was curled up like a baby. He had an urge to smell her breath. Little-girl breath was like puppy breath, a touch of cinnamon. Maybe it'd counter the kerosene fog rising up from the mess cheap liquor was making of his stomach lining. He'd probably trip, fall onto her, wake her up, hurt her.

Gerard envisioned it anyway. Kneeling down, just perfect, sliding Pontiac into his arms so gently she didn't wake, and carrying her straight out of the swamp, northward, till the fragrances of sweet olive and Confederate jasmine ceded to the smell of concrete and glass.

Pontiac wasn't even on her mattress. She was on the dirty floor. Gerard indulged in annoyance—it covered up the scrape of his guilt. What if the Oil Man had swung by again and seen Pontiac sleeping on the floor? If Gerard wouldn't sign the Oil Man's papers, the Oil Man could get Child Protective Services and boot Gerard's ass out the shanty.

"Re'veiller, cher."

Pontiac's eyeballs rolled beneath her lids.

Gerard got impatient. Wasn't fair to the girl, but the liquor was starting to curdle like it always did when daylight hit his skin. He underhanded the baseball so it bounced against Pontiac's hip.

"I'm up," she murmured.

Pontiac rolled over. Gerard winced. The girl had a hand down the front of her pants.

"Had a dream," Pontiac sighed.

Gerard dropped his exhausted butt into a chair.

"Dat why your hand's in your caneçons?"

Pontiac's eyelids pulled open through crust. She blinked downward, noted the irrefutable evidence, and removed her hand like she used to from Janine's cookie jar. Gerard felt the lack of Janine's presence like never before, a physical absence big as half the shanty. He knew what he had to say, as well as how poorly he'd say it. His odds were worse than German Rusnak's hundred-to-one.

"My own daddy called dem de Fats o' Life," Gerard sighed. "I don't reckon Mama told you none of dose t'ings?"

Pontiac sat up and shrugged.

"Fuck-damn, Daddy! I don't want to talk about it!"

"Now, *dat*—dat's what you learned from your daddy. Whole pile of cuss words and not much else. No, cher, you stay sittin. I don't relish me dis none more den you, but I gotta teach you somet'in. Word passes you been workin up at Doc's. Dat okay wit' me. But I know you too damn curious not to be pokin your head back behind dat curtain. All dem videotapes wit' naked folk. Way I figure it, you been lookin dem tapes over and wonderin how boy parts and girl parts fit togedder. Why it all looks so scary but also interestin too. Stop your squirmin and let me finish. I don't care if you look at dem boxes. I don't even care if you watch dem tapes—you gonna watch dem eventually. What's important, cher, is knowin dem tapes ain't de Fats o' Life, you hear? De Fats o' Life ain't no more complicated den how batter and eggs make pancakes. A man's got special stuff he squirts out his pecker and it mixes up wit' special stuff inside a lady. Dat's what makes babies, c'est tout. You female, Pontiac, whether you like it or not. You got no choice but to be careful round peckers. You do it wrong, sex ain't no better than any udder nasty-sugar. It break you down. You want to know what a broke-down man look like, you don't gotta look no further den your daddy."

Gerard's gaze had slid sideways. In the watery dawn, the shanty looked like the wreck of a ship. As captain, he ought to have steered better.

When he looked back at Pontiac, she was taking notes in her log.

"Ça va, cher. Nothin I say official enough to be scribin down."

Pontiac didn't look up. "Did God fix it this way on purpose? De Fats?"

Gerard spat. Hurt. Alcohol in his lungs burned like sprayed magma.

"Ain't no God, cher. Only t'ing a pastor or priest do is fill you up wit' fright. Fright of how de devil's gonna have your ass on de coals for doin exactly whatever sinful shit he talked you into doin. Ain't no need for it. We swamp rats got frights peeking out behind every cypress. One thing we good on is fright, non?"

Pontiac frowned thoughtfully. Gerard braced. Half the girl's questions these days flew way over the top of his head.

"Doc says some dead folk have restless spirits. We need to be afraid of them too?"

Dawn's shadows elongated into fangs, sunk through Gerard's skull, and pierced his throbbing brain. He should be a good daddy, stay awake, keep answering questions. But his body had gone nocturnal like a hedgehog and wanted to burrow. The booze was gelling in his stomach.

"What Doc's talkin bout is voodoo stuff. Dat's somet'in I ain't educated in. All I know is voodoo folk keep more gods den de ocean has fish. One god for de eart', one for de stars, one for de lightnin, one for de sea, one for de folk who sail it. And on and on. Too much for me, cher. I got enough trouble wit' one."

Pontiac got back to writing. Gerard shut his eyes, listening to the scratch. He was aware, just barely, of the subsequent noises of Pontiac getting dressed, padding around the shanty, and clinking dishes. He registered the springy closing of the screen door a few minutes after it happened. Shit. He cracked open his right eye.

Evil sunlight was everywhere now. His girl was gone. It was Saturday, which meant she was off doing stuff with men who weren't him. Gerard forced himself to open both eyes and stand. He felt the hangover push through this aching veins.

Water was what he needed. But there wasn't nothing cold in the icebox. He started opening cabinets. He tried to get jealous of Doc Devereaux but it didn't work. Doc was as old as one of those voodoo gods. He couldn't have much to offer a girl like Pontiac except a few dollars.

Nothing in the cabinets. Gerard realized, and accepted, that he wasn't searching for water. He squatted and opened lower cabinets now. Nothing but old circles where full bottles used to stand. He tried the last resort of the cabinet under the sink. All he saw were products to mock him. Lysol to clean the floors, something he hadn't done properly in years. Zep for wiping windows. Clorox for bleaching clothes. Drano for draining drains—

Now what was this?

Gerard picked it up. Coke bottle, looked like, but done over in black paint, wee shells, mirrors, and twine. Could be a voodoo thing, which might explain Pontiac's questions. Then again, Gum Jenkins had been known to get creative in packaging his shine. Gerard shook the bottle. Sure enough, something sloshed within.

Gerard sat on the floor and worked the stopper. Stubborn sumbitch. But his thirst was ballooning past what he could control. He pressed harder, turned harder, tearing up his hands no longer a concern. Burred metal hissed and he felt falling flakes of rust graze his hands. Followed by a sticky strand of saliva. He was drooling.

The bottle didn't give up yet. Twine looped through metal eyeholes secured the stopper to the glass. Gerard scrabbled a butter knife from the sink and sawed its baby teeth over the twine till it gave with a puff of black dust. Gerard tossed the stopper, then picked it back up and stuffed it in his pocket. He didn't want Pontiac to see it. He burned with shame, but the burn of thirst was worse.

He peered into the bottle.

Black. Nothing to see.

Hold up. Did he see a flash of white?

Gerard brought the open end of the bottle to his eyeball. Didn't help. He put it to his nostrils and sniffed. A pickled odor with an edge of gamy meat.

He frowned into the under-sink space. Had he acquired the bottle years ago, stashed it, and forgotten? Could it be Janine's, some kind of hoodoo juice to make him believe she was the best lover who ever was? An offensive thought; Janine hadn't needed no help. Gerard was left to conclude the bottle had come here honestly. Which meant it wasn't nothing to fear.

Gerard brought it to his lips, chalking up another white flash to imagination.

He tipped his head back and the bottle too, and got his tongue out of the way. Liquid filled his mouth. Hot, which he didn't expect, and thick as syrup, and sweet to boot, but not smooth, flecked throughout with what felt like almond slivers but tasted like the sharp marrow of chicken bone, chased by something that *wiggled*, he swore it, flopping down his tongue like a tadpole, a shock he didn't know what to do with besides swallow it down quick.

Gerard reached to set down the bottle.

He missed the floor by three feet; it fell hard but did not break.

Gerard lay a hand over his throat. He felt a series of light abrasions like it was a bottle cap going down. He seized tight, letting the thing hang mid-gulp. Didn't dare even breathe. He sat there, probably dying, faced with the choice of trying to cough it back up, whatever it was, or letting is splash down and dealing with it on the other end.

A drunk like him always preferred to deal with things later.

He swallowed hard.

He gasped. He held still. He listened to his body.

Nothing.

Gerard chuckled. Wasn't a bottle cap he ingested. Not no tadpole either. Just a glob of sugar gone bad, pretty normal for backwater shine. Spoiled sugar could upset your belly, but what of it? Getting sick from booze was already on his day's agenda.

The thing was, he didn't feel sick at all anymore.

In fact, he felt fine. Strong, even.

Now that was some good nasty-sugar!

Gerard licked his lips for any he'd missed, then stuck his tongue inside the bottle to lick up any that might be in there too. Wasn't the first time he licked the inside the bottle, but it was the first time he didn't feel ashamed about it.

He sighed a big sigh, a healthy boom he hadn't heard from himself in a while. He looked around the shanty. Nothing really wrong with it, now that he saw it with a clear eye. A fine place to live. To be brought up in. He was proud. Pontiac should be proud too. The shanty oughta be enough for her. That it wasn't a demerit to her character. He should find her, scold her. Had she said she was off working at Doc's? For a rod and reel? No, that didn't add up, not in a brain that was going like firecrackers. Pontiac must be fixing to hightail it from the Point, same as all the other traitors signing the Oil Man's papers. Who'd put such ideas in her head?

Gerard knew who.

André Saphir. Somewhere out there, daddying Gerard's girl, making her believe there was more to living than what the bayou had on offer. It was a lie. You mark off any square foot of marsh and wait a while, and everything on Earth will cross it. Down in the delta, whole universes fit inside other universes, a whirlpool, a black hole.

Gerard stood. Stretched. Flexed muscles he hadn't flexed in a spell. When was the last time he'd hunted anything but pirate booty? Never dug up any, a frustration that might be quelled by choosing a target he knew to exist. Tall fellow, bronze skin swirled with tattoos, black knit cap on a shaved head, leather wristbands, doubloon earrings, always fishing. Fishing—that was good.

When a fisherman drowns, don't too many think nothing of it.

~ 33 ~

PETE WAS INTO HIS THIRD CUP of Texaco coffee, one cowboy boot up on a fire hydrant, fancying himself looking like the Duke resting on a fence rail. Spuds sat in the car five feet off, looking green through the lowered window. While jockeying horses had given Spuds no problems, the Highway 90 straightaway to New Orleans always made the deputy motion sick.

The NOPD cruiser showed up an hour late, creeping into a painted spot without the slightest urgency. It was a Crown Vicky like Pete's, only newer and smaller, therefore lacking the gravitas of the Melbourne Queen. Pete swished his mouth with the coffee-flavored swill, spat it, and tossed the paper cup into the car. He leaned back against the sun-heated hood, tilted back his Stetson, and hooked his thumbs into his belt like John Wayne sizing up some big-for-his-britches gunsmith.

The driver's door flung open and out stepped a uniformed woman, Black, heavy-set, radiating irritation. Being half Pete's size didn't affect her supercilious swagger. She thrust her bottom jaw and pressed down on her utility belt. Leather squeaked. Handcuffs rattled. Pistols clinked—two of them.

Pete grinned the grin that said he weren't really grinning.

The woman flashed one even faker and sized him up like he sized her.

"You Roosevelt?"

"Ma'am." He cricked his head at Spuds. "Deputy Ulene."

"Hi," Spuds said.

"Detective Pat Wilkes," she said. "I understand you called in a couple 10-57s."

Pete grimaced. "I, ah . . . it's been a while, ma'am, since . . . we don't really use codes in the—"

"Missing person."

"That's right," Spuds said through the window. "Billy May and Pork Fat!"

Spuds's guileless sincerity made Pete shift feet. He wobbled on a boot heel. Shit-balls! He hadn't misstepped in a cowboy boot misstep since he was a knee-high to a junebug.

"I was tryin to call up Terry Thurmond was all."

Wilkes squinted. "Thurmond's dead."

"I was told."

"Wouldn't have been much more helpful if he was still kicking. Thurmond spent more time making dumb-blonde jokes than he did policing."

Pete laughed. "Sounds like old Terry."

Wilkes pointed at her mouth. "It look like I'm laughing? That shit was tiresome."

Pete sealed shut his smiling lips. He felt knocked off *both* heels now.

"Easy, now, lady. Terry Thurmond was a friend of mine."

Wilkes's smile could have frozen the whole bayou.

"Detective Wilkes is what I go by in pleasant conversation. I have no doubt Thurmond was a good buddy of yours. The Old Boys Club. Runs deeper than plantar warts down here."

"I got a plantar wart," Spuds offered.

Pete adjusted his hat from the easygoing back of his head to the shit-kicker front.

"I don't recall signin up for no membership, Detective Wilkes. What I do recall is how to give a dead man a smidge of respect. Could be that's an outdated swamp-rat tradition that's lost favor up here in the city."

Wilkes smiled and pushed down on her gun belt again.

"If I were in your parts," she said, "I might make myself go missing too."

Pete narrowed his glare like he was a sharpening a knife. Gave him a second to gather his bearings too. He aways felt off in the city. People swarmed like fire ants, buildings piled atop buildings like a turkey tail fungus. The unholy stench of scorched oil, turned seafood, and tourist sunscreen. Too damn noisy too.

"'Out of these deerskins and into our foofaraw,'" Pete drawled.

Wilkes blinked. "Huh?"

"It means 'let's fight,'" Spuds deciphered helpfully.

"Says who?"

"John Wayne." Pete nodded. "*The Alamo*. Directed that one too."

Wilkes unleashed a long sigh. "I got better things to do than trade quotes from some country-western asshole."

Spuds goggled up at Pete. "Does she mean *John Wayne*, Pete?"

Pete inflated his chest. "John Wayne was a great American. Maybe the *greatest* American."

Wilkes rolled her eyes. "Lord, grant me the grace."

"What do you know about the Duke?"

"Only that he was a closed-minded bigot who didn't think highly of anyone any darker than him." Wilkes smirked. "Probably didn't even like the horses he rode."

"John Wayne owned a horse ranch!"

"I've seen westerns. All those horses piling on the ground during Indian fights."

"That's called the Running W! It's just a tripwire for horse stunts!"

"No real cowboy likes to see horses fall like that."

"I'll have you know, John Wayne didn't only play cowboys. Ain't you ever seen *Brannigan*? *Tycoon*? *Wake of the Red Witch*?"

Pete stabbed himself by mentioning *Red Witch.* The screen he'd saw it on at age nine flashed before his eyes: the Duke's battle with the octopus Tarutatu, Pete turning to find his mother gone and Gee Putnam killed.

"I haven't," Wilkes replied. "But then again, I've never seen any John Wayne flick. A record I intend to maintain."

Pete gave a haughty sniff. "Who's closed-minded now?"

"My advice to you, Roosevelt, is to chalk up those 10-57s of yours to people getting their asses out Crocodile Haven. You have a blessed day, now."

"Alligator Point!" Spuds correctly genially. "Bye!"

Detective Wilkes touched an invisible cap and started back to her cruiser, squeaking that belt. Pete's bravado left his body like two lungfuls of cigar smoke. What the hell was he doing? Spuds had it right. This situation didn't call for a pissing match. He should have played it nice with the detective from the start.

"Hey," he called. "Ma'am. Wilkes. *Detective.*"

Fourth try was the charm. Wilkes planted a heel and swiveled on it. Her expression said, *Amuse me.* Pete took off his hat to wipe off sweat. Then kept it off, a sign he was, for the moment, defeated.

"Detective, we got two residents missin. It's true, some folk flee the damp. But with these two, it don't add up. Specially when the whole town's gettin bought up by the oil company and folk are finally seein a light at the end of a dark, despairin tunnel. They're dead, detective. I know it all over my skin. I just don't have no bodies to show. Just a few ribs that may be a generation old. If it'll help put the minds of my citizens at ease, I'll eat whatever crow you want to serve. Me and Spuds are on this case by our lonesome. We could use help. Whatever help you feel fit to offer."

The look she leveled? Abraham's shit. Could've knocked Pete through the rust-bucket Queen.

"All right, Sheriff. Or not-Sheriff. Whatever you are." Wilkes checked her watch. "I got a free fifteen. Tell me what-all you know and what-all you don't."

Pete exhaled in relief. "Obliged. Let me think now where to start."

Wilkes lifted a finger.

"Hold tight. Let me just grab a cup of Texaco's finest first."

~ 34 ~

PONTIAC ONLY KNEW TWO KINDS OF MORNINGS. Ones where she had to tiptoe around Daddy's collapsed body without making a ruckus and ones where he wasn't there at all. This morning appeared to be the latter, until Pontiac opened the door and saw Daddy standing outside the shanty.

He stood on a plate-sized patch of bog, black water leaking up between his toes, a curve to his spine like he was an idiot. Grinning like an idiot, too, big and loose, and staring at Pontiac like he'd been laying in wait for hours.

Daddy stood inside a cyclone of skeeters. There wasn't a skeeter anywhere else in sight.

"You're gonna get gobbled, Daddy."

He didn't seem to notice.

"Cher. Where you skedaddlin so early dis beautiful morn?"

"It's the last day of school, Daddy."

He nodded and grinned. "Oh, dat's good. C'est en sirop."

Pontiac nodded back, but kept a careful eye. "You feeling okay?"

"Not a day in my life did I feel finer. You goin to Doc's after?"

She couldn't help but brighten. "Sure am. I'm gonna walk away with that Whiz-Bang today. I mathed it out."

Daddy's grin grew so big Pontiac could see the pond of saliva inside. Going brackish, by the sheen. Pontiac spotted a dead skeeter floating there and her stomach flopped.

"You goin to try it out after Doc's?" Daddy asked. The saliva sloshed but didn't run.

"I don't know," Pontiac admitted. "Could be kinda dark."

"De dark is when de fishin goes best. Say, now, cher. You figure dat ol André Saphir be out there fishin too?"

"Maybe," Pontiac said, though she was downright counting on it.

"Guimbarde, do you figure, cher? Where dat ol rascal likely to be?"

"I guess." Pontiac was puzzled. "You want me to say hi for you, Daddy?"

Saliva sloshed at the levee of Daddy's bottom row of teeth. Sure enough, a skeeter had become lodged between the two front ones.

"No need, cher. I t'ink I be seeing Saphir sooner den later."

Sounded creepy to Pontiac, but she shrugged, came down the stairs with her book bag, and started along the path. Five steps in, she turned around.

"Daddy, you ain't seen a fancy bottle around, have you?"

"Fancy bottle?" Multiple skeeters now, blacking his bared teeth. "Nope."

Pontiac frowned. She couldn't find it this morning. Had she left it outside yesterday? Had Doc come over to claim it? Had the zombi bottle rolled its way to freedom? She kept on the path, troubling over it. It was her fault regardless. She figured taking care of a zombi astral was more important than taking care of a pet, and she screwed it up.

At her school desk, she wrote down all she could remember about the zombi bottle. When Miss Ward entered, humming as usual, Pontiac drew a horizontal line on the page and started keeping track of the teacher, writing down every observable detail. Miss Ward wore the same gray dress Pontiac had seen a million times with no sign of anything gauzy beneath. Her movements as she chalked the board transmitted no tingles to Pontiac's nether regions. She had her glasses back on too.

Just regular old Miss Ward again.

Pontiac relaxed. Smiled, even. She loved Miss Ward, she realized. More than any lady since Mama.

Miss Ward turned from the board with flair. The class gasped. She'd chalked the word *COKE* in the same loopy script as on Coke cans. She hummed Bizet's *Carmen—hand 'em in—*and the students passed their drawings up the rows. Some had been working on them for months. Others had waited till this morning. Yet everybody, Pontiac bet, was dreaming of that first-place prize of a portrait painted by Miss Ward.

Pontiac felt a bit of smugness. She'd figured out the riddle two nights ago. The fact that *this* Miss Ward didn't remember it proved that *that* Miss Ward hadn't been Miss Ward at all.

The teacher made a point of saying nothing until she had glanced over all the drawings. The only sound was the shifting of paper. Finally she tapped one.

"I have chosen the winner."

The class stirred. Pontiac forgot her log. She heard nothing but her own breathing. She'd done the drawing yesterday, and done it good. On a piece of black construction paper, she'd used gray and white charcoal pencils to outline the bottle and sketch in its relevant characteristics: the lip at its mouth, the thicker glass of the base, the ribs curving up its sides. Plus, of course, the words *Coca-Cola* raised from the glass, the answer to the riddle.

"First prize goes to . . ."

Pontiac pictured her painting hanging in the shanty. Daddy would be so proud.

". . . Alice Chilcote."

Alice, that stuck-up suck-up, squealed like air being let out of a balloon. Half the class groaned; half applauded; the noise was enough that no one heard Pontiac mutter, "Fuck-damn the hell *what*?"

Miss Ward displayed the drawing. Not one smudge of charcoal to be seen. Markers. Fat markers. Skinny markers. An array of colors and quality of markers Pontiac wouldn't have access to if she lived to be three hundred years old. Some of those markers even glittered, making the bottle look resplendent in the sun. Alice had solved the riddle as sure as Pontiac had. She'd used the most dazzling markers to emphasize the *Coca-Cola* blown into the glass.

It *was* better than Pontiac's.

Pontiac stared down at a desk scrivened with the fruitless marks of generations of swamp kids like her, none with any hope of making shit of themselves. How could they when everybody else had the advantages? Today, it was better markers. Tomorrow, it'd be better cars. Better jobs. Better food. Better houses. Better families. Better medicine. Better deaths.

A third of the class was gone now, their families having signed the Oil Man's papers, the illiterate ones making whatever mark signified their intent. For the first time, Pontiac wondered if the Oil Man's contract might, in fact, be the best deal going. She'd never make her own mark, not here in the swampy depths. Getting out of the Point was her only chance.

~ 35 ~

TAKING THE WHIZ-BANG FROM THE window felt reverent, the removal of a relic from a holy chamber. Spiderweb snapped. Felt like something inside Doc snapped too. Was it just six weeks ago Pontiac had showed up at the Mercantile calling him a *falsifying prevaricator*? The six best weeks he'd had in the past seventeen years, truth be told. And it was a truth he would certainly not tell. Who was there left to tell?

He cast away the cobwebs.

"If this don't catch you the biggest fish in the bayou, you're the worst fisherlady who ever was."

Closing time had come. Pontiac had scrubbed the joint with excited force all night, despite there being little left to clean. Doc had sent her into the back room for the stepladder, quietly hoping she'd finally notice the dusty sheet over the gatorskin journals, but she'd been too distracted. She'd lugged the stepladder into the store, got on top, and dusted the ceilings.

Now she was hopping up and down.

"Hand it over, old man! And just call me *fisher*. *Fisherlady* sounds dumb as hell."

"You know where we keep the Spindrift. Fetch it yourself."

"I'm holding it in my hand!"

"The bobbers too."

"I'm holding it my other hand, you blind old bat!"

Doc wasn't blind. He could hardly look at the girl, that's all. Trying to get used to not seeing her, he supposed. She'd be back, of course. You couldn't live on the Point and not require the occasional whistle-wetter. But they'd be quick visits, Pontiac taller each time, recalling less about Doc each time, till she didn't recall much at all, or Doc was dead, or Pontiac moved away with Gerard after he signed the Oil Man's papers. By then, she wouldn't recall him enough to say goodbye.

He handed over the Whiz-Bang. Pontiac gave it a few pretend casts.

"I'll show Saphir who's boss now."

Saphir—already the girl had moved on.

"I practically gave you those bobbers for free," Doc complained. "Probably just felt bad sticking you with the zombi bottle."

Pontiac's next fake cast didn't reach the fake lake.

"Hey, Doc. What would happen if I lost that zombi bottle?"

"That depends. If it wasn't your fault, like how I had it in a box all them years, or if somebody robbed it or some such, I don't suppose the zombi astral could blame you."

"What if I, you know . . . just sort of lost track of it."

"You? Lose track? With that log of yours? You're the last person in this swamp who ought to lose track of anything!"

Pontiac bristled and drew her rod, reel, and bobbers close.

"I'm not saying I did! Now get out of my way, this fisherlady's got fish to catch!"

"Little girls are godawful liars. What'd you do with that bottle?"

"I don't know, man! One day it was there, and one day it wasn't!"

"You see anybody come round your shanty?"

"Course not!" Pontiac reconsidered. "I mean, I thought I saw Miss Ward one night. But it wasn't her."

"Miss Ward? Way out at your place?"

"You're deaf as a bat too. I said it *wasn't* her."

"What time of day?"

"Middle of the night. But you ain't listening!"

Doc felt a low ache in his skeleton, like his spine had been struck with a tuning fork. He crossed his arms to settle the icy,

arthritic throb and tried to think. Deep in those gatorskin journals was something like this. Folk arriving at other folk's windows
during some witching hour, and those visited folk vanishing for
good. Made Doc think of that boy Billy May. That girl Pork Fat.

Cold mud slid over Doc's flesh. He'd gone seventy-five years
without slipping into a pool of quick, but this had to be how it felt:
a thick black blanket pulling over the sun.

Doc snatched up his hat and cane.

"Let's pay that schoolteacher of yours a visit."

"Doc! I told you! It was a dream!"

Doc opened the door, the clapper-less bell cracking on wood.
Molasses-thick air oozed over him. Cypresses tossed. Toads chanted
for their gods. Doc snapped for Pontiac to snap to it.

"Don't snap at me, old man! I got fish to fish!"

Doc snapped again.

"No one on the Point even knows where Miss Ward lives!"
Pontiac insisted.

Lord, did this child think he was born at three o'clock this
afternoon? Doc snapped so hard his arthritis plunged like safety
pins into his finger-bone marrow. He ignored it. That sort of pain
wasn't permanent. It was the other sorts you had to watch out for.

~ 36 ~

IF YOU WERE HOOFING IT from Bullock Elementary to Mr. Peff's
library, you'd go for fifteen minutes down the mud path locals called
School Road, hang left at the path called Library Lane, and there'd
you be. Unless you had a full-blown phobia of speaking to anybody
over twelve years old, in which case you'd be Miss Ward, and you'd
use the covert, diagonal, and more direct path she'd beaten through

the swamp over a quarter century. Kids curious about her secrecy had tried to follow her over the years only to end up befuddled. The second she left their sight behind the old water oak, she removed a plate of dead bark, went through the trunk itself, and under a bough of groundsel bush. From there, she dodged a thorny patch of scaly gayfeather, moved through a cascade of Texas bluebonnet, and skirted a fen of carnivorous pitcher plants. A live oak with a trunk so thick and tubed it looked like a giant black heart offered her enough cover to wait till the coast was clear before hurrying to her door beside the library.

To say the least, Miss Ward wasn't in the habit of respond-ing to knocks on that door. This particular knock wasn't the I'm-selling-encyclopedias kind either. It was adamant. Miss Ward started sweating. She had a method of peeking through her drapes at night. She even had a method of dumping buckets of water when the situation required it, which it did most Halloweens.

No tricking kids tonight.

Below stood an old white man and mixed-race child.

Was that Doc Devereaux?

Was that Renée Pontiac?

Never a stranger pair had Miss Ward laid eyes on. Doc kept knocking. Miss Ward turned to the portrait of Jack, searching for help in that streak of Raw Umber W550 on his cheek. If it were Jack knocking on her door, she'd let him in, all questions about his resurrection tabled until she tasted his lips, his skin, everything one more time.

"Miss Ward?" Doc shouted over the wind. "If you're hearing me, I'd sure appreciate a chitchat."

Miss Ward stood in the dark for several minutes. She hadn't spoken to old Doc in fourteen years. Yet she felt more kindly toward him than anybody else on the Point. As the last person to speak to Jack before he died, there was a chance Doc had something related to say.

She crept down the covered stairs and angled her head toward the door to hear past the screaming wind. Pontiac was fussing about fishing and Doc was telling her to cram it. Miss Ward smiled, a reaction so drastically opposed to her pounding heart that she impulsively acted upon it.

"Doc? That you?"

The bickering cut off.

"Yes'm. It's me, Miss Ward. Are you . . . how have you . . . ?"

His voice, this close, this hesitant. Miss Ward shuddered and let the locked door take her full weight. Doc's voice had sounded just like this at Lady of the Sea General Hospital—*I'm sorry, Miss Ward, Jack's gone, he couldn't hang on*—soft yet somehow lifted above the drone of air filters and the squeak of a janitor mopping up what was probably Jack's blood.

"I'm . . . okay," she said into the door. It was sourly lacquered. "And . . . you?"

Doc's age was in the asthmatic whistle of his chuckle.

"I'm surviving."

Miss Ward could not open the door. She knew she couldn't. He didn't ask and she thought she might love him for that.

"How can I . . ." Miss Ward began. "Is it about . . . ?"

"No. It's got nothing to do with Jack. Unless . . ."

Miss Ward's heart took the worst beat it had since the 1984.

"Yes?"

"Unless it does, I guess. Miss Ward—and this is a mighty peculiar question to be pestering you with after a decade and change—but by any chance, any chance at all did you go barefooting up to

Gerard Pontiac's shanty Friday night?" Doc's voice quickened. "If you did, it's none of my beeswax why. You, me, and Gerard are grown-ass adults. The last thing I'm trying to do here is butt into somebody's private affairs. I sure hope you understand that."

Miss Ward gave the inference a second to sink in.

She and Gerard Pontiac?

Like any small town, Alligator Point ping-ponged with illicit sex. Even cloistered as she was, Miss Ward overheard enough student whispers to know that Lurlene Wilson was bedding down with her employer, Zeno Prior, and that Mr. Prior's wife, Goo Goo, had been screwing around with Stale Cookies for going on fifteen years, despite that Stale Cookies had been caught, literally with his pants down, with Juicy Lucy's Lucy in 1979 right there in the bar, a famous incident immortalized in a photo Rawley Deevers snapped of the incident and Lucy, a woman of good humor, kept framed on her wall, which never sat well with her son, Benoit, who, so it was said, worked out his feelings on it by sexing up anything on two legs, or even one leg, a condition not so rare in in gator country. The Saloon Committee estimated Alligator Point divorce rates were fifty times the national. So, too, was its marriage rate, half of them by the same two-timers who just got divorced. Things were rough in the damp. Folk liked having other folk with them, even if that meant ducking the occasional pot, the periodic pan.

Miss Ward laughed lightly. "I was right here Friday night. Watching my programs. I don't even know how I'd get to the Pontiac place."

Doc's sigh was greasy exhaust from a clockwork contraption.

"All right. That's what I was afraid of. Thank you."

Wrinkling her forehead against the door hurt. Doc had *hoped* she was having an affair with Gerard Pontiac?

"Doc, what's going on?"

"Don't you give it another thought. I'm real sorry to have bothered you. I won't do it again. You keep your windows shut tonight, you hear? A big wind's coming off the Gulf. Have yourself a good night, and a good—well, I hope all the rest of your nights are good."

Another way of saying farewell forever. Miss Ward didn't feel the relief she expected. Instead, a rising anxiety.

"Doc!"

The shuffle of clumsy feet. The softer bump of a rubber-footed cane. Miss Ward's heart clenched. Doc was old. She was old too.

"Yes'm."

"You . . . signed those papers yet? The Oil Man papers?"

"Not yet, Miss Ward. But I . . ."

"Yes?"

"I see them. I see those papers all over. I see some right now, blowing down the road. I suppose that means they can't be avoided for long. Yes'm, I've been dwelling on it. You?"

Miss Ward put her hand flat to the door. Nights like this, the door sweated like a person. She pressed harder. Maybe she'd feel Doc's shoulders, Pontiac's head, or push further and feel the mud-crusted hair of Jack's arm. She exhaled and imagined those arm hairs ruffling back, a miniature field of wheat. She could almost talk to Jack. She pretended to do so now.

"Folks have been talking about shutting down the school since the day I started teaching. The costs were too high, they said. The cost of new equipment. Of maintenance. Of salaries. Of insurance. Putting different grades in the same room helped some. But the only thing that ever really saved Bullock Elementary was the cost of bussing students to Dawes. The cost and the risk of those roads. Half my students will be gone come fall. That makes the calculation a whole lot simpler. The budget's almost nothing. Why not make it exactly nothing? No, I haven't signed. But I see now that I should. There will be no more school here after today. If there's no school, there's no point for me being here. There's no point to me *being*."

The cane *tap-tap-tapped*.

"Now, Miss Ward, don't talk like that."

Doc didn't say she was wrong, Miss Ward noticed. She pictured the new path she would track through the swamp, a one-way journey. She smiled against the door. With the decision so easily made, she felt relaxed and heedlessly affectionate.

"Pontiac, you're more quiet than I ever heard you."

"Just seems strange is all," the girl mumbled.

"What does?"

"Kids said you lived in a hidden shanty. Or paddled out from a pirate island. I never figured you were just over the library."

Miss Ward laughed. "I've seen you visit that library many times. Mighty big books you lug out of there."

"Yeah, but Doc ruined it. Told me Lovecraft was a bigot."

"That didn't ruin anything. What you have inside your head is yours. That's why learning, *always* learning, is the most important thing in the world. No one can take it away from you."

The cicadas screamed. After a while, Miss Ward noticed, you get used to hearing screams and they begin to sound like songs.

"We really done having school, Miss Ward?"

"I'm afraid so."

"So I won't ever see you again, Miss Ward?"

Miss Ward tasted a tear rolling down the wood.

"Probably not."

Miss Ward closed her eyes. It was black under her lids, though really, when she concentrated, it wasn't at all. It brown and orange and red and blue and gray and purple.

And umber.

The gulf wind shrilled, then relented for a breath. Miss Ward heard the fuzzy shush of Doc screwing on the hat he'd taken off in deference to the lady present, despite that lady keeping the door shut between them.

"I got one last thing I want to say to you," Doc said.

Miss Ward took off her glasses and squeezed her closed eyes tighter. Closer to true black now. She held her breath and hoped it was her last.

"It's not just the school coming to an end, Miss Ward. It's the whole Point. All of it dying. Maybe from what the Oil Man's doing. Maybe from whatever's been showing up at people's windows. But I keep thinking of your Jack. I do. Because I was there, holding his hand, my bones grinding to dust in that grip of his. Till the last minute, till the last *second*, Jack O'Brien kept fighting. You hear?"

Doc left then, two feet, one cane, and Pontiac left with him.

Miss Ward, though, kept thinking of umber.

She climbed the stairs. She went into the kitchen. She stood before the portrait of Jack O'Brien. Doc was right. Jack had been a warrior and that streak of Raw Umber W550 had been his war paint. Miss Ward felt something inside her growing, like she'd swallowed a pollen that had germinated in her stomach, and now was flowering, and flowering fast.

That tube of Raw Umber W550 was inside this apartment somewhere.

Maybe she could find it. Maybe she could be like Jack.

Maybe she could go down fighting too.

~ 37 ~

WHAT HIS LITTLE GIRL WAS doing with Doc Devereaux after hours, Gerard didn't have the foggiest. But the rickety old shopkeep didn't have the energy to be up to anything unseemly. Gerard watched from behind a holly tree as Doc gave Pontiac a talking-to, his skeleton finger going up and down. Pontiac nodded, exasperation clear as day even though it was night, and a windy one at that, maple leaves flying and Spanish moss whipping, along with a whole ballet company of paper, legal forms it looked like, the stamp of an oil company like a secret society's seal.

Old Doc clearly hadn't learned much about children from the time he'd spent with Pontiac. The girl was promising him she'd head home. But the way her hand clenched that brand-new rod? The girl was going night fishing, come hell, high water, or both.

Gerard slipped away. He had to get there first.

He'd gotten a late start. Hadn't felt like himself since knocking back that black bottle of sludge. Felt worse in some ways, like something inside was swelling. He wondered if this was how Janine's tumors felt. In other ways, though, he felt better, clear-eyed like it hadn't been hooch in that bottle but one of the harder drugs he'd seen folk like Gully Jimson and Rawley Deevers get hopped up on.

Focused. That's how he felt. Like he could see in the dark. A night hunter. Something whose eyes glinted pale when a flashlight hit them.

Gerard had never moved through the swamp at such speed! His bare feet knew every hole and how to hop it, the thick clay lips of crayfish holes, the dime-sized pits of vole holes, the larger holes he'd dug himself, all those wasted years trying to dig for Lafitte gold, when in truth all he'd dug was his own graves, one for each useless part of him.

When he reached Guimbarde Beach, it was like the old baseball diamond still existed, daystar white in the purple night, and he was running it down, stretching a single into a double, a triple, an inside-the-park homer, and back to first for a second greedy round.

Much as the field had sunk, so had Gerard's memories of eating pork belly here with Janine and Pontiac. All he could picture now was a drowned family, the bleary underwater sway of their waterlogged corpses. Janine's murderer was up for debate. Pontiac, though? One man alone was dragging her body to the depths.

The blue-gray colors of the moon outlined the lithe shape of André Saphir at ocean's edge. He looked comfortable in the smashing Guimbarde tide, casting his hook, teasing the line, reeling it back.

Saphir was better at fishing than Gerard had ever been at anything.

The sludge in his belly rolled itself into a long, soft worm. It pushed into his intestines, stretching them wide. Gerard felt like he had to take a dump, but if he did, it would rip his asshole open and keep going, unzipping him to his neck. He heard the worm's voice in his head, words that hadn't changed from when he'd first heard them from the puddle of puke on his shanty floor.

I could have killed you that night
Instead I helped you win back your marbles
Win back your pride
You owe me, Gerard

To hell with that. Gerard owed *himself*. The Brothers of the Spear marble was in his pocket same as ever, but instead of being a comfort, it felt like the ball of buckshot he'd carried in his thigh

from age eight to eighteen, the result of his daddy taking an irre-
sponsible shot at a black bear. The buckshot worked its way out
one day in the bath. *Plink!*

That was André Saphir: deeply dug in, needing to be pried.

Gerard reached into his other pocket.

An old buck knife with the Sinclair Oil logo on it. He unfolded
it. The old blade shone prettier than the sea.

Gerard crossed the spongy knee of second base and continued into shortstop territory, right leg sinking shin-deep into a
warm, sandy mucus. That shit could snag you like a glue-trap
does a cockroach. The trick was to keep moving. Up splortched
one foot, down splortched the other, each leg its own derrick digging new wells. Gerard was knee-deep in center field before he was
forced to turn a shoulder and break the back of each gust of wind
before carrying on.

The roar of the wind met the roar of the sea.

Saphir's knit cap hung from his back pocket. Moonlight shone
off his salt-sparkled scalp. The steel loops of his earrings swung
wild. But the weather did not shove Saphir as it did Gerard. The
fisherman's Douglas fir stance mocked the drunkard's heaving,
bedraggled lurch.

Gerard made a final forward stagger. He stood but a foot
behind Saphir. The fisherman's shirt was slicked to the long muscles
of his back as they flowed through the motions of casting, teasing,
reeling, and armpitting the rod to pinch a catch from his hook and
drop it in a bucket that bobbed amid the breakers. Gerard wiped
his wet hands on his shirt and regripped his knife.

Might take a lot of stabbing to bring this fellow down.

* * *

~ 38 ~

THE GUIMBARDE WIND SLUGGED AT Pontiac with what felt like hundred-pound tentacles. Pontiac bore it without thought of turning back. The Whiz-Bang was a knight's sword at her side. She had herself a dragon to slay.

She came at the beach where the home team dugout used to be and skimmed along the foul line into the bog of left field. Her puny height never did her any favors and it was the same bullshit today. Mud up to her calves. Wind blowing buckets of warm gulf water into her face. Gobs of thick, spongy plant stuff tangling up her legs and goobering across her face, salty as an empty plate of fries.

The nighttime beach was band of lunar blue rounded with the planet's curve. The tide was as sensational as Pontiac had ever seen it, like the Point was a snow globe and some god was upending it. Foamy crests popped from the water like the spines of prehistoric beasts, then exploded into Pontiac and spattered her skin with drops as sharp as chippered wood. She squinched her face tight to avoid splinters to the eyes.

None of it stopped her from drawing back the Whiz-Bang with a matador's flair, making rapid assessment of wind speed and direction, and flinging her arm forward like she was roping a steer. The glow-in-the-dark bobber sailed like a night dove, darting through rising waves and grasping spray. Thing of beauty! If only Pontiac could hear the landing's faultless *splish*!

Instantly came the tug of whirling water. Pontiac grinned with teeth dribbling salt water. A fight was what she'd come for. She looked northward, hoping to see Saphir slack-jawed in disbelief, but all she saw were dead palmetto leaves kiting in the wind.

Sharp nips at her bare fee snared her attention. She bent down while struggling with her line, but the shallows were too murked with silt for Pontiac to see much. Until the nipping objects kicked upward off her legs, twinkling like jewels before the undertow snatched them back.

Seashells! Hopping like mullets! Fun to witness, though an old warning from Daddy tempered her thrill. A surf thick with shells testified to dramatic shit going out at sea. Currents bulldozed across seabeds a thousand miles off, like a shark never troubling the surface, scooping shells, stones, and plants to ultimately spew them upon a shore.

Pontiac reeled in her empty line and relished the Spindrift's well-oiled action. She regripped it and pushed her face into the wind for a fresh calculation. Before she could form one, a shell leapt from the surface, flashing just long enough to grab her attention.

A Junonia.

Pontiac looked down, saw the scroll-shaped shell whirl like a top, then saw the cash it represented, superior to any bragging rights she might hook. A hundred bucks, twice as much if she was lucky. Money like that, Pontiac could get Mama's drapes cleaned. Fill the cabinets with the best stuff Doc kept stocked. Pay a detective to hunt down that zombi bottle. Or, hell, hand the Junonia over to Saphir to replace the one she broke. Of all the ways she'd imagined apologizing, none felt better.

The Junonia rolled impishly inside a funnel of surf. Pontiac lodged the Whiz-Bang under an arm, bent her knees, and extended a hand. The shell twirled inches out of reach. Pontiac sidestepped after it. She felt unexpectedly ungainly and ogrelike as the wet beach sucked her feet down to the ankles. She leaned into the wind, squinted against sheets of sand. She reached for the shell again. Her middle finger grazed its top row of brown dots—what Saphir interpreted as the writing of the dead, but Pontiac only read as dollar signs.

She had a nasty-sugar need for it, like Daddy needed his booze.

The twenty-foot rogue wave was soundless in the howling wind but Pontiac had lived on the Point her whole life. She ought to have seen it coming. Moonlight blinked out like a blown bulb. She turned and found a cliffside of water falling toward her. The idea of running was pointless, an academic exercise like one of Miss Ward's riddles.

The world collapsed.

She felt fly-swatted, the wind in her lungs expelled.

Pontiac lost all orientation inside a triple somersault. Salt water hewed her lips apart and pushed down her throat where it collided with sister water driving up through her nose. Her feet felt nothing, then spongy floor, and she planted them and cycled her legs, but for every foot she gained toward land, a throttling undertow dragged her back five more. She was pitched like a cork and spiraled through an outer space studded with stars the way Saphir's belt and wrist bands were studded with gems. Slimy weeds garroted her neck, unless it was something else.

The roar she heard wasn't a roar. It was the ocean filling her ear canals, a vice of pressure against her skull. Everything else was irrelevant. The quitting urge spread fast, Pontiac's frantic horse kicks reducing to flicking frog-legs, arms not struggling so much as waving goodbye.

The blackness of the water birthed an underwater aurora.

A cottonmouth whiteness.

Coming for her.

Swallowing her whole.

Being pulled from whips of slashing waters was like being a blanket pulled from an electric drier, a nifty thing Pontiac had seen at a birthday party at Alice Chilcote's house. Pontiac's body crackled, each salt grain on her skin a conductor of raw energy. Air made her gibber like a feral pig impaled on the spikes of a trap. Crap was barfing from her lungs but it felt like she took no part in it.

Dolphins, was her strange thought. *I'm being rescued by a pod of white dolphins.*

The white was a person. Saphir's white shirt, it had to be. Pontiac's arms shot out and held tight, violent, desperate, only it didn't feel like cloth, it felt like—

"You tearin off my ears!"

Pontiac felt another tidal surge, but this time it was the landward lurch of the man carrying her. Together they crashed to sand, more breath walloped from lungs, and then, additional insult, she was rolled like a hotdog in a gas station warmer, wet body coated with sand. She spat but the sand inside her had turned to wet cement and it caught in her throat.

Fingers in her mouth. Pontiac bit on instinct, teeth to knuckles, but the fingers didn't relent. They scooped wet sand from her tongue while a different hand whacked her on her back.

"*Cher! Don't leave me!*"

Pontiac looked up. Eyes blurry.

Wasn't Saphir.

It was Daddy. Eyes bugging, mouth coated in black slime, ears bloody from her grip.

"*You can't leave me! It ain't your time! I won't allow it!*"

Pontiac spat sand. A pinhole of clean air opened in her trachea. She screeched breath, a lot of it grit, but sprayed that grit with her next exhale, her next. She held on to Daddy's shirt, tried to speak. Her words broke into pebbles.

". . . Da . . . dud . . . dy . . ."

He scooped her off the sand and into her arms.

"I t'ought you was gone, cher, dat I lost anudder one."

"My . . . Whiz . . . Bang . . ."

"Don't t'ink bout it. I gonna get you de best rod and reel dere ever was."

". . . my . . . log . . ."

"Dat too, baby." Daddy broke into laughter. "You good at keepin track of everyt'ing but dat wave, non?"

Pontiac looked to the Gulf. The waves had lathed smooth. The palmetto leaves had settled. The lights of the distant oil derricks were visible where before they'd been hid. She'd survived. What had she survived? Something powerful, that's all she knew. Powerful enough it should have drug both her and Daddy out to sea. Instead, somehow, Daddy had emerged the victor. He draped his arms around her, breathing like he'd inhaled the windstorm.

"Cher, s'il vous plaît? I been a bad papa to you. A terrible papa. When your mama left, I reckoned I could do all right. But I couldn't, not wit' just we two. De only face I had to look at was yours. And your face is part her face. Part my face too. Didn't matter if I broke every mirror in de shanty, I still had to look at faces I couldn't stand seein. I went bad. Real bad. Only reason I'm on dis beach right now was to do evil. But you saved me, cher. Saved me by makin me need to save you."

Pontiac couldn't fully follow but didn't think she had to. Daddy was holding tight like he'd been the one drowning and Pontiac had been the one to pull him free.

"I want to stop failin, cher. Real and true. But I can't, not here in de damp. But if we leave? Den I t'ink I can. I can stop with de drinkin. De drinkin and de sinkin. Sinkin down, down, down. All de pirate booty I dug for, cher, was just damn silly was what it was. You de treasure. You de gold. And I'm keepin you."

Pontiac tried to see and think straight.

"We're signing the Oil Man's papers?"

Daddy shook his head, flopping wet, cold, stringy hair.

"We ain't dare dally dat long. Come on to de shanty now. We fetch us some dry clothes and what money we can, den march us to de bus depot in Dawes. Once we on dat bus, den we can relax. We got a good, long ride ahead of us."

As Pontiac's exhausted brain tried to make sense of this, a graceful form parted the rolling waves. It was André Saphir, shaking off salt water and grinning, back from a swim nobody but him would have dared, not on a night like this. In one hand Saphir held the Whiz-Bang, bent like an elbow but surely willing to be repaired. In the other he held Daddy's buck knife, which was impaled through the center of the strange fish Saphir had been hunting: black, rectangular, and sodden, but maybe open to repair as well.

It was Pontiac's fuck-damn log.

QUEEN
COTTONMOUTH
~ OR ~
RED WITCH
TRIUMPHANT

RIDING FROM BAYOU COUNTRY INTO the inland dry was like watching Daddy skin a rabbit. The foliage, thick and furry, peeled back to reveal a musculature of orderly landscaping, road-sign tendons pointing absolute directions, concrete bones painted with lines straighter than anything ever seen in the swamp. Evisceration reached completion in New Orleans, and by the time the Greyhound rumbled off Blues Highway onto Interstate 10, the beast Pontiac had lived inside for nearly a decade had been rendered into cloverleaf interchanges, blue-glass office buildings, entire off-ramp empires of flat-topped big-boxers, white brick and riveted steel and industrial plastic, not a living thing in sight. That was before the sun came up! Nighttime in Alligator Point was pure hog guzzle, blacker than black compared to the lucent ley lines of what Miss Ward called *modern civ*. Even along the townless stretch between Bilox and Mobile, thousands of highway lamps acted as monster lightning bugs straight out of Lovecraft, unfathomable and unblinking over dinky-shit cars, axel-gadget trucks, and grumbly Greyhounds. Dawn exposed how scared inland folk were of the old gods at continent's edge. There were paved escape paths by the hundreds.

From the depot in Dawes to Pensacola, Florida: the exact three-hundred-mile path Pierre Lafitte took in 1806 when fleeing to escape his debts. It was the farthest Pontiac had traveled by a long shot, and required so much track-keeping she had to beg around the bus till a lady coughed up a pencil from her purse to replace Pontiac's lost original.

The log had dried fast in the arid bus air, which stung her eyes like the perfume Doc sprayed in the bathroom after he'd produced a "movement." It was only Pontiac's pencil past that had saved the log's contents; ink would have run in streaks. Beginning anew, however, was complicated. The pages had dried yellow and with armadillo scaling. She had to press like a fucker to effectively map their journey.

Daddy, meanwhile, wasn't doing jack but rolling his Brothers of the Spear marble through his fingers, smooth as a magician. Pontiac preferred it to all the puking. At the start of their journey, Daddy had puked like the Mardi Gras Fountain off Lake Pontchartrain. Puked on the path to Dawes, puked in the depot bathroom, puked out the bus window at sixty-five miles per hour. Other riders had given them the evilest eye possible and changed seats. Pontiac didn't mind. She'd seen Daddy puke so many times she had different words for different kinds of puke, like Miss Ward said Eskimos had for snow.

This time, though, it felt like Daddy had puked it all out.

What was *it*? Pontiac had an idea, an icky one. Could be all the cheap hooch Daddy had drunk had formed something evil in his gut, a cruel imitation of Mama's tumors. Maybe this Evil had forced Daddy to keep feeding it with nasty-sugar. Only at Guimbarde Beach had Daddy pushed it from his system like Doc said he'd once passed kidney stones out his wiener.

Now Daddy gazed past Pontiac like he was seeing something beautiful. Truth was, he looked beautiful. Not *Mama* beautiful, naturally, but the dirty window diffused the light the way lemonade did a lemon, evening it out and warming up Daddy's ashen skin. He got a big, awed grin on his face each time he spotted a Bojangles', or a Waffle House, or a Shoney's, like they were Egyptian pyramids, something he'd waited his whole life to see. Pontiac figured he'd seen them before but never seen them *plain*, not through liquor's warp.

Been a long time since he saw *her* plain either, Pontiac guessed.

She oughta feel lucky. She knew that. She was glad to see Daddy looking happy, healthy, and hopeful, she was. Only there was a problem. A big problem.

Pontiac didn't really want to leave Alligator Point.

She knew all the reasons to scram. The shanty rot, the bayou floods, the oil company takeovers. One day not too distant, the Point would cease to exist.

Running away, though? That felt like shit Billy May would've pulled. Pontiac hadn't even gotten a chance to deliver a proper au revoir to Saphir. To Doc. To Miss Ward. To Salazar's dog. To that big old turtle that'd been visiting their shanty all her life. To Mr. Peff's library. To her favorite climbing tree at Skunk Hole. To her and Billy May's secret meeting place in Chickapee Basin. To the cochon de lait at Juicy Lucy's. To the stash of racy pictures wrapped in a Wonder Bread bag at Lake Laurier. To her zombi astral, wherever it had gone to. To the finest octopus carving in the swamp, the one in the crepe myrtle right outside the Mercantile.

Four hours into the trip, Daddy nudged Pontiac awake from a nap she hadn't meant to take and pointed out the window at a sign reading WELCOME TO FLORIDA. Gopher shit. Purely gopher shit. If Pontiac were going to insist they turn around, she should have done it back in Dawes. Not now, when Daddy looked more like a Daddy-shaped cabin with a warm fire crackling inside.

Daddy scrambled to a different seat so he could hang his whole fool head out the window. Pontiac dug in her pocket for the one item she'd grabbed from the shanty: Billy May Part II. She made sure nobody on the bus was looking, held the mangled baseball up to her lips, and whispered.

"You were too scared to go to Bob Fireman's, Billy May. Well, now you and me's gone a whole lot farther than that."

~ 40 ~

TO FOLK WHO DIDN'T KNOW BETTER, Louisiana summers and Florida summers were comparable: hot, humid, Southern. Gerard knew better. Louisiana heat was a broth that seeped through your pores and filled you like a bowl. By barefooting round, you stirred that broth into a roux, till your blood was good and salty and your meat parts nice and tender. Made you food, in a way.

Florida heat, now that Gerard felt it and remembered, was oil dancing in a frying pan, still wet, still hot, but navigable. The heat sizzled on his skin but no deeper the instant he stepped off the Greyhound on Burgess Road, right between Wendy's and McDonald's. Pontiac followed, flicking the heat like skeeters the whole forty-minute walk to Sunshine Trailer Park.

The park hadn't moved an inch in ten years. Neither had the forty-foot trailer. The roof drooped like a horse with a bad spine and one window frame was covered with cardboard. But age was only age. Other details indicated pride in the habitat. Each fern heading up the four steps was at a different stage of dying, like the Stations of the Cross, but the pots were hand-glued with costume jewelry. The trailer had a fresh coat of pink paint. A jubilant flowerbed hugged the front end and a newish grill was chained to the undercarriage.

Gerard marveled. In the swamp, all flower-planting bought you was front-row tickets to their strangulation by vines and weeds. He stole a look at Pontiac. Her jaw hung low, another thing you couldn't do in the swamp. Dragonflies, wasps, skeeters, and flies were liable to zip inside, in search of hotter, stickier berths. Pontiac was just that astonished.

You can have nice things here, cher, Gerard thought.

He made a quick search of the trailer's wooden parts just to make sure the right person still lived there. He found the proof he needed at the end of the stairway rail, a rough etching of an octopus—old Alligator Point juju meant to placate some lethal force. Gerard had never been sure which one.

He kneeled in front of his daughter. Though knee pressed hard into the grass, it didn't draw water. Florida, not Louisiana.

"Dis here's my mama's place. Name's Eulalie."

"That's what I'm supposed to call her?"

"You call her *Mère*. Better yet, call her *ma'am* till she tell you udderwise."

"How long we staying?"

"Ain't no tellin yet."

"Forever?"

"I told you. I can't say."

"I'm not staying forever, Daddy. I got business on the Point."

"What type of business a pee-wee like you got in de playree?"

"*Keeping track* kind of business."

"That be a dyin business, cher."

"Plus it's almost St. John's Eve. Bob Fireman's gonna be setting up in Chickapee Basin. Me and Billy May go every year."

"Billy May ain't goin nowhere. Dat somet'in your heart gotta accept."

Pontiac's jaw flexed, masticating the idea. She glanced up at the trailer.

"You think she'll be glad to see us?"

Gerard wiped his face with the inside of his sleeve. "Seein dis ol trailer again, I ain't sure of nuddin. But here we be. No choice now but to toc-toc de door and see what-all ensue."

Pontiac drew back. "Ensue? Daddy, that's a word I ain't ever heard you say."

Gerard smiled. "Wit' dat rot out my gut, I rememberin all sorts of t'ings."

The steps were old but not shanty-old. The door was bright white metal, not a spot of rust. Gerard didn't think he'd seen nothing so new in his life. Made a good, clean, shimmery sound when he knocked too. With his other hand, he held tight to Pontiac.

The woman who answered the door was a stranger. Gray updo too buoyant, flowered blouse too colorful, teeth in better shape than anybody her age on the Point.

"Gerard," she gasped.

Mon Dieu, the years away from the bayou had done her good.

"Comment ça se plume," Gerard greeted, a chirrup of cracked happiness. He guessed it was the lack of fortifying booze in his blood that made both his eyes pour tears, fast stripes hot down his face. He stood sobbing, arms flat at his sides, and it was only by her embrace that he knew for sure it was Mère. Though Père had died of bone cancer in '69, Gerard felt his grip, too, the hand that had chucked Gerard's marbles, oui, but also the hand that had taught him how to clean a muskrat, to steer an airboat, to treat a puncture from a catfish spine. The truth reverberated through touch. Eulalie and DeLoach: they'd forgiven Gerard for ten years of being dead.

Mère's voice still had a banjo bounce. "Don't tell me this is—"

"Don't say it," Pontiac interrupted. "I go by Pontiac, ma'am."

Through the teary blur, Gerard saw Mère cackle at Pontiac's proffered handshake before giving the girl a body-swallowing hug.

Emotions came rough enough that Gerard felt nine rounds into a fight by the time he found himself sitting inside the narrow trailer at a table even narrower. He blinked around in disbelief. It was so blamed *dry* in here. No gray mold trailblazing from the corners, no rain forcing its way through the ceiling. He could feel his sweat dry on his skin instead of just getting wetter.

Mère slid a glass of sweet tea into his hand. He tried to pick it up but his dry skin kept sliding through condensation. Mère sat across the tiny table. No third chair existed; Pontiac sat atop an industrial barrel of kitty litter, property of a tabby named Baron Samedi. Gerard felt faint waves of heat from the other mammals. It made him a different kind of dizzy than from drink.

"Why'd you come?" Mère asked. "What happened?"

Fair question. But a different one raced around Gerard's skull. Why had *Mère* left the Point? Gerard had spent twelve years too laden with nasty-sugar to speculate. Eulalie had pulled anchor from the Point two years after DeLoach died. She'd tried to get Gerard, then twenty-two, to come with her. The Point was deep-down rotten, she'd said, and you'll rot too if you stay.

Young Gerard had been intractable as a vulture. He wasn't afraid of no swamp. Plus, a shanty all his own was an appealing idea at that age, when all you wanted to do was invite drinking buddies over. The single time he visited Mère in 1988, with Janine in tow, there'd been a blowup. Mère again begged him to stay. *Him.* Maybe she hadn't meant to exclude Janine but Gerard sure accused her of it, alleging that Mère didn't like how the Pontiac shade of skin didn't perfectly match up with Janine's. He'd stormed off, dragging poor Janine by the wrist, but Mère had threw the trailer door open and gotten the last word.

There's too many old outrages on the Point! You stick around there, mon fils, someday there'll be the Piper to pay!

Abraham's shit. Had Mère really warned him of the Piper way back then? The same way Gerard had taken to warning Pontiac? It was both miracle and madness how a child grew into the shape of his parent no matter how many miles stretched betwixt. Mère had been right in '88. Gerard had failed to save Janine from the Point but he'd be damned if he didn't save Pontiac.

With both hands, Gerard began to raise the glass to his lips.

His fingertips wiggled through the dew. The glass jagged. Tea sloshed. It came to him why. Shaking hands—alcohol withdrawal. It had been over eight hours since he'd had a swallow. Gerard tried to concentrate on his mother's question: *What happened?*

"De Piper," he replied. "It nearabout drunk us down."

Gerard Pontiac had blacked out many times in many places from many kinds of beverage. But this was the first time that beverage was his mama's own sweet tea.

~ 41 ~

PONTIAC HAD LIVED A NINE long years in proximity to things hiding in the dark. Gators under duckweed. Cottonmouths in carny trucks. The Cajun named Papoose who liked to pop up from underbrush and show schoolkids his ding-dong. The thing that looked like Miss Ward but wasn't.

This was the first time the thing was her daddy.

Mère's trailer had three spaces: main room, bathroom, and bedroom, which is where Daddy was. Pontiac assumed he was only taking a nap till Mère nailed metal latches to the door and frame, and looped a padlock through both.

"You holding Daddy hostage?" Pontiac demanded.

Mère crunched the padlock shut. "He's holding himself. I'm following his instructions."

"What if he gets thirsty?"

"He filled up every bottle he could find."

"What's he gonna eat?"

"There's food in there too. Bland stuff, easy to keep down."

"What about peeing?"

"I gave him a bucket."

"A fuck-damn *bucket*? That's some messed-up shit!"

"We need to discuss your language, young lady. Pensacola is not Alligator Point."

Things went sour fast. Within the hour, Daddy started moaning. Started gagging. Started crying. Started shouting. Started cussing. Started sobbing. Started kicking the furniture. Started turning the doorknob. Started squeaking the bedframe, then outright torturing it. Started weeping, soft and pitiful. Three hours had passed, only three.

"Can't we give him just a little?" Pontiac asked Mère. "A sip?"

Mère had to shout over the food she was cooking, or dishes she was washing, or plants she was potting, or repotting, or re-repotting. Pontiac knew busywork when she saw it. None of this was easy for a mama to do her boy.

"Your daddy needs you to hang tough, okay? Before it gets better, it's gonna get worse."

The DTs, Mère called them. Something that attacks your body when you quit drinking all at once. Mère said it all calm and scientific but it sounded to Pontiac like Daddy was being torn apart by gators in there. Wood splintered. Glass shattered. Daddy screamed. He kicked the door till there were cracks. He got low and begged right through the crack under the door. It was awful how he begged, especially when Pontiac happened by.

"Cher. Listen to your daddy now. Mère's fixin to kill me."

Didn't much sound like Daddy at all.

"Y'hear, cher? Dat t'ing in de dark, all dem times, maybe dat was her."

His fingertips, bloody and bruised, wiggled from the crack.

"Won't you lemme touch you, cher? I promise I won't pull you under."

Pontiac backed off. Why would Daddy mention pulling her under if it hadn't crossed his mind? She pictured her hand jerked under till her wrist lodged in the crack, then Daddy pulling so hard her wrist bones crumbled and her whole arm went under, the bottom of the door rinding her muscles off bones like chicken off a drumstick.

A hand on her shoulder—Pontiac leapt aside but it was only Mère.

The old lady had tearful eyes but the tears didn't fall.

"That isn't your daddy talking," she said.

They ate boudin while Daddy kept raging.

"Your daddy's daddy, my DeLoach, went cold turkey a couple times," Mère said. "Right now, you're daddy's seeing things that aren't there. He's working up a bad fever. His whole body's running harder than it ever has. Good thing, too, because he's being chased."

The spicy pork was tasty but Pontiac couldn't work up a hankering.

"Sounds like his heart's gonna explode," she said.

CRACK!

Something hard struck the bedroom wall.

Mère flinched, took a breath, arranged her hair, and kept eating.

"I don't think his heart's gonna explode," Mère replied, and Pontiac didn't like the word *think*.

The *CRACK!* sounds kept on. Sounded like Daddy was trying to chip his way out with an icepick. It got so Pontiac and Mère got used to it, the tick of a deranged clock. When bedtime came, Mère pulled out the sofa mattress for her and Pontiac to share. At first, Pontiac couldn't quit grinning. It was like sleeping on cotton candy, the nicest thing she ever felt. By the time Mère was snoring, though, Pontiac was twitching bad. She crawled out, laid down a bath towel, gathered up her log and Billy May Part II, and curled up on the floor near to the locked bedroom door. Baron Samedi joined her.

The *CRACK!* blasts waned in ferocity.

After a while, they stopped, and all Pontiac heard were Daddy's wheezes.

Much better. Daddy had wheezed lots of times before and still woke up the next day. Pontiac snuggled to the wall and curled an arm around the cat. The cat knew what she knew: the floor was the safest place to sleep, where your body could know the rumbles of woe long after your brain switched off.

- 42 -

PONTIAC WOKE TO THE CRACKLE and aroma of a mudbug boil. Mère, in a pastel housecoat, poked a spatula at meat spitting from atop one of the large white appliances. It wasn't a wheeled propane boiler like how mudbugs were supposed to boil.

"That a stove?" Pontiac mumbled.

Mère chuckled. "I expect you and Gerard are still coaxing along that old wood-burner. I know, I know, a stovetop boil isn't the same. But I tell you, nothing made me happier about moving to the dry than being able to get a stove going without a fight."

Pontiac sat up.

"There's not nothing else you miss about the Point?"

"I'd sell my soul for some cat and craw that's no more than a hour dead before it hits your tum. Me and DeLoach and your daddy

ate like royalty in the Point. Jambalaya. Gully-whumpus. Pigs feet
and kraut. Lamb kibbeh and cow's gut. I wouldn't even try those
dishes out here. Out here, you gotta be a whiz at spices to make your
vittles half-tolerable. Had to learn the difference between a *pinch* or
a *drop* or what they call *a whole bunch*. Never needed nothing but
salt back in de damp."

De damp. A bit of Mère's old Cajun creeping back.

"Smells good," Pontiac offered.

Mère looked pleased. "C'mere, I'll show you how to scramble
eggs that taste like Jesus and grits like the Holy Ghost."

Daddy woke up when they started to eat.

CRACK! CRACK!

Though not quite as hard now. Mère smiled from behind but-
tery steam.

"Abraham's shit, my boy is beating it."

Abraham's shit? Mère was a Pointer, all right.

By lunchtime, the *CRACK! CRACK!* had lessened to a *crack!
crack!* Despite the lickin she'd given to Florida seafood, Mère ran
off to the local shops for all the fixings for a celebratory jambalaya. One ingredient after another was piled into an old lobster
kettle. Mère stirred it with a tire iron and winked at Pontiac's
bugged eyes.

"If you stir it with a spoon, it's not thick enough. This tire iron
used to rattle around DeLoach's jitterbugging old Fairlane. I guess
it still makes me feel safe to hold, just in case."

"In case of what?"

The stirring sounded like blood and bones.

"Case of anything that might come peeking at your window,"
Mère said simply. "DeLoach used to talk about All Feathers,
No Meat."

"The fuck-damn is that?"

"Your language."

"Sorry. What the *shit* is that?"

Mère shook her head like Mama used to, like she didn't know what to do with Pontiac.

"I don't know, precisely. He used to talk about it like it was a place. A place you could get stuck. Said it could be anywhere. Iceland, Greenland, Wonderland. He was in a war when he was a young man and spent a whole day hiding in a river, just his nose peeking from the water. Said that was the closest he ever came All Feathers, No Meat."

Pontiac pondered. "Is that why you moved away?"

"What do you mean?"

"Because the Point was All Feathers, No Meat?"

Mère tapped the tire iron on the side of the kettle.

"There never was a place on God's green earth with less meat than the Point. It didn't have to be that way either." Mère frowned. "What are you writing down?"

"Just what you're saying."

Mère nodded briskly. "Good. Been a long time since I saw a body keep track."

"I shoulda kept better track of Daddy."

"Well, darling, I should have kept better track too. We all could have kept track of somebody better. You're at least trying. It's the only way to make sure it doesn't happen again."

"That what doesn't happen?"

"Another All Feathers, No Meat. Another Alligator Point."

A light *clack* interrupted the quicksand gurgle of the cooking food. Both Pontiac and her grandmother looked toward the front of the trailer.

The Brothers of the Spear rolled from under the bedroom door.

Baron Samedi skittered alongside it, light-pawed, whiskers fanned, arched for play. The marble gristled across specks of sand Pontiac and Daddy probably brought with them. It was a slow roll the throw rug should have stopped. Yet the marble had just enough momentum to crest it. Either that or it was the combined courage of Dan-El and Natongo.

The marble came to rest at Pontiac's feet. The cat touched it with its nose.

"The Baron didn't recoil an inch," Mère said happily. She withdrew a key and slapped it on the counter. "Go on ahead. He's ready."

Pontiac looked nervously at the buckled bedroom door. She was the one who wasn't ready. Then again, she hadn't been ready to leave the Point and look at her now, Billy May Part II nearly forgotten, galivanting with an old lady she'd never met, salivating over a tire-iron jambalaya. She might be ready for all sorts of things she didn't realize.

She closed her log, picked up the Brothers of the Spear, and crossed to the door. She put her ear to it. The thing in the room hadn't sounded like Daddy for a long-ass time. Now, though, she didn't heard squat.

Pontiac held her breath, undid the padlock, and opened the door.

For a bright, shiny day, the room was gloomy. Laundry had been shoveled over the windows like soil. One bar of sunlight razored through, hitting what had to be the bathroom bucket. The smell wasn't too bad, which made Pontiac think her daddy had dumped his vileness outside. Her eyes adjusted. Poor Mère—the room was busted to shit. One of the bed's feet had been cracked off, making the bed lay slanted. A dresser had been gutted like a deer, drawers disassembled, clothing strewn like innards. A mirror frame was empty with its glass shards below, half of them dull with dried blood. The wall separating the bedroom from the rest of the trailer was cratered like the surface of the moon, marking every time Daddy had hurled the Brothers of the Spear with a *CRACK!*

"Cher? C'mere? S'il vous plaît?"

New day, new room, same old scene.

Pontiac stepped up the side of the bed. Daddy was curled limp atop the naked mattress in a posture that looked angelic. His face had an exhausted grace, like ladies Pontiac had seen in movies who'd just given birth. Daddy reached out his hand. It wavered like he was blind. Pontiac gave him her left hand. But she made a fist out of her right. You never know.

"Guimbarde Beach." Daddy's voice was gravelly and gentle.

"Yes, Daddy."

"I went dere hopin to kill dat André Saphir."

Pontiac felt oddly serene.

"Why, Daddy? Saphir never hurt nobody."

"I know dat."

"Except fish. He's a serial killer when it comes to fish."

Daddy chuckled. Looked like it hurt, and that Daddy liked that it did.

"Dat wuddn't me, cher. It was da bottle I drunk."

Understanding flowed easy in the serenity.

"You drank it. My zombi bottle."

"Oui. I believe dat's so. But what was in dat bottle wuddn't what made me go after Saphir. It was what *stopped* me. All dem *udder* bottles I drunk leadin up was what made me go bad. Even dat's not de honest trut'. All dat nasty-sugar did was push me along de track I already was on. I was jealous of Saphir. Dat simple. He been more a daddy to you den I ever been."

Pontiac wanted to say, *It's not true, Daddy!* But she couldn't. The truth, if a lawyer wanted to gather it, was all written down in her log.

"Me and Saphir were as near as a dog's balls when I raised my knife. Dat's when dat black bottle gunk fought its way outta my gut. Kickin and screamin and carryin on. I dropped right dere in de surf, chokin and dyin. Still holdin dat knife, t'ough. Saphir oughta let me die. But he a good man, cher. Dat fisherman helped me choke up what I had to choke—a zombi if dat's what you say. And dat fisherman carried me to de beach. And dat fisherman cry over me till I was better. I reached up and held dat's man face, I did, like I used to hold de face of your mama, and right dere on Guimbarde, wit' dem tempêtes rollin in, I asked dat fisherman to be your parrain, cher— your godfather. Cuz André Saphir, from the look of him, he gonna live forever, when I know I ain't long for de world, not wit' all de t'ings I done to dis old body. Dat fisherman, he don't even blink. He say, Oui, monsieur, and nuddin I heard in my life ever made me feel better. If somet'in happen to me, and somet'in happen to Mère, if de good life we fix you up here in Florida goes bad? You know how to take dat' Greyhound back to de Point. You got it wrote all down. You ride back there, find dat fisherman, and he take care of you. He gave me his solemn oat."

Pontiac was too old to cry. So she didn't.

But inside her whirled a hurricane.

"Okay, Daddy."

His smile wilted his bruised face like a rotten pumpkin.

"What you got in dat hand dere?"

Pontiac didn't recall. She opened her palm. The laser of sun hit the marble. Dan-El and Natongo lit up like tiny titans. A thousand years old and this marble was still birthing new stars.

"My old friends." Daddy sounded awed. "Dey yours now."

Pontiac shook her head firm.

"No, Daddy. You need them more than me."

His jack-o'-lantern grin got bigger till it folded in on itself. He was crying. But he was dried out too. Only two sad trickles came out, salty enough to leave sparkly trails. He picked up the marble and gazed as it like he'd once gazed at baby Pontiac—she'd seen the photo herself. He turned it over, and over. Every turn did him good.

"I ever tell you how we called dese marbles *hardtoget*?"

"Yes, Daddy."

"I ever tell you how I shot dis marble good enough to take German Rusnak's hoard?"

"Yes, Daddy."

Daddy looked half the weight he'd been before Mère locked the door, all his soft parts carved away. Not much of him left, Pontiac thought, but what remained were the best parts.

A tire iron banged off a kettle.

"If y'all are finished, I got a jambalaya here spicy enough to burn off any devils left in ya."

- 43 -

MUST HAVE BEEN THREE IN THE A.M. when Spuds Ulene finished sweeping and mopping at Juicy Lucy's. It didn't matter if it was cleaning for Lucy, deputying for Pete, or brushing his horse roomies at the Fontaine stables: there was nothing Spuds liked better than work. Once he locked in? Goll, folk had a heck of time unlocking him.

Belly full of Lucy's leftovers and pocket thick with cash, Spuds limped down a spindly trail burning phosphorous white with moonlight. Fronds and boughs filtered the light till the trail was a dull gray. Two years back, a band of coyotes killed a Fontaine foal and dragged the intestines sixty feet. The trail kinda looked like that.

Ugly thought, but Spuds did a lot of ugly-thinking these days.

According to Lucy, regulars Rawley Deevers, Wee-Wee Sly, and Gully Jimson had all signed the Oil Man's papers. The bigger shock wave was the announced closing of Plum Peppers, Juicy Lucy's storied competitor. Lucy hadn't taken it as a victory. She was scared. Spuds noticed her paging through her own copy of the Oil Man's papers. It got Spuds thinking what Pete called "unproductive thoughts."

If Juicy Lucy's closed, how would Spuds eat?

The Pelican would close third, and without taverns, Alligator Point would shrivel up. Everybody would pull up stakes. This included the Fontaines. Spuds imagined himself abandoned in the gooey damp, scrawny and naked on all fours, eating bugs, biting into rats still kicking. He'd become a creature of legend. Until, of course, his nightmare came true—and the quicksand got him.

Spuds let himself be lulled by a rhythmic racket as fine as any by Zydeco Chowder. The backbeat groan of frogs and the timpani splashes of puddling toads, the cricket maracas and fiddle caws of sleepless hawks, the piano plinking of night birds and the call-and-response of a mated pair of owls, layers rising and dropping, a drone as rich as the ocean.

It was a wonder a human voice could pierce it all.

"Spuds?"

Spuds stopped. His trick knee juddered like always.

"Spuds Ulene? That you?"

Spuds lifted the bill of his Astros cap to see better. He turned. Nothing but mangroves and sea grapes. He decided to reply anyway.

If he'd just been hearing things, it wasn't like there'd be anybody around to poke fun.

"That's my name, anyways. Where you at?"

"Hellfire!" Southern accent, but citified, not swamp. "Imagine *me*, running into *you*!"

Spuds kept turning. "Y'all know me from someplace?"

"You kidding?" The voice laughed. "I was there that day!"

"What day'd that be?"

"That day y'all took roses up at Gretna Downs. Same day you got walked on by that pissant gelding."

Spuds's throat dried. Same as when anytime Gretna Downs came up.

He completed a full circle. Now he saw white clothing radiating from the dark maybe ten feet ahead and ten to the left of the trail. A getup that white was going to get ruined in there, but Spuds supposed that, when natured called, you had to respond.

"Horse didn't mean it," Spuds croaked.

"It done it, is all what matters. If I'd-a had my gun that day, hoo-ee! I'd-a shot that hoss dead on the track for it what it done."

As much as Spuds hated talking about that day, he believed he heard respect in the voice. Spuds didn't get a whole lot of respect on the Point.

Spuds cleared his throat. "You, ah . . . seen me ride?"

"More'n a hundred times! Up Gretna. Over Montfort. At Chantilly. Could tell on day one you was a winner. Hoped and prayed y'all would get to ride a hoss that had some high-test gasoline in her, not those glue-factory nags. When y'all took them Gretna roses, I was hootin and hollerin. Not just cuz I had fifty dollars riding with ya. I was hootin and hollerin for you, sir! Cuz I thought ya'll had found yourself a good animal at last."

Spuds felt old pain ghosting around his prosthetic knee.

"Didn't catch your name, sir," he said carefully.

"Come a little closer," the voice said. "Be my honor to have us a proper introduction."

Few things made Spuds nervouser. The Point's trails were guide ropes laid down by Lafitte's pirates. You didn't stray outside them unless you had a real good reason. Did flattery count? Spuds didn't know; he'd never heard it before. Even as a jockey, the best compliment he ever got was *You'll do.*

He swished the flattery round his mouth.

Finally, he'd found a nasty-sugar to his liking.

Spuds pushed back a branch of pignut hickory and stepped into the dim. The ground squelched. A fellow could lose his shoes in gunk like this if he didn't keep it snappy. He powered on, taking curly pondweed to the face. The white-clothed person grew bigger and clearer. Spuds rounded a patch of bushy bluestem and abruptly was face-to-face with the only fan he'd ever had.

White man. White hair. White seersucker suit with fine black stripes. Two-tone blucher Oxfords. Big straw Panama hat. A tiny purple flower waved hello from the suit's lapel. The man looked straight out of the olden days, but so did many of the sporting types who frequented flat-tracks. What's more, he didn't have a single speck of mud on him. There was something familiar about the man. Spuds couldn't help but smile.

Shock flashed over the man's soft, shaven face.

Spuds's reflex had been learned young. He tried to make himself even smaller than he was, a harder target to hit. Quickly, though, the man in the seersucker suit repaired his face into a grin. Happened like a filmstrip run in reverse.

"You're just a little, well, *older* than I remembered," the man chuckled.

Spuds let himself expand a little.

"Yes, sir. I'm twenty-seven now. That's pretty old and I apologize."

The man laughed and held out a hand.

"Name's Booker."

Spuds glanced at the hand. Smooth as the man's face, like it hadn't gripped a tool in its life. Even the nails were round and soft. Spuds took it and gave it a shake.

It felt cold and scaly.

Spuds got his hand back quick as he could. Did Mr. Booker have a problem with circulation? Did he have a mess of callouses Spuds hadn't noticed in the dark? No chance to tell: Booker propped both hands on his hips and shook his head in disbelief.

"Spuds Ulene! Shoot! Where you riding now, sir?"

Spuds got smaller again. Truth was, he was riding truck beds, mostly, on the way to Juicy Lucy's when he could thumb one. Other than that, the passenger seat of the Melbourne Queen.

"Nowhere, Mr. Booker."

Spuds made a fist and rapped his fake knee. It thudded weird.

Unrolling his fist, Spuds noticed an itch on his hand. Same hand he'd used to shake hello. Maybe a skeeter had zipped between the hands and given a dying bite.

"Crying shame." Booker snapped his fingers. "I won't ever forget seeing y'all sittin Hot Yeller in the Runyon. I though he was a winner certain. Ran quicker'n Seabiscuit on a track slicker'n a sick dog's shit."

Spuds felt his face twitch in a smile. Hand itch forgotten.

"You know how that horse got its name?" he asked.

"I do not, sir!"

"That horse's owner was a fellow called Jake Cramer. One day Jake went to the stables to check a shoe job and that horse just cut loose. Pissed all over him!"

Booker slapped his seersucker thigh. "Sheeeee-it!"

"Jake tried to call it Hot Piss, but the boys up at the regional tore down the signs with their bare hands. Said it wasn't decent!"

Booker was laughing so bad now he had to hold a cypress to keep upright. Even the man's laughing sounded familiar. It was the kind of breathless sputtering that always got Spuds laughing too. He giggled and chortled and whooped. It had been a spell since he'd laughed so hard. That he'd made somebody *else* laugh so hard. Felt so good that Spuds didn't mind the itch on his palm. The hot and twisty itch.

Booker wiped happy-tears from his eyes.

"Can't I buy you a sippa somethin? Conversate about the old days?"

Spuds didn't drink booze. Tasted terrible. But he could sure go for a Mountain Dew. At the same time, Spuds realized that this Booker fellow had planted a notion in Spuds's gut. Alligator Point was disintegrating. As much as Spuds liked being longside Pete, it wasn't gonna last. He oughta get back to the horse tracks. If not as a rider, a trainer.

Abraham's shit! He'd hitch a ride tomorrow to Gretna.

"I'm gonna have to decline," Spuds said proudly. "Early morning."

"That's my boy," Booker said. "Always knew you'd make somethin of yourself."

Spuds stared. And thought. He wasn't real good at thinking. He tilted his head to the right—that helped sometimes—and thought harder. Gradually, Booker's face changed a little. Or else Spuds just finally saw it for what it was.

". . . Daddy?"

The man's chicken-cutlet cheeks pudged into a soft grin. His happy-tears were back.

"Booker Ulene," the man confirmed. "I wasn't sure you'd recognize me, son."

Goll, Spuds's heart was racing now. He'd never known Pa's name. Truth was, Pa had been awful rough on Spuds before Pa took off for good. But look! Look how he'd cleaned up! Besides, he'd never actually left. He'd been there in the stands, cheering Spuds on every time.

Pa Ulene's happy-tears refused to fall. They became magnifying glasses over his eyes, making his pupils as big as silver dollars. Pa's smooth hand slipped beneath seersucker, wiggling the lapel flower— a lilac, Spuds thought. The hand returned with what looked like a pint of whiskey. Except the label was obscured under what looked like black paint. Booker uncapped it and held the bottle out to Spuds.

"Always carry a sippa on me," Pa said. "Do me the honor?"

Spuds's nods sent his own tears cascading down. Spuds reached out. Pa handed over the pint. It was cold, like hefting one of Lucy's ice blocks bare-handed. Awful odd thing here in the sweaty swamp, though it felt nice against the itch on his palm, which was starting to feel like it was swelling up. Must have been one mean skeeter.

Spuds drank fast. Ice-cold going down too.

"Ain't the first time we sucked at the same tit," Pa chuckled.

Spuds finished and gasped. "Goll, that feels good."

Booker's black-pupiled eyes shined. "Better'n a busted knee, I expect."

"Yes, sir, Pa. A whole mile better."

"Musta hurt like a sumbitch, what that hoss did."

Spuds took another pull. The coldness coated his insides.

"Did at that, Pa."

"Almost like it was mad at you for winning."

Pete always told Spuds how too much drinking made your vision spin. Something like that was happening now. Instead of spinning, though, Spuds's sight was hinging like a wind-slapped weathervane right before it got whirling. Back, forth, back, forth. Now, then, now—

Then: he saw Gretna Downs. Just like it had been that fateful day. He was a fill-in jockey at 50/1 odds, crossing the finish line first on a five-year-old gelding named Ergoteur. For four, maybe five, seconds, Spuds knew what it felt like to be a winner. Then Ergoteur bucked out of nowhere, pitching Spuds over its mane.

The instant Spuds looked up from the track, he knew what the animal was going to do. It was going to run for the stables. And Spuds was right in its path.

There was no time for him to get out of the way. If Spuds bunched up small, he might multiply the targets of a single stomp. If he kicked and crawled, he would only increase the possibilities of getting stomped in the first place. His best move was to not move at all.

He shut his eyes real tight, as if gathering flesh over his lids, brows, and cheeks might provide a kind of padding if the horse were to step on his face. A second later, one of Ergoteur's iron-shoed back hooves, bearing most of the horse's 1,500 pounds, came down on Spuds's left knee. The pain was incandescent. Spuds somehow held still until he felt the passing of the horse's shadow and the rumble of its getaway sprint.

"Ya hurled up," Pa Ulene said.

"Did I?" Spuds asked.

He'd never looked at the knee that day. It was too much. It was all too much. The pain. The lost opportunities. The endless gall of the metal knee docs had built and shoved inside him.

"Big puddle of all the nasty-sugar you had inside ya," Pa chuckled. "Looked purty much like . . . well, like that puddle yonder."

Pa pointed. Spuds looked.

Quicksand.

Only six feet off. How had he not noticed it before? The quick was the color of oatmeal. The consistency of oatmeal. It even bubbled like oatmeal when you set the heat too high. Veils of steam danced upward and exuded the smell of lilacs. Or could be that was Booker Ulene. His voice had drained of its accent, become colder, older, ageless.

"What your knee looked like cannot be put into words. But you must be curious to see it. I can show it to you. I can show you right now."

Spuds dragged his eyes from the bubbling quicksand to the man in the seersucker suit. The pools of tears over Pa's eyes had thickened into gelatin, magnifying the pupils so much the white of his eyes were gone, leaving nothing but oily black holes. He was holding high the hand Spuds had shaken. As Spuds watched, the smooth, pale flesh dripped away like candle wax, leaving behind braids of raw meat. Individual hand bones wiggled, then began to tumble, one after the other, the whole hand in rapid collapse.

Pa pointed the stump at Spuds. The insides were hollow. But not empty.

Packed tightly within was what looked like black tar.

The itch on Spuds's palm crawled upward, cording around his wrist and threading into the muscle of his forearm. Lord, he wanted to scratch it, though he knew if he did, it would only itch worse. He looked away from it, the same as he'd looked away from his jellied knee six years back. But the man in the seersucker suit was right. He *was* curious.

Spuds lifted his right arm. It had dissolved to the elbow, a shallow sleeve of skin cupping a red gumbo of bone chips, tendon flaps, balled veins, and muscle hanks. Spuds watched the mess boil over, then he fell to his knees and screamed, because his bad knee was still his bad knee, and it hurt terrible. Spuds began to crawl, blind with pain, no direction in particular. His crawling got slower, then stopped, as the itch dissolved his other arm and his legs as well.

The head and torso once known as Spuds Ulene came to a rest at the edge of the bubbling pit of quicksand. It didn't seem so bad now that he was beside it. A smooth hand stroked Spuds's hair. That meant Spuds had lost his Astros cap. The Astros cap Pete had awarded him the day they met. This made Spuds cry more.

"Shh," Pa whispered. "I know."

"When that horse stomped me down," Spuds sniffled, "down I shoulda stayed."

The hand was colder and scalier against his temple.

"I know. Shh."

The best thing Spuds could do, he decided, was finish himself off quick in favor of the long, slow death the swamp had planned. Hadn't that been what Pa had tried to do to Spuds when Spuds was small? Finishing off a dumb kid wasn't a crime. It was a mercy. Sounded kinda nice, actually. No more mopping. No more fretting the future. No more reminders of what could have been. Only Spuds didn't want his best buddy Pete having to clean up a mess. So he started rocking his limbless torso. Back and forth. Hot pudding bubbling against his cheek. Back and forth. Vision swirling sick with each sway. Back and forth. Topsy-turvy now, like when he'd flown over Ergoteur's head.

Spuds rolled into the quick, grateful this version of his fall wouldn't hurt for long.

It was one more disappointment in a life full of them.

It hurt for a long, long time.

~ 44 ~

THE SOLE CHURCH IN ALLIGATOR POINT was the Bread of Life, nondenominational by default, a one-room, ten-pew structure as old as Lafitte's shanties but with ten times the architectural integrity. Though it had been built on dry land, two centuries of a rising gulf now had the church's stone foundation sheering into brackish waters. The eighteen-foot steeple was fully coated in kudzu, making it look like the swamp had an upright appendage. Blasphemous locals, and that was most of them, called it the Point's Boner. The cross on the top? Why, that was the Prince Albert.

Miss Ward had heard schoolkids tell that joke for seven years without understanding it. Jack, laughing himself red, had to explain to her what it was. Miss Ward had gone redder than him, even as the vulgarity had excited her. Vulgarity always had. Jack had been the only one to know that.

No one else ever would. Miss Ward expected her investigation into Alligator Point would kill her the same as it had killed him. With the school doomed, that was acceptable. She may not have Jack's know-how, but she had his skiff, shotgun, Bowie knife, machete, and gris-gris. Once she set her mind on something, it was ironclad.

Jack had been the only one to know that too.

Miss Ward hiked to Bread of Life with confident strides that surprised her. It helped that she'd dug up the magical old tube of Raw Umber W550 and was rhythmically squeezing it inside her dress pocket. But her muscles seized upon spotting the Point's Boner through the foliage. Up ahead, folk were milling outside the church in their finest, which on the Point meant something that had, or had once had, buttons. They'd see her. They'd recognize her. They'd stare agog. The rumors would begin.

You know that hermit teacher lady? Well, she come right out of the woodwork. And for what? Spuds Ulene's funeral, that's what!

Hearing steps from the trail behind her, Miss Ward did what she was used to doing. She slipped past a pear tree and squatted in Yankeeweed. Her thighs shook. Cold sweat rolled down her jawline. Steam fogged her glasses. The swamp's sweet smell sickened her. If folk saw her, they'd ask why she hid all those years. Why she came back. She'd say nothing. She *was* nothing. All the songs she'd hummed had vaporized. All the paintings she'd made would be discovered at an estate sale and pitched into a fire.

She squeezed the raw umber at the speed of her heartbeat.

Then squeezed it slower. Her heartbeat followed. Interesting.

Before the folk on the trail had passed, Miss Ward was scolding herself. Think like Jack. Like *Jack*. If she couldn't show herself to fellow Pointers, how would she show herself to Evil? Anger was a fuel Jack had always made use of. Miss Ward got up and fought through Virginia fern to emerge into the Boner's shadow at the church's south end. Catch a breath, that's all she needed. She leaned against turquoise moss and tilted her head up.

When she looked back down, she was holding the tube of umber.

She squeezed a daub onto her finger. Don't think about it.

She placed that finger on her left cheekbone. Don't think about it.

She wiped the paint diagonally across her cheek. Don't think about it.

Miss Ward's spine was live oak as she bucked herself from the side of the church. She charged around front. An ill-looking lot of smokers stared right at her, then her cheek. What did it matter? Some folk smeared their makeup. Some folk had scars. She had both sets beat: a slash that lent her the boldness of her beloved.

Miss Ward hurled open the Bread of Life doors.

The smallest of narthexes. A guest book atop a lectern. Miss Ward adjusted her glasses and read the current page. Twenty-one names featuring the usual potpourri of swamp-rat scratchings: embarrassed squiggles, all-caps alarmists, best-guess phonetics, illiterate X's, and the ostentatious calligraphy of the proudly educated.

The first signature on the page stuck out. Written in ink so luscious it looked like unrefined crude, it had a sawtooth pattern that conveyed sophistication, the kind of signature, Miss Ward intuited, that came from signing a lot of checks. No one on the Point had cause to write like that. Which meant . . .

Miss Ward stepped into the bare-bones sanctuary: ten rows of pews unvarnished by generations of butts but enlivened by two bouquets of wildflowers in urns. Not even swamp folk wore hats in a church, which made it easier for her to scan for a head of perfectly gelled hair. Or a black, tailored suit. A well-knotted tie. A coruscation of glossy leather shoes.

Nothing. The Oil Man wasn't there.

But he'd been here. Miss Ward was sure it of it. It wasn't only the signature. It was the phantom of cologne unlike any of the mouthwash funks she'd smelled before on the Point. This was fresh-cut grass and tea leaves, a hint of sandalwood, a ghost of plum. Though she'd only spoken to the Oil Man through her door, she could see him as well as she could visualize a painting. He shimmered just out of sight, fumes from a gasoline fire.

A handful of loungers passed a flask. Musicians by the looks of them, especially the one in the pink rhinestone suit. She felt an adolescent draw toward them: she was a musician, too, not that they'd ever believe it with her traditional cornflower dress. Nobody had yet to notice her. That, at least, made it easier to start investigating.

What was it about Spuds Ulene that had drawn it? The thing? The Evil? The Piper?

Miss Ward filled her lungs with mothball air and made her way up the center aisle. Any second, every eyeball would fly at her like darts. Any second now. Any second.

No casket, but she'd expected that. The vent beside her bathroom toilet was a direct line to Mr. Peff's checkout counter, and until the night of Doc and Pontiac's visit, she'd only ever listened through the vent by accident. Now she spent so much time beside it she'd given the toilet an extra-intense scrubbing and put down a rug to make eavesdropping more comfy. A book borrower had told Mr. Peff that Spuds Ulene had vanished, and vanished folk didn't warrant caskets, not in impoverished puddles like the Point.

Where the casket might have gone was an ornamental stand hosting a single framed photograph and a small, shiny object. It was this stand folk were paying their respects to while shaking hands with the primary mourner. Miss Ward had prepared a response in case anyone in the Ulene family asked why she'd come. She was running the script when the mourners shifted.

The person shaking hands held a telltale Stetson at his side.

Of course there weren't any other Ulenes. Of course the closest thing Spuds had to kin was Pete Roosevelt. Miss Ward's heart took off like backyard rabbits. Her forehead stung from the viscosity of sweat bulbing from her hairline. She tried to picture Jack for strength but couldn't recall what he looked like. The church spun. Fifty Jesuses riding fifty crosses.

She squeezed the umber tube. Think like Jack. Think like Jack.

Miss Ward proceeded forward. Her ankles wobbled with each landing of each foot. Pete's big, broad, sweaty, useless face loomed closer. Miss Ward imagined the weight of Jack's knife, machete, shotgun. She could do this.

She reached the stand and brought her shoulders back. Pete was shaking the hand of somebody wearing a vest with no shirt, but he lifted a wary eyebrow at Miss Ward. Pete's pale blue eyes were as empty as sky.

"Pete," she greeted stiffly.

Pete tipped an invisible hat at the departing well-wisher, inflated his blimp chest, and pivoted to address Miss Ward. Booze. Not overpowering but it was there, stinging her eyes from behind a veneer of coffee. Pete surveyed her as if expecting her to be on fire.

"Miss Ward." Pete had his teeth bared. Bracing for comeuppance.

In the decade-and-a-half since Doc Devereaux had broken the news of Jack O'Brien's murder to Miss Ward, she and Pete Roosevelt had faced off but once, at Jack's funeral, right here at Bread of Life. The greeting line had been a mile long, folk from all over the delta. When Pete's turn had come to offer Miss Ward his condolences, she'd pressed her arms to her sides and took the most aggressive action of her life.

She'd spat in his face and asked him to leave.

Miss Ward regretted it. Not for how it made either of them feel, but on the off-chance Pete believed it had been her final word. Perhaps that's how men did it. A loogie to the face, a punch to the gut, and then it was the glad hand, everything forgiven. Miss Ward was no man and was glad. Her hatred was what had kept her alive.

Pete licked his lips and looked pained.

"What's that on your cheek?"

Miss Ward had to flex her jaw and feel the raw umber's pinch before remembering.

Strength blew back into her like gusts off the Gulf.

"Paint," she snapped.

Pete nodded like he thought he was being suckered.

"You . . . knew Spuds, did you?"

"I came to pay my respects. As a member of the community."

Was that what she was? The notion put iron in her blood, even as her muscles cankered from the irony. Joining the community as the community was being picked apart like carrion was Miss Ward's luck in a nutshell.

"It's just . . ." Pete squinted. "I ain't seen you outside the school in . . ."

He trailed off. Miss Ward only stared. Jack had taught her there was power in silence. An unanswered question was like an ignored sexual overture. It made the person who did the asking feel foolish.

Miss Ward turned from Pete's liquor aroma. What a dark, purple thrill it was to discount him so easily! She adjusted her glasses to focus on what she was here to see, the framed photo atop the stand, darkened by Pete's goliath shadow.

For four years, Miss Ward had seen Spuds Ulene anytime she saw Pete Roosevelt. Not only had the younger man looked to be Pete's physical opposite, he exuded contradictory qualities. Spuds seemed welcoming, optimistic, guileless, and honest. Miss Ward didn't know what she expected to see in the photo, but it wasn't the dearly departed in red-and-yellow jockey silks, giving a deer-in-the-headlights stare to the photographer as he held the reins of a sorrel quarter horse in matching blinkers.

Spuds looked baffled. But hopeful too.

The grief of it sideswiped Miss Ward. Not just Spuds's death but the inescapable charnel house of the Point, amplified by the folk congregated here, their every breath, swallow, and drop of sweat providing evidence of encroaching extinction. Miss Ward steadied herself with the stand. It rocked on an uneven base and the framed photo skidded an inch; the shiny object next to it rolled right off the platform.

A big paw caught it.

Only now did Miss Ward notice particulars of Pete beyond his pickled breath. Red eyes, gray sockets, deep trails of pain mapped at the temples. He gripped the shiny object like a baseball, and Miss Ward pictured the gutted ball she'd found in Pontiac's desk. What she felt for Pontiac and her missing friend was bleeding over to Pete and the loss of his. Nothing else explained the bolt of sympathy. Miss Ward hated it and coughed up a question as cover.

"How . . . how did he . . . ?"

Pete frowned at his contorted reflection in the metal object.

"Cottonmouth. Brown recluse. Loggerhead turtle. Take your pick. Or coulda got caught on a fishin line or crab trap and drowned. That's the kind of death folk expected of him. Everybody hereabouts thought Spuds was dumb. I guess he was, but only when it came to trusting folk. Boy never met a body he didn't hand his whole heart to. Seems just as likely to me it was a person who done it. Who lured him off the path. Spuds was real scared of goin off paths."

Miss Ward checked again to ensure she hadn't missed a casket. "If you didn't find his body, then how do you know . . . ?

Pete flashed a grim grin. "Spuds had mettle. But not enough to dig out his own bum knee."

Now Miss Ward recognized the object Pete held.

A prosthetic knee.

"However he died," Pete continued, "I suspect a gator ate up the tasty bits—and left this."

Nobody had cleaned the knee. Polychrome light from stained-glass windows brought tactile definition to an orange sheen of dried blood. Otherwise, it was pristine. If a gator had chewed this thing with its eighty teeth, it would be dented if not destroyed.

Miss Ward felt tears at the corners of her eyes. Jack had been right all along, even near the end when she'd been sure he'd lost his mind. She took off her glasses and used her inner elbow to hold her tears in place. If she cried in front of Pete Roosevelt, she'd never forgive herself.

Seen through her nearsighted eyes, the sanctuary acted like a bead of paint hit by the first drop of water: it diffused into abstract blobs of color. Miss Ward tried to ground herself with the nearest object, the framed photo. A brown horse-shaped oval behind a pale child-shaped oval.

Child-shaped.

What felt like cold, molten steel poured through her chest.

Jack O'Brien had been chosen to fight the Evil for a reason. Now Miss Ward saw the reason she had been chosen to take up his fight.

She fumbled her glasses back on and whirled toward Pete.

"Children," she stammered. "It's after children."

Pete wrinkled his forehead. "*It?*"

"Billy May. Pork Fat. Spuds."

"Spuds was twenty-seven."

Miss Ward pointed at the photo. "But he *looks* like a child. He *looks* like one."

Pete bristled. "He was born that way, lady. Wasn't his fault he—"

"If you were nearsighted like me, and looked at him, you'd think—"

"Lotta these old Cajuns have bad eyesight from Usher syndrome," Pete sighed. "But they're not gonna go stumbling around the—"

Miss Ward grabbed Pete's sleeve. She couldn't stop herself.

"There's a monster in our swamp killing children!"

The sandy buzz of church chatter hissed to halts. Miss Ward gazed across ten pews of faces. Alarmed. Confused. Appalled. Most of all, tired. Yet she felt no urge to apologize, no matter that she'd made the loudest sound of her life, with the possible exception of whatever noises she made after Doc told her Jack was dead. What was wrong with Pointers? Glued in place like fungus on deadwood, waiting for the ax to fall. Where were the urges to stand up? To save one another if not themselves? She inhaled, ready to yell again.

Pete was faster. With a twist of his wrist quick enough to attest to some actual policing skill, he broke her grip on his sleeve and cinched his big hand around her arm. He planted the Stetson and charged down the aisle, dragging her behind.

~ 45 ~

ON THE THUMB OF LAND between Bread of Life and a black gutter of bayou water, Pete released her. Miss Ward careened sideways and bashed through a gelatinous clump of sticky bladderwort. She went down on her side. Brown water jetted. Her right leg, hip, and shoulder went instantly wet. She growled and fought back to her feet, wringing out fabric.

Pete didn't appear to give a shit. He waved a sausage finger at the church.

"Spuds Ulene was as close to a saint as this dunghill ever saw! I won't have you wrecking the only peace he ever had!"

Miss Ward staggered forward.

"There's a reason you haven't turned up a single clue, Pete. And it's not just because you're stumbling around drunk."

Pete reddened.

"We're not set up for murder cases here. I'm bringing in help."

"Are you? I don't see any."

"I'll find that killer. Mark my words."

"Your record on finding killers is not encouraging."

Pete's face curdled. No swamp monster could be uglier.

"You don't know half what you think you know," he snarled.

"I know Jack was shot. In the chest. By one of those human killers you think are so easy to find. Except you didn't find that one either, did you? Or you did—and just didn't do anything about it."

Pete took a grizzly lurch forward, hands clawing at something invisible.

"What the hell do you know about keeping the peace? About weighin the grief and terror of one person versus another? Of holdin in your hand the ability to ruin only one life versus two or three? All due respect, Miss Ward, but you're a *school* teacher. I'm sorry you lost your beau. That's tragic. But the truth? You barely *know* tragedy. I'm damn *floatin* in it, woman."

Pete's laugh sounded half-wild. He slipped a hand inside his jacket and took out a small liquor bottle. Not even hiding it now. He took a swig and held out his arms to both sides as if luxuriating in a cool rain. If only they were so lucky.

"*I'm goddamn drownin in it!*" he bellowed.

Miss Ward felt chastened. Oh, she hated that. She crawled a hand to her left cheek and plumbed fury from the well of Raw Umber W550. Pete might know nuances she didn't, but that didn't bring sight back to blind eyes.

"You go ahead and drown, Pete. In the quick or the bottle— your choice. This whole town can go ahead and drown with you." She pointed at the naked swamp; it writhed and dripped summer dew as if pleased to be seen. "I'll be out there, hunting. If anybody in this town gave a damn about anybody else, they'd do the same. They'd keep track of what was going on. They'd keep track of *each other.*"

Pete put his hands on his hips and stared at the ground. All Miss Ward could see was the dent atop his cowboy hat.

"You go out there alone, it'll be your body I drag in next. Your body *parts.*"

"Don't be so sure. I'm neither a child nor as short as one."

Pete huffed angrily. "Look at you. Covered in mud. You can't keep upright on *land.*"

Miss Ward looked away. It was true, of course. She'd never had an ounce of Jack's coordination. It might well be her downfall in those twisted marshes.

"All the same," she said, to Pete but also herself. "I'm going out."

"At least tell me where you're gonna go. So your parts are easier to find."

Miss Ward stood straight. "I have Jack's things. His, you know . . . his alligator hunting equipment. I'll take his boat to the worst places I can find. And I'll call it out. It will answer me, Pete, because no one's had the courage to call it out since Jack."

"What words will you say, exactly?"

"That's not for you to know."

Pete slitted his eyes and shook his head.

"Too bad you didn't know Spuds. In this matter, you were two peas in a pod. He said the Point was like a tater with a brown spot nobody dug out yet. The Piper, he said."

Speaking of his dead friend appeared to sand Pete's edges. He looked hangdog now.

"I believe that's what it is," Miss Ward said softly.

"And that it's your job—the schoolteacher's job—to go get it."

Miss Ward heard the squish of footsteps before she realized she was the one on the move. She walked straight up to Pete Roosevelt. Stood inches before him. Had a notion to reach out to him, despite what he'd done, despite the liquor funk, and cradle his cheek, pink and abraded from shaving too hard for this funeral.

She didn't. A secret creek ran through this spot of swamp, and she and Pete stood on opposite banks. A smile, though? She could afford him that.

"I've been caring for the Point's children for twenty-five years. I won't abandon them now. Not when they need protecting more than ever. If that takes miracle thinking, so be it."

Pete looked resigned at last. Miss Ward brightened her smile, a gift he didn't deserve, but one she was willing to give in case it was the last time she saw him. For reasons that bedeviled her, Miss Ward wanted the ex-sheriff to remember her in a positive light. She wanted everybody to remember her in that light. All that was left was to paddle through the Spanish moss into the realm of the bald cypress, find the source of that light, and claim it.

~ 46 ~

PETE'S SKIN BAKED BESIDE THE WINDOW of the easternmost Dunkin' Donuts in Orleans Parish, dipping donut holes into black coffee and slurping them down. Pure sugar, but it none of it penetrated his brain. For that, he needed the occasional splash of whiskey, which he did, secretly at first, then out in the open. Everybody here wanted to do the same, staff included.

Parked outside the window was the Melbourne Queen. It took all Pete's fortitude to stay put, dunking and slurping, instead of retreating to the Crown Vicky, burning rubber back to the bayou, and kicking down every shanty door till he found his missing folk.

Instead, he had to sit here like a school kid and apologize. There weren't much in the world he liked less.

The door dinged and Detective Pat Wilkes bowlegged in like a gunslinger.

Same way, four years back, Pete bowlegged into Juicy Lucy's and saved Spuds.

"You," she said.

Pete plugged his face hole with a donut hole so he wouldn't get smart.

Wilkes swaggered forward like she had at the Texaco, jaw out to here, pushing down her belt. Leather squeaked like before. This time, though, there was no handcuff rattle or pistol clink. Pete squinted through whiskey-scented coffee steam. It was a regular belt. Wilkes wore the light blue shirt and dark blue pants of a copper, but it was costuming. Nothing in the way of badges, tags, patches, or radios. She planted her feet beside the booth.

"Had to call me *today*," Wilkes grumbled. "You know how to pick them."

"What's wrong with today?"

"You fucking with me? It's June 23."

"Yeah. I figure that's right."

"St. John's Eve?"

Pete shrugged. "Explains why Bob Fireman's Carnival is setting up in Chickapee Hollow. Drove by on the way out of the Point. I'm not real conversant in this particular holiday."

Wilkes groaned as she slid into the booth.

"You *are* aware this is New Orleans, right? Some folks call the holiday Midsommar. Others call it Summer Solstice. For voodoo sorts, it's St. John's Eve. Started in the 1830s by Marie Laveau. Tell me you've heard of Marie Laveau."

"Some kinda voodoo priestess, right?"

"Some kinda is right. I could barely get out of my house. We got a few thousand people decked out in white heading to Bayou St. John right now. Going to sing them some hymns. Do some dances. Have a head-washing ceremony. That's why I'm late."

Pete didn't know much about voodoo holidays, but he knew a half-lie when he heard one. A detective in flashing police lights didn't struggle to get through a crowd, St. John's Eve or not. When Pete gazed past the Melbourne Queen, he didn't see an official vehicle of any kind. He felt a wiggle of his old strut.

"You got canned," he guessed.

Wilkes ran her tongue over her teeth.

"Downsized. Ax drops, guess who they come for first?"

"I supposed you're gonna tell me *ladies*."

"Try *Black* ladies."

Pete smirked. "Nah, I'm good. Tried you, didn't I? Enough to scare me straight."

Wilkes came damn close to smiling at that.

"More specifically," Wilkes said, "Black ladies who waste too much time investigating 10-57s in some bullshit backwater."

"I got some good news for you, detective. We happen to be hirin down on the Point. Not officially, you understand. No pay, benefits, none of that mess. But anytime you get a hankerin to tromp the damp for our killer, you're more than welcome."

"That's the conclusion settled on? Two residents uproot from your charming little piece of heaven and suddenly we got a killer?"

"Three," Pete said. "And this time, we found a part. And not an old part like those ribs."

"What kind of part?"

"A knee."

Wilkes's scorn went steely. "Human remains. You got to report that shit."

Pete had gotten so used to the feel of the object in his pocket that he barely felt himself drive it to the tabletop with enough force to make fallen donut sugar leap. Spuds's prosthetic knee. He liked the heft of it. He liked the sound of it when it hit stuff. He even liked the skein of dried blood, no matter the hygienics of it.

Wilkes didn't appear to care for it. She eyed the knee, then Pete.

"You don't carry a bloody body part unless you're drunk."

Pete shaped a grin from lips that felt like cold clay.

"'I got a touch of a hangover, bureaucrat. Don't push me.'" He pointed at heaven. "Mr. John Wayne in *McLintock!*"

Wilkes raised her palms. "I don't waste time with alkies."

Pete pretended to hail the donut seller. "'None of that cow purge. Give us some whiskey.' *Rio Lobo*—John Wayne."

Wilkes started to get up from the booth.

Pete scrunched his face. The hell was he doing?

"Don't go," he pleaded. "I ain't drunk. I'm trying to get *outta* being drunk. It's not goin great. But it's a good cause, ain't it?"

Wilkes gave a thin-ice glare before easing herself down.

"I did that search I promised. That search that got me *fired.*"

Pete picked up his Stetson so he could tip it. "Apologies, ma'am."

"There's zero on the May boy. Nine years old, why should there be? Now, Mr. May has a rap sheet long as the Ouachita River. But it's nonviolent through and through, not so much as a thrown punch. Mrs. May's clean, of course."

"Oh, the ladies are always innocent." Pete pictured the mud-spattered Miss Ward.

"Trust me, when women reach their breaking point, they break hard. They don't just kill an asshole. They chop that asshole *up.* Make a Christmas tree out of his body parts. Use his dick for the star on top. Bitches get creative."

Pete shrugged. "Maybe our suspect's a bitch. What's happenin feels awful creative."

"Gillian Marie Le Blanc—who I guess folks called Pork Fat? I found something on her. The day after she disappeared, she was scheduled to audition for the Kessler School for the Arts. Kessler is big-time, Roosevelt. The head of music there was all aggrieved Pork Fat didn't show. A school like that? Would've changed that girl's life."

"You're startin to think like I'm thinkin."

Wilkes didn't look thrilled by that. "All I'm thinking is a girl doesn't drop off the planet on the biggest day of her life. She was in a band, right? Any chance of a jealous bandmate?"

Pete pushed his throbbing brain to think it through.

"Well, the time-honored way of quitting Zydeco Chowder is to die on stage at the end of a four-hour set. Look, detective, most of what I've been doin down there is establishin alibis. Pink Zoot's got a solid one. Blue Tuna Fish Jesus, Bottle-o'-Gin Jerry, Six A.M., Suck-Up, Bunny Rabbit—they all were together when Pork Fat disappeared."

Wilkes massaged her eyes. "That town's worse than Dog Patch."

Pete offered a weak smile. "This mean you're gonna help?"

Wilkes took herself a donut hole and stuffed it in her mouth hole. She frowned and chewed. Looked like she might take all day with it, too, like a cow with cud.

Pete held up his hands.

"Before you answer, let me speak. Me and you got off on a bad foot. That's my doing. I called you, not the other which-way. You got me fired up bad-mouthin the Duke like you did and I got spoutin fightin words, which I oughtn't of done. But bad-mouthin's a lady's prerogative. We gotta come together, us two. 'We water our horses at the same trough.'"

Wilkes swallowed the dough.

"You're too dumb to come up with a line that good," she said.

Pete sagged guiltily. "*Angel and the Badman*. John Wayne. Sorry, detective, the Duke's lines, they're dug in me deep."

Wilkes produced a toothpick and levered it between teeth with a force that made Pete wince. If this was a big-city intimidation tactic, it worked. Wilkes let go of the toothpick so it popped upward from her mouth like a silly cigarette. Just like that, the detective's glowering steel buffed to a pewter softness.

"Truth is, Roosevelt, that day at Texaco, I might have bull-dogged more than I should. It was a long-ass day. Didn't get home till eight, hadn't ate since breakfast. I fixed me a Cup of Noodles, kicked up my feet, turned on the tube . . . and there he was. Right on my screen. John Motherfucking Wayne."

Pete had been underwater since Spuds's death. Finally, a lure bright enough to bite at.

"No kidding? Which flick?"

"*The Cowboys*. I sat on my exhausted ass and watched something called *The Cowboys*."

Pete felt like his corpse had been plugged into a socket.

"'It's not how you're buried, it's how you're remembered,'" he said.

"Say what?"

"Best line in the movie." Pete was leaning over the table. "What'd you think? You like it?"

"Hell, no, I didn't like it! John Wayne cattle-drives with a bunch of little boys? Stupidest thing I ever saw. Only part I liked was when John Wayne kicked the bucket."

"You got lucky there. He died on-screen only nine times in 167 movies."

The toothpick was really getting gnashed now. "Few days later, same thing. Long day, Cup of Noodles, tube—and there that drawling old son-of-a-bitch was again."

Pete was delighted. "The Duke!"

"Something called *Red River* this time. I had not one goddamn reason to watch it. *JAG* was on over on CBS. And I love me some *JAG*."

Pete slapped the table. Utensils hopped.

"*Red River!* Shoot, movies don't get much better!"

"Another cattle drive. Except this time your Mr. Wayne's a full-on psychopath who tries to kill his own son."

"He loves his son, though," Pete insisted. "You can tell at the ending."

"The *ending*? You call that an *ending*? Sixty seconds of happy-crap tacked to the ass-end of a serial killer story!"

"Listen to you. You liked it!" Pete laughed. He actually laughed.

Wilkes spat the masticated toothpick. "I didn't say I liked shit."

"Saying you didn't like the ending means you liked the rest of it!"

"Who died and made you Siskel and Ebert? John Wayne, he's just . . . always on."

Pete puffed up his chest. "That's cuz John Wayne is America made flesh."

"Big and loud? Gun-crazy? Thinks he owns everything? That sounds like America, all right. I guess I haven't appreciated how this whole city is full of John Waynes. Lucky me."

Pete, though, felt dreamy. "One of these days, I'm gonna visit the house the Duke was born in. Little white house no bigger than this Dunkin'. Winterset, Iowa. Can you imagine how cold it is there? How dry? Just listen to that word—*Winterset*. If there's an opposite to Alligator Point, I bet that's it."

Chiseling winds blasting powdered snow across slate plains, wicking sweat from his skin for the first time in his life. Pete reveled in the fantasy. One day in Winterset and he'd be siphoned of a fifty-two-year stock of nasty-sugar. He'd be fifty pounds lighter. Not a care in the world. He'd walk out any door, like the Duke at the end of *The Searchers*, and not turn back, not ever.

When Pete looked again at Wilkes, she was pensive. Pete gave her the Duke's squint.

"You saw a third movie," he guessed.

Wilkes ran a finger through donut-hole sugar.

"This one was different. It was the day I got canned. Couldn't sleep. Had to be two a.m. when I turned on the tube. Some movie, didn't catch the title, but it looked safe. No cowboy hats, no horses getting tripped, no poor Indians getting shot up. Nothing but the open sea. Then there he was again, like one of those bad-penny criminals that keep coming up in this city. John Wayne in a captain's hat, standing on the deck of a ship. I could have kicked in the screen. But this movie . . . I don't know, Roosevelt. Made me wonder if I'd lost my nut. It pulled me right in. There were tropical islands, treasures, sunken ships . . ." Wilkes frowned. "Roosevelt, you okay?"

- 47 -

COLD IOWA WINDS SCOURED PETE'S BONES.

Pat Wilkes had seen but three of the Duke's 167 films. *The Cowboys* and *Red River* made sense. They were classics, film prints scratched and source tapes desaturated. But this third film? Pete could barely believe his ears. He picked up his cup to cover his shock. Coffee slopping over the rim ratted him out.

"*Wake of the Red Witch*," he managed.

Wilkes chuckled at his expression. "You look like that movie killed your mama."

Pete took a gulp of coffee. Tasted like motor oil. He swallowed it anyway. He could still smell the stale popcorn on the floor of the Liberty Theater. Mixed with the stink of cigarette smoke. And the slight gaminess of fresh blood.

"First John Wayne movie I ever saw," he stammered. "That's all."

"Who you talking to, Roosevelt? 'That's all' my ass."

Pete glugged more motor oil. He hadn't ever told nobody about it. Not even Spuds. Never saw the sense of it. A cheap way to buy somebody's sympathy was all it was. Now, though, he kept seeing a rerun in his mind, not of the Duke but of Miss Ward outside Bread of Life. Saying how they all had to start depending on one another, keeping track, if anything was going to get any better.

"My mama killed her pimp while I watched that movie."

There. He'd said it. He'd finally said it.

Pat gasped and drew back.

But she didn't hightail it through a side exit. The house lights didn't come up to reveal Pete was all alone. The corpse of Gee Putnam didn't break through the floorboards and try to drag him under. Donuts kept being peddled and Pete kept breathing—just a little harder was all. He felt his nasty-sugar drain from an invisible tap. He was half his old weight, and hadn't needed to travel to Winterset to lose it.

"Damn, Roosevelt," Wilkes said. "Is that a cold case that needs opened?"

Pete shook his head. "Lacombe. Outside our jurisdictions."

"Back when we had jurisdictions."

Pete smiled. How remarkable it felt to smile.

"You and me's probably the only folk left alive who've seen that movie," Pete said.

"That fight with the octopus? Tatatonga?"

"Tarutatu."

Wilkes whistled. "Pins and needles. And when Angelique died? I'm not the swooning type, Roosevelt, but her last words . . ."

"*This isn't the end,*" Pete quoted. "*It's the beginning.*"

Wilkes fanned her face. "I'll tell you *what.*"

"The Duke loved that movie. He might have won an Oscar for *True Grit.* But he named his company Batjac after the trading company in *Wake of the Red Witch.* What does that tell you?"

"It's got a magic, all right." Wilkes looked askance. "Still racist, though."

Pete frowned, but felt good regardless. "You still on that?"

"What were those island people supposed to be? Some kind of Polynesians? Except the ones with speaking roles. Looked like they had an awful lot of bronzer on. Just saying."

Pete felt he at least needed to act offended. He upended the Dunkin' cup. The motor-oil taste was on the wane. He considered another splash of whiskey before realizing he didn't need it. He stared through the window at the Melbourne Queen. *His* Melbourne Queen.

"My partner, Spuds, had this theory. Now, Spuds, good a man as he was, weren't the crispiest chip in the bag. But he was a damn fine observer, and I always told him, observin's the best skill a deputy can have. He saw so many folk drinkin themself dead, me included, he figured they were trying to outrun the Red Witch that would otherwise nab them. What they'd done, Spuds said, was what he called *wicked porkin*."

"Like gay stuff? See, now you're talking prejudiced like John Wayne again."

"Gopher shit. I don't care what parts folk poke into other folk. What Spuds was talkin about was . . . a kind of mass suicide, I guess. Like Pointers had done somethin bad a long ways back. And the bad they did got passed down in their blood through porkin. That's the wicked part. Rather than face up to that, they got to drinkin. Drinkin and dyin."

Wilkes looked at the metal knee. Either she'd known all along or figured it out just now.

"Spuds was your third 10-57. That's rough, Roosevelt."

Shrugging it off was what men like Pete did. Inside him, though, flowed lava. Wilkes looked like she knew it too. She folded her hands and looked outside. She gestured with her forehead and Pete looked. A Caucasian couple in white tunics and white headscarves walked hand-in-hand through the parking lot.

"Folks forget how much of New Orleans voodoo is based in trickery. The slaves who brought it here only *pretended* to worship

Christian saints. Each of those saints was a stand-in for the gods they actually believed in. Pretty good, right? Back then, the whites didn't let the Blacks gather in groups. Afraid of another revolution, like the one in Haiti. That's what made Marie Laveau's St. John's Eve so clever. They let her have her big parties because she was famous and let the whites come too. Rumor has it, it was a feint. Gather all the white folk in one spot so the real worship could take place deep in the swamp."

Wilkes raised an eyebrow at Pete.

"Always kinda wanted to see those swamps," she said.

Pete raised an eyebrow back. "That right?"

Wilkes laughed. "I guess we're bonded, Sheriff."

"*Longside*, Detective, is what we call it on the Point."

Pete felt a prick of boo-hoo crying and coughed it away. This blew donut sugar against the knee. It caught in the swirls of dry blood. Looked kind of pretty, like white hankies waved at a parade. Pete missed Spuds something fierce. If he'd ever found a way to pay his deputy, Spuds wouldn't have been trekking home from Juicy Lucy's that night. Pete didn't deserve another partner. Goll, though, the world had a funny way.

Maybe Miss Ward was right. Maybe it was time for miracle thoughts.

"I'm no sheriff, by the way, " Pete added. "Haven't been since '93."

"And I'm no detective," Wilkes replied. "Haven't been since sometime last week."

Pete grinned and stuck out his hand. "Call me Pete."

Wilkes shook it. "Howdy, Pete. I'm Pat."

"Howdy, Pat." Pete's grin hung in there. "What say we tootle off to the bayou and see if we can't scare us up a witch?"

~ 48 ~

GERARD WOKE UP ON ST. JOHN'S EVE to the aroma of Eggs Sardou. He sat up on the sofa. Peeled cat hair from his tongue. Staggered to the bathroom and pissed. Yawned and piled some of the eggs Mère had saved for him on a plate. Stood by the window and ate while he looked outside.

Mère sat in a plastic purple lawn chair. She wore a straw hat and sunglasses. Before her stood Pontiac and a kid named Cole from a few trailers down. Mère had matched the pair earlier in the week. They were both nine. Come fall, they'd attend the same school. But things were going compliqué. Pensacola was one giant suburb. Kids here hadn't gone barefoot a day in their lives.

From the looks of it, Cole had a grievance. He was crying and holding his elbow, even though there wasn't no blood and the elbow had probably quit hurting a while back. Gerard couldn't hear specifics, but Mère was clearly explaining to Pontiac how things worked in civilized society. Pontiac had her arms crossed tight as shoelaces and looked like she might pop Cole again just on principle.

Gerard smiled. Wistful, though. All Mère did anymore was explain. How a young lady ought to care for herself: soap, moisturizer, shampoo, conditioner. Pontiac accepted the soap, but squirted the moisturizer at Baron Samedi and said Mère didn't know fuck-damn about her hair. How to dress: skirts, fitted tops, things with frills and waists, things lacking sleeves. Pontiac said the outfits were straitjackets. How to use good manners. *Please* and *thank you* sounded insane coming from Pontiac. How to enjoy fancy foods, sleep on soft beds, make friends, and conform—just a little—so the first thing people noticed about you wasn't how good you were at catching mice with your bare hands.

Cole pointed at Pontiac. Pontiac pointed at a hole in the ground.

Gerard snickered. These holes were his fault. After his bedroom incarceration, he'd been filled with jittery energy. He'd realized he needed to dig. Like he'd dug in Alligator Point. He'd found a shovel, gone out after midnight to the weeds behind Mère's trailer, and started digging. Felt good. He hit his typical depth of three or four feet, turned around, and started over. He'd dug six holes by the time dawn light revealed Mère watching from the lawn chair. He'd expected to hear a chill in her voice, her son worse off than she thought. All she'd done was light a cigarette.

"Better fill those in. Park owner will have a fit."

He filled them in, dug more, filled those in too. Gradually the holes, empty and filled, spread around the trailer, making neighbors think Mère had adopted a relentless dog. They were good to trip on, and that's what Pontiac was claiming happened to Cole.

Mère, though, wasn't having it. She gestured for an apology. Pontiac obeyed through gritted teeth. She jabbed out her hand. Cole shook it. Mère beamed. *The old lady had a lot yet to learn about Pontiac*, Gerard thought. She wasn't the type of girl you could simply tell not to fall into holes. Pontiac had to fall into them and climb out herself before she'd learn.

The girl's faded, water-damaged log lay on a chair. Usually the sight of the ragged old thing made Gerard feel lousy but today he had reason for optimism. He'd asked Mère to buy Pontiac a new notebook and she had: bright red, spiral-bound, and college ruled—Pontiac would love those narrow lines. He'd hidden it in a drawer so he could present it special.

Gerard glanced outside. Pontiac and Cole were investigating a trash can under Mère's supervision. He picked up the battered log. Stiff pages crackled as he opened it and a wealth of detritus fell out: beach sand, a dragonhead leaf, foil from a stick of gum, a fortune-cookie fortune, and several pencil-lead points. Gerard smiled. Not too far a cry from a special marble. Kids made their luck from whatever was handy.

Gerard peeled apart two stuck-together pages. The top of the left page tracked the hourly activity of a raccoon out by Skunk Hole. Beneath was a list of Pointers whose shanties had ever caught fire. Next to that, a sketch of a tree with an octopus carving and a grid tracking how many pieces of mail the Pontiacs received in December 1997. At the top of the right page, a heavily under-lined question—*WHO IS LURLENE WILSON???*—followed by three potential answers: *1) Cleans for Fontaines, 2) May be dead, 3) Related to Lawton Tuthill?* Under that was a recipe for shrimp boulettes. Beside that, a sketch of the kind of crane that lords over offshore oil rigs.

The pages had sopped a lot of water. Now Gerard's tears as well.

Pontiac had insisted on the Greyhound she had unfinished business on the Point. But Gerard was the one with affairs to con-clude. He couldn't mooch off Mère forever. Not when the Oil Man was trading good money for bad land. Gerard had property to sell. Apologies to make. An address to give André Saphir. A long good-bye to bid at St. Vincent de Paul Cemetery #3.

He had to go back to the Point one last time. He knew it like a kick to de couilles.

But to take Pontiac with him? That'd be a crime.

The Point had gotten dangerous. The rogue tempête that had nearly stole Pontiac. All the missing folk, some trudging north with oil money, others plain disappearing. The odd things growing in the swamp like misbegotten births. The black bottles with myster-ies inside. The soft, lulling sounds coming from the night, which might be bad-dreaming, or memories of Janine, or something else come to collect a fee.

Gerard knew he'd be lucky to make it back to Pensacola alive. Too many ill elements against him, the worst of which were the familiar, seductive places he'd spent his last three years inside, lifting every glass that other folk, old friends holding up marbles, bought him. One drink and he'd be done for, for good.

Death would be worth it if his corpse fertilized Pontiac's growth.

Saphir would make sure his goddaughter got any Oil Man money she had coming, and anything else besides. Gerard figured, oui, Pontiac would mourn his passing. But not for long. She'd have more than she could handle here in Pensacola. The soaps, perfumes, and dresses Mère foisted upon her wouldn't stick, but other stuff would. When it came to fostering the kind of smarts evidenced by Pontiac's log, Pensacola soil was far richer than the Point's boue pourrie.

Folk would *notice* Pontiac when Spanish moss wasn't covering her up. Maybe at first it'd be because of her strange name, the way she spoke, the way she dressed. Pretty soon, though, they'd notice that *she* noticed. Noticed everything.

It unspooled before Gerard, a movie he never saw on a TV he never owned.

Pontiac's legs would shoot up like chickweed.

Cheekbones would push out of her pillowy face.

Maturity would leaven eyes that were as wide and sticky as spiderweb.

She'd grow tall enough to be seen and loud enough to be heard.

Having kept track of every wrong choice on the Point, she'd make good ones.

Nobody she ever linked up with would hold her reins. She was, and would forever be, the girl who tromped out to the Gulf coast with a fishing rod in the middle of the typhoon night without a trace of fear.

Gerard cried into his elbow, then scrubbed the elbow to clear his eyes. Pontiac and Cole were far down the road now. Mère was deep in complaint with an aggrieved neighbor.

He had all the time he needed.

Gerard started gathering his stuff. What stuff? Pants, a wallet. In the wallet, he tucked a fold of cash from Mère's not-so-secret stash, leaving a mea culpa that he needed it for bus fare and would pay it back. He put on his pants, felt the Brothers of the Spear in the pocket, considered leaving Dan-El and Natongo for Pontiac, then decided his girl was too smart for him to ignore her plea: *No, Daddy. You need them more than me.*

His last act was to imitate his daughter. He took up the wrinkled old log and slid it into the back of his waistband. He replaced it with the crisp red notebook. Inside the front cover, he scribbled another mea culpa. She'd be pissed he took her old log, but wouldn't be able to resist opening the new one and getting back to business.

~ 49 ~

OPERATING A G.P. REQUIRED EXPERTISE in scientific parlance, medical jargon, pharmaceutical patois, and insurance balderdash. Doc thought he knew his fine print. But the Oil Man's papers read like a cursed manuscript. Paragraphs on remuneration death-spiraled inside escrow mazes and subsidy labyrinths. Subsections on tax transactions referred to Notice of Transfer attachments that referred to schedules that referred to authorizations that referred to certifications that referred back to the original sub-section. Something called "the Termite Report" kept popping up. Compliance was demanded, only to be undercut by gentler-sounding "agreements," only to be socked in the jaw by boldface laws.

Doc glanced through his bifocals at the Mercantile's dusty shelves. The capes of cobweb over the comic-book spinner. The boxes of his most recent and final order, sitting untouched with no Pontiac to unpack them.

Would have been busywork anyway.

It was June 23. Half of Alligator Point had signed the Oil Man's papers. Come fall, the town's forty-seven shanties would hold but ghosts. Ghosts didn't buy snack cakes. The intricacies of the Oil Man's contract didn't much matter. Doc flipped to the last page, uncapped his pen, and put the moist, winking ballpoint upon the signature line.

He began, his palsied first loop mocking his age.

The clapper-less doorbell thwapped the door.

Doc looked up. Had to push up his bifocals and look again.

Miss Ward stood just inside the door, backlit by an iron dusk. Her white fists clenched and reclenched like she was taking her own blood pressure. Her cheeks pulsed with the grind of her jaw. She swayed like she was about to nose-dive. But Doc did not hustle around the counter to help her. His shock was too total.

It wasn't that Miss Ward was out in public, though that was startling.

It was that Miss Ward had gotten old.

Doc hadn't seen her face since, what was it? 1983? 1984? When he'd held her in that hospital with hands still red with Jack's blood, Miss Ward at her peak beauty because she was in love. Those weren't fourteen years of wrinkles on Miss Ward's face. Those were twenty-five, thirty, thirty-five, a hundred. The hair band she must have worn for teaching was not up to the task of extended time outdoors. Her hair was frizzy and glossed with sweat. Doc's physician eye saw a physique close to malnourished, elbows like billiard balls, clavicles like drumsticks, cheekbones like hatchets.

If Miss Ward was old, Doc was a fossil.

"Miss Ward," was all he could say. "Oh, Miss Ward."

"Doc," she said, and she pitched forward, waist striking the counter, arms angling over it, unsure of what they wanted. He scrabbled for her wrists as he had in the hospital, his knuckles crying out in arthritic ache. They were two skeletons fighting to see which one could be buried first.

Somehow they ended up beside the bread display, holding each other's arms, staring shyly through tears at each other's beaten faces. Miss Ward seemed as speechless as Doc felt. He forced a smile and gave her an up-and-down look.

Miss Ward wore a man's belt, the buckle's prong inserted into a punch hole she'd drilled far up the strap. Still, it sagged halfway down her left hip from the weight of a giant, wedge-shaped sugar-cane machete.

Doc had seen it before. Same with the Bowie knife strapped to Miss Ward's scrawny calf. The strap between her breasts, too, which across her back sleeved an old Remington 870.

"You can't," Doc pleaded.

"I am," Miss Ward replied.

"You'll die out there."

"Then I'll die."

Doc released her like she was covered with maggots. He caned past her, facing the door. He pounded a fist on the counter.

"Why tell me about it, then? So I can have another regret? Look at me. I'm too old to stop you. I'm too old to do anything."

"I need you to tell me where you found Jack. I'm picking up where he left off."

Doc laughed at the absurdity. Jack O'Brien might have been a skilled gator hunter, but he'd been certifiable to go swashbuckling into the swamp alone. Even worse, his madness hadn't died that night. He'd impregnated the town schoolteacher with it, and today was the day of delivery.

Doc had delivered plenty of babies. Plenty of stillborns too. And plenty of the third category, the ones nobody liked to talk about, the babies born with anencephaly, severe spina bifida, neural tube defects, hemoglobin disorders, and the deformities that seemed to flourish like invasive privet hedge down here: heads without skulls, hearts outside the chest, fetuses tapered to fleshy blobs by stronger twins who'd leeched their nutrients.

He'd never snuffed one out, not even when the mother begged.

Could he snuff this one?

"Are those the Oil Man's papers?" Miss Ward asked.

Doc looked at his fist. It had landed atop the contract. He lifted the fist. Its underside was smudged from the single letter he'd penned, like he'd smashed a juicy bug.

Miss Ward cleared her throat. "Did you see him?"

"See who?"

"The Oil Man. Did you actually *see* him?"

Doc hobbled a one-eighty and gave the teacher a squint.

"I got his papers, don't I?"

Miss Ward chewed her bottom lip.

Doc tapped his chest. "I *saw* him. I did. Down the path a ways, sure. Must have been a minute after he dropped these off. Black suit, black tie, shiny-ass black shoes."

"But his face? Did you see his face?"

Doc cocked his head. "Why the hell would I need to see his face?"

"It's just . . . I know people who've talked to him, and spotted him from afar. But no one who's actually looked him in the face."

"Suddenly you know a lot of people, do you? That's a new development."

Miss Ward stared at her feet, delicate canvas flats that wouldn't last an hour in the real-deal marsh. Doc gave himself an invisible lash. That was a cheap blow. What was wrong with him?

"Comes a time when fighting stops making sense," he sighed.

Miss Ward bowed her head. Doc didn't like it. Submission didn't fit a woman kit out to kill.

"I'm not the only one who was there that night," Doc grunted.

"Pete's drunk. He's also still got handcuffs. He's liable to lock me to a radiator."

Doc planted both hands atop his cane.

"You want me to send you off to your death, you better give me a good reason!"

Miss Ward sagged. Pontiac used to sag like that. When Doc told her no, he was not knocking a few bucks off the Whiz-Bang; no, she could not help herself to a roll of Wint-O-Green Life Savers; no, she could not call the chat line advertised in the back of one of the gentlemen's magazines he carried.

Pontiac always listened, though, and so did Miss Ward. She took a weary but courageous breath and, in a monotone that had to be opposite of how she spoke to students, unleashed a preposterous tale. That there was a capital-E Evil in the damp responsible for the Point's many plagues, from cancer, to drink, to despair, to the loss of Billy May, Pork Fat, and Spuds Ulene. Old-timers had kept this Evil reasonably at bay, but old-timers—like me, Doc thought—were running out. Hence Jack's forays to confront this Evil and kill it, or else discover which rituals had been forgotten and reinstate them.

Daylight had faded from Miss Ward by the time she'd finished. Doc was glad. He didn't relish being well-lit as he did the shameful act he planned to do next: lock the door and keep Miss Ward right here until he could get Pete Roosevelt to impound her till her suicidal plan had passed.

Doc caned toward the door as fast as he could.

"Doc!" Miss Ward cried. "Listen to me! You can't—"

The door banged open, striking against arthritic fingers. Doc stumbled, cane aslant, and grabbed the icebox to keep himself upright. A man stepped in, chased by blades of grass from a gale wind that hadn't been blowing twenty minutes ago. The man stunk of gasoline and sweat. Matted hair, wrinkled clothing, red eyes—and not the hangover-red Doc was using to seeing in those eyes. It looked more like the man had been reading in a moving vehicle all day, which, Doc was soon to find out, was exactly what he'd been doing.

The man held up a battered old notebook.

Doc's old heart throbbed. Pontiac's log.

"Dere's a monster in dis here playree," Gerard declared. "And accordin to what my girl wrote, you got some gatorskin books in de back dat might be de best chance we got."

~ 50 ~

DOC RIPPED THE SHEET FREE. It rippled away, a sail from a mast.

Miss Ward and Gerard Pontiac fanned aside clumps of dust. Doc, though, leaned into it. He hadn't laid eyes on the journals in sixteen years. The gingerbread brown of the bony scutes were silky beneath the room's bare bulbs, and the thick, brown-and-white stitching had a brutish beauty. Fifty journals, forty-nine of them filled, a compendium of everything Doc had kept track of during his twenty-six years with Emily.

"They're wonderful, Doc," Miss Ward said.

Doc stroked a volume. Man skin, gator skin, both crusted with age. He made a fist to hide his trembling fingers. Wonderful, were they? There were 163 asterisks in these journals that insisted otherwise. Doc forced a chuckle. Dust rolled out of the way.

"That girl of yours, Gerard, poked her snout into more holes than a puppy. I guess I'm kinda relieved she got herself an eyeful of these, even if she kept it secret."

"She wrote dey was pretty," Gerard whispered. "But I t'ink dey de prettiest t'ings I ever saw."

Doc stole a gander at Gerard as he gawked. Gerard Pontiac might not have Miss Ward's agoraphobic tendencies, but he wasn't habituated to asserting himself in company more sophisticated than the Point's most dedicated drinkers. To stand beneath the lights of the Mercantile and spout fantastical theories took a Miss Ward level of courage.

"Tell me what she wrote," Doc encouraged. "Exactly."

Gerard glanced shyly around.

"Ain't no *exactly* way of puttin it. I don't t'ink my girl had no idea what she was writin. How it all add up, I mean. Every soul dat died in da Point she's got wrote down. Not just durin her livin years eidder. She got it back twenty years if a day."

Doc patted gatorskin. "Between the two of us, we got the whole century covered."

"Yessir. My girl wrote you was keepin track long before she started. Wrote dat she wanted to be just like you, sir."

Doc let the words slug through his veins, slow like cholesterol. That lovely brat. Who gave as good as she got. Who'd been a daily pain in the ass to Doc, thank god, so he'd never had to admit how he loved her, that he wished she was his own grandkid and that Emily was alive so they could both encourage her to never change. Pontiac loved him back? Doc thumbed a tear. He hadn't figured another living soul would love his dusty skeleton ever again.

He felt pride. That long-lost swell of pride.

Hellfire. Time had come to make Pontiac proud of him as well.

"Pointers have been keeping track since Lafitte's day," he graveled. "Not always on paper, you understand. Lot of it was passed down mouth-to-ear. Oral traditions. Work songs. Hymns. Symbols, or buttons, or shells. Bedtime stories, stuff you tell kids they figure is make-believe till they grow up and the power of the story sinks deep, and they feel the truth of it way down in their bones."

Gerard paged through Pontiac's log. Looked to Doc like it had been dunked in the sea.

"I iddn't much a reader." Gerard glanced at the schoolteacher. "Çe me fait."

Miss Ward smiled. "It's like Doc says. Reading's only one way to pass knowledge."

"De whole bus home I read like I never done before, seein how it was my girl that done de writin, tu vois? De t'ing I wanted to show y'all, t'ough, it iddn't so much writin than picture-drawin."

The last page flipped with a sandpaper snick. Gerard held it up. Amid the persnickety penmanship Doc had come to love was a cluster of sketches. Both he and Miss Ward adjusted their glasses and leaned in.

"Are those octopuses?" Miss Ward asked.

"Oui," Gerard said. "Pieuvre."

Miss Ward frowned. "Pierre?"

"Pieuvre."

The sketches lost focus. Doc felt as if sinking into cold jelly.

Pieuvre. French for "octopus." The translation rang a bell broken for longer than the one on the Mercantile door. Doc started yanking volumes off the shelf. Several toppled to the bed below. Doc didn't stop. He threw open gatorskin covers, pipsqueak shrieks crying from each sleepy spine, and checked the dates on each opening page. Too old, too new, too old. He pitched the losers to the mattress. Bedspring squawked.

"Doc?" Miss Ward asked.

"I kept track of this. Round the time Emily and me repainted my waiting room. 1962, I think it was . . ."

Before the cliché of a doctor's handwriting took full hold, Doc's penmanship had been as orderly as Pontiac's. There were the words he wanted to see, printed at the top of a page.

"August 1962," he announced.

His knees gave out. Doc twisted so he sat hard onto the bed, his spine unhappy with the rough surface of two dozen hardcover journals. He chucked several to the floor with enough force that Miss Ward and Gerard had to double Dutch to dodge them. Doc licked a dry finger and started paging. He wouldn't need to lick a second finger. The investigative zeal of his youth, the audacity with which he'd gone tumbling into Alligator Point arcana, flooded his old veins, a vitalizing transfusion.

The moment he saw the first few words of it, the legend came back to him with the suddenness of a resurfaced dream.

Which it was, wasn't it? Hadn't youth been a dream? Hadn't love?

Make it real, he prayed. *Make it all real again.*

"Here." He tapped a page. "La Pieuvre. The Octopus."

Concern wrinkled Miss Ward's face, despite her weaponry.

"We have . . . octopuses in Alligator Point?"

"Hindus, Buddhists, and Ancient Greeks called them gods. Vodouisants called them lwa. None of them, I don't think, had claim over La Pieuvre. First mention I found was in the journals of Jean-Baptiste Le Moyne, the French governor who founded Nouvelle-Orléans. May 1720, he writes: *The sailors insist their boats were destroyed by an eight-limbed beast as big as the moon.* It goes further back. La Salle's 1682 expedition report: rumors of a, quote, 'octopus god' snatching traitors tossed overboard. 1542, an aid to De Soto writes of an entire encampment crushed in the arm of a gigantic octopus. The original people of this area were the Chitimacha, and archaeologists have recovered cypress canoes carved with the symbols that are in Pontiac's log. Circa 700 AD. And y'all thought *I* was old."

"Jack was chasing after . . ." Miss Ward looked dubious. ". . . an *octopus god*?"

Doc shrugged. "Something like? La Pieuvre was always represented with eight arms. Could be that's where the comparison started. In her eight hands were eight mirrors. Legend said she was so obsessed with her own beauty she became nearsighted."

Miss Ward touched her glasses. "That's what I thought at Spuds Ulene's funeral. If you couldn't see properly, you'd think he was a little boy. If something was trying to draw in children . . ."

"Drawin in." Gerard clucked his tongue. "Sounds an awful lot like de Piper."

"Pieuvre, Piper," Doc said. "One and the same."

"Why attack us?" Miss Ward asked.

Doc indicated his old writing.

"She's not attacking. She's *protecting*. La Pieuvre was a seducer, true. But she was also a fierce protector of those who sailed her seas. And an avenger for those who died there unjustly."

"But we're the ones dying," Miss Ward protested. "And we haven't done anything."

Gerard looked morosely at his daughter's log.

"I t'ought de same. For a long while I t'ought it. What we Pointers ever done to dis swamp but fish it? Hunt it? Try to keep one dry hummock for ourself? But de last pages Pontiac wrote in her log, dey about t'ings she charre wit' you, Doc. About dem pirates. About what dey done." Gerard shook his head. "Makes me sorry how I dug for t'eir gold. Any gold of t'eirs be cursed."

Miss Ward wobbled. Doc started in alarm, but Gerard already had an arm out to steady her. The teacher pressed her palm to her temple. Beset, Doc knew, by the ache of the truth.

"It's not what we did," she said softly. "It's our ancestors. Those pirates."

Doc stared at the opposite wall, imaging the Gulf beyond.

"Whole lotta Lafitte slaves died in our waters."

Miss Ward frowned. Doc sympathized with her resistance. She'd put all her stock in the mission Jack O'Brien had undertaken, believed in the monster he'd been sure he was chasing. It was a hard turn to take, learning the monster was you.

"All the Pointers who've died, in Pontiac's logs, in your journals," Miss Ward said. "They were taken *slow*. Over years. Over decades. So slow you wouldn't pick up on anything unless you were keeping track."

"Folk dyin faster now," Gerard said.

"I got a notion why," Doc said, displaying the ink smudge on the bottom of his fist.

"What does the Oil Man have to do with this?"

Gerard spat at the name. Doc grunted at the rudeness, and Gerard, a swamp rat through and through, wiped the spit up with his shoe, which only, of course, spread it around. Doc sighed and gave his guests a heavy look.

"You gotta look at the situation like you're a god, a lwa, some kinda ageless thing. There's this place you don't like, see? Place called Alligator Point. Populated by folk descended from pirates who filled the sea, *your* sea, with innocent bodies. So you whip yourself up a plan to get back at them. Hurt them. Over multiple generations, even, cuz it isn't like the evil they did stopped short. No, sir. It reverberated. They kept venerating their pirates, giving places their names, waving flags with skulls and crossbones. Cancer's a good choice if you're playing a long game like La Pieuvre. Comes slow. Kills slow. Lotta suffering along the way. Then one day you wake up and everybody, and I mean *everybody* in Alligator Point's signing contracts and hightailing inland, out of your reach. Suddenly cancer's too slow. Suddenly you need to kill a whole lot faster."

Both Miss Ward and Gerard tried to squash their emotions but Doc knew what despair looked like better than most. He'd seen it in the mirror since the day of Emily's diagnosis. As if to cover it, Miss Ward quickly picked a volume from the shelf.

This was different. It was sealed with duct tape inside a water-tight bag. The fiftieth journal, the one Doc had never gotten around to, which he'd kept safe for reasons that depressed him. The pitiful chance that someday he might return to keeping track, and when he did, the bagged volume would be waiting. Miss Ward ran her fingertips over the plastic.

"You said the old-timers used to pay homage to La Pieuvre," she said softly. "Maybe that's what you were doing. What Pontiac is doing. Keeping track honors the dead, maybe. Maybe helped keep La Pieuvre at bay. For a time."

"Did I do bad movin my girl away?" Gerard sounded panicked. "Was she de only t'ing keepin dat octopus from—"

Into the group's silence yowled a tempest, followed by the rubbery creaks of pinwheeling branches. Wood popped inside the Mercantile's decaying walls. Shingles peeled from the roof with a rasp like serpents over concrete. Rain opened up as if from a turned faucet, pounding timpanis against windows. Didn't seem to matter which way a window faced either. The storm was coming from all directions at once.

The lights blinked out. Then fluttered back on.

All three Pointers rolled their eyes toward the cracking roof beams.

A tree branch, or something worse, shouldered into the store's north side, a snap like the detaching of worlds. Doc leapt from the bed and in the fluxing light tangled with his cane and tripped. Gerard snagged his torso and kept moving, and with his other hand pulled Miss Ward with them. The trio nearly went down as one, but a surprising strength persisted in Gerard's wiry muscles.

Small objects pelted the south wall. Sticks? Rocks? Hail? Birds?

"I know dat sound." Gerard sounded scared. "Marbles."

Doc: "Huh?"

"All de marbles my papa dumped. It spittin dem back out."

The corner by the bed shook and groaned. Boards buckled inward. Paint flaked. Nails ejected. The lights went out, on, out, on.

"She's moving faster," Miss Ward gasped.

"She knows we know," Doc hiccupped.

"St. John's Eve," Gerard muttered. "Dis would be de night it all happen."

A leathery slither as Miss Ward unsheathed Jack's machete.

Doc and Gerard exchanged glances. Miss Ward noticed and nodded.

Doc took Jack's shotgun. Gerard took Jack's Bowie knife.

The three of them held the weapons like the folk they were: strangers to any objects in their grip but a price-tag gun, a piece of chalk, a bottle of liquor. Doc looked at the shotgun, so cold and strange in his hands, and old words drifted back to him.

"*Shoot your shot,*" he said.

The store shook and shrieked.

Miss Ward glanced at him. "What?"

"Jack's last words. I'm sorry I never told you."

The lights strobed, a flip-book by candlelight.

"Shoot your shot?" Gerard sounded like he'd heard it before. "*Shoot your shot?*"

A window exploded out in the main room. Then a second, a third.

"We should call Pete Roosevelt," Doc managed.

"Pete doesn't believe in this," Miss Ward hissed. "In anything."

"When something bad's on its way, you tell the sheriff," Doc insisted. "And now, before we lose the telephone too."

~ 51 ~

"PETE! TELEPHONE!"

If you'd asked Pete in years past if it was the liquor or the company that kept him visiting the Pelican, he'd have spat his liquor in hilarity, then probably licked the liquor back off the bar top, because the answer, you dumb-ass, was *the liquor*. Now he weren't sure. Gerard Pontiac, one the hardest drinkers on the Point, had left town, so the barflies said. Must have signed the Oil Man's papers, scrounged up that girl of his, and headed for higher land.

Felt like the end of an era—the final era. Without the good-hearted raised marbles inspired by Gerard's presence, drinking felt, well, dry. Back in the day, Pete had all sorts of drinking buddies: Firmin Polycarp, Hortense Ewell, Boudreaux Boudreaux. But throat cancer had fixed it so Firmin couldn't drink, a fate worse than death for Firmin until actual death, which came a three gnarly years later. It was liver cancer that torpedoed Hortense; Pete wished he could forget watching Hortense down a shot, then gibber in horror at how the shot glass had refilled with his own blood. And Double-B? Pete never found out what kind of tumors were inside Double-B. All he knew was that he and Spuds had cut him down from a suicide noose outside his shanty.

Stand-up fellows, the whole lot. But Gerard had been the sun they'd circled.

Or the black hole.

"Sheriff! Phone!"

At Pete's elbows tonight were Pink Zoot, melancholy since the loss of Pork Fat, and Gully Jimson, so low on teeth that most his well whiskey spilled down his chin. This unappetizing view of his future made Pete's reflection the best company left. And sorry-ass company it was. Could be the curvature of the beer glass that made him look like he did. But could be that his crime-fighting days were kaput. His jowls drooped. Gin blossoms germinated on his nose. He no longer bore much resemblance to the Duke. The Duke near the end, maybe. The Duke when there weren't nobody left to lose to but the Red Witch.

Only thing of value Pete had left was his signature. With his left hand, he threw back some swill. With his right hand, he withdrew the Oil Man's papers from his jacket, slapped them to the wet tabletop, and tried to smooth the wrinkles. As luck would have it, he had a pen in that pocket too. He flicked the plastic cap with a thumb and it rocketed off behind the bar, lost in a tabernacle of labeled bottles.

He blinked his blurry eyes and searched the contract for a horizontal line.

What else was he supposed to do? Plod back to his Airstream? Fetch *The Shootist* from his fancy cigar box, pop it in, and try not to think about Spuds? Or how about Pat Wilkes? He and the ex-cop had spent the day barging into shanties and scouring them for any trace of the missing Pointers.

The only shit they'd found was more empty shanties than Pete expected. The Point was past resuscitation. The Oil Man had won. Pete had swung the Melbourne Queen into the Pelican lot and lied to Wilkes that he had a probing question to ask Moses Goingback. Instead, he'd tipped his Stetson to Moses, plopped down at the bar, and asked Wilkes to pick her poison. Her eyes, flaming all day, had dimmed back into her old, distrustful glower.

"I'll be in the car," she'd said. "Come back when you pull your head out of your ass."

Gonna be a long wait. Pete's head was in and staying in. Half the folk whose doors he'd kicked in today were at the bar with him. They knew there weren't no sense in grudges when you were all going down together. They probably had Oil Man contracts in their pockets too. Pete would pass his pen once he was finished.

Pete started signing.

A big golden hand slapped down in his pen's path.

Pete glared upward. Booze always shortened his fuse. It was Moses, gray ponytail pulling back his hair so he looked as severe as ever. Sober as ever, too. Word had it Moses had never sampled the draff he served, a fortitude that made Pete feel like a slug. Moses held out the wall phone's handset, the spiral cord stretched taut. Pete gestured at his contract.

"Can't you see I'm busy?"

"Can't you see *I'm* busy?" Moses's flat tone bashed through the bar's clacks and splatters. "They keep calling. Tying up my line."

Pete scrubbed his bleary face. First thing he was doing when he got done here was frisbee-ing his hat into the swamp. His belt and boots after that. Maybe roll the Melbourne Queen into Bayou Lafourche. Anything that made folk think he was still sheriffing had to go. For now, Pete couldn't piss off the person serving him the sloshing he needed. He snatched the receiver.

"What."

"I knew you'd be at a bar," a voice replied.

A call from his black subconscious. Pete only identified Miss Ward's tone of sharp disgust because of their face-off at Bread of Life. Least that's what he told himself. It was no fun admitting he'd never forget Miss Ward ordering him out of Jack O'Brien's funeral service.

"I'll tell the Saloon Committee," Pete snipped. "They'll work you up an award."

"I need you sober. We all need you sober right now."

Pete grinned. There was a certain kind of fun to giving up hope.

"Lady, I'm fixing to sign me a contract right now. Reap me some of those American spoils I've always heard about. Buy my Airstream a few new tires, hitch it up, drive my ass all the way to Winterset, Iowa. How's that grab you?"

"Don't sign, Pete. The Oil Man, he's not . . . I don't know what he is but—"

"Mighty kind of you, Miss Ward, for the financial consult, and after business hours, no less. But not all us swamp rats inherited daddy's shrimp-boat fortune. We gotta take our payouts where we—"

"Shoot your shot," Miss Ward interrupted.

Pete frowned. "Wuzzat?"

"*Shoot your shot.* Does that mean anything to you?"

Pete's flippancy sizzled off. Yesterday, Miss Ward had worn a slash of paint on her cheek. Had shouted, *There's a monster in that swamp killing children!* Had, in general, behaved nothing like the teetotaling milquetoast Pointers had taken for granted for a quarter century. Maybe she'd gotten into some nasty-sugar. Or plumb lost her mind. Loads of potential reasons: grief, isolation, the psychic upset of losing the school.

"Law enforcement don't shoot *any* shots if we can help it," Pete said carefully.

"*Shoot your shot.* Jack had one leg through death's door when he said it. It's a message, Pete."

Blood congealed by too many meals fried in cajun spices throbbed in Pete's temple. Unfair. The hard part of drinking weren't scheduled to come till morning.

"Here's your message, Miss Ward: go home. Jack didn't talk to you from no magical realm. He was just a good man who made a bad decision. That's it. That's all. He shot *his* shot, Miss Ward. And now it's you who's gotta live with it."

The line crackled. The line buzzed.

"Hello?" Pete checked.

Through snarling static, Miss Ward's voice was cold and controlled.

"A swamp god called La Pieuvre—the Octopus—intends to stamp out the Lafitte bloodline. It's going after our children. It's going after them *tonight*, Pete."

Pete did something he'd never seen outside movies. He held the phone in front of his eyes and stared at it, like the hardware had gone haywire. No way could Miss Ward have gone so batshit so fast. He brought the phone back to his ear.

"I'm hanging up, Miss Ward."

"You've heard this before. Think, Pete."

"Good night, Miss Ward."

"*Think.*"

Pete dealt with lots of nutcases. If he hung up, Miss Ward would call back, pissing off Moses and delaying Pete's plan to drink himself stupid. He started winding his hand in the phone cord in order to yank it clean from the wall. Tipsy, it took a few bumbling seconds, long enough for Pete to do what every schoolkid on the Point did: obey their teacher.

Think, Pete.

Spuds's voice drifted back, insightful in its way. *What I'm saying, Pete, is it might look like it's just Pointers doing evil to other Pointers. But we ain't evil folk. I know we ain't.* Pink Zoot said much the same. *You know how it watch from de water, Pete. Lookin like a cottonmouth head, bout eight inch tall. Deep under, t'ough, it eight feet. Squeezin what left of folk down it t'roat.* William May Sr. knew it too: *Dat t'ing out dere, it finished hidin, Pete. It creepin out of de damp, Spuds. You start talkin bout it like you two talkin bout it, it disposed to start talkin back. And you know what happen after it start talkin. Folk start* followin.

What if Pete was the last one holding the door shut against the truth?

"Miss Ward," he croaked. "Where are—"

Miss Ward screamed.

And the Pelican went as black as grave dirt.

The overhead lamps cut out hard, the strands of holiday lights faded quick, the register glow snuffed, and the beer signs cooled their neons to black. The jukebox cut out mid-banjo breakdown, a shock of silence before everybody in the bar inhaled at once. A hard pop cracked from the phone receiver Pete held, and that was it, no dial tone, nothing.

Blinded drinkers put down their glasses, a horse stampede worth of hard clops. Pete let go of the phone and its cord slung away to death-rattle along the floor. Out of nowhere, a vast chain mail of rain sideswiped the Pelican. Pete swiveled on his stool in time to see an entire vascular system of lightning thread the sky through the windows, burning his retinas in cold white light—

—and glinting across the wet face of Pat Wilkes.

Pete gasped. "Jesus, lady!"

Lightning died, Wilkes vanished. Her voice remained.

"This storm came out of nowhere!" she cried.

Pete started to swivel back to the bar. "This ain't the weather complaint department."

Wilkes grabbed his shoulder, spun him back.

"This *storm* dumped on your rust-bucket like a wheelbarrow of cement!"

Pete's senses sharpened. "The Melbourne Queen okay?"

"She's *not* okay! No vehicle out there is okay! You see what I look like?"

The swamp saw fit to spike another trident of lightning into the Point. Wilkes lit up again. Face beaded with rain, hair half-flattened, clothing slicked to her skin. Pete tried to dig himself from nasty-sugar quicksand.

"The rain . . . broke . . . the windshield?"

"That stuff I said about Marie Laveau and St. John's Eve? How the real shit went down in the swamp? I'm starting to believe it, Roosevelt. What's going on out there isn't weather. It isn't any kind of weather at all!"

"Not . . . weather?"

"More like a—I don't know—a tentacle. A big, fat tentacle of water coming off the Gulf and smashing a bunch of cars it didn't want going anywhere."

Pete felt detached. Had Miss Ward said something about a tentacle?

"La Pieuvre," he said.

"The Octopus," Wilkes translated.

"How'd you know that?"

"Salade de pieuvre grillée." Wilkes's silhouette shrugged. "I like French food."

Pete sniffed dismissively. "Just something a crazy lady told me."

"*I'm* a crazy lady at this point. What'd she say?"

Pete kicked the bar's foot rail, an obstinate child.

"I don't know. Some swamp god? Fixing to kill all our kids tonight?"

Moses Goingback was lighting candles. Pete didn't approve. Gave the cozy environs the flickering threat of a prehistoric cave.

"That does sound crazy," Wilkes admitted. "It's not like all y'all's kids are in the same place or anything."

Oh, Pete hated hearing that. Hated it. He booted the rail again.

"Well."

Wilkes's shoulders tightened again. "Well, *what*?"

Kicked the rail harder.

"*What*, Roosevelt?"

One last kick and the old rail snapped from its brass post.

"That carny we drove past," Pete snapped. "Bob Fireman's."

"What about it?"

"Every kid in town is there," Pete grunted.

Wilkes took a fistful of Pete's jacket. Felt like a punch.

"Up," the detective said. "We're going."

Pete steamed. Even with no badge, this was his bayou. He didn't take orders from nobody in Alligator Point.

"I ain't goin nowhere but back to the tap. Barkeep!"

Wilkes's fist tightened. "Up, Roosevelt."

"'I'll just take a ginger beer,'" Pete chuckled in a bad accent, his favorite line from *The Long Voyage Home*, John Wayne young and handsome, straight off of *Stagecoach*, playing a lightweight Swede sailor innocent of the inside of a bottle.

His ribs rammed into the bar. Empty glasses overturned and rolled in tight arcs.

Now *that* was a punch! Right into shoulder blade! If it weren't so dark, folk would notice and intervene, toss this copper into the deluge. Wouldn't they? Drinking buddies were still buddies, right? They didn't just come here so they wouldn't have to die alone, did they?

A second punch, this one to the arm. Pete guarded his face, the likely next target.

"Daggonnit, lady!"

"We're not done yet, Roosevelt!"

"We busted into every shanty on the Point!"

"You asked me to help! I'm trying, Roosevelt! I'm trying!"

"You think draggin me into a monsoon is gonna help?"

"I do, in fact, think it."

Pete looked over his smarting shoulder. Lots of candles now, jack-o'-lantern flames glissading across the cop's dark skin. She'd kindled herself a fire no rain could dampen. Pete pictured himself out there. The silver shelves of rain. The cold water down his throat. He might drown. He might be cleansed. He might rediscover what had gotten him into sheriffing in the first place, his hope of correcting the injustice of his upbringing by bringing justice to others. It didn't matter if Miss Ward was crazy, if there were children to be saved tonight or not. Rushing off to Bob Fireman's right now might save *him*. If he lived, others might live, too, for little while longer, even if the Red Witch caught up to them one day down the long, marshy road.

"How long does it take to get to Dawes?" Wilkes asked.

"Eight-minute drive."

"Roosevelt. *Pete.* You need to believe what I said about your car."

Pete heard his name. Blinked. Woke up some more.

"Forty-minute walk. Most folk, they walk."

Wilkes struck him again, twice. Pete winced. But they weren't punches. They were two handfuls of his jacket—what strength this women held in her arms and hips. She hoisted the nearly three-hundred-pound sheriff like no one had before. Abraham's shit. This lady was truly longside him, and he longside her. The Pelican's candles were inside him now, flickering hot.

Pete moved to gather the Oil Man's contract, then chose to let it bloat in spilled spirits.

"Let's go," Pete and Pat said at once.

* * *

~ 52 ~

RIGHT BEFORE PONTIAC REACHED THE high lip of Chickapee Hollow, the swamp funk of damp moss, muddy algae, bat guano, and stagnant sulfur was overrun by a rolling fog of sugar: funnel cakes, kettle corn, cotton candy, deep-fried everything.

Shit-balls. St. John's Eve. Pontiac cussed herself out. Two weeks in Florida was all it had taken for her to forget her homeland rhythms.

The squiggly trail to her shanty, and hopefully Daddy, was through the hog guzzle off to the right. Straight below her, though, was a temptation no nine-year-old could resist, a pyrotechnic galaxy of colored lights wheeling, rocking, and leaping in every direction. Bob Fireman's Wagon Wheel Carnival snagged her better than the Whiz-Bang could have snagged anything. To be caught thrilled her, then scared as she realized she had unfinished business.

The Chamber of Dragons.

She couldn't help the Point if she didn't first conquer her fears.

Pontiac hurried down the gentle grade. The fluttering of her embarrassing flower-patterned skirt put her undies at constant threat of being flashed, but the dress *was* nice and cool—Mère had been right about that. For the sort of heroics Pontiac was hoping to execute, however, the getup was impractical.

She hadn't had time to change into anything better. Directly after finding the note Daddy left in the new red notebook, the note talking about being brave and doing what was right even if it didn't benefit you personally, Pontiac knew she had to give chase, if only to show Daddy she'd been this brave all along.

Also to get her fuck-damn log back!

Pontiac had gotten her chance thirty minutes later, when Mère tootled off in her car to pick up a bucket of chicken, leaving Pontiac with Cole. Pontiac liked Cole okay. But he was no Billy May. No Saphir. No Doc. Pontiac used the oldest trick in the book, hide-and-seek, to fool Cole into sprinting away. Pontiac dashed inside Mère's trailer, no time to dump the dress, pocketed Billy May Part II, and opened the hidden stash Mère was so terrible at hiding. There she found a note Daddy had left saying he'd borrowed money. Runs in the family, Pontiac figured. She grabbed some cash and added three words of her own.

ME TOO! PONTIAC

She hadn't wanted to keep track in the red notebook. It offended her sense of closure with her original log. But a second bus ride through four states was an opportunity her scribbling fingers couldn't deny. She filled seven pages with observations before the Greyhound reached New Orleans and nighttime descended.

Pontiac passed under Bob Fireman's archway. She smelled the blue raspberry Sno Balls she and Billy May had favored, accented by the rubbery odor of balloons. There it was, the wall of balloons no dart could pop. The basketball hoop with a rim too small to sink a basket. The shooting gallery with wonky guns. The dunk tank with the howling clown. The Coke bottles you tried to throw rings around. If you did, did the zombi astrals within fly free?

Her old nemesis drew her past the whole mess.

There it stood. The gray panel truck. The wooden stairs with the octopus carved into the lowest step. The metal stool. The demon in the red mask fanning himself with wrinkled bills.

"You," Pontiac said.

The demon nodded. "Hiya, pumpkin."

"I'm nobody's pumpkin."

The demon's white-circled mouth couldn't move, yet somehow smiled.

"That's right. You're the one named after the automobile."

Pontiac tried to slide her new log into the traditional spot at the back of her jeans. But there were no jeans. She had to hold the log at her side, her other hand making a humiliated fist. The demon quaked in silent laughter. Red paint flaked off the mask. The papier-mâché beneath looked like dry mummy.

"Six bucks," the demon said.

"Last time it was five," Pontiac protested.

"Things cost more when you're older."

"I don't turn ten till September."

The demon chuckled. Eyes hollow.

"You're older, all right."

The dress had pockets, at least. Pontiac reached past Billy May Part II for her cash.

"I got three," she said.

The demon tapped a long, dirty finger against a red chin.

"One dollar off for being named after a car."

"I'm not afraid of you," Pontiac warned.

"One dollar off for wearing a pretty dress."

"Take that mask off if you're so tough."

"One dollar off for fainting in the Chamber last time."

Pontiac glared. He remembered that, did he? Luck alone had kept anyone Pontiac knew from finding out about it. Pressure vised down tight. If she fainted a second time . . . if the demon had to drag her out again . . . the truth would get out to anybody left who mattered. She couldn't imagine responding to that disgrace by doing anything but turning tail back to Pensacola.

She handed over all the cash she had.

The demon took the three singles, rolled them into the shape of a cigarette, and inserted it through the hole in his mask. It vanished into the black. The brittle newspaper pulp of the mask expanded, ancient paste crumbling, like jaws beneath were chewing. The demon's throat bulged with a swallow. Pontiac goggled in disbelief. The demon held up a finger for Pontiac to wait. Seconds later, a small piece of paper emitted from the mouth's black hole.

A ticket. The demon pinched it with his fingers and held it out to Pontiac.

Shit-balls. Fuck-damn. Hellfire. Skunk.

Pontiac took the ticket. It was as hot as a stovetop.

The demon, always so thick and hunched, stood and, joint by joint, unfolded a body of shocking height and thinness. It was horrific, the kind of metamorphosis Miss Ward taught in science lessons. The demon, willowy now, bowed like a regal gent and gestured toward the Chamber of Dragons. Pontiac scrambled up the steps, gripped the door handle, and threw a look back.

From the higher angle, Pontiac could see the demon's outfit.

Black suit. Black tie. Shoes blacker than both.

Pontiac didn't know what these details meant. Or who the demon really was. All she knew was she had to escape his blacker-than-black eyes, deeper than any treasure pits her daddy ever dug, and that meant opening the door to the Chamber of Dragons and stepping inside.

* * *

~ 53 ~

THE CALL ENDED WHEN THE phone was torn from Miss Ward's hands.

When the front counter of Doc's Mercantile was ripped into the sky.

Even constrained to the school, her apartment, and the walk between, Miss Ward knew a vastness of Barataria Bay noises. But no bloop, squirt, dribble, sprinkle, spray, warble, splash, plop, trill, whoosh, drizzle, croak, whistle, flap, babble, groan, grunt, snort, blurt, chatter, growl, gulp, squeal, mutter, clap, whoosh, crunch, swish, gasp, cheep, bray, tweet, ribbit, buzz, purr, cluck, howl, screech, hiss, twang, whine, sputter, scrape, roar, sniff, rattle, honk, fizz, slurp, or whimper prepared her for the bone shake and eardrum pierce of every piece of wood, metal, plaster, and shingle of the store's north side hurling into the sky.

Miss Ward gripped the nearest object, an ice-cream cooler. She caught the blurs of Doc and Gerard diving from the soaring obliteration and taking hold of the candy rack, the coffee island. Miss Ward watched the men's hips and legs lift off the floor, sucked skyward by whatever was inhaling the store, before she realized her back half was floating too. She may or may not have screamed; there was nothing to hear but the undoing of the world.

Bags of chips, cardboard cups, jugs of spilling detergent, a flock of paperwork including the Oil Man's contract, it all swirled up into the vortex. Miss Ward's legs, though, touched down, a hesitant return of gravity. Keeping a hold of the cooler, she squinted through the downpour and saw Doc and Gerard still existed. Rain was falling into the store as hard as rocks. And so were marbles, just as Gerard had said, a busted solar system of tiny, bright planets coming down, a blue one striking Doc's bald head and drawing blood, a gold one hitting Gerard's thumb with enough force to splinter the nail.

Miss Ward hinged her neck up into the deluge, praying to avoid marbles to the eyes, and looked through a halo of her own whipping hair out of the opened roof.

She expected to see a tornado.

What she saw resembled a single wave isolated from its ocean. Miss Ward taught her students about weather, pedestrian and extreme, and knew tsunamis regularly exceeded the height of houses. This one was beyond the fifty-one-story One Shell Square in New Orleans. Here was a skyscraper in the marsh, dizzying to behold, blotting out a huge swatch of twinkling stars, the topmost curl so distant it would be invisible if not for the glow of the moon.

Doc's Mercantile, and everything and everybody inside it, would be annihilated, the remnants flooded toward inland levees. But a wave that tall might take a full minute to land. Miss Ward and her oddfellows should have enough time to tabulate their regrets.

It didn't take her long. She only came up with one.

Not stopping Jack. They'd misunderstood the thing in the swamp all along.

Miss Ward slopped wet hair from her eyes. The marbles and rain kept falling but the wave did not. It dipped slightly, curved slightly, turned slightly, as if it curious about the three fleshy ants wiggling below. Miss Ward shielded her eyes from rain bullets and examined the colossus.

Made of water, yes. But it was not a wave.

La Pieuvre. The Octopus.

It was a tentacle.

The tentacle undulated lower. Its perceived size swelled, first the width of a semi-truck, then of an interstate highway, then Miss

Ward stopped trying to comprehend and let the cosmic impossibility overwhelm her. As the tentacle dipped, Miss Ward saw that it held something. Though the dimensions of a basketball court, it was razor thin, invisible seen from the side. Its ovoid shape recalled the palette Miss Ward wore on her left hand while painting. Like her palette was a bouquet of colors dabbed over decades, this object, too, held depths of shimmering tints, all the rainbows of an oil slick.

Perhaps La Pieuvre was a painter of worlds.

But if La Pieuvre was anything like Miss Ward, it would throw away paintings that it no longer had room for, in either its home or its heart. Alligator Point might be just such a painting.

Inside the flat object, Miss Ward saw the reflected innards of the Mercantile and the mesmerized faces of Doc, Gerard, and herself. A mirror—Doc had said La Pieuvre was always depicted holding mirrors. Miss Ward had the dreadful thought that there might be seven more of these tentacles draped over the Point, each one holding a copy of this thing—not a mirror as humans understood it, but a item with parallel properties.

The tentacle's tip, thick as the store itself, curled above the destroyed roof. Each drip of ocean water that slid from it was a waterfall with enough force to flatten food racks and snap floorboards. The tentacle swayed as if observing, like Doc used to observe, like Pontiac still did. Surface tension was its skin, and it rippled in concentric rings. Miss Ward trembled beneath a great, lowering shadow. Deepwater cold: her exposed skin raced into goosebumps.

She looked away, down at her clasped hands. Rain fell from her face.

A liquified bead of Raw Umber W550 dropped onto her hand.

Jack had been wrongheaded in his hunt for this being. But he never would have bowed before it. Miss Ward fumbled his machete from its sheath and tossed it away. She began an attempt to stand. Juddering knees, slippery floor, loose marbles.

The tentacle dipped closer to Miss Ward like somebody leaning down to inspect an upended beetle. For the briefest moment, the top of Miss Ward's head grazed the hovering tentacle. It felt like passing through a spray of breakers. In that instant, she saw a negative universe of grasping skeletons, tasted ten thousand tears, heard a chorus of furious screams, and was overpowered by the scent of the salty sea. Of lilacs, too, syrupy and sickly-sweet.

Then she was back in the world she knew, inches from the tentacle's immaculate crystal and foaming fathoms. It angled its massive mirror. Miss Ward caught flashes of Alligator Point, but other things too—lots of water, lots of blood. She did not let it stop her. She lifted her body under her own power and locked her knees against the blasting winds. She was here at the end, and it wasn't by chance. She'd earned this, through patience, through love.

She would die standing up.

~ 54 ~

SPRINTING SWAMP PATHS DURING THE sort of storm folk would recount to their grandkids was suicide. Trails disintegrated, boue pourrie loosened, quicksand expanded, and chasms of soil-black water, grabby with root systems, opened like whale mouths, ready to truck your sodden corpse to the Gulf.

Pat Wilkes didn't appear to give a shit. Didn't understand the swamp's danger, that was part of it. Not all of it, though. The metropolitan ways of working Pete had shunned all his life held strains of dedication and duty rural folk only thought they had. Wilkes's tilt into pummeling palms of rain spoke it simple: until the folk at the carny were confirmed safe, it didn't matter what befell the saviors.

Pete lagged at a protracting distance, heart a bowling ball, lungs two big bruises struggling to sieve air from water. It was darker than ever before, impenetrable pitch. An escape, in a way, from pain. Pete thought about quitting. Again and again. Slumping over, letting cold mud ooze over him, surrendering to whatever took Spuds. The despair of reaching out for nobody was more crushing than never reaching at all.

He collided with a warm body. Wilkes grabbed him.

"Roosevelt! Roosevelt!"

Lightning lit up Wilkes's face. She'd been sliced by palmetto leaves. Drilled by slash pine. Gouged by honey locust thorns. Blood welling from punctures was instantly washed away.

"No path!" Wilkes was gesturing. *"There's no path!"*

Pete was gagging on rain. Drowning standing up. He felt Wilkes's fingers in his mouth, tasted vomit but didn't feel it in the flood. He heaved and spat. He shoved rain from his face like it was a burlap bag. He squinted. Wilkes was right. No path. Not even ground through which a new trail could be blazed. Only what looked like a boiling lake.

"What do we do?"

Pete shook his head. Buckets of rain slid off his Stetson brim. Nothing to be done.

Wilkes shook him as the sky shattered.

"You know this swamp! You need to go in front!"

Shaking his head, shaking everything.

"... I ... can't ..."

Wilkes punched him in the chest. Something hard pounded his ribs. Wilkes whooped.

"Feel that, Roosevelt? What's that?"

He didn't want to reply. But he did, a dribble of spit.

"Knee." Gasp, wheeze. "Spud's knee."

Only Wilkes's grinning teeth were visible.

"No, man! That's your badge, Roosevelt! You're back on the payroll!"

Pete puzzled. That weren't right, was it? He'd lost his badge in '93. What was a badge, though, really, but the authority to act against what was wrong? Spuds's knee was proof, real physical proof, of the greatest wrong he'd ever known.

He stood taller. Took a step past Wilkes. Water halfway up his cowboy boots. Glaring through the rain and dark. Wilkes slapped him on the back.

"Lead on, Sheriff!"

She didn't have to shout twice.

Pete plunged into the lake. Wilkes was right. He *did* know this swamp. This was Durber land. If that fence was the fence he thought it was, they were just east of the pigpen. Up ahead was Dale Bouchet's property, that big cement driveway he'd poured himself. Swerve right from there and they'd be plodding along the relative high ground of the Fontaine stables.

The going began okay, Pete stomping, Wilkes shouting regalement. But the storm cranked louder and the water kept rising. Each raindrop was the size of Spuds's knee, bombarding him, driving him shin-deep in mud. His left foot uprooted without its boot but there was no going back for it, momentum was everything. He spilled forward and felt through his sock the suck of greedy soil, the squirm of slithery things seeking a toenail to slide under.

Pete pushed, his knees all bone but hardening toward metal every second. Muscle fibers peeled from his thighs. Tendons stretched thin. Hip sockets cracked. This might be the last path he ever walked. He wished he could still hear Wilkes but the screeching wind had stolen her voice. He had to find somebody else to push him. Who was up to the job?

Pete grinned. His teeth ached in the cold rain.

Marion Robert Morrison, that's who.

Stage name: John Wayne. AKA the Duke.

"I can whup you to a frazzle," Pete huffed. *The Searchers.*

"There's quitters to be buried." *Red River.*

"I'll do the masterminding around here." *The Sands of Iwo Jima.*

"There's some things a man just can't run away from." *Stagecoach.*

"I won't be wronged, I won't be insulted, I won't be laid a hand on." *The Shootist.*

On second thought, no, these weren't John Wayne's words. By Wilkes's account, the Duke weren't so great a guy in the end. Kind of an Andrew Jackson type, come to think of it. In Pete's true-burning state, he realized this only made the actor *more* of an emblem of America, its faults and evils included. The words that moved Pete now, and had always moved him, were the words of Ethan Edwards, Thomas Dunson, John Stryker, the Ringo Kid, and J. B. Books. Characters, that's all. Pete was grateful to them nonetheless, for how they kicked his ass now and dared him to live up to acts of courage beyond his natural ability—like Bob Hightower, the character the Duke played in *3 Godfathers*, carrying an infant through a desert, mile after grueling mile.

The marshland angled upward. The fight against gravity got harder. But less mud now, and both of Pete's feet started doing what he told them. Dead ahead, a chintzy barbed-wire fence. Pete kicked it over, forgetting to use his booted foot. He went down all the same. He glanced back, saw Wilkes right where he'd hoped she'd be, and offered a hand. She took it with both of hers and he hauled her up like she was a doll.

They turned together.

Bob Fireman's Wagon Wheel Carnival cavorted from Chickapee Basin, a million lights blinking in code as oily engines, beveled gears, circulating treads, and tortured screws tossed cargoes of children around in frantic rehearsals for death.

Pete had seen the carnival fifty times. Something looked off. The place looked more vivid than it should, like it existed on a brighter plane of reality. He didn't understand it till he walked, with Wilkes apace, another ten feet, out from under the curtain of rain.

Pete stopped. Stared at his feet. His drenched body dripped onto dry dirt.

He looked up and shared disbelieving blinks with Wilkes. They both turned back.

The rain that had trounced them the whole walk to the basin stopped in a line straighter than the blade of a butcher knife. Pete stared down along the smooth wall of rain until it lost itself in foliage. From there, he titled his head upward.

Emerging from the rain, a thousand feet into the night sky, was what looked like a pale brontosaurus neck. It swung in slow motion, surveying the carnival below. It seemed to Pete that it was made of water. Within it, he saw a sea's worth of currents, ripples, and whirlpools.

"It's a river," he whispered. "A river in the sky."

"River my ass," Wilkes said. "That's a fucking *tentacle*."

~ 55 ~

Here it was—All Feathers, No Meat—the place where Pontiac might be waylaid forever. The gross darkness made eternities of floor, walls, and ceilings. The terrariums extraterrestrial with violet blacklight. The tin lids dinky, jointed to the glass by bent paper clips. The stink of candy and smoke. The dearth of anybody else, like the Chamber of Dragons wasn't a public exhibit at all, but a gauntlet inside Pontiac's heart.

Nothing had changed. Except her. The last time she'd waded into this inky pool, her best friend had been flesh-and-blood, not a clump of horsehide, yarn, rubber, and cork. Her teacher had been a steady inspiration, her school a reliable sanctuary. Her daddy had been there—drunk, but there. Her shanty had been the safest place in the world, before she'd known anything of trailers with locks, neighborhoods with gates, Florida.

Life had gotten tough. But she'd gotten tough along with it.

Least, that's what she hoped.

The Komodo dragon, Gila monster, baby gators, and snapping turtles were like the previews they showed at the Blind Bayou Drive-in in Dawes. The snakes, as before, were the headline shocker. She felt the python's motion, heard the rattler's rattle, smelled the mamba's sticky tongue, tasted the coral's broiling scales. Their restless curlicues were no different from the Pentecostal convolutions she'd heard inside Bread of Life now and then. The snakes praised their god, which lounged in the tank along the back wall.

The old label was curled as if by fire.

COTTONMOUTH

Pontiac crossed the lightless span. Her toe stubbed a raised board and she pitched. The visions came fast and dire. Her face through terrarium glass, the shards slicing her flesh, the cotton-mouth, crazed by blood, darting into her mouth, filling her cheeks with scales, thickening her throat as it fanged its way down.

She caught herself, whipping forward, then back, and heard two things: the gentle slap of her hair against the terrarium and the harder slap of her new log hitting the floor. She made fists and felt cold blood flow. She wanted that log back but no way was she all-foursing it in this dungeon. She swished her foot around. Nothing.

Pontiac swallowed. Her skin prickled.

Forget the log. Live now, only now.

Pontiac raised up on tippy toes and stared straight down into fear.

Usually fear was a thing she saw at oblique angles. Her pal's head under Guimbarde waters. Her teacher naked in the swamp outside her window. The same held here, no cottonmouth yet to be seen, though its existence was evident from the ripple of sawdust like an ocean wave, the tossing of wood chips like flotsam.

"Hi," Pontiac said.

The shape kept rolling, slow as honey except for what had to be its tail, flicking sawdust.

"You don't scare me no more."

It was a lie, but Pontiac felt she might build a truth on top of it, like pirates built shanties atop mere hummocks of solid earth. She just had to repeat the lie. Get used to hearing it. Believe it down to her toes. The Piper, whatever it really was, had been terrorizing folk since the day the Point was born. A stillbirth, more like, the folk here never really having learned to properly walk. It wasn't right and Pontiac might as well be the one to tell it off.

"You been haunting the Point too long. Making folk too scared to do what they gotta do. There ain't no reason for it, snake.

Whatever we did to you, you gotta get past it. You gotta stop being so angry. Look at you, trapped in a box. Look at *me*—I'm in a box too. Neither of us is happy. It don't have to be like this."

The sawdust motion had ceased.

Pontiac rapped on the glass with a knuckle.

"Hey. Piper."

Nothing. Just its outline, harder to discern the longer it stayed still.

Pontiac knocked with her whole first.

"Show yourself, coward!"

The damn thing was trying to wait her out! Pontiac wasn't having that, no, ma'am. She grabbed the right-side paper clip holding the lid in place and yanked it out. The lid's right side fell inward onto wood chips. Pontiac didn't care. She straightened the clip into a wire, pinched it in tight, and start scraping against the glass—a shape she'd drawn fifty times in her log.

An octopus.

If this snake had shit-all to do with the Piper, this oughta show it who was—

Sawdust exploded as the cottonmouth struck.

Under normal conditions, it wouldn't have mattered, but nothing about this St. John's Eve was going normal. Pontiac jerked backward, same as she'd done on January 8, only this time the paper clip caught the eave of the blacklight, closer now due to the slanted lid. The blacklight was anchored in the terrarium.

The whole thing slid off the table, right at Pontiac.

The tank hit her in the stomach. She went straight down, trying to hold the terrarium upright, keep the snake inside, keep the snake inside. She hit the floor too hard. The terrarium shattered against her chest.

First, the awe of it. That she could be so stupid, cause such disaster all on her own. Cold floor under her now, other terrariums looming like eight alien moons. Survival instinct: she lifted her arms from beneath glass shards to see if she felt either pain or the flow of blood. She felt neither, but before she could find any solace in that, a drift of sawdust spilled across her neck, disturbingly warm.

The cottonmouth rose up.

Flat, diamond-shaped head. Barklike scales. Paired white spots. Steel-rivet eyes. A single second of affectless regard before the mouth sprung open a full forty-five degrees, the inner cheeks white enough to burn holes through the dark, its deep throat ever so barely pink, like a drop of cherry sauce mixed into a bowl of cream. The interior folds looked silky, nearly sexy, Miss Ward shedding her nightie outside the window, fanged and beckoning.

Pontiac tensed and made fists.

She never had a chance. The cottonmouth shot forward like a diving eagle. Its fangs sunk into Pontiac's right arm above the wrist. Instantly, volcanically hot, the fangs like fork tines dipped in molten metal. Pontiac tried to scream but air only swept inward. She whipped her arm but the snake bore down like a second set a biceps, a brand-new limb with its own designs.

Pontiac thrashed her arm against the floor. The cottonmouth torqued but held fast. She felt the grotesque rubber of her wrist flesh yawning open as the fangs sickled deeper and poison pumped from salivary glands. The bite was so hot it went icy, freezing the radius and ulna, bones she'd learned about from Miss Ward.

Could be the poison, but Pontiac believed she saw eight black-lights flicker as the Chamber's other creatures fought for freedom. It made no sense, really, that the Piper would let a cottonmouth alone serve as proxy. The Piper was the Gila monster, the Komodo dragon, the gators, the turtles, the snakes; it was Ayida, Chikangombe, Monyoha, and Ol' Splitfoot. Even more upsetting was that customer faces reflected in terrarium glass might reveal that they were the Piper too—wronged, sorrowful, forgotten, and furious.

Daddy's old warnings bubbled up along with blood. Soon the pain would go radiant. Pontiac would barf, go limp, start suffocating as the poison enflamed her tissues. She had seconds to act if she were going to have a ghost's chance.

Her free arm swept an angel-wing pattern across the floor. Nothing to help till she bumped her own thigh, the dress Mère bought, the pocketed object. Pontiac's hand knew what to do even if her mind didn't. It weaseled into the pocket and uprooted Billy May Part II.

A baseball was built to survive a hell of a lotta hits.

Pontiac slammed the ball onto the cottonmouth's head. The snake spasmed. Pontiac slammed again, again, hearing bones snap, hopefully the snake's but she couldn't be sure. The spatter of snake blood across the new log would write a more truthful account than her pencil ever could. Not a bad final entry, truth be told: defending not only herself but the town she loved. Pontiac kept smashing, even as she felt drops of poison bead along her nerves.

The cottonmouth's head was wet gristle by the time Pontiac felt somebody toss aside the limp snake and start to lift her off the floor. Billy May Part II, nothing but a handful of bloody fabric and string now, plopped from her hand. Again she'd lost her best friend. This time, though, she felt a whole lot better about it.

They'd fought longside each another one last time.

Pontiac was off her feet and into the air. She felt as flimsy as the Oil Man papers Daddy had never signed. Daddy—she tried to coalesce her convulsive thoughts into a coherent goodbye but could only rake together a batch of the sneaky winks, surprised smiles, and proud nods he'd given her over the years. Mama's crypt rose like the moon behind him, doors open, welcoming Pontiac home.

The Chamber's blackout gave way to carnival's kaleidoscope. All Feathers, No Meat—she'd escaped! If only Mère could see it! But the venom was altering Pontiac's chemistry; she was greased in sweat, slipping through the arms that held her. But her bearer was strong and capable. The arms hitched her up and kept moving, away from Bob Fireman's lights into darker, cooler pools. A sudden maniacal rain drove down on them like nails. It hurt, but cooled her too.

Pontiac tried to see who had her before she passed out. No red face, no black suit. That was all she could tell, and was grateful for it. In a few minutes, she'd die, and while it might not be in the arms of an angel, it sure wouldn't be the arms of a demon. Laissez les bons temps rouler, non?

~ 56 ~

LA PIEUVRE SEEMED MESMERIZED BY Miss Ward, the wet, willowy human who dared stand before its abysmal power. The water tentacle rolled; it swayed; it angled its mirror-thing as if trying to decipher the teacher's secrets. Pure speculation, of course. All Gerard knew for sure was that La Pieuvre was preoccupied.

He stood up. Tougher thing than he would have guessed. His clothes were so soaked it felt like he was deep in the quick. The store floor was slick with the laundry detergent, dish soap, window cleaner, mop solution, bleach, and other products that had exploded from their containers. It slopped underfoot as Gerard clambered over a shipwrecked candy rack.

The marbles, of course, were a crueler impediment. Over a hundred immies, steelies, corkscrews, clearies, and milkies seeded the Mercantile floor, old friends that had turned against him after spending thirty-eight years in the quag, the ultimate hard-togets. Now they rolled beneath his staggering feet, less angry at DeLoach for jettisoning them than they were at Gerard for failing to tear apart the swamp to find them. Should he have? Were they, and the friendship they represented, the gold he should have dug for?

Gerard searched for Doc. The coffee island was upended and the old man's bony fingers were still clamped to it. Doc was coated in liquified issues of the *Times-Picayune*, the newsprint spotted red from bloody wounds. His eyes were half-closed. His ribcage ballooned and deflated. There was no telling the severity of Doc's injuries.

Also no telling where Doc's shotgun was.

Last thing Gerard recalled was arming himself with Miss Ward's Bowie knife while Doc took the Remington 870. The shotgun must have been lost in the destruction, same as the knife. But it had to be close! Gerard crept eastward, where most of the Mercantile's materials had flooded. He pushed aside a shelf of soaked scratch-tickets. No shotgun. He kicked past a bin of individually wrapped beef jerkies. No shotgun. He didn't hear rain anymore, only a tribe of mad drummers beating hysterical patterns.

Added to that, gradually, was the sound of being watched.

City folk might not believe in such a sound. Swamp rats counted on it for survival. Gerard had looked directly at silent watchers on hundreds of different late-night muddles through the marsh. A nutria staring from a cattail fort. A gator's golden cat-eyes visible just over a sticky tarn. A fellow drunkard collapsed on the trail, maybe harmless, but maybe plastered enough to stab the next passerby for grub money.

Gerard stood straight and began to turn around. He saw Doc, coughing blood, staring up high. He saw Miss Ward, frozen with fear, looking the same direction. Gerard clenched his teeth and finished his turn.

The tentacle had forgone Miss Ward. Now it hovered over Gerard, swaying as if giving him a doggie sniff. Gerard's hands and feet prickled. His skin went cadaver cold. What he felt was less fear than surrender. There was no comprehending this entity.

A sound emitted from the tentacle. Or from the thing behind the tentacle. Or from the swamp behind the thing, La Pieuvre's veins and vessels intertwined with every root, stem, axil, bud, and blade. A voice of multitudes purred through alligator weed, Virginia creeper, and buffalo grass, and creaked like the boughs of bald cypress, southern magnolia, and crepe myrtle. Undertones, those. The tenor and soprano were bullfrog, dragonfly, hawk, mosquito, crane, woodpecker, cricket, bobcat, rattlesnake, alligator, wren, beaver, parakeet, owl, and wolf, predator and prey aligned, all part of the same refrain of life, death, rebirth.

It asked a question.

WHAT ARE YOUR CONVICTIONS?

Gerard recoiled at thunder cannonades and squinted through rain. The tentacle dipped slightly, fifty feet closing to forty. La Pieuvre's voice lowered.

NO CONVICTIONS IS WORSE THAN MALEVOLENCE.

"I don't know de t'ings I supposed to say," Gerard pleaded.

SO MANY DEAD—ON ACCOUNT OF THOSE LIKE YOU.
THE CONVICTION-LESS.

YOU HAVE HAD GENERATIONS TO ADMIT YOUR WRONGS.

TO ACKNOWLEDGE YOUR ILL-GOTTEN GAINS.

TO TOURNIQUET THE BLEED OF COMPOUNDING GRIEVANCE.

Gerard's guts were empty of alcohol but caught fire anyway. He'd spent his life burbling to barfly buddies, wheezing weak lessons to Pontiac, weeping futilely at Janine's grave. Here was his chance to stand the way Miss Ward had stood. If he went down shouting, maybe it would give Pontiac, wherever she was, the headstart to outrun this thing. He whipped his head upward with a sawblade of gray rainwater.

"I never hurt nobody! Nobody but my own self!"

THE DEAD NEVER HURT ANYONE EITHER.

AND YET THEY REMAIN DEAD.

IN THE WATERS THAT ARE MY HOME.

"I'm just one man! It ain't my fault! None of dese deaths are my fault!"

YOU THINK THE FAULT LINES END.

THEY DO NOT EVER END.

THERE MUST BE OWNERSHIP. ATONEMENT. REDRESS.

"Empty my pockets, octopus! Tear down my shanty! You'll see I don't got nothin!"

YOU DROWNED YOUR SINS IN NASTY-SUGAR.

SO YOU NEVER HAD TO FEEL THEM.

THERE ARE OTHER WAYS TO PAY.

Gerard shook his head. Not if it meant taking Pontiac. Not if it meant taking any of the boys and girls who didn't even know the wicked lineages they belonged to. In a lightning flash, Gerard was eleven again, lowering himself into a storm-frenzied lagoon, feeling around for lost marbles till a cottonmouth showed up. Gerard hadn't backed down then.

The words flew from his mouth verbatim.

"Do it, snake! You hear?"

Did swamps have memories? The tentacle aped the cottonmouth of Gerard's youth, tilting its erstwhile face and giant mirror like a dog tilted its head upon meeting an unexpectedly feisty varmint. Gerard kept shouting the shouts of his past.

"You t'ink dat scares me, snake? You t'ink you can take somet'in from me dat everybody else ain't already took? Y'all ain't shit, snake! Y'all ain't shit!"

All the while, his hands did what they'd done thirty-eight years back, digging deep, not into lagoon moss and sweet grass, but his own pockets.

Shoot your shot, Doc had said.

What Gerard found in the lagoon back then, today he found in his pocket.

The Brothers of the Spear. Better than a Remington 870. Better than a Bowie knife or sugarcane machete. The loyal marble had saved him before. Saved a lot a folk, actually. Gerard held the marble in his right fist, cold as an ice chip. He pushed his thumb into that fist so it touched the glass. It was his thumb, after all, that had beaten German Rusnak's hundred-to-one-odds and brought hope back to the blighted boys of Alligator Point, at least until harsher forms of nasty-sugar started sinking their still-breathing bodies.

Shoot your shot.

With Doc and Miss Ward looking on, somehow the whole Point looking on too, Gerard reared back and hurled the Brothers of the Spear.

~ 57 ~

FEW REVELERS NOTICED THE TENTACLE lording over Chickapee Basin. The jamboree of midway lights made the tentacle appear to be nothing but a ripple of cloud. Kids spent their allowance, played rigged games, bought greasy food, and cavorted between queues. It made Pete think of the Ceremony of the Pearls from *Wake of the Red Witch*. Festivity and frivolity, with ignorance of the tragedy waiting on deck.

"What we we do?" Pete asked dumbly, rain dribbling off his lips.

"Protect and serve," Wilkes said.

The cop took off so fast rain flew from her in pennants. She went directly for the ill-lit slums of carnival trailers, maybe in the belief that Bob Fireman actually existed. No: she accosted a quintet of lounging carnies. She didn't tell them about the tentacle, too hard to make out and too confounding to behold; Pete didn't know *what* she told them. But the roustabouts perked up with the thrill of deputization. They sprinted off to five different destinations: the carousel, house of mirrors, bumper cars, Ferris wheel, Wombat Scrambler. Pete watched in wonder as the carnies tore apart queues on their ways to stop the rides.

Wilkes ran a slant across the carnival's neck, some kind of crowd-control technique, hollering and making traffic-cop gestures away from the wall of rain. Back when the Point was a official town with an official payroll, Sheriff Pete often bewailed his lack of staff. Even if he'd had a full complement of colonels, majors, captains, and rank-and-filers, they could not have sheep-dogged this crowd better than Pat Wilkes. People saw her, paid heed, and began to drift northward.

"Standin here like a spot on a dog," Pete scolded himself.

Who cared if he lacked Wilkes's training? He'd always been more of the brawler anyhow, stomping through brackish waters sans galoshes or ripping apart leathery rush with his bare mitts, anything to get him closer to where he had to get. Too old a mutt now to learn new tricks.

He galloped to the nearest group he saw, four little girls.

"Get out of here! All y'all!'

"Hello, Sheriff," Alice Chilcote said.

"Scat! You hear me? Thataway!"

"But the cotton candy's that way," Melissa Montagne said.

No time for respecting personal space. Pete wrapped his big arms around the quartet and bowling-balled them north. Corn dogs, soft drinks, and hair clips went flying.

"GET!"

They got. Pete bolted to the next group. A little boy, two parents: the Durbers. Same routine. Next the Beatty kids, the Tournier family, the Dauber twins, the Fontaine brats. All these faces he knew down to birthmarks and scars. Most of which had yet to fill out into the grown-ups they had every right to become, no matter the regrets and despair that were adulthood's dowry.

Pete bellowed, and pulled, and pushed, and in one instance kicked. The carny deputies, meanwhile, had darkened half the midway booths and every ride except the Wombat Scrambler, a rollicking baton studded by hundreds of crimson lights, still making riderless circulations. These lights lit the tentacle from below as it dipped closer, the reflective face of its mirror going a blinding, catastrophic red.

The Red Witch, Pete thought. *It's come for me at last.*

Half the attendees were still on the grounds, booing the ride blackout and only starting to notice the thing reaching over

Chickapee Basin. Time had run out for Pete to inveigle them to skedaddle. He had to face up to the Red Witch, just like the Duke's Captain Ralls had faced up to the wreck of the Red Witch ship. It had caused Captain Ralls's death, but with his beloved Angelique already gone, what did it matter?

Pete had nobody left to live for.

Except Wilkes, he supposed. Pete realized he *did* want the big-city copper to know what a good backwater sheriff was capable of, even if it was the last thing he did.

With the nose of the tentacle craning downward over the Wombat Scrambler, Pete hooked his thumbs into his belt loops, stuck his chest out, and strode hips-first, just like John Wayne, to the center of the carny's clearing. Only had one boot left, so Pete made it count, stomping it twice as hard. Each stomp into dry dirt sounded like a hard heartbeat.

Never in his whole stupid life had he been so scared.

He weren't alone in that. Finally, screams from every direction, fleeing footfalls. Plenty of folk, though, especially little ones, looked immobilized. They crouched against vendor stands and game tables, waiting for somebody to save them.

The tentacle hovered fifty feet overhead. Made entirely of water. Broad as a blue whale. Of infinite length. Looped so it could hold the large, flat, reflective object. It had no face yet looked directly at Pete. A noise groaned up from its whirlpool depths, a billion tributary voices thundering into a single seething river.

WHAT ARE YOUR CONVICTIONS?

Pete winced through spatters of salt water. He glanced left and right, and failed to find a funhouse that might have broadcasted the shivery voice. He wiped his face and stared into the tentacle's liquid cosmos.

It was an elegant question, but the Point weren't a total stranger to eloquence. Hell, you get a few drinks into somebody like Gerard Pontiac, he'd sermonize you something gorgeous. That'd never been Pete's way. If he had something to say, he said it short and direct.

Maybe that was the answer.

"I believe in telling it straight." Pete scarcely recognized his frightened voice.

The water stirred, bubbled, fermented.

TELL IT TO THOSE WHO WERE DEAD BEFORE DYING.

Either Pete, or the world, or both, had gone mad. He accepted it.

"I . . . don't know who you mean."

THOSE HUMANS RIPPED OF THEIR HUMANITY.

"I keep the peace. That's all I ever tried to do."

THEY HAVE NEVER KNOWN PEACE.

THEIR BONES LIE DEEP IN MY WATERS.

ROLLING AND ROTTING IN CHAOS.

CONFESS. ATONE. REDRESS.

Pete tried to think through the curdling fear. What awful things had he done? Who had he wronged? Letting Jack O'Brien's killer go was all he could think of, and he still believed that didn't qualify. He tried to think beyond his own actions. The Red Witch felt ancient; might that mean the wrong was ancient too? Pete considered his mother, slashing her pimp's throat. Neither Rose Roosevelt nor Gee Putnam was worth this being's wrath. Further back, then. The settlers of Alligator Point, the Pirates Lafitte. Distinguished anti-heroes round these parts, though a parallel narrative scuttled about the edges. The Lafittes as slave traders, boating souls across the Styx of the Caribbean.

"You talkin about . . . slaves?"

CALL THEM BY THEIR PROPER NAMES.

"I don't know . . . their names—"

COME LEARN THEM, THEN.

HERE AT THE BOTTOM OF THE SEA.

PAIN WILL BE YOUR PENCIL.

KEEP TRACK OF THEM FOR ETERNITY.

Pete did not follow what the Red Witch was saying. Yet he felt yoked with guilt and shame. He opened his mouth. To confess? Atone? Redress? He didn't know how. He felt he had to say something to start draining the pus from the infection of this putrid land. Unlike John Wayne, however, he didn't have Hollywood's finest writing his lines. Sure, he could go on borrowing them. *Reap the Wild Wind* had a juicy line he could imagine telling the Red Witch right now: *You haven't enough sand in your craw to stand in front of me alone.*

End of the day, though—and this might be the end—he weren't John Wayne.

He was Pete Roosevelt. Sworn to protect the folk of Alligator Point. Didn't seem likely he could defeat this gigantic thing. But if he talked big enough, he might just buy his Pointers time enough to scamper free.

It was time to start playing reruns his *own* legends.

One stuck out. Pete's *True Grit*, you might say, the performance of which he was proudest. August 1, 1994, Juicy Lucy's, the day he'd met Spuds Ulene. Spuds had held his own that day. Could be he hadn't needed Pete's help. But, hellfire, it had been Pete's greatest honor to help him anyway.

"One big fella against one little fella," Pete said, modifying his old Juicy Lucy's dialogue. "Them scales seem tipped."

The tentacle rotated slowly, observing with invisible eyes.

"You look real hard, Witch, you might see yourself a couple old pinholes on my shirt here. That's where my badge used to hang. Maybe I don't got the force of law behind me no more. But I got somethin better. I got the will of the people. They believe in me, you ugly thing." He tipped his Stetson for old time's sake. "I ain't sure *any* of us believe in you."

The tentacle angled its mirror. Red light from the Wombat Scrambler fired back at Pete. Hurt so bad tears squeezed from his eyeballs. But he didn't look away. He'd held his ground for Spuds. He'd hold it now, too, for Alligator Point. He broadened his legs, lifted his chin, swagger incarnate.

"Now, it's true, I ain't been allowed to carry a gun since '93. But I got other ways of fightin. Try me, Witch. Just try me."

The tentacle made a gradual midair loop, a rope trick in slow motion. Like it was not only hearing Pete, but gauging his words. Pete swallowed hard. It was all bluster. He didn't have the first clue what he'd do if that thing came swooping down. But did the Duke have a plan in *Wake of the Red Witch* when he jumped into the lagoon and wrestled the octopus Tarutatu? No, sir. But he'd beaten that beast, spurring the islanders to dub him "Son of Tarutatu." Like *he* was the monster now.

If fighting made Pete a monster, too, so be it.

The tentacle jolted closer, mirror glaring. Pete's instincts held true: he reached for whatever he had. Five years back, it'd been a gun. More recently, the pair of handcuffs he'd kept, or the can of soup a grateful townsperson had given him, or the sharpened pencil he carried for notes he never took. He patted his body down double-time, felt a solid object, and whipped it out.

Spuds's metal knee.

Pete heard Miss Ward's voice, through the Pelican's phone.

Shoot your shot.

Something galvanizing about those words, no matter who they'd come from.

Pete gripped the knee. A lot like gripping a baseball. Used to play on the Guimbarde Beach diamond with other Pointers back in the day, even pitched a few games, fancying himself Babe Ruth. The tentacle swayed like a snake about to strike. Pete knew he had to strike first. He reared back with the knee, all those old muscles recalled, and shot his shot.

~ 58 ~

WHAT'S A MARBLE WEIGH? A tenth an ounce? Not enough to resist a gentle breeze, much less a walloping tempête. The tiny marble embedded with the images of Dan-El and Natongo didn't carry ten feet before it blew left. Gerard felt a loss of vitality, like he'd been stabbed in the chest. All winds, though, were crosswise now. A second gust blew the marble to the right. That should have been the end of it, the marble sinking into the Mercantile's soggy lumber. But a northern draft lifted the Brothers of the Spear skyward, over the crumbled west wall. Still thirty feet from the tentacle until a darting snakebird batted it with a black-and-white wing, boosting the marble fifteen feet, and just as it began to dip, it struck the wing membrane of an upswishing brown bat, and suddenly the marble was there, right in front of the tentacles, a billion-to-one odds, though the marble had lost all velocity, until a four-inch kingfisher, blue as a summer sky, rocketed into it, head-butting the marble with enough force to kill the beautiful bird, firing the marble with all of Gerard's original strength, not into the tentacle itself, which had slithered yards away, but into the large, flat, reflective object it held like a mirror.

It was as if the swamp's beasts wished to give the Point what La Pieuvre didn't.

One last chance.

The Brothers of the Spear speared the mirror. It shattered, brighter than lightning, a downpour of flashing daggers.

~ 59 ~

THE KNEE MIDAIR WAS A CHROME COMMA tumbling across a page of black paper. Its odd shape caught the wind with aplomb, like a football, a thing engineered to be thrown. Impressive distance, but Pete was no Jim Everett. Hell, he was no Heath Shuler. The knee strayed toward the back left of the end zone. A moment before it began a downward trajectory, a rogue gust bumped it skyward, though even farther to the left, all the way into the realms of the only machine still running, the Wombat Scrambler. The ride's cycling baton missed the knee by inches. The knee dropped straight down into the oily socket of the Wombat's grinding engine. Pete had time to feel a pang of grief, his sole physical remembrance of his best friend gone, before then the Wombat's gears coughed hard and spat the knee like a sunflower seed. The knee zinged off one of the ride's rising compartments, which clocked it like a golf club bashing a Titleist from a tee. The knee flew rightward with twice the speed of Pete's original throw.

Spuds's knee kneed the mirror. It exploded. Reflected shards of the carnival pinwheeled over the carnival, a red cataclysm, the Son of Tarutatu crowned via destruction.

~ 60 ~

BRIGHT DARKS: A WORD COMBO Miss Ward might have called a contradiction, but Pontiac couldn't think of a better way to describe taking a hit—a real *hit*—whether falling noggin-first from the monkey bars, or getting tossed by a Fontaine pony, or landing bad when the best tree limb at Skunk Hole broke under her. Each time she got hit like that, there came a black explosion, and explosions were fuck-damn bright no matter what color they were.

Same thing getting snake-bit. Ten seconds after the cotton-mouth got her, the bright darks blasted away everything else in sight, until inky fireworks were all she saw. Before she faded out, two sensations engulfed her. First, the poison, the way it crawled through her blood like a train of fire ants, stretching each vein and trailing what felt like the paprika bayou chefs slathered on mudbugs. Second, the rain, falling like cold metal rods, alarming but fortunate. It was the only thing keeping Pontiac's skin from bursting into flame.

There was no nice, drowsy waking up with venom inside you.

Pontiac gasped to life, half drowning, rain so thick there were no breathing spaces between drops. Without individual points, the rain felt softer, unless it was her flesh that had gone to pulp, the rain having knifed through muscle on its way to scrimshawing her bones.

Wasn't rain at all, turned out. Pontiac peeled open eyelids sealed together with yucky crust in time to see an ocean wave come at her, the breaker curling like the top jaw of an even larger cottonmouth. It crashed against Pontiac's legs, detonating into white surf that washed over her, cold and creamy. The tide heaved south, taking with it Pontiac's sweltering, choking fever.

She rubbed salt from her lashes and looked around.

No carnival. She was at a beach. Guimbarde Beach.

The ocean thundered. A storm raved.

The next wave, already ballooning, would drag her out.

But for the hand that gripped her tight.

Pontiac looked straight up and caught a glimpse before the wave blotted out sight.

André Saphir.

Under two feet of thrashing surf, Pontiac clung to the scene Daddy had painted for her back in Pensacola. Daddy taking Saphir by the face and asking him to be Pontiac's parrain, and Saphir replying *Oui, monsieur.* Though she was only under the ocean for four or five seconds, picturing the two men she loved holding each other that way imbued her with a stimulant better than any anti-venom. Shit-balls. *Anything* could happen in this swamp.

The wave retreated. Pontiac gasped.

Saphir was backlit by the moon, but his face was lit too. Guimbarde had a native illumination—bioluminescence, Miss Ward called it. A six-syllable augury that let Pontiac see Saphir's wide eyes and tentative smile, his slender body unflagging in tossing gales, tattoos as black as fresh oil, earrings tambourining, black hat gone from his shaved head, white cotton shirt soaked to his skin.

"Okay, catin?" he shouted.

Pontiac blinked, taking stock. She didn't feel okay. Where the cottonmouth got her felt like butane fire. Her neck was swollen and rubbery and her mouth tasted like rotten mint. Breathing made her lungs feel cheese-gratered, and she didn't think her heart would ever stop beating like this, the wings of an ascending red-tailed hawk.

But she *was* breathing. Even gagging on gulf water, she was breathing.

What had Daddy said about cottonmouth bites?

Eidder you got de stuff to survive it or you don't.

What had Saphir said about Guimbarde Beach?

Dese waters got magic, catin. No tellin if it bad magic or good. Or if dere's any difference to de ones who make de magic happen.

Which of her father figures had it right? Both, Pontiac decided. It had been both who'd raised her, who'd showed her what the swamp could take from you if it wanted, and what you could take from it.

"Okay," Pontiac replied—

A glugging splutter as a third wave bashed into her. The knobs of Saphir's callouses pressed into her back as he lifted her from the splash. Felt familiar. Two years after Mama died, when Pontiac was eight, Daddy got baptized outside Bread of Life. He didn't believe in God, Jesus, none of that junk. He was desperate, that's all, casting about like Saphir with his rod for something to save him. Daddy insisted on being dipped in water like they did it in movies, and came up slimed in duckweed and with a leech on his forehead.

Seconds before that, though, Pontiac had been struck by how peaceful Daddy looked, like the baptism might have Jesus-ed the nasty-sugar right out of him.

Pontiac felt that now. Jealousy of goody-goody Alice Chilcote, washed away. Weird lust for Miss Ward, gone. Guilt for not being there when the Piper got Billy May, grief for not having Mama around, shame of taking money from Mère, all of it flushed like swamp crud from her shanty's shower. Daddy's mistake, she figured, was getting baptized in waters the oil companies had fouled. They were fouling the Gulf, too, but the Gulf was bigger. It still had life to spare, and didn't mind handing some out now and then.

Saphir held her like a baby in the foaming surf.

"Sorry." Her weak whisper added to the ocean's hiss.

Saphir grinned. "For what you apologizin, 'tit couyon?"

"Getting bit. That was dumb."

"Lots of t'ings gonna bite over a life. Wit' each bite you inch closer to immunity, non?"

Pontiac nodded, head twice as heavy with drenched hair.

"Gotta get you to hôpital," Saphir said. "Now dat you all cooled."

Pontiac was cold, all right, but had fire enough to resist this plan. Wasn't much she hated more than doctors. Before she could hell-no the notion, there came a hard tap against her butt. Would have figured it for an ocean pebble if it hadn't been followed by a tap to her leg, to her back, to her neck.

"Skunk. Something's pecking me."

"Oiseau?"

Saphir rose himself to his knees and with his wiry strength swung Pontiac to his right hip. This faced Pontiac to the sunken baseball diamond, away from the Gulf. All Pontiac had to go on was her godfather's expression. Confusion, then concern, then shock, and then, the last thing Pontiac expected on a dumb-dilly night like this, a look of stark, blank, dazzled awe.

"Mon dieu," Saphir cried. "Coo-wee!"

~ 61 ~

THE MIRROR'S SHARDS TURNED to ocean when they hit the ground, breaking like water balloons, each splash so laden with salt they felt like tacks thrown into Doc's face.

The tentacle, that umbilical cord attached to nothing nearer than the moon, swung like a pendulum, west to east, hitting Gerard Pontiac like a truck and emitting an aerosol of ocean spray. Gerard tumbled over the store's demolished east wall like one of the Mercantile's cheap cloth poppets. Only by luck was it Gerard's right leg, and not his head, that crashed through jagged remnants of the roof. Doc saw that leg flap and fold, broken into segments only banded together by skin. Then Gerard was gone inside the gray-brown storm, a fate Doc had no time to consider, as a half-second later, the tentacle hurled Miss Ward the same direction, backward through a window that was, at least, already shattered. She followed Gerard's flight toward Dawes as if attached to him by rope.

The swamp inhaled. Exhaled.

Digested, perhaps.

No longer burdened with carrying the mirror, the tentacle was more agile and, apparently, angrier. It reoriented in midair, snake physics that defied gravity. Doc felt a doomed weight when the eyeless, faceless thing focused on him. It craned forward through the rubble, stopping at a ten-feet distance.

La Pieuvre waited. The railroading rain bounced off the tentacle and left the evidence of silver steam. Inside the tentacle, ocean water contracted in untroubled galactic spirals.

Doc knew he was in bad shape. The time when he could walk off pain like this was long gone. He had broken bones, some from rifled marbles, and at seventy-five those wounds wouldn't heal right even if he survived. He tried to move the coffee island but his wrist was shattered. Doc sobbed once, then used his shoulder to slide the island through the slippery skim of spilled product. He squirmed his left arm under him and pushed. He had to pause his scream a few times so he could snatch what air he could.

He made it to a sitting position, palsied against wet cardboard boxes. He thought about looking for Jack O'Brien's shotgun. What would be the point? Shooting this tentacle would be like shooting into the ocean.

Doc was a goner. But it didn't have to be for nothing.

"Kill me," he said.

The tendril floated a few feet closer, electric with rejected rain.

"Me. Just me. Leave everybody else alone. I'm begging."

La Pieuvre's steam thickened like the exhale of a feral hog.

I AM TOO NEARSIGHTED TO SORT THIS INSECT FROM THAT.

TO MEASURE INNOCENCE BY THE GRAM.

IF ONE GOES, THEY ALL MUST GO.

BUT I UNDERSTAND YOU ARE A MERCHANT.

A MERCHANT LIKES TO MAKE DEALS.

I, TOO, AM A DEALMAKER.

YES, MERCHANT, LET US BARTER.

Doc didn't follow, but nodded, gratefully, frantically.

"They didn't mean it. They didn't mean to break your mirror."

The tentacle tilted in a way Doc read as amusement.

TWO OF MY MIRRORS HAVE BEEN BROKEN TONIGHT.

IT IS IMPRESSIVE.

I DID NOT EXPECT SUCH A SHOW OF SPIRIT.

IT TEMPTS ME TO REWARD YOUR PEOPLE.

I DO NOT HAVE TO.

I HAVE SIX MORE MIRRORS.

I COULD BRING THEM TO BEAR ON YOU RIGHT NOW.

The idea was horrific. Doc nodded. He would take the terror and death.

"Bring them all. Show me all of you."

YOU CANNOT FATHOM ALL OF ME.

THE OCEAN'S SURFACE IS ALL YOU ARE CAPABLE OF SEEING.

I WILL MAKE NEW MIRRORS.

Doc squinched through the downpour. The old legends. La Pieuvre's vanity. Could be a sore spot to poke, a way for Doc, and Doc alone, to draw its ire.

"You think you're beautiful? You're ugly. A big, disgusting worm."

More tilting, more amusement.

THE WEEVIL CALLS THE SNOWY EGRET UGLY.

DO YOU THINK THE SNOWY EGRET MINDS?

AS IT CIRCLES ITS HEAVENS?

ONLY AT THE BEGINNING WERE THE MIRRORS FOR ME.

OVER TIME, I TURNED THEM TOWARD YOU.

SO YOU COULD SEE WHAT YOU HAD DONE.

SEE IT IN YOUR OWN FACES.

HEAR IT IN YOUR OWN VOICES.

FOR A WHILE, YOU REMEMBERED.

Doc coughed up gluey blood. Tried to breathe. To think. The drawings in Pontiac's log. The likeness in the crepe myrtle outside the Mercantile. The sigils all over the Point, carved as reminders to do better, stay vigilant. But all the symbols so old now, just like him.

"How long do we need to remember?"

YOU TELL ME, MERCHANT.

WHAT CONTRITION APPEASES MILLIONS ENSLAVED AND MURDERED?

IN MY WATERS.

MY WATERS.

La Pieuvre's voice sizzled. The water in its tentacle boiled. Doc's fluids were anemic by comparison, but they boiled as well. He pounded his fist to the floor. Water jetted up, hot as arterial blood. He howled in grievance, disbelief, impotence, and plain old age, and saw the result in the tentacle's reflective skin: his *own* ugliness.

"What are we supposed to do? Tell me how to make it right!"

La Pieuvre's tentacle surged forward.

BECOME A MUDBUG, MERCHANT.

COOK IN YOUR OWN FURIOUS JUICES.

THE INJURIES WERE NOT DELIVERED BY ME.

YOU MUST HACK THROUGH YOUR OWN JUNGLE.

YOU MUST DIAGNOSE YOUR OWN SICKNESS, DOCTOR.

YOU MUST SEE YOURSELF FOR WHAT YOU ARE.

YOU MUST SEARCH FOR THE DEAD.

FIND THEM.

SEE THEM.

KNOW YOUR NATION AS A BUTCHERY.

KNOW YOURSELVES AS THE BUTCHERS.

WRITE IT DOWN.

TURN THOSE WRITINGS INTO BLUEPRINTS.

REBUILD EVERYTHING AS IF YOU WERE LEVELED IN BATTLE.

START HERE.

START NOW.

Doc gagged for air in the deluge. He choked and nodded.

"Keep track."

TOO FEW DO.

DOWN HERE, ONLY A LITTLE GIRL, TOO YOUNG.

THIS IS WHY I TURN TO YOU.

DOC DEVEREAUX.

"What . . . is it you . . . want me to do?"

CHOOSE.

"Choose what?"

THE FATE OF ALLIGATOR POINT.

"What . . . what does that mean?"

I COULD RETREAT INTO THE OCEAN.

DISTRACT MYSELF WITH THE AFFAIRS OF FISH.

OR I COULD WIPE THIS TOWN OFF THE PLANET.

THIS, OF COURSE, IS MY PREFERENCE.

"Then why give *me* the choice?"

THE SWAMP.

HOW IT EXASPERATES ME BY INDULGING YOU.

ENCOURAGING YOU COWARDS TO STAND.

HELPING YOU TO BREAK MY MIRRORS.

BUT SUCH IS THE WAY OF THE SWAMP.

STUBBORN. FRACTIOUS. RECALCITRANT. UNGOVERN-ABLE.

IT IS THE MOST LIKE YOU.

AND HOW DO YOU THANK IT IN RETURN?

YOU DESTROY IT.

Doc surveyed the splinters and shavings of what had served as his home for sixteen years. His eyeballs pulsed when he saw a soggy white lump the size of the Oil Man's contract. Doc was glad he hadn't signed it. He'd die with that conviction in place, at least.

But did he have to die? Did anyone? La Pieuvre's offer seemed explicit. Curse Alligator Point and the octopus would do what she had come to do: scoop the town from the bayou, roll it into a ball of mud and shanty and flesh, and pitch it into the same forgotten depths of those devastated by the Pirates Lafitte.

La Pieuvre called Doc a merchant. But it wasn't a capitalist code he'd aligned himself with as a young man. It was a code more Hippocratic. First, do no harm—shouldn't that be the ideal? Not only for him. Not only for the Point. For everybody, no matter whose bloodline their bodies had bloomed from.

A healer healed. Bloodthirsty revenge couldn't be the answer.

Either that or Doc wasn't strong enough to pull the guillotine switch.

THIS IS THE DEAL, MERCHANT.

LET US SEE IF YOU MAKE THE RIGHT CHOICE.

WILL YOU PASS THE BUCK?

OR WILL YOU PAY THE PIPER?

Doc parted bloody lips to speak the words he knew would forever haunt him: *Pass the buck.* He'd damn himself to save Alligator Point. *Pass the buck.* He puckered his lips to say it, finally say it. *Pass the buck.*

A thin voice sparrowed into the ruined Mercantile on a slip of wind.

Doc didn't know the voice, yet instantly knew its origin.

A second voice joined the first, a moaning duet. Another made a wailing trio, another a shrieking quartet. Each voice its own but united in outraged lament.

When Doc practiced medicine, it never paid to hesitate. Draw the blood, snip the mole, do the tests. He didn't hesitate now. He scrounged his rust-burred stethoscope from the dark drawer of his mind, inserted the headset, and held the diaphragm to the chests of the arriving ghosts.

~ 62 ~

Pelting Pontiac and Saphir were Junonias.

Pontiac's mind spiraled with the whorls of rain. Two hundred bucks for a Junonia at She Sells Sea Shells, just one, and here were twenty—no, fifty, shedding from collapsing waves—no, a hundred Junonias, two hundred, a hailstorm driving horizontally from the

Gulf—suspended in the salt-sprayed, moonlit air it looked like five hundred, and that's without the shells that had to be making landfill up and down Guimbarde—could be a thousand, two thousand, five thousand, they kept coming, spitting from the sea like blood from a puncture, slapping her face, slicing her lips, nicking her cheeks.

Saphir's arms enclosed her waist. His bare feet appeared on either side of her, heels digging into wet sand, pushing the two of them back from the gnashing surf, each heel divot filling with its own tiny sea. Saphir collapsed ten feet back, Pontiac an upturned turtle on his chest. The surf, sharp with shells like a sink of broken china, stretched for them and reached their knees, not enough for an undertow kidnap, not yet.

Junonias piled against Saphir's legs. Dozens of small, cream-colored, scroll-shaped shells, then dozens more. They spilled over Saphir's thighs and onto Pontiac.

She rolled off Saphir, hands sinking into beach, and turned her shoulder to the onslaught. The shells bit at her skin. She felt the chill of blood. Saphir, too, smelled of fresh wounds. That didn't explain what she saw in the water. Under the pale moonlight, the entire Gulf was red, as if as many bodies bled beneath the water as shells were tossed above it.

Pontiac pulled her arm from under a fresh dozen. They tumbled and clinked like terrarium glass. Her eyes focused on the Junonia's rows of brown markings. *Writin dat means to tell us what to do, which-a-way we ought to turn.* Under a fresh barrage, Pontiac picked one up. Feather-light. Lotion-soft.

"Read it!" Saphir cried.

A broken Junonia slashed Pontiac's forehead.

"I don't know how!"

"You do, catin! You do!"

She held the shell closer. The day she'd found Billy May Part II here on Guimbarde, Saphir had told her she could read them like books. *You got de eye too*, he'd insisted. *Lotta ladies do.* She'd scoffed. No way she had the skill, or even the right, to read mystical shell-writing. She'd been a nine-year-old punk good-for-nothing but upsetting the Durbers' hogs, collecting late fees from Mr. Peff, and scratching crap into her log.

But between the Battle of New Orleans holiday and St. John's Eve, Pontiac had faced a red-faced demon, acted a puss with a cottonmouth, lost a friend, found his head, sketched the best Coke bottle, got a job, made a new friend, owned a zombi, lost that zombi, resisted a fake sexy teacher, bought a fishing rod, nearly died using it, took the longest bus ride ever, met her grandmère, played with Florida kids too dumb to go barefoot, took the longest bus ride ever *again* and by her lonesome this time, faced the red-faced demon a second time, stood up to the cottonmouth like Juno the warrior-goddess, and, oh yeah, defied death.

She could read, all right. She could read *anything*.

Pontiac didn't think hard on it. Just opened her mouth. Her mind. Her heart. Her feelings—the hardest thing of all to open. Tears came flooding from her eyes. For Mama, for Daddy, for herself and all the time the three of them never had. Then that personal stuff was gone, like the hard plug you gotta blast from a mustard bottle before the good stuff starts flowing.

Words came. Other folk's words. Slow at first but, hellfire, she was only nine. Right quick, her mouth picked up the patterns, her teeth and tongue learned to danser le gigue. Voices that didn't belong to her, yet felt kin to her, pushed from her gut, spurred up her throat, plucked her vocal cords like a harp. For a few moments, the voices were joyful. Made sense to Pontiac. They hadn't been heard in a long while.

The tone eclipsed into a harrowing howl. Pontiac's eyes didn't quit crying; they cried harder. These were the wails of the drowned, mad as hell. Everything had been taken from them. All that had made it onto this patch of marsh were drops of their blood. These drops pollinated and spread as wide as a root system. A root *universe*, nerve lines tying every living thing together in agony and offense.

The longhair sedge cried out.

The rabbitsfoot grass cried out.

The mustang grape cried out.

The trumpet creeper cried out.

The laurel oak cried out.

The chanterelle mushrooms cried out.

The camphorweed cried out.

The valley redstem cried out.

The maidencane cried out.

The Spanish moss cried out.

Pontiac cried out, too, only a puppet now, but an articulate one, a speaker for those who hadn't been allowed to speak. The voices became ospreys and whooping cranes and wood storks and mallard ducks, and found gaps in the canopy of water oaks, elms, and tupelos, and soared into the storm, raging against the night that was and any dawn that might yet be, a chorus of the haunted, their seeds gone unplanted, their livelihoods never acquired, their pleasures never enjoyed, their properties never owned, their wages never paid, crying, cussing, complaints of excruciating specificity, documenting every crime in hopes that somebody might hear and keep track and repeat the judgment until others paid attention, and as the cloudbound voices braided into a physical mass, a sobbing groan louder than any thunder, they aligned to say four words in simple sequence.

~ 63 ~

THIS IS A RECKONING.

~ 64 ~

DOC WOULD HAVE BET HIS last breath nothing could overpower La Pieuvre. He had, in fact, bet exactly that. But he was wrong. The gorgeous atrocity of the voices, translated in a tone that sounded eerily like Pontiac, swept in on slashing rain, each raindrop an incensed soul screaming its tragedy. One drop was no more irksome than a locust; Doc might have emulated his pirate forefathers and flicked it away, not given it another thought. Together, though, the locusts made a plague. Everything they touched was devoured.

Half the choir filled Doc's ears, hewed through his sinuses, scoured his brainpan. Half poured down his inundated throat, plunked his ribs like xylophone keys, laid fresh eggs across the purple quiver of his heart. Once the music was inside you, Doc found, there was no faking you couldn't hear it. Hundreds of years belated, their pain became his. He was buried by it even as it lifted him up, allowed him at last to truly see over the jungled foliage.

Through the dolorous furor, La Pieuvre's question persisted.

PASS THE BUCK?

OR PAY THE PIPER?

Doc didn't deride himself for having almost vocalized the former. No, sir. No, ma'am. Protecting your own was as natural an instinct there was. It was high time, though, to do the unnatural. A good man didn't remove a curse from those who brought it on themselves. The unfairness of it didn't matter. The spectacle of horror would be just that—a spectacle. It had to be, if anybody was to see it.

He chuckled from the near blunder, even though it hurt him in every broken place. The so-called "Evil" that Jack O'Brien hunted had never skimmed beneath duckweeded waters. It had been the reflection *in* the water. Jack's face. All their faces. La Pieuvre, or the Piper, or the other aliases Doc had never heard before but now murmured in his head—Pierre, Blind Bull-Belly, Booker Ulene—it didn't matter what you called it. Just don't call it Evil. If anything, it was an angel. An avenging one, perhaps, but an angel all the same.

With any luck, Doc would see Emily soon. He'd explain to her the choice he made. He'd use medical metaphors to assist. Evil was hatred. Hatred was a cancer, something you should feel, like he should have felt the tumors in Emily's breast. What you did with cancer was rip it out. And you didn't stop there. You nuked the whole area so it couldn't rise up again. That was La Pieuvre's proposal. Die, just a little, in hopes that folk would *see* the deaths this time and bring themselves into confessional lockstep. Fear wasn't the ideal emotion to kickstart this kind of action, but the time for *ideal* expired three-hundred-some years back.

Emily would be angry. But Doc had to believe she'd understand in time. That the whole fuck-damn country would understand in time, and the buck, at long last, would stop being passed. Their common enemy was *right there* and had always been *right there*. Greed. It was what killed Emily. What took people from their homelands. What ruined the Earth.

Doc looked up. Through the icy picks of silver rain. Into the protean orb of the tentacle's face. Tears flooded his cheeks, fresh water into salt. Stupid to cry now, but he couldn't help it. To his surprise, even delight, the tentacle mirrored him, releasing two trickles of ocean water, drop for salty drop. It understood. Even sympathized, maybe.

But it did not forgive.

DO YOU HAVE AN ANSWER, DOCTOR?

He who pays the piper calls the tune, Doc thought.

He smiled. Lord, it felt good, those old zygomaticus major muscles flexing after so many scowling years. He pictured Emily's smile, Pontiac's smile. Happiness was a gift to be given, and anybody who received even a token ought to be grateful. He smiled wider and felt each missing and jacked-up tooth. The rain's loamy odor gave rise to the scent of lilac. Emily liked lilacs. Doc nodded and replied, and was startled to hear the reply come out amid laughter. Doing the right thing—what a wonderful way to die.

"Pay the Piper," Doc Devereaux said.

~ 65 ~

THE TENTACLE LORDING OVER Bob Fireman's Wagon Wheel Carnival retracted several yards, and for a ludicrous second Pete Roosevelt believed he'd snipped the octopus battle from *Wake of the Red Witch* and pasted it into his world, and that he, Son of Tarutatu, had defeated it, not with the Duke's dagger or a former sheriff's revolver, but with the more profound projectile of Spuds Ulene's prosthetic knee.

The tentacle was only coiling. A cottonmouth about to strike.

Pete's heart lobbed. It felt leathery, careworn. He hoped the minute or so he'd bought had been enough to save folk. Not all of them. Not even close. From his peripheral vision, he saw plenty of carnival-goers still cowering. A lawman knew the grim facts of collateral damage. The terminal infection of trauma was more pervasive than outright death. Put you in the grave the same, only with slower shoveling.

The tentacle fattened. But didn't lash out as Pete expected. With a sound-barrier concussion, the tentacle's skin vanished, and suddenly the sky over Chickapee Basin held what looked like fifty miles of water in the shape of a tornado funnel, enough to fill Lake Pontchartrain. For a surreal instant, the body of water floated in space.

Then fell all at once.

In officer training, Pete had been forced to look at photos of folk who died by suicide off bridges, to see what hitting water at such speed did to a body. That was bad enough. But when the water hit you? Your whole town? Pete didn't have a clue, but figured there weren't gonna be much left.

The dropping lake filled the sky, blocked the moon, swallowed Pete in shadow.

Alligator Point had seconds left to exist. Pete was gonna die, right here where he'd spent twenty years living. Least he could go out like he wanted. The climactic scene of the Duke's final film, *The Shootist*, flashed at the back of Pete's eyes. The old cowboy, riddled by cancer, choosing to go out in a blaze of glory. Pete tipped back his Stetson. Dangled his thumbs from his belt loops. Stood loose, jangly as all get-out, jaw thrust, chest forward, waiting for a cocky desperado to try to outdraw him. All while grinning the half-grin he'd emulated a thousand times before.

The lake blasted to the earth, a hurricane volume of water in one go. Pete heard a sliver of shrieking metal, rides twisting beneath the drenching tons, before his consciousness was stolen. No pain, only abrupt silence, same as any time he'd dove into a body of water. The difference was disembodiment. He was not clobbered into the dirt, not crushed into midway debris, not in the present or past. It had to be death.

Somehow it weren't. Not yet.

Pete squinted through what he believed was a whirlwind of carnival wreckage but was only his fluttering eyelids. He was alive, though he knew right off it was only barely. He was cognizant of his pulse because his blood had never pulsed this way, like a long-held dam had given way. Not a bad feeling, really, the guttering of his candle's flame. All wicks reached their finish.

His brain ground as slowly as his breathing. Sensory input came in dribbles. The rain had stopped. The wind had ceased. Pat Wilkes was looking down at him. She was doused in mud. Blood dripped from a long cut down from her temple to chin. Her eyes were bugged. Her mouth moved but Pete didn't hear words. She was holding him in her lap. Like Pete's mother never had. Like no one ever had.

There was no illumination but the moon. All carnival lights was gone. Pete rolled his eyes. Well, one eye rolled. The other reported nothing. Pete believed it was gone altogether. With his one eye he saw a giant, curved path of shattered lumber across the basin, like kelp smeared along a high-tide line. It was what all the shanties on the Point must look like now. He saw helixed heaps of metal, too, from pulverized rides. They looked a half-mile away. He had been washed that far in the torrent.

The edge of the mud plateau where he lay was cairned with moist lumps. Pointers. He didn't have to be any closer to know they were dead. A glint of recollection: being atop a fifty-foot wave that was half meat with tumbled corpses. Another: watching manhole covers far below shoot a mile into the sky with the instant flooding of the sewers. He mourned all of it. Even as he knew his part in the drama had finished.

His head was redirected by the chin. He caught a glimpse of his body. Abraham's shit. He didn't have no legs. His belly had been opened like a lid taken off a pot. Instead of a crawfish boil were his red, shining guts. The grip of his chin tugged until his good eye was facing Wilkes.

She had constructed herself a encouraging smile, not near good enough to hide the despair. Pete was a goner, they both knew it. Wilkes placed a hand on his cheek. Pete couldn't feel it but was obliged all the same. He could tell by the pattern of her lips that Wilkes was repeating something. He nodded like he understood. He wanted this good detective to think she'd reached him, though his vision was darkening like roux.

His eye lost focus on Wilkes and snapped to a figure looming behind her. Could be five feet behind or fifty. Without two peepers, he had no depth perception. It was a man, standing in the center of the carnage, equidistant to a dozen survivors wailing over their gored dead. The man looked haggard, as if he, too, had taken some sort of powerful blow. Pete coughed and struggled. Was he seeing this right?

The man wore a mask. Red papier-mâché. Black horns. A white-ringed mouth.

Pete was a sheriff to the last, rummaging for clues. The man's suit was the tip-off. Looked city. Tailored. Expensive. Not a speck of mud. Not even damp. Nobody had ever worn a suit like that this deep into the damp. Except one. Here he was at last, closer than anybody had ever reported seeing him.

The Oil Man.

Pete had no idea if what he saw next was real. Could be that seeing things was all part of dying. There was a jag of white lightning in the sky, quiet and distant. Lasted two seconds. In those seconds,

Pete didn't see the Oil Man's mask or suit. He saw *inside* the Oil Man, like the lightning was Doc's old X-ray machine. The Oil Man didn't have no skeleton. All he had filling him was bright things. What looked like diamonds. Jewels. Coins. Gold, too, maybe the pirate doubloons Gerard Pontiac had forever chased.

Mostly, of course, the man's insides were filled with oil, coursing in circulatory filaments that exited out the soles of his feet and squiggled through the mud like weed runners. These secret streams of oil connected the Oil Man to every living person in sight.

Pete felt a lonely, sinking, aching regret that folk everywhere, himself included, had been fighting the wrong fight all this time, slaying neighbors in hot red blood while the real villain strolled in their midst, clean-cut, dapper as a penguin, smiling pleasantly while filling his briefcase with lives traded for nothing. At the end of the day, nothing.

Lord, how Pete wanted to stare the demon down while it was hurt. But his eye couldn't hold. A generation better than Pete's would need to find the Oil Man themselves, perhaps by the scent of greed, and focus their rage upon him. Pete weren't sure it could be done. But in the dry, vine-like pulls of his final breaths, he tasted the sweet lilac of hope.

Motion, blackness, motion. Wilkes hitching him closer. Tears smudging the bloody slash on her face. It recalled to Pete the line of umber Miss Ward had painted across her cheek. It was Miss Ward who'd gotten Pete off his drunk ass and down to Chickapee Basin. Miss Ward and Pat Wilkes. Goll, as Spuds would have said. What an honor it was to have known such women.

Pete tried to speak. He pushed his tongue, folded his lips.

Wilkes nodded him on.

Pete realized he was no longer breathing. The light was dimming. Same as they had in the Liberty Theater when he was a kid and *Wake of the Red Witch* had played before his astonished eyes, the glow of the silver screen letting him believe that good lives were possible, and good deaths too.

He went limp. He died. Pete was pretty sure, though, that he'd gotten the final two lines of dialogue out, right before the closing credits.

"This isn't the end. It's the beginning."

~ 66 ~

DOES A WRONG AVENGED BRING SATISFACTION TO THE WRONGED?

No.

Does terminating a bad bloodline prevent the rise of a worse one?

No.

Can a mass death change minds?

The odds are against it.

Humans tend not to learn their lessons.

Look at all the dead before me.

I could name them.

But the dead in my waters were never named.

Now look at the survivors.

There are a few.

They will brood over this catastrophe for the rest of their lives.

Was it a freak anomaly?

Or did it have a deeper meaning?

Most will conclude that no, it did not.

Even as their lives collapse into ruin.

Even as their bodies yield to black pods of death.

Entire peoples have been ravaged.

An entire world is being despoiled.

The damages must be paid for.

Further damages must be prevented.

There is a chance someone will understand.

A chance someone will spread that understanding.

Now and then, there are things to admire in these people.

Their magic is young and their totems creative.

A marble.

A baseball cap.

A streak of umber paint.

A stack of gatorskin journals.

A prosthetic knee.

A baseball.

So I did them a favor they did not deserve.

I did not only destroy their town.

I destroyed the oil rigs.

I destroyed the refineries.

Both will rebuild.

But there is a chance.

If people move fast enough.

If they can work together.

If they can do the right thing.

If not, there will be no stopping the sinking.

The bayous first.

There is no saving the bayous.

The Houmas are nearly gone.

The Cajuns are nearly gone.

The oyster beds are nearly gone.

The shrimp and crab fishing are nearly gone.

The coasts will go next.

The valleys third.

The plains fourth.

The mountains last.

Imagine it.

The world will be water.

Even I will lose track of the dead.

All I will have left is to look at is myself.

I will grow ever more nearsighted.

Until I am blind.

Blind in an endless ocean.

Is that a life worth living?

You should know.

It is the life you live now.

Raise your head above the water, human.

Look across dry land while there is still land that is dry.

See what you have done.

What you are doing.

This is a reckoning.

Open your eyes.

~ 67 ~

PONTIAC'S RECOLLECTION WAS TANGLED LIKE mangrove roots.
Saphir carried her waterlogged body to the flatboat he'd looped to
a sugar maple, and gunned his Evinrude into the same waters that
had bombarded them with shells. Seemed ill-judged to Pontiac, but
Saphir made it all the way up Bayou Lafourche. Folk at the Dawes
shipyard helped them onto the dock, jabbering about the titanic

tentacles they'd lording over bayous to the south. Even soaked and tired as she was, Pontiac had to hold her tongue.

Tentacles? Shit-balls. Tempêtes, more like. Waterspouts probably looked like tentacles if you were a dumb dry-lander.

She and Saphir spent the night in the lobby of a police station that reeked of burnt coffee, not even chicory coffee, before being escorted to the local school. Seeing it, Pontiac thought she was being pranked. The school was massive, two stories tall with long cold halls like a museum. They'd filled the gym with cots as comfortable as cypress roots. By then, batches of swamp folk were arriving, bandaged to hell from a tidal bore they claimed wiped out Bob Fireman's. They hailed from sundry boondocks, everyplace but the Point. Hardly nobody from the Point had made it.

It was the lowest time in Pontiac's life, and not only because she'd been forced into another dress, the only item of donated clothing that fit. No survivors meant no Daddy. The thought of no Daddy messed her up. Five or six times, she got close to crying and hid under the gym bleachers. Mama had herself a fine crypt, but Daddy? His body was floating out there, likely being munched by with the serpents set free from the Chamber of Dragons.

Not the cottonmouth, of course. Billy May Part II had killed it good.

Kind of a surprise, then, when three days after landing in Dawes, Saphir came into the gym from the parking lot, earrings jingling, grinning like he had a secret. Pontiac stood up on fawn legs. She knew the secret before she saw it.

Daddy limped in on crutches. His right leg was packed in a cast that looked a half-foot thick and was girdered by interlocking scaffolds. Looked like one of those derricks in the Gulf. Come to think of it, she hadn't seen any of the oil rig lights the night she and Saphir had escaped. The tsunami that got Alligator Point must have gotten offshore rigs too. For some reason, this made Pontiac happy. The rigs would rebuild. But that rebuilding might buy people time.

Daddy loped up to her. Did a good job hiding how much it hurt. He hated doctors even more than she did. They probably told him to stay in the hospital and he probably said yes, and the instant they'd turned their backs, he'd crutched his broken ass out of there. The rubber tips of his crutches squeaked as he halted in front of Pontiac. He looked like he was crying without tears. Like he was all dried out.

"Don't you hug me now, cher. You'll hurt dis busted leg o' mine."

"You know I don't hug, Daddy."

Truth was, she wanted to.

"I know it. But I figure you might be glad to see me. A wee bit?"

Pontiac shrugged. "Yeah, it's all right."

She'd never been happier in her life.

Daddy's lips were quivering.

"I mighty pleased to see you too. Dat parrain of yours, he tell me he boated y'all here."

Pontiac looked for Saphir. He wasn't there. She turned in a circle, looking harder. All she saw was the gym door settling shut. Saphir had left, and Pontiac had a feeling he wasn't coming back. She wondered where he was going, what he was going to do. Help out in the recovery, probably. Folk were gonna want to fish what bodies they could from the bayous. And there wasn't no finer fisherman this side of the Mason-Dixon.

Pontiac knew she might never see André Saphir again. She felt real sad for a minute. But the sadness didn't last. Saphir had left her for a reason. He was Pontiac's godfather, not her father. Somebody else still held that job.

"I guess he's gone," Pontiac said.

"Man like dat ain't ever gone," Daddy said. "He de opposite of dat pirate gold I spent most my life diggin for. De time come you need Saphir to be dere? Den dere he be. Don't serve a body no purpose to ask how or why."

Pontiac reached out. Then got shy, and redirected to take gentle hold of a crutch. It was as cold and hard as the rail on Saphir's boat. She had a hunch it might protect her just as well, no matter how rocky the waters got.

"What do we do now, Daddy?"

Daddy gazed across the gym. Folk eating bland vittles, glugging water from bottles, redressing wounds, crying the dead, waxing colorful for news folk with video cameras. The gym was bright, the rubber flooring clean. But it was a fractured place. There might as well be an earthquake crack jagged through midcourt.

"How you feel bout goin back to Pensacola?" Daddy asked.

"To live with Mère?"

Daddy shrugged. "Till I get dese feet under me."

"Gonna be a while. One of them's broken to shit."

Daddy laughed. "Dat true. But I get it under me all de same. Den we get our own place. Fix it up how we swamp rats like it. How dat be?"

"Would I have to play with Cole?"

"What wrong wit' Cole?"

"He's a suck-head, that's what's wrong."

"All right. You don't have to play wit' no suck-heads."

"Do I gotta wear dresses? I ain't going if I gotta wear dresses."

"No playin wit' suck-heads and no dresses. Dis my solemn oat."

Pontiac dwelled hard on it. Pensacola was three hundred miles east. Still bordered the same gulf, though. That seemed important. Of all the things worth keepin track of, water seemed the most crucial. Every night here in Dawes, she'd heard the Junonia voices, only to wake up not recalling what they said. All she could grasp was four words, and she didn't know what they meant.

Gopher shit—she had time to figure it out. When she did, it might help to be in a place a mite more sophisticated than Alligator Point. Pensacola, Florida, was a place where a girl could say something and folk might actually hear it. If she had her maps right, there were lots of places around Pensacola stuffed with potential listeners. Montgomery. Tallahassee. Jacksonville. Tampa. A little farther, Atlanta. Nashville. Charlotte. St. Louis. Washington, D.C., even. She'd keep one ear to the waves, keep track, and take what she learned all the way to the capital.

"Okay, Daddy," she said.

Somebody gave Daddy a bottle of water. He drank it in one guzzle. Must have been just the moisture he needed. One fat tear rolled slow down his cheek.

Finding Daddy, losing Saphir, and admitting the Point was gone forever was a lot to take in. The surprises weren't finished. Some thirty seconds later, Pontiac saw another person she knew under a basketball hoop being respectful and giving Pontiac time with her daddy. She looked small bundled inside a man's coat. Her hands and face were dotted with bandages like she'd showered in broken glass.

Pontiac waved at Miss Ward.

Miss Ward waved back.

A few hours later, they stood at the Dawes depot: Pontiac, Daddy, and Miss Ward. The last three Pointers alive, Daddy wagered, and only by luck. He said the storm had tossed him and Miss Ward from Doc's Mercantile onto the Dawes side of border, the side where not so much as a single leaf had gotten wet.

Pontiac wasn't sure she believed that but she was too busy to interrogate it. Long ago, Mama had taught her how to take photos in her mind, and she was running out of time. She twisted her neck in the bright sun. She needed to memorize the periwinkle flowers by the post office. The sourwood bark that sloughed like elephant skin. The sticky burrs of green-white sedge dotting her pants. Dawes was no Alligator Point. But it was as close to a final glimpse of home as she was gonna get.

"You keep rollin dat fool head, cher," Daddy said, "it gonna roll right off."

"Skunk," Pontiac muttered.

She hitched up her bag, full of nothing but donated clothes, and squinted up at Daddy. He was gazing south where their life used to be. Pontiac took one last photo in her mind: Daddy looking peaceful with the swamp he loved behind him.

Pontiac looked at Miss Ward next. She looked pretty in the pink morning. Pontiac had asked twice if Miss Ward wanted to come live with them at Mère's. Miss Ward had shared an amused smile with Daddy both times.

Distantly, the skronk and jeer of a Greyhound in slow approach.

"Miss Ward, where are you going to go?" Pontiac demanded.

Miss Ward kneeled beside Pontiac. Her bandages made her prettier, braver.

"North," she said.

The bus gunned a block away. Pontiac bounced impatiently.

"*Where* north?"

"There's a lot of country out there. I haven't seen any of it."

"But how are we gonna find you?"

Miss Ward smiled. "You won't."

The bus blacked out the sun. Metal rattled and exhaust blurted as the Greyhound shuddered to a stop. The door hissed open and folk started climbing off. A lot of folk, actually. When Pontiac had debarked in Dawes last week, she'd been the bus's final rider. This Greyhound was full. A bunch of folk wore neon vests. A few wore hardhats. Some had equipment belts. The ones holding briefcases grimaced at the humidity. Pontiac supposed they were here to see the Point's slimy grave. Study it, build barriers, maybe, to keep New Orleans safe.

Barriers wouldn't do it. Pontiac could have told them that.

What they needed was the opposite.

Miss Ward gave Pontiac a hug, real quick before she could gripe about it. Pontiac felt Daddy's hand on her shoulder, positioning her to board. Pontiac wrenched her head for one last look at her teacher.

"Next year—St. John's Eve," Pontiac cried. "Promise to be somewhere! So we can find you! In case things go bad again!"

"But Pontiac. I told you—"

Daddy pushed Pontiac at the bus. Her shin struck the first step. She had no choice but to tumble onto it. She was still looking back, though.

"Just pick a place, Miss Ward! A place we can call and find you!"

Miss Ward blinked, thought—then lit up.

"Winterset, Iowa. The John Wayne Birthplace Museum. I knew somebody who always wanted to go. I'll go for him."

Miss Ward looked pleased with herself. The same way she'd often looked while watching her students respond to her hummed instructions. Pontiac was suffused with warmth. She'd been the one to pose a riddle this time, and Miss Ward had solved it quick. Made sense. Teachers were the smartest folk there were.

Pontiac chose a row in the middle of the bus.

The Greyhound groaned like Daddy did when he came to, drunk and bewildered. The vehicle shook so bad Pontiac's teeth rattled. The bus swung into a hard U-turn that pitched Pontiac into her daddy's side. He pointed out the window.

"Quick, cher. Say au revoir."

Goodbye. To the swamp. Her swamp. She struggled to see it. The sun through the filthy window stung her eyes with a blush-colored light. The Greyhound finished its turn and, just like that, the swamp was behind them. Pontiac felt a sparrow of panic and an impulse to scramble to the back of the bus.

Daddy applied pressure to her arm.

Let it be, the hand said.

Pontiac exhaled, shook out her limbs, and settled into the soft seat.

The bus picked up speed. Dawes proper rose up, and then five minutes later melted like butter into the land. Trees, grasses, streams, ditches, flatlands. The road convalesced from blacktop to pavement. If Pontiac remembered right, the major highway wasn't far. Then it'd be New Orleans, Interstate 10, Biloxi, Mobile.

Her thoughts accelerated with the bus wheels. She'd escaped Alligator Point, avoided All Feathers, No Meat. Had she done so without paying the Piper? She inspected the cottonmouth scar on her right arm, visible thanks to the stupid sleeveless dress. A doctor had come to the gym and checked her out. Proclaimed it a marvel that she'd survived such a deep fanging. Pontiac didn't know what to make of it.

What she hoped, though, was that Saphir was right and the bite was an inoculation. Maybe it had given her just enough poison that she could tell others what it felt like. You can have poison in you and do good with it. Maybe you could even become a queen. Pontiac was sure of it, growing surer every mile.

Daddy dug into his duffel.

"Got you somet'in."

"Is it pants?"

Daddy snorted. "It ain't pants."

He wrestled free a rectangular object swaddled in a plastic bag and handed it over. Pontiac turned it over in her hands.

"Ouvre-le."

"On the bus?"

"Oui. I t'ink you gonna want it for de ride."

A plastic bag was hardly holiday giftwrap. But Pontiac wasn't accustomed to presents. She unfolded the plastic with care, the acorn color beneath growing richer with each layer. When she found strips of old, yellow tape, she picked at them with her fingernails, a rigamarole that took her past New Orleans to complete, past the Highway 45 turnoff to Lafitte National Park, the town of Jean Lafitte, the town of Lafitte, all those names written in blood.

Daddy smiled all the while.

Pontiac defeated the old tape as the Greyhound passed the forested edges of Bayou Sauvage. She reached inside. Her fingertips grazed the unmistakable, segmented smoothness of gatorskin. She pulled out her prize and set it in her lap.

"It's a book," she said.

"Ouvre-le."

Pontiac did. The pages were blank. All but the first page, which had *#50* written in black pen in the top corner. She knew the handwriting from every sales slip at Doc's Mercantile. Doc—she missed the growly old bulldog more than she would have ever thought. Best she could do in life, she figured, was to honor him by growing some bulldog qualities of her own.

"This my new log?"

"To make up for de one I lost."

"How'd you get it?"

"Me and Miss Ward weren't de only t'ings dat ended up in de dry."

Pontiac stroked the thick, woodsy pages.

"You got a pencil?"

Daddy produced one from his jacket pocket.

Pontiac took it. It was a mechanical, the kind of pencil that never went dull. She gave it a good long clicking while Daddy crossed his arms, closed his eyes, and got comfy. Pretty quick, he was snoring. This left Pontiac to alternate looks between page, pencil, and the world speeding by too fast to register. The only way Pontiac knew to slow it down was to write.

First, though, she checked on the bus driver. He wasn't looking. She checked on Daddy. He was snoozing. Pontiac made herself smaller than she was, leaned against the window, and started drawing on the wall. It wasn't a good drawing. Way worse than her Coke bottle sketch. But a pencil wasn't charcoal and a quaking bus wasn't a piece of paper. It helped that she'd drawn this symbol so many times before.

Maybe the symbol—a warning was what it really was—would protect the Greyhound as it zoomed up and down the coast. There was no telling, though Pontiac intended to keep drawing octopuses everywhere she went till she'd replaced all the ones that had gone under with Alligator Point. Maybe folk would start noticing them. Maybe they'd start drawing reminders too. Maybe it'd satisfy the thing in the swamp just long enough for folk to start making things right.

She finished the octopus.

She stared down at the empty page.

What to write first? What she'd seen? What she hoped to see?

Neither, she decided. She'd write about the folk she knew. The folk who were gone but needed remembering. A spindly whisper of Junonia voice glided through the cracked-open window. The voice had much to tell her. To tell everybody. About a different kind of storm that was brewing. All Pontiac could do was keep track of it.

"*When we think of white supremacy, we picture COLORED ONLY signs, but we should picture pirate flags.*"

Ta-Nehisi Coates, "The Case for Reparations,"
The Atlantic, 2014

AFTERWORD

If you've read the author's note in *The Living Dead*, my previous collaboration with George A. Romero, you know the twists and turns that went into shaping that posthumous novel. The existence of the novel itself, however, was no surprise. It had been reported for a decade that Romero had been chipping away at it.

Pay the Piper is a different story. During the two years of working on *The Living Dead*, I grew close to George's wife, Suzanne Desrocher-Romero, and joined the board of the George A. Romero Foundation. Prior to my joining, the GARF's first major piece of news was the acquisition of George's archives by the University of Pittsburgh.

Under the guidance of Horror Studies Collection Coordinator Benjamin J. Rubin, cataloging efforts began in early 2019. In August 2019, I was granted permission to be the first person outside library staff to sift through the collection. My goal was to aid in the university's efforts to publicize the collection, though I made no secret that spending a week inside George's head was a dream come true.

At that point, twenty-six boxes had received preliminary cataloging but had yet to be arranged into any chronology. This made the discovery process, for me, all the more startling. In one envelope might be George's handwritten notes for an early version of *Dawn of the Dead* starring O. J. Simpson, and in the next might be an unproduced screenplay called *Funky Coven*.

On the final day of my visit, inside the final box I opened—T-Box 7, SL15, to be exact—I came across two thick envelopes marked *PAY THE PIPER*. Inside were a combined 348 pages of a novel. At first I thought it might be complete. As I sat down to read, I learned that was not the case. George had clearly delighted in breaking his story ever wider, chapter by chapter, only to stop cold just when it came time to start knotting the threads.

Context clues from George's manuscript suggest his draft was written in 1998, though it's possible the true date is 2004 (one year before Hurricane Katrina). It is unclear why George kept the project secret. Perhaps he feared the reaction to a work that had nothing to do with zombies (except, in brief, the Vodou kind). By this point in his career, that had become the standard reaction to Romero, and one that, I regret to say, remains in place. Strides, however, are being made. For instance, the celebrated release of George's lost 1975 film, *The Amusement Park.*

If *The Living Dead* was the novel George felt he had to write, *Pay the Piper* was the book he *wanted* to write. It is filled to the brim with the sort of stuff George had adored since youth: pirates, treasure, westerns, and jungle adventuring. He was clearly having a ball throwing everything he loved into the pot. Leaving me, twenty-five years later, to autopsy what he had left, study the clues, and find a method in the madness that would carry the novel to conclusion.

Though George left no notes on the project, the wealth of subtextual coincidences insist he had a plan. *Pay the Piper*'s story nods at the 1815 Battle of New Orleans, which involved the infamous Pirates Lafitte. Pirates play a big role in the largely forgotten film *Wake of the Red Witch,* to which a whole chapter of Romero's manuscript was dedicated. *Red Witch* starred John Wayne, and a character in *Pay the Piper* is obsessed with Wayne, particularly Wayne's death, on screen and off. After reading a couple John Wayne biographies, I discovered that Wayne called the cancer that ultimately took his life "the Red Witch." This revelation pulled tight many of

George's loose strings. Some of the other clues I will keep to myself (though I might tell you about them if you ask).

Given Romero's status as the godfather of zombies, it is notable that *Pay the Piper* touches upon aspects of vodou/voodoo zombis. If there was any doubt about George's interest in the subject, one need only see his introduction to the 2016 edition of William Seabrook's 1929 book, *The Magic Island,* often credited as the text that first brought zombis to the attention of the western world. The intro must have been one of the last things George wrote before falling prey to his own "Red Witch" of lung cancer.

Finishing *The Living Dead* was the greatest honor of my career. Stumbling across a second (and, by all indications, final) novel was a coda I never saw coming. My hope for this work is that it continues to broaden the popular view of George A. Romero's capabilities. He was more than zombies. He was an artist, plain and simple, and a great one at that.

Daniel Kraus
October 2023

ACKNOWLEDGMENTS

Special thanks to Chris Roe and Suzanne Desrocher-Romero for letting me to be part of this book's overdue completion, to Richard Abate and Claire Wachtel for making the project a reality, and to the University of Pittsburgh Library System's Horror Studies Collection Coordinator Benjamin T. Rubin for leading me to T-Box 7, SL15 (now Box 44, Folder 1-2 for the curious) of the George A. Romero Archival Collection, where I first stumbled across the half-finished manuscript of *Pay the Piper* in 2019.

I am also in debt to two readers who gave crucial creative input on the novel: Stephanie Kuehn, author and psychologist, and Sarah Juliet Lauro, an author and professor at the University of Tampa, where she specializes in postcolonial literature and modern-day narratives of slavery and revolt.

In addition, thank you to Barbara Berger, Matt Blazi, Hannah Carande, Tananarive Due, Zach Fontenot, Lisa Forde, Edward A. Galloway, Lisi Harrison, Richard Hazelton, Adam Hart, Amanda Kraus, Jenny Lu, Sandy Noman, Grant Rosenberg, Michael Ryzy, Igor Satanovsky, Julia Smith, Alison Skrabek, Patrick Sullivan, Christian Trimmer, Jeff Whitehead, and Ada Wolin.

ACKNOWLEDGMENT

ABOUT THE AUTHORS

GEORGE A. ROMERO is often considered the greatest horror director of all time. His classic "Dead" movie cycle began with the groundbreaking *Night of the Living Dead* and *Dawn of the Dead*, which were followed by four sequels. He also directed *Creepshow, The Dark Half, The Crazies,* and created the TV series *Tales from the Darkside*. Romero died in 2017 after a fifty-year career in film.

DANIEL KRAUS is a *New York Times* bestselling author. With Guillermo del Toro, he wrote *The Shape of Water* (based on the same idea Kraus and del Toro created for the Oscar-winning film) and *Trollhunters* (adapted into the Emmy-winning Netflix series). Kraus followed his science thriller *Wrath*, coauthored with Shäron Moalem, with the widely acclaimed *USA TODAY* bestseller *Whalefall*. His novel *The Death and Life of Zebulon Finch* was named one of *Entertainment Weekly*'s Top Ten Books of the Year.